MIRANDA GAINES

FEARLESS



Published in the United States by Bookwing Press, a division of Zollmania, LLC.

www.bookwingpress.com

ISBN 979-8-9888935-1-6 (hardback)
ISBN 979-8-9888935-0-9 (paperback)
ISBN 979-8-9888935-2-3 (ebook)

Library of Congress Control Number: 2023943916

*To Caroline Eschenberg Brown*

*5/31/60 - 4/5/17*

*My dear friend, your kindness continues to shine further than you will ever know, and I am forever grateful.*

# Chapter 1

*June 21st, 1593*

Magic and mystery—that's what the day of the summer solstice promised, but so far Branwen had only seen sheep. She sighed, leaning on her shepherd's crook as she stared across the sloping fields of her family's pasture. To the west, she could see the bronze steeple of the village church peeking above the treeline, and beyond that, the ancient hill-forest of Bryn Celli Ddu. Pale mist enshrouded the hill's base as the warmth of the morning slowly evaporated the night's dew. Dark trees loomed both foreboding and alluring against the blue-gray sky.

In a few hours, the men and elders from the village of Llanddaniel Bryn would make the trek up through the forest to the stone cairn hidden at its apex. There, they would conduct the binding of Bryn Celli Ddu, a ritual to bless the land and keep evil at bay. As *iachäwr*—village healer—Branwen's mother was the only woman allowed to accompany the sacred procession.

For years, Branwen had wanted to join her, to witness the mystery of the mound in the dark woods. The desire of that knowledge burned a hole inside her. What exactly did the elders do there? Why did they keep it so secret? A full third of the village adults went up to Bryn Celli Ddu every year, yet none of them ever spoke a word about it. Of course, that didn't stop the stories—tales of magic and missing girls, of strange creatures and blood sacrifices. Branwen had heard from neighboring villages that the forest was cursed, that it was the home of the old gods and the faerie folk.

Such tales frightened children, but Branwen had never been scared. As a young girl, she'd listened to all the stories of the fae with fascination, wondering if binding the tomb at Bryn Celli Ddu really did keep the insect-like pixies, toad-skinned kobolds, and shape-changing kelpies at bay. When she'd turned twelve and was finally old enough to apprentice, she'd insisted on training to become an *iachäwr,* too. She'd hoped to walk alongside her mother to the ruins, but each year, the older woman told her to stay behind with the promise of, "Maybe next time."

Five years, her mother had been saying that. Five years was long enough.

Branwen's grip tightened on her shepherd's crook. *I* will *go to Bryn Celli Ddu. Today,* she swore to herself. Soon, she knew her mother would send her to the village of Gaerwen or even as far as Bangor to complete the final two years of her training as *iachäwr.* Two *years*. If she didn't discover the secret of Bryn Celli Ddu today, she'd have to wait at least that long for another opportunity.

*I feel like I've been waiting my whole life already*, Branwen thought. *Seventeen years and I'll finally know the truth.*

One of the sheepdogs barked and Branwen reeled in her gaze just as her older brother Madden approached from the lower field.

"I brought a visitor," Madden told her, his sky-blue eyes twinkling with mischief beneath the blond haystack of his hair.

From behind him, their younger sister Colwen rushed forward. The six-year-old was winded from trying to keep up with her brother's long stride, but that didn't stop her from talking.

"Papa said I could come help watch the sheep," Colwen told Branwen in the span of a single, wheezing breath. She clutched her favorite rag doll in her fist, her fingers tight around the toy's lumpy waist.

Its yarn hair was honey-colored and full of cowlicks—just like Colwen's. Two summers ago, Branwen and her sister had made the doll together. They called it Hyll which meant "ugly"—because it *was*—and Colwen loved ugly things.

Branwen smiled. "Good. I needed some help," she told Colwen while giving her brother a sly wink. "Madden can take the dogs and the lambs while you and I stay with the grannies by the creek. How does that sound?"

The grannies were the oldest sheep in the flock—ewes well-past their lambing days, but still valuable for wool production. More importantly, the grannies were the *calmest* of the flock. They wouldn't mind when the six-year-old inevitably ran circles around them, pretending to be a sheepdog. And when Colwen got bored—as Branwen knew she would—the younger girl could venture into the creek to play while remaining within Branwen's line of sight.

"Sounds perfect," Madden interjected before Colwen could raise any protests. "Thanks, sis," he told Branwen, then whistled sharply. The two sheepdogs snapped to attention, gathering up the proper sheep at Madden's command. "Pa said he'll bring the rams up in a little while," Madden added as he led the flock away. "I'll be in the north field if you need me!"

*Of course,* Branwen thought. Their family's northern-most pasture shared a fence with the wool-dyer's eastern field where the wild madder root grew...and where Ifanna—her best friend and Madden's fiancée—would be gathering herbs for the solstice festival.

Branwen smiled as she called after her brother, "Tell Ifanna I said hello!" She could see the gleam of Madden's answering grin even from a distance.

"Oh, I will," he said. A swift breeze carried back the sound of his laughter as he disappeared over the next hill with the sheep.

Branwen laughed, too, pushing back a few dark, wind-snarled curls that had escaped her braid. When she looked up, she saw her sister bolt past her, already heading toward the creek. The grazing sheep scattered out of the little girl's way, but only briefly; the grannies let few things come between them and their food.

"C'mon!" the six-year-old shrieked as she kicked off her shoes. Colwen paused only to tuck Hyll safely behind a rock and out of her splash range before she plunged, skirts and all, into the knee-deep water. "Come play with me!"

*Why not?* Branwen thought as she glanced back at the sheep. The grannies had returned to their grazing patterns. Half of them even dozed as they ate. They weren't going anywhere.

"I'm coming!" she called as she took long, even strides down the hill, using her shepherd's crook for balance. Near the creek, Branwen jabbed the end of the cane into the soggy ground, then tucked up her skirts and headed for the water. She crouched by the edge of the creek and thrust both hands into the cool, burbling stream as she prepared to splash her sister—then she stopped.

Something wasn't right. The water turned to ice against her skin, sending shivers up her arms and down her spine. Further along the creek, she could still see Colwen tromping through the water, still hear her laughing as she chased tiny minnows. Nothing seemed amiss and yet....

Branwen looked down at her hands again. Then she saw it—no, *them.* Paw prints in the creek bank. Fresh ones. Big ones. Too big to belong to a sheepdog. *Much* too big. If she didn't know better, she would think they had come from a—

*Wolf!* The word yelped in Branwen's mind. Her heart pounded in her chest even as she told herself, *That's impossible. The last wolves were hunted to extinction nearly a hundred years ago! They're just stories now, like all the tales of Bryn Celli Ddu.* Still, she leapt to her feet.

Behind her, the sheep started bleating—softly at first, then more frantic. She glanced back and saw them all huddled together, seeking protection in numbers. A few feet upstream and to her left, she saw Colwen. The six-year-old was no longer splashing through the water, but stood stock-still and stared into the bushes at the far edge of the creek. From her angle, Branwen couldn't tell what Colwen was looking at, but she could see fear ripple through her sister's body.

Colwen screamed.

A lean, dark shape lunged from the bushes. Amber eyes burned within a body of living shadows, and Branwen dashed forward, desperately trying to thrust herself between the black beast and her sister. She made a huge splash as she landed in the knee-deep creek. The shadow-creature flinched away from the sudden sound and surge of water, hissing and spitting as it darted out of her range.

*Wolves don't hiss!* The thought rang like a gong in Branwen's mind and she felt the cold dread of its warning seep into her bones. Instinct had already told her this creature couldn't be an ordinary wolf, but she'd let her rational mind hold sway and now she didn't have time to waste being surprised. She plowed through the water, making as much commotion as possible to keep the beast at bay until she could reach her sister. Only a few feet away, Colwen stood utterly motionless in the middle of the creek, her mouth gaping wide as she continued to scream.

Branwen clamped her hands on her little sister's shoulders, cutting the younger girl's shriek short as she yanked her to the side. Then, Branwen stepped in front, using her own body as a shield to block the shadow-wolf's access to Colwen. She stomped her feet in the creek and flailed her arms through the water, splashing as much of it as she could at the beast, trying to drive it back.

"Get!" Branwen shouted, her voice pitched low and commanding as though she addressed a disobedient sheepdog. "Go!"

But the shadow-wolf didn't move any further away—it only skittered from side to side, becoming more successful at dodging the arcs of water Branwen flung at it. Any moment now the beast would catch her rhythm, she knew, and then it would be the *wolf's* time to attack.

*I can't let that happen*! Branwen thought, her mind scrambling for another option. *I have to move—now!*

"Colwen, run!" she bellowed even as she hurled herself toward the wolf. She didn't have time to turn and look, but for once, she knew her sister obeyed. She could hear the girl's desperate splashing as she bolted for the shore. She could smell the musty scent of churned earth as Colwen's bare feet dug into the muddy embankment. Out of the corner of her eye, she could see a flash of honey-blonde against white and green when her sister finally raced up the hill from the creek. The sheep fled ahead of her.

The shadow-wolf caught the movement, too, but just as its gaze shifted to follow Colwen, Branwen shouted, raking her hands through the water and slinging it at the beast's face.

WHOOSH!

A blast of heat and steam exploded from around the wolf, nearly blinding Branwen, and she staggered back, blinking desperately to clear the fog from her vision. She couldn't see for all the vapor in the air, but she could hear the shadow-wolf—hissing and howling in agony. The sound made her skin crawl and the marrow of her bones ache.

*What just happened?* For a moment she stood, too stunned to move. Her muscles strained against the eastern flow of the creek as she realized, *It doesn't matter—now's my chance to run!*

Before she could pivot toward the shore, two glowing amber eyes cut through the lingering mist. Their harsh light burned like twin will-o'-the-wisps, beckoning Branwen to follow them to her doom. She stared in horror as the steam faded, revealing the full effect of her attack.

Red-charred skin peeled back from the side of the wolf's face and head where the water had splashed, exposing the layers of muscle and bone beneath. The gray-white dome of its skull glistened under the early morning sun, and the beast's teeth gleamed between the shreds of its jaw muscles. Smoke rose from chunks of black fur still stubbornly clinging to the creature's flesh; the white tendrils hissed as residual heat escaped.

*That's the sound I heard earlier*, Branwen suddenly understood. It wasn't the wolf hissing, but the sound of water dissolving fur and skin and bone. Only then did she remember an ancient saying still recited by some of the grandmothers in her village—"running water drives away evil." *But if that's completely true, then why is that* thing *still here?* Branwen questioned.

Impossibly, the shadow-wolf walked toward her. Its massive paws gouged deep ruts into the mud along the creek bank, though it was careful never to touch the water. The beast's red tongue lolled out of the burned side of its mouth, panting hungrily, and its eyes smoldered with hatred.

*Is this it?* Branwen wondered as the wolf marched inexorably forward. *Is this the face of Death?* Something within her immediately balked at the notion. Her jaw clenched and she stared back at the shadow-wolf in staunch rebellion.

"This is *not* how I die," she told the beast. Without taking her eyes off the wolf, Branwen took a step back, deeper into the creek—her fortress and her weapon. She held her arms out wide, palms up as if to say, "Now what?"

The wolf stopped its advance.

Branwen held her breath.

She could see intelligence swirling behind the creature's unearthly eyes. The shadow-wolf tilted its head when it looked at her, reminding her of a sheepdog...if that sheepdog were a nightmarish fiend bent on her personal destruction.

After an agonizing second, the beast seemed to come to a decision, and Branwen watched with her heart in her throat. Her body tensed, ready for anything.

Slowly, the wolf turned, following the trail of its footprints back up the creek.

*Is it leaving?* she dared to hope. *Have I beaten it? Are we safe?* She thought of Colwen and glanced up the sloping field. Her sister wasn't as far away as she'd expected. *She should be halfway to Madden by now.*

As she watched, Branwen could see the trouble: Colwen's dress. Water-logged from playing in the creek, the thick, woolen garment weighed her down and clung close to her skin, catching between her legs as she tried to run. The six-year-old could only go a few feet before the sagging cloth made her stumble. Despite her struggle, Colwen had nearly made it to the single ash tree at the top of the hill. A few more yards and she'd be over the ridge and out of the shadow-wolf's line of sight. Their ordeal was almost over.

Branwen let out a slow, shuddering breath, turning her gaze back to the wolf. The beast had walked another fifteen feet further up the creek bank where the waters grew shallow as they neared the source-spring. The creek itself was only three feet wide at the point where the shadow-wolf stopped again, turning perpendicular to the flow of water. Then, it glanced back at Branwen.

The muscles of the creature's maimed jaw stretched into a wicked grin and its fiery amber eyes darted directly to Colwen as she continued to fight her way up the hill. Saliva dripped from the beast's mouth and its red, red tongue ran across its teeth in anticipation.

Branwen could have no doubt that the shadow-wolf's long legs and lean, muscular body would easily overtake her sister. Terror filled her heart. She screamed, "No!"

The wolf jumped across the stream.

Branwen watched in horror as the beast's shadow-swift form raced up the hillside even as she dove toward the shore, clawing her way up the embankment.

"Colwen!" Her sister's name ripped from her throat, piercing the air, and the younger girl glanced back. Branwen saw her gait falter briefly and knew she'd seen the beast gaining on her. "Don't stop!" Branwen shouted, her own legs pumping as fast they could, propelling her up the hill. With each billowing breath, she surged forward, taking the hill at an angle in the hopes of intercepting the wolf, but the shadow-creature moved faster still. It would be upon her sister in seconds.

*I won't make it. I won't reach Colwen in time.* Branwen knew the truth of those words, but she couldn't give up. She had to *do* something—she had to find a way! Her heart pounded in her chest. The sound of it pummeled her eardrums. She could barely hear her own voice as she cried out, "Colwen—the tree!"

In her frantic dash for safety, the six-year-old had nearly passed the solitary ash tree at the top of the hill, but at Branwen's words she stuck out her hand and grasped the trunk. The young girl's momentum slung her around the base of the tree, changing direction too quickly for the wolf to adjust. The beast barreled forward, its teeth snapping on only air as it lunged for where Colwen used to be.

The force of its efforts carried the shadow-creature over the ridge of the hill, and Branwen saw dark chunks of peat and sod go flying as the beast tried to scramble back up the slope. By the time the wolf gained traction, Colwen had managed to clamber halfway up the ash tree. Branwen had never felt more grateful for her sister's adventurous spirit than in that moment when she saw the way the young girl's nimble feet and fingers found easy purchase in the smallest knots and whorls of the tree's tall trunk. The lonely ash had always been Colwen's favorite climbing tree despite their father's warnings against its creaking boughs.

As she ran, Branwen let out a gasp of breath. Faint tendrils of relief coursed through her body. Her lungs burned as fresh air rushed in, driving away the weariness in her chest and legs as she continued to bolt up the interminable hill. The sloped field seemed to stretch on forever, growing steeper with every stride.

*That means I'm nearing the top!* Branwen thought, her spirit rejoicing until she realized she had no idea what to do once she got there. She had no weapon to speak of—the stones lying about were too big for throwing and there weren't any conveniently-downed tree limbs to use as a makeshift stave. Her only other option—her shepherd's staff, meant for this very purpose—she'd left down by the creek in her rush to save her sister. She could see it in her mind's eye, jutting from the ground like the great sword Excalibur.

*And just as unobtainable*, Branwen thought with an internal grimace. At least, the staff was *real,* but it couldn't do her any good from where it stood a hundred yards away. She certainly didn't have time to go back and get it. Her sister had escaped the wolf—for now—but Branwen could see the beast circling beneath the ash tree, clearly preparing for another assault. The wolf's fierce amber eyes never once strayed from Colwen as she climbed further and further up the tree.

Below her, the shadow-wolf stopped circling and approached the tree, stretching its front feet up the base of the ash. Colwen yelped as the wolf made its first attempt to scale the tree. Its teeth snapped at the heel of her dangling foot, but missed, and the beast's black body slid back down the trunk, carving deep fissures into the bark with its claws. The ash tree wept from the injury, leaking sap like lymph from an open wound. The wolf leapt again.

To Branwen, time slowed to a crawl as she watched the shadow-wolf fly through the air. Her own limbs dragged and the wind felt like lead against her skin as she finally crested the hill, but she didn't stop—*couldn't* stop. Her sister needed her!

Colwen yanked her foot up, placing her full weight on the base of the branch as she half-stood, her movements desperate as she tried to haul herself up to the next level and out of the shadow-wolf's reach. She had her torso and one arm slung over the upper boughs when the branch beneath her cracked and fell. The sound of it roared in Branwen's ears like thunder.

"NO!" Branwen's own shout drowned under Colwen's shriek of terror.

The six-year-old clung to the higher branch, her fingers white with the strain. The sodden wool of her skirt weighed her down, making it impossible for her to pull herself into the upper boughs without support from below. Her body swayed from side to side and her bare feet peddled the air, blindly searching for a new foothold.

When the traitor-branch fell, it collided with the shadow-wolf, knocking the creature to the ground, but the beast recovered quickly. It scuttled out from beneath the leafy cage of the branch, then used the girth of the fallen limb as a step to launch itself higher up the tree.

Branwen couldn't allow it to get that far. *I have no weapon. I* am *the weapon,* she thought and without hesitation flung herself at the wolf. Her arms latched around the creature's chest, then she threw herself backward as hard as she could, using the force of her own weight to reverse their momentum. Despite the beast's impressive size, it had barely any mass at all—as though it were truly formed of nothing but smoke and shadows. Branwen had no trouble letting gravity and the natural slope of the hill take over, tumbling them back toward the creek. She ducked her head as she rolled, keeping herself shielded as best she could against the frenzy of tooth and claw. Behind her, she could hear Colwen screaming for Papa, Madden—*anyone*—to help, but Branwen knew they were all too far away.

The wolf snarled, turning its head to snap at her face, but in the tumult it only managed to tangle its teeth in the thick braid of her hair. Dark strands ripped from her scalp as the beast yanked its mouth free. The shadow-wolf broke her grasp then, and tried to scramble to its feet, but Branwen didn't let it. She lunged after the creature, throwing herself onto its back once more in an attempt to pin it to the ground. The beast twisted beneath her and sent them both rolling further down the hill.

Branwen clung to its back, digging her hands into the wolf's shadow-black coat. Its fur slid between her fingers like oil. She nearly lost her grip, but fear turned her hold into a vice. If she let go of the beast now, it would turn on her, ripping her face and arms to shreds. And when it had finished with her, it would dart up the hill and vault into the ash tree after Colwen. In her mind, she could already hear her little sister screaming, could imagine the soft, wet squelch of the wolf at her throat, followed by earth-shattering silence.

*I can't let that happen!* Branwen thought in a panic. She needed to get the shadow-wolf as far away from her sister as possible and, once she did, she needed a way to *fight back*.

Her eyes widened, desperately trying to glimpse her surroundings as she and the wolf continued to tumble down the hill. The world spun by in waves of color: green, blue, black.

Grass, sky, shadow. Then—*yes!*

Only a few feet away, she could see the large stone by the creek, and next to it, her shepherd's crook, gleaming like a ray of golden hope in the sunlight. *That's it!* She hooked one arm around the shadow-wolf's chest and threw her weight forward and to the side, forcing their locked forms to accelerate and veer to the left. One, two, three rolls and then—*crack!*

The beast's breastbone slammed directly against the rock, stunning it for one vital second.

Branwen didn't waste any time. She fell off the wolf, scrambling back on her heels, her arms reaching out behind her. She didn't dare takes her eyes off the shadow-beast as she frantically searched for her shepherd's staff, but her hands patted only grass.

She couldn't understand. It had been right *there*—why couldn't she find it? The tip of her finger bounced against something solid and she grabbed it, squeezing tight. Her heart plummeted as the object compressed beneath the force of her grip. It wasn't the staff, but she didn't have time to search again—the wolf was rolling to its feet, chest heaving. The shadow-beast lunged at her, mouth wide and gaping, and she thrust the object forward, stuffing it into the wolf's open maw.

The beast's amber eyes bulged in fury and surprise as a bundle of rags and yarn clogged its jaws.

*Hyll.*

Branwen would have laughed if she hadn't already been on the verge of tears. Her sister's ugly, lumpy doll was lodged in the wolf's mouth, choking it with thick tufts of wool that spewed from ripped seams.

The beast shook its head, flinging the doll aside, and Branwen seized the moment of distraction. Leaping to her feet, she turned and grabbed her shepherd's crook—it had been only an arm's length away the whole time. She brought it to bear just as the shadow-wolf rushed in. The beast's teeth clamped around the staff, leaving deep impressions in the oak shaft instead of Branwen's forearm.

She shoved back—hard—jamming her shepherd's crook into the corners of the wolf's mouth, then twisted it back and forth. The motion played on the creature's predatory nature, triggering the instinct to bite down and pull just as it would if rending meat from bone or like a dog tugging on a piece of rope. Branwen hadn't been sure the trick would work, but she was glad it did—at least for now. Every second she kept the wolf occupied was another second Colwen remained safe, another second bought until help arrived.

Madden *had* to have heard Colwen's cries even in the north field. Regardless, he would have known something was wrong when all the granny-ewes came rushing into the far meadow... wouldn't he?

*And Papa*, Branwen thought, her muscles straining as she pushed against the wolf. *He should be here soon, bringing up the rams.* She wished. She hoped. She prayed...because she didn't know how much longer she could hold the shadow-beast off.

Purple bruises bloomed along her skin and blood flowed from three gashes atop her left wrist where the wolf's claws had caught sometime during their tussle. Branwen hadn't even felt the injuries happen with everything else going on, but she felt them now. Warm blood trickled down her hand and seeped between her fingers, making her grip on the shepherd's staff slick and wet. The tendons in her wrist quivered with pain and her whole body ached.

One look at the wolf and she knew it could sense her weakness. Its amber eyes gleamed with anticipated victory.

"Oh, no you don't," Branwen growled, bracing herself for the beast's final assault—but not well enough.

The shadow-wolf released its hold on the shepherd's crook and Branwen stumbled at the sudden lack of opposition. She thrust the end of the staff into the ground to keep from falling, but the action left her wide-open for an attack. The wolf darted forward, teeth bared in a wicked, hungry grin.

*Thwak!* Out of nowhere, a chestnut-sized rock struck the shadow-beast in the eye. The creature howled and flinched away, giving Branwen time to regain her balance. Looking up, she saw her brother yelling and racing down the hill. He had a shepherd's sling in one hand, loaded with a small, jagged rock. It spun round and round poised for flight. As the wolf began to recover, he loosed the second projectile, bashing the creature on the burned side of its face. The shadow-wolf staggered and Branwen ran toward Madden, trusting her brother to keep the beast off her back. To her left, she heard her father's low voice, shouting, though she couldn't make out the words. The pasture gate clanged shut behind him with the rams, forgotten, on the other side.

Branwen skidded to a halt. "Papa, watch out!" she cried as she saw the wolf's dark shape dart toward the small, swarthy man from across the field.

Her father bent low, charging the beast with his own shepherd's crook raised above his head like a broadsword. He swung the staff down hard, cracking it across the shadow-wolf's shoulders.

Madden met their father halfway, pelting the beast with rocks as the older man kept slashing at it with his shepherd's crook. The wolf dodged most of their attacks, but Branwen could see the effort it took as each action wore the creature down bit by bit. She hadn't noticed before in all the commotion, but the wolf favored its left hind leg badly and the burn to its face finally seemed to be taking a toll.

"The water!" Branwen gasped, their path to victory suddenly evident. "Papa, Madden—push it into the water!"

Her father's eyes never once left the wolf, but Madden looked back at Branwen in confusion.

"Just do it!" she shouted, pitching her voice above the sound of Colwen's still-frightened cries behind her. She couldn't comfort her sister—not yet—not until she saw this evil *ended.* Branwen took up her own staff and jogged back down the hill.

The shadow-wolf must have sensed her intent. It took full advantage of Madden's momentary inattention and darted through a gap in his coverage. Branwen's father bolted after the beast, but she knew he could never catch it.

*He won't have to,* she thought. *It's given up on Colwen. Now, it's coming straight for me!* She picked up speed until she ran toward the beast, her bones jarring with every step.

Eyes glowing with menace, the shadow-wolf leapt as soon as she was in range, but Branwen was ready. She swung her shepherd's crook with all her might, catching the beast mid-air. Her staff snapped in two with the force of impact, but the wolf's shadow-born body went flying. Branwen ran after it, watching as it landed at the very edge of the embankment. The beast dug its claws into the peat-laden shore, trying to haul itself up from the ledge, but Branwen would have none of it.

With her bare hands, she shoved the shadow-wolf into the creek.

# Chapter 2

A geyser of steam erupted from the knee-deep creek as the shadow-wolf plunged beneath its surface, and Branwen leapt back, trying to avoid the scalding water that rained down around her. Hot droplets splattered across her arms and she could feel them seep through her hair, burning her scalp. Her pale skin glowed with angry red dots, but her pain was minor compared to the wolf's agony.

The roar of boiling water did nothing to block out the beast's final howl. The spine-numbing sound pierced through the hiss of steam, sending spasms of panic across Branwen's entire body.

*What if it doesn't die?* she thought in desperation. *What if somehow—some way—the creature claws its way out of the creek?* She half-believed in that possibility even as the water melted away the beast's flesh and fur. Layer after layer sloughed off, revealing hard, white bones and glistening gray organs. At last, she heard the gurgle of water in the shadow-wolf's throat followed by the wet rasp of liquid filling its lungs.

The howl drowned with the wolf, sinking into the churning tumult of the creek. For a moment, Branwen thought she caught a glimpse of amber glaring back at her from beneath the roiling waters, but then she blinked and the eyes were gone. Nothing remained of the shadow-wolf but wisps of black smoke curling up from the still-bubbling surface of the creek. A cool morning breeze caught them, and the dark tendrils drifted away, dispersing in the wind as though they had never been.

Branwen stood beside the creek, gasping for breath as she stared into the water. Her father and brother rushed to her. She could hear her sister calling her name from atop the hill, but she couldn't respond.

"*What* was *that*?" Madden blurted, his blue eyes wide as he watched the swirling tide of the creek. His gaze darted back to Branwen, maintaining his expression of disbelief. "Are you all right?" he asked, his sand-colored brows drawing tight with concern, but Branwen just shook her head, speechless.

Her whole body quaked with the aftershock of the morning's events. Her father wrapped his lean, hard arm around her waist just as her knees buckled. His solid grip gave her strength and she recovered, drawing herself upright by sheer force of will.

"I'm fine," she said, trying to pull away. Immediately, she wobbled and grasped onto her father's shirt to steady herself.

"You are *not* fine," her father replied, his voice as deep and firm as bedrock. He stepped in close to her side and looped her injured arm across his narrow, wiry shoulders, so he half-carried her as they moved toward the large rock by the creek. Madden followed close behind them, his tall form looming anxiously.

"Sit," her father commanded, lowering her onto the flat end of the stone.

Branwen obeyed, her eyes fluttering briefly shut. Her hands still grasped her father's sleeve tightly, unwilling to let go. In that very moment, all she wanted to do was curl up in her Papa's arms like when she was a little girl—to let him protect her and tell her everything was going to be all right, that the big, scary monster was gone and would never come back.

*But I'm not a child,* she thought, prying her fingers loose one by one. *I fought the monster. I killed it.* I *did that.* Sucking in a steadying breath, she opened her eyes.

Her father returned her gaze with a look of quiet appreciation. "That'll do," he murmured in her ear and Branwen's heart swelled with pride. In her family, the phrase meant a job well done, and coming from her father, it was high praise. "I'm going to get Colwen," he announced, giving Branwen's shoulder a gentle squeeze as he straightened. His eyes hardened as he looked over at Madden and added, "When I come back, I want to know *exactly* what happened here."

Branwen watched the color drain from her brother's face. "Yes, sir," Madden said with a near-audible swallow, but their father had already turned and started marching up the hill toward the ash tree. As soon as he was out of ear-shot, Madden turned to Branwen, his expression desperately pleading as he knelt by her side.

"I am *so* sorry," her brother began. "I should have gotten here sooner. I heard Colwen screaming, but I thought she was just playing, so I kept talking to Ifanna." Shame colored his face and voice as the truth continued to tumble out of his mouth. "I wasn't watching the flock like I was supposed to. I didn't even *see* the grannies come over the hill. Ifanna had to point them out to me before I realized something was wrong and—"

Branwen stopped him with a single raised finger pressed to his lips. His sky-blue eyes crossed comically as they tried to focus on her outstretched hand. Then, she saw a look of pain pass over his face as he spied the three gashes on her wrist. He winced in sympathy, his eyes tracing the deep, red lines one at a time.

"I'm fine," she insisted again, removing her finger. She tucked her injured hand into her lap, concealing the wound within the folds of her skirt. "Colwen's fine," she added with a nod up the hill toward their little sister. "If you hadn't come when you did...." She let the rest of the thought linger in the air, unspoken, but Madden knew.

He frowned. "I still should have been there," he said, far from placated.

"Yes," Branwen agreed. "But you don't need *me* telling you that. You're about to hear an earful from Papa on the subject."

Her brother moaned, his expression petrified, and Branwen thought she understood. Madden had been so distracted with Ifanna because of their recent engagement. *Papa only just decided Madden was responsible enough to propose*, Branwen knew. *But now, after this....* She wasn't sure what their father would say. Poor Madden could do nothing but wait.

They both stared up the hill, watching as Colwen climbed out of the ash tree. The six-year-old practically rolled down the hillside and flung herself into her father's arms as he approached. He scooped her up, holding her tight for a long moment before he turned and headed back toward the creek, still carrying his daughter. Branwen didn't think he could have put Colwen down even if he'd wanted to—both her arms hooked around his neck and her spry, young legs clung to his hips like a vice. She was really too big to be carried around anymore. Their father wasn't a tall man; if Colwen had straightened her legs, her feet would have nearly dragged the ground, but she held on. Not even the jostle of her papa's walk could loosen her grip.

When he arrived back at the creek, he tried to set Colwen down on the rock beside Branwen, but his movements were awkward as she still clung to his neck. Beside her, Branwen could see the remnants of tears streaming down her sister's face and snot still dripped from her nose. The young girl sniffled ingloriously, then finally looked up.

"Branwen!" she yelped, bursting into new tears as she scrambled out of her father's arms and fell into Branwen's lap.

Her little sister's bony elbows and knees pummeled Branwen's bruised and tender body, but she didn't care. She hugged Colwen, filled with the relief and joy of knowing her sister was safe and unharmed. Whatever kind of creature the shadow-wolf had been didn't matter; it was gone and they were going to be all right.

When Branwen glanced up, she could see her papa standing a little ways off—to give her and Colwen some space, she presumed. As her sister calmed, their father's expression changed from one of fierce protection to that of cold fury as his eyes darted to Madden. She could feel the chill in the air as her papa's gaze turned as hard and sharp as flint.

*Here it comes*, Branwen thought and grabbed her brother's hand in warning.

Madden looked down at her with something akin to resignation in his eyes. He gave her hand a squeeze, then extricated himself from her grip. He straightened his shoulders, bracing as he turned to face his father.

"Your sisters are safe—now—but where were you?" the older man demanded, his voice tight with restrained anger. "Where were *you* when they were in need? Where were *you* when the girls were fighting for their lives?"

Though Branwen knew he'd expected it, Madden flinched. "I'm sorry, Pa," he began, but their father cut him short.

"I don't want apologies, Madden," he said. "I want an answer. Where—were—you?"

Madden murmured something indistinct, and lightning flashed in their father's peat-brown eyes.

"Where?" the man repeated, his voice like the crack of thunder. Even Colwen noticed, turning around in Branwen's lap. The young girl scooted off to sit beside her on the rock, half-hiding behind her and yet just as unable to look away from the coming storm.

Madden spoke up. "The north field."

"That close?" Their father stared at him incredulously. "I could hear Colwen cry for help as I was coming up from the village. You were less than half that distance away. You should have been there!" He gestured toward Branwen as he said, "Maybe if you had, your sister wouldn't be hurt!"

Madden flinched again at the accusation, but before he could say anything, Branwen tried to interject.

"Papa, that's not—"

"Enough, Branwen," her father interrupted, his voice sharp. "I won't have any excuses for him—not this time. That *thing,* that"—he hesitated before saying—"*dog* could have really hurt you. It *did* hurt you. I'd hate to think of what an animal that size could have done to Colwen. What if it was rabid?"

As he spoke the words aloud, a new fear lit into his eyes and his gaze flashed over to Colwen and then down to Branwen's wrist. She felt the weight of her brother and sister's eyes on her, too. They all stared at the three deep marks obscured by the now-slow drip of her blood.

*The gashes could be anything, really*, Branwen thought with a sense of quiet dread. She hadn't felt the wounds when they'd happened; so much else had been going on. They *could be* tooth marks scraped sideways across her skin.... *No*, she decided, *the lines are too regular. They're definitely from the wolf's claws...right?*

She clamped her hand over her wrist, gritting her teeth against the pain. The salt of her sweat stung the wounds as her fingers lined up with the deep grooves in her flesh, covering them completely.

"It's a scratch. A nasty one," she admitted, "but still just a scratch."

"It looks deeper than a scratch," her father said, his voice dubious. His dark brows furrowed with concern.

Branwen shrugged, trying to down-play her injury for Madden's sake. Her brother carried enough guilt over his part in the matter, and their father didn't need any more ammunition for blame.

"It was a big...dog," she said at last, echoing her papa's description of the beast.

Beside her, Colwen shifted, and Branwen stole a glance at her sister. The six-year-old caught her eye and they shared a *look*. They both knew the creature that had attacked them was no dog. They also knew that now was not the time to debate the fact. Their father's patience had worn thin enough. Already, he'd begun to turn his attention back on Madden.

"And what of the sheep? Were they attacked on your watch, too?"

"The sheep are safe," Madden answered quickly. He paused only briefly, then rushed on with the rest of the truth. "I left them and both dogs with Ifanna in the north field."

*Good,* Branwen thought, proud of her brother's admittance. She gave him a subtle nod of encouragement. *With Papa, the truth is always best, even if it isn't exactly* good.

"Ifanna." Their father said the girl's name slowly, sucking in his stubbled cheeks. His thin lips pinched and his eyebrows raised as he seemed to put together what had really caused Madden's slow reaction to danger. "Is that right?" he asked. It wasn't a question.

Madden didn't answer, but instead ducked his head and lowered his eyes in a gesture of repentance. Their father barely acknowledged it.

"Well, you made *one* wise decision," the older man muttered, then raised his voice as he said, "Not long ago, I said you were a grown man, ready to take on the responsibilities of your own household, but after this..." Their father shook his head, pain and disappointment etching themselves into the crags of his face. "Clearly, I was wrong. You're not ready. Therefore, I rescind my permission—"

Madden's face had grown paler with every word, but at this last pronouncement, he blanched pure white. "Pa!"

The name seemed to jump from his lips in protest, but the look on his face was one of instant regret. Branwen watched as her brother covered his mouth with his hand, holding back the rest of what he wanted to say as their father's eyes flashed in warning.

She knew Colwen recognized it, too. Though their father's ire wasn't directed at the younger girl, she scooted back on the rock, using Branwen's form as a shield.

"Madden." The older man's tone stopped her brother cold. "Go collect the sheep," he commanded, "and while you're there, you can explain to Ifanna why you will *not* be allowed to marry her. After today, I do not want you even *speaking* to her until you've proven you can put the needs of your family above your own desires. Do you understand?"

Anger and indignation flushed her brother's face red as he choked out his response, "Yes, Pa."

Branwen could see tears brimming in his sky-blue eyes though he stubbornly refused to let them fall even as he turned away and trudged up the hill toward the north field. Her own heart plummeted at the conditions. They were far worse than anything she could have anticipated. Extra chores—or a month of Colwen-watching duty, she would have understood, but this? She tried to think about it from her father's perspective.

*Papa must have been terrified when he heard Colwen screaming, but couldn't find her. And then he saw the shadow-wolf attacking me.* She watched the way her father clenched and unclenched his fists, his fingers trembling as they extended. *With rage*, she thought at first until she realized: *he's still scared—scared that he could have lost us all.*

Colwen peered around Branwen to stare at her papa and Madden's retreating back, obviously not quite comprehending what had happened between them. She looked at Branwen questioningly, but Branwen just shook her head.

"Later," she mouthed and the six-year-old sat back down beside her, leaning her honey-blonde head on Branwen's shoulder.

Their father sighed, his breath shaky as he, too, watched Madden go. As his son disappeared over the hilltop, he turned to Branwen. "I've got to go get the rams," he said, gesturing vaguely toward the road. His hands still quaked with anxious tremors, so he busied them with gathering his shepherd's crook as he added, "Branwen, you should head home and have your mother take a look at those scratches. Come—I'll walk you two to the fence."

Colwen moved first, eagerly jumping off the rock, and Branwen followed after, more slowly. Her hill-tumbled bones had settled as she'd sat and now her joints creaked and popped, shifting back into their rightful places when she stood. After the fall she'd taken, she knew she'd be sore for a few days, but she was grateful.

Gingerly running her fingers over the gashes on her wrist, she thought to herself, *Things could have turned out a whole lot worse.*

They'd barely gone more than a few feet when Colwen shouted and darted off to the side. Branwen and her father both startled at the sudden movement, bracing themselves for another attack. Branwen recovered first, laughing when she saw what Colwen had gone after.

The six-year-old came tromping back up the hill with her mangled doll held proudly aloft.

"Hyll survived, too!" the young girl shouted, a wide smile beaming across her face. She thrust the doll at her sister for inspection.

"*Survived* might be a very generous way to put it," Branwen commented, turning the rag doll over in her hands.

The already-ugly Hyll had become even more hideous. One of doll's button eyes hung loose and both were chipped where the shadow-wolf's teeth had clamped down on them. A single thread kept Hyll's right arm attached and half the stuffing had come out of her lumpy torso. The honey-colored yarn of her hair had fallen out in clumps while the few remaining strands tangled themselves into inextricable knots.

While Branwen held the doll, Colwen began gathering lost chunks of wool from the grass, following the trail of white fuzz where the wind had blown them across the field. As she moved, she tucked the wool safely away in her pockets for later.

*She'll want the doll repaired, not replaced*, Branwen thought as she and her father trailed after the young girl. New stitches would mark the doll like scars, adding to Hyll's intense ugliness, but Colwen—being Colwen—would only love the doll even more.

On a whim, Branwen held the rag doll out to her papa.

"Hyll had the worst of it," she said as he gently took the doll from her hands. "Colwen and I...we're bumped and bruised, but we're all right—thanks to Madden. If he hadn't been there when he was with his sling..." She shook her head, trying to banish the thought. "You couldn't have gotten to us fast enough."

Her father didn't respond, but she knew he'd heard her. He brushed his thumb over the tear in the fabric of Hyll's wrist, an injury nearly mirroring Branwen's own. For a long time, he looked at the doll without saying a word.

"Papa..." Branwen began again, though she knew full-well what his reply would be. Her father didn't disappoint.

"No, Branwen. My decision is final," he stated. "It's nothing against Ifanna. You know I love her—she's practically family already—and she's been so good for Madden." Her father loosed another gusty sigh, shaking his head before he added, "I just want what's best for them both. For all his size, Madden is still just a boy on the inside. How can he take care of a family of his own if he can't protect the one he's already got?"

He looked to her for agreement, but Branwen strategically kept her silence. She arranged her face in the most neutral of expressions, letting her father's own words hang in the air. It was a trick her mother used to make Branwen and her siblings think about what they'd said during a heated argument. Branwen knew it was working on her father; she could almost hear the echo of his words in his own mind. The harsh light in his eyes softened as he looked at her.

"I know what you're doing," he said, his craggy cheeks lifting in a crooked grin. "Your mother would remind me that I—that *we*—were young once. So young, so...*stupid*."

He laughed and Branwen grinned, too, knowing she'd made her point.

"I will relent," her father confirmed, "but only a little. And don't you spoil it—I want him to stew for a while. Madden still has a lot of growing up to do. He needs to learn that his actions have consequences and not just for him. When you're married, everything you do *matters* to someone *else*."

"I won't tell," Branwen promised, looping her uninjured arm around her father's neck and kissing him on the cheek. His beard tickled her face as she told him, "I love you, Papa."

"Love you, too," he replied, giving her a fervent squeeze.

They walked side by side to the gate, passing Colwen along the way. The younger girl had gotten bored at their lagging pace and stopped to weave a flower crown for Hyll.

Their father pushed the gate open, waiting for them, and Branwen turned back, holding out a hand to her sister. "Colwen, are you coming?" she summoned more than asked, and her sister raced to catch up.

As the six-year-old neared, she reached over and grabbed their father's hand instead, extracting Hyll from his grasp so she could wrap her own fingers around his broad, rough palm.

"I'm going to stay with Papa," she said. "He might need help with the grannies. I'll bet they're still scared after...." She shuddered, then twitched her limbs as though shaking off the memory of the shadow-wolf. Branwen wished it were so easy for herself; when she blinked, amber eyes stared back at her from the dark. "Anyway," Colwen added when she'd settled, "I keep finding pieces of Hyll everywhere."

"All right," Branwen agreed, smiling at her sister's resilience. "I'll see you at the festival, then? Mother should have me patched up and we can get some sweet buns at the market stalls."

"Mmm...sweet buns." Colwen licked her lips, then held up her doll. "Hyll loves sweet buns, don't you Hyll?"

Their father piped in. "Don't encourage her," he warned, but Branwen could see the smile teasing at the corners of his mouth.

"Bye, Papa. Bye, Colwen. Tell Madden I'll see him later," she said as she walked through the gate by herself. She could hear the rams' low bleating from further up the road. Despite all the commotion, they hadn't strayed far. Her father would have no trouble gathering them up again and taking them to the pastures at last.

Her family waved after her as she started down the sloping path toward the village, marching homeward. With every step, her wrist throbbed, constantly reminding her of the pain and fear she'd experienced...and reminding her, too, of the thrill of victory when she'd finally vanquished the shadow-beast. Her blood sang with remembered adrenaline and her heart skipped in her chest, knocking erratically against her sternum. With the threat of the wolf gone and her family safe, she felt invincible.

Invulnerable.

Branwen looked to the west where the hill-forest of Bryn Celli Ddu rose above the soft curve of the tree line. The sun had burned away the morning mist that earlier enshrouded the hill's dark base. Its golden light burnished the treetops along the hill's crest, forming a crown of glittering yellow against emerald green. What had once looked ominous in the cool, dim light of the early dawn now seemed vibrant and welcoming in the glow of the mid-morning sun.

*I'm going there. Today*, Branwen reiterated her decision. *Right after Mother helps me get these gashes stitched up.* As *iachäwr*-in-training, she knew better than to go gallivanting through an unknown forest with open wounds, but any of her other reservations had simply vanished. She thought she believed the rumors about Bryn Celli Ddu, now—well, at least some of them. The tales of magic and mystery...they couldn't all be just stories. After seeing the shadow-wolf, she knew things existed beyond the realm of human explanation. She'd witnessed pure, devouring evil in the form of a wolf and she'd destroyed it. Whatever the burial mound at Bryn Celli Ddu held, it couldn't be worse than that.

She had nothing left to fear.

# Chapter 3

Branwen knew for a fact that her family possessed the largest dining table in all of Llanddaniel Bryn. And for good reason. As home to the village *iachäwr*, hardly a week went by when some farmer's son wasn't hauled into the house right before supper time and plonked on the end of the long oak boards for emergency care.

Her mother had to be prepared to set bones and tend wounds at a moment's notice—especially in the spring when the rams were frisky and prone to butting heads with more than just each other.

*Well, today it's my turn*, Branwen thought, clenching her teeth against the pain. She sat at the very end of the dining table with her injured limb stretched across the tabletop. Her mother sat on the other side with her head bowed in concentration as she sewed up the gashes on Branwen's wrist.

Seventeen stitches. Seventeen times the hook-shaped needle had to pass through her skin to close up the marks left by the shadow-wolf.

*One for every year of my life*, Branwen considered as her mother tied off the last suture. Tiny knots dotted the curved red lines on her wrists like stars forming a morbid constellation.

Because of her mother's skill, Branwen knew the wounds would heal quick and clean, leaving behind only the thinnest of scars, but right now they still *hurt*.

In addition to the dull, throbbing pain of her torn flesh, she could feel the phantom stab of the needle lingering along the wounds' edges and her skin felt uncomfortably tight where the thread pulled them together. The numbing sensation of the mint oil was beginning to wear off.

"Here, chew this," her mother said, reaching across the table to hold a few thin strips of willow bark to Branwen's lips. "For the pain."

Reluctantly, Branwen obeyed, chomping down on the dry strips and drawing them into her mouth. She hated the bark's bitter flavor, and its rough texture made her wonder if it was possible to get splinters in her tongue, but she couldn't deny the willow's pain-reducing effect. Still, she grimaced as the now-wet bark began to exude its acerbic aftertaste.

Her mother must have seen her expression. "Keep chewing," the older woman insisted. She pressed another small bundle of the bark shavings into Branwen's uninjured palm. "That's for later."

Branwen dutifully placed the willow bark into the pocket of her over-skirt, but her mind was already churning over ways to sneak the bits of wood back into the jar on the mantle. She had more than enough in her mouth already. The juices of it threatened to dribble down her chin, so she quickly swallowed the excess liquid. Her nose scrunched and her mouth pinched at the renewed bitterness.

Seated in a wicker highchair at the head of the table, two-year-old Magrid peered down at her and giggled as she tried to mirror Branwen's look of disgust.

"Yucky!" the little girl exclaimed, slamming both of her small hands on the table for emphasis. Chunks of that morning's porridge clung to the fine, blonde silk of her hair.

Branwen laughed. "Yes," she agreed, wrinkling up her nose for fun this time. She stuck her tongue out, provoking another giggle from her youngest sister. "Yucky."

Her mother stood, playfully rolling her eyes as she collected her surgical supplies from the table. "You know, your Great-Aunt Esther always said—"

"—healing rarely comes without pain. I know," Branwen finished drolly. To prove a point, she made a show of swallowing another mouthful of willow bark juice.

Apparently, Great-Aunt Esther had said a lot of things, but that bit of wisdom seemed to have been her favorite...or at least Branwen's mother's favorite. She quoted it all the time, along with a myriad of other sayings when the situation permitted. Her mother used the phrases so often, Branwen was beginning to suspect she'd never had a Great-Aunt Esther at all, but that the woman was just a construct her mother used to add weight to her own medical pronouncements.

In a small village like Llanddaniel Bryn, people didn't trust new ideas, especially when it came to the mysteries of the healing arts, but if "Great-Aunt Esther" had said it...well, that was all right, then, wasn't it?

Branwen's mother smiled. "As in all things, the best solutions are often also the hardest," she said, quoting another of Esther's sayings. She tilted her head, looking directly at Branwen. "You'd do well to remember that."

"Yes, Mother." Branwen sighed, but accepted the advice, tucking the words into the back of her mind for further contemplation. Later. Now that her wounds had been stitched up, she was anxious to leave—to take every spare moment she had to explore the cairn at Bryn Celli Ddu.

Before long, the solstice festivities would begin. With her parents and Madden all taking part in the procession, Branwen would be expected to look after Colwen and Magrid. She couldn't just leave them to satisfy her own curiosity about the forest-tomb, but if she could sneak away beforehand, she could return before anyone knew she had gone. Branwen's jaw clenched at the prospect, grinding the stringy remains of the willow bark into a fine pulp before swallowing.

She stood, pushing back from the table. The stitches in her arm pinched at the movement, but the willow bark was starting to take effect. The sharp pain had dulled to a localized ache.

"I need to talk to Ifanna," Branwen announced, turning toward the front door. "I want to make sure she's not angry at me for what happened with Madden."

"Ifanna? Angry?" Her mother scoffed. "I don't think that's possible. Ifanna doesn't have a stern bone in her entire body. How could she be angry? She'll know it wasn't your fault. And besides, I'm not done with you yet. Sit down."

It wasn't a tone that begged for questioning. Branwen sat.

She kept her silence as her mother gathered strips of clean linen and a small clay pot of ointment, but with every second Branwen could feel her opportunity slowly vanishing. She knew once her mother had determined to treat a patient, nothing could get in her way.

Well...almost nothing. After seeing her father's reaction to the shadow-wolf and the fear he'd had for his children, Branwen thought she finally understood one thing.

"Mother," she blurted, "why are you afraid of letting me go to Bryn Celli Ddu?"

At the question, her mother's entire body tensed. Her warm, hazel eyes flashed wide with shock...and something else. *Guilt?* Branwen wondered as she watched a series of convoluted emotions flicker across her mother's face.

For a moment, she thought her mother would deny the truth. Branwen could see the words forming on the older woman's lips, but at the last instant her mother's mouth clamped shut. She took a step toward Branwen, sitting next to her on the bench. The ever-so-slight tremor of her mother's hands belied her otherwise calm facade. The lid on the ointment jar rattled as she set it and the linens down. At the head of the table, Magrid continued pushing around the remains of her porridge with her toddler-sized spoon, oblivious to the change of mood in the room.

"You're right. I am afraid," her mother admitted, breaking the silence. She took Branwen's hands in her own, clasping them tightly.

The older woman's thumb rested just above the last stitch on Branwen's wrist. Her touch provoked the memory of the shadow-wolf, and Branwen's heart raced as visions of the beast's dark hunger echoed through her mind. *The wolf is dead,* she reminded herself. *You killed it.* She took in a deep, steadying breath as her mother continued.

"There is a presence at the ruins of Bryn Celli Ddu," the woman said. "A vast power watches everything within the shadow of that hill. It blesses us...and it curses us. You know the story."

Branwen had heard hundreds of rumors and folk tales regarding the hill-forest of Bryn Celli Ddu over the course of her lifetime, but the vaguely haunted look in her mother's eyes left no doubt as to which story she referred.

"You're talking about Eirlys," Branwen stated.

Every child in Llanddaniel Bryn knew the legend of poor Eirlys, daughter to one of the previous wool-dyers—Ifanna's great-grandfather—and the last girl to vanish from Bryn Celli Ddu just over fifty years ago. Each year on the anniversary of her disappearance, the eve before the summer solstice, the old women of the village would trot out the well-told tale of how the young, beautiful Eirlys walked into the forest and never returned. Bryn Celli Ddu took her, the old women said, just as it used to take young girls in the ancient days when the old gods and the fae demanded payment for protecting the village.

Until now, Branwen had never really believed in the story of Eirlys. Ifanna had never mentioned anything about her, and Branwen had figured *she* would know, seeing as how Eirlys was supposed to be her great-aunt. Branwen had always assumed Eirlys was just another construct—another great-aunt like Esther—meant to keep children from going into the woods.

But now....

Branwen shifted uncomfortably in her seat. Earlier that morning, she would have scoffed at her mother mentioning the tales surrounding the mound at Bryn Celli Ddu, but after her experience with the shadow-wolf, she knew better. If a beast made of darkness and hunger could exist, why not the strange magic of Bryn Celli Ddu? Somehow, the thought didn't scare her. Branwen felt excited, instead.

"Your father's mother Medb knew the girl," her mother said, drawing her attention back.

Branwen looked up at her, startled. "What?"

Her mother nodded. "They were friends much like you and Ifanna," she explained, picking up the small clay pot of ointment once more. As she spoke, she used a flattish spoon to dip the goo out and spread it across Branwen's inflamed skin. "Medb liked to push the boundaries—of *anything* and *anyone*—and Eirlys always followed her wherever she went. They liked to sneak around the edges of the forest and see how deep they could go into the woods before they got too frightened. Your grandmother told me she'd always talked about going all the way up to Bryn Celli Ddu, but Eirlys actually did it. That was the day she disappeared."

"Oh." Branwen paused. *What do you say to that?* she wondered. *Was Grandmother Medb part of the reason Eirlys went missing?* "I'd never heard that before," she finished lamely.

"Your grandmother didn't talk about it much," her mother said as she began wrapping Branwen's salved wrist with the thin strips of linen to create a layer of protection. "I think she felt guilty. Ashamed. When you were born, she asked me to swear that I would never let any of my daughters into the forest. No one but the men, elders, and *iachäwr* were allowed beyond the border, anyway. I thought I could keep my vow, but then you decided to apprentice as an *iachäwr*...."

"And one of the village *iachäwr*'s most important duties is presiding over the ritual binding of Bryn Celli Ddu," Branwen finished for her mother. Of course, she was well-aware of that fact—it was one of the main reasons Branwen had decided to become an *iachäwr* in the first place.

The older woman sighed, tucking the end of the linen wrap beneath the other layers of bandages to secure it. "You remind me so much of her—your grandmother."

It wasn't the first time Branwen had heard the comparison. Her mother and the few remaining villagers from her grandmother's generation often commented on how strongly she resembled a young Medb with her moon-pale skin, leaf-green eyes, and wild, dark hair. Yet this time, she didn't think her mother was referring to just her looks.

Her mother shook her head, as though settling something within herself. "I made a promise," she told Branwen. "I will never take you to Bryn Celli Ddu. I won't risk it. I pray that in a few months when you go to Caernafon to finish your *iachäwr* training, you'll put it from your mind entirely. You'll find a nice boy from Gaerwen or even Bangor maybe, get married, settle down, and never think of that place again."

At her mother's words, Branwen felt her heart drop down into her shoes, but she knew better than to protest. *Never?* whispered the crush of her dreams. To her mother, she said only, "I understand."

The older woman smiled. "Glad that's settled," she said, patting the back of Branwen's hand.

Branwen could only manage a closed-lip smile in return and hoped her expression read as reassuring. She said nothing.

She couldn't think of anything *to* say that wasn't an outright lie. Things were *far* from settled. Branwen wasn't going to give in to her mother's—or grandmother's—desires so easily. With everything she'd been through that morning and now learning that at least part of the story of Eirlys' disappearance was true, she wanted to explore Bryn Celli Ddu more than ever. She wanted to see with her own eyes the mysteries of the tomb in the dark forest. Her mind churned with the possibilities.

At the other end of the table, Magrid clapped her small hands together, demanding the rest of her family's attention.

"Want down," the two-year-old insisted, wriggling her small body within the confines of the wicker highchair.

Her mother stood, scooping the child up with outstretched arms. Branwen followed suit, pushing back from the table. Her wrist twinged a little at the pressure, but it was bearable. Her injuries shouldn't impinge on her anticipated trek through the forest. If the old men of the village made the journey every year, the path couldn't be too difficult.

"I'd better get going," Branwen announced. "Papa probably won't let me tend the sheep—he'll have Madden do it—but maybe I can lend Ifanna a *hand*." She smiled at the small joke, waving her uninjured wrist. The linen wrapping on the other one made it more difficult to move.

"That would be nice, dear," her mother said, her attention focused on Magrid as she tried to pick the bits of porridge out of the little girl's blonde curls. The toddler would have none of it, twisting her head this way and that.

"Bye, bunny," Branwen said, distracting the little girl just long enough for her mother to accomplish her goal.

Magrid grinned, showing off her pearly teeth with their slightly prominent incisors. "Buh-bye!" the toddler shouted happily.

"Make sure you're home in time for the counting!" Branwen's mother called after her as she headed toward the door. "The procession won't start if all the children and young women aren't accounted for."

"I know," Branwen said, doing some quick calculations in her head.

The entire celebration of the binding of Bryn Celli Ddu usually lasted three hours from the beginning of the procession to their return. Assuming the actual ceremonies took up the majority of that time, she thought the journey itself couldn't take more than half an hour one-way, or an hour total. It was nine o'clock now and the procession always started at noon, so even if she took it slow, she could make it to Bryn Celli Ddu and back before anyone would ever miss her.

Branwen couldn't help it; she grinned. "I'll be there," she assured her mother. She blew a kiss to Magrid, then walked out the door.

She moved calmly through their front yard, unlatching the white-washed, picket fence and closing it behind her as she stepped out onto the dirt road. The path split at the north edge of her family's property.

One branch trailed back up the hillside toward the pastures; the other continued east, eventually becoming the main thoroughfare of Llanddaniel Bryn.

Branwen took neither.

She went down the road just far enough to be out of sight from the house—in case her mother had grown suspicious of Branwen's easy acquiescence.

*Mothers seem to have a sixth sense about that sort of thing*, she thought as she peered back at her family's cottage from the cover of a small copse of trees. She was proven right as the drapes on the window at the side of the house fluttered, and she could see her mother—with Magrid on her hip—gazing toward the path that led to the fields.

A twinge of guilt pricked at Branwen's heart—a reminder of her disobedience—but as the curtains closed, her sense of adventure came rushing back. She swerved left, cutting through the trees and circling around her house. She tucked up her skirts and ducked between the slats of the old, board fence at the back of the cottage, darting behind the sheep barn and chicken coops to remain unseen. She did *not* want to explain to her mother why she had said she was going to help Ifanna in the fields, yet somehow ended up in the opposite direction.

She made it over the fence at the other side of the yard without disturbing a single one of her mother's hens; the over-feeding from Colwen that morning had made them sleepily content. There were no windows on that side of her family's cottage, so Branwen didn't hesitate to follow the dirt road as it curved a quarter-mile around the village lake and up toward Bryn Celli Ddu.

As she neared the shadow of the forest-hill, the path grew rough, no longer worn flat by the steady trod of human feet or crush of wagon wheels. Small stones kicked from beneath her heels and overgrown grass tangled around her boots. Ahead, she could see an area where the village elders had hewn back the undergrowth, making an entrance to the forest. It loomed like a dark door before her.

*Anything could be lurking beyond there*, she thought, and the image of amber eyes flashed through her mind. *The wolf!* Branwen jerked to a halt, peering intently into the gloom-veiled grove.

Something rustled within the scraggly brush of the forest's edge and Branwen bolted toward the lake, throwing herself behind a stand of cattails. Water and lake muck came up to her knees, soaking into her recently-dried dress, but she didn't care. Her heart hammered in her chest and her fists clenched tight, making the newly-stitched wounds on her wrist throb as she stared at the dark hill.

The entrance to the forest rustled again and Branwen crouched lower just as three men strode out from the bushes, laughing and joking. She recognized them right away: Dafydd the milliner, Old Thomas the wheelwright, and Jacob, his son. The small, rowan-handled axes at their belts told her they were part of this year's designated Pathwalkers—men of good standing within the village chosen to clear a path through the forest up to the cairn at Bryn Celli Ddu.

Branwen relaxed at the sight of their smiling, familiar faces, but didn't move from her cover. None of the villagers allowed their young women near the forest, especially during the summer solstice. If any of the men spotted her, she knew she'd be hard-pressed to explain what she was doing there, but they passed by, too occupied with their own witty banter to notice the few extra ripples her movements had sent across the lake.

When they disappeared beyond the curve of the road, Branwen clamored up from the shore, shoes squelching as she went. She stood in front of the forest-hill once more, glaring into the darkness. *The shadow-wolf is dead*, she told herself. *And the Pathwalkers would have been carrying a lot more than wood axes if they'd expected trouble. The way must be safe,* she concluded. *There are no wolves in the forest. I have nothing to fear.*

Still dripping, Branwen straightened her shoulders and, with the rising sun at her back, marched straight into the twilight wood.

The Pathwalkers had done their job well, cutting a clear swath up the side of the hill. The wide trail snaked through the woods like a dry riverbed, following the natural ebb and flow of the forest's growth.

Every few feet, Branwen saw stakes of rowan, hawthorn, and ash driven into the ground at the edges of the pathway, marking the boundary between the sacred road and the forest. Remnants of braided wool wrapped around the tops of some of the stakes and small, rusted bells littered the ground around them. Branwen plucked at the stray fibers, picking out dried bits of savory and rue enmeshed in the ragged plaits.

*Herbs of protection*, she knew as she dropped the wilted braid to the ground. The stakes themselves were all made from trees symbolic of safe travel and shielding from evil. Someone had gone through a lot of trouble to ward off the power from Bryn Celli Ddu. *This must all be a part of the binding process*, Branwen thought as she continued up the path. *The elders will probably re-tie bells around the posts with braids of wool and herbs as they ascend.*

Beyond the path, the forest grew dark and wild. Every so often, rays of sunlight pierced the forest canopy, illuminating patches of emerald moss or citrine briars. In the distance, she thought she heard the gentle splashing of a stream as it tumbled down the hillside—the source-spring of the lake, she assumed as the trickling noise echoed through the hush of the woods. Yet, the longer she listened, the more distinct the sound became, transforming into a curious, fluting melody. The silvery tune played among the forest's upper branches, bouncing off the pale undersides of the leaves.

*Almost like a bird call, but not...quite,* Branwen thought as her eyes darted from canopy to canopy, trying to locate the source of the sound. The cadence flowed like water, pouring from one sweet note to the next as the melody wove between—soft and muffled at first, but growing clearer and clearer with every passing second.

The sound—*music*, she decided—originated somewhere deep within the woods. *From Bryn Celli Ddu*, whispered her secret desire. *Maybe this is all part of the preparation for the ceremonies?* she wondered, but wasn't fully convinced. Something in her heart told her this music was too beautiful to be made by human hands. It infiltrated her mind and Branwen's feet moved of their own accord, stepping forward to the rhythm of the song. Her heart quickened with the allure of adventure as she walked on, her gait light and sure as she let the music guide her up the winding path to the crest of the hill.

Sunlight shone through the tree line, indicating a wide, open space ahead and Branwen plunged forward. The music of the forest swelled around her in a brief crescendo as she crossed the threshold from darkness to day. She blinked against the sudden brightness of the mid-morning sun after what seemed like an eternity in the dusk of the woods. When her eyes finally adjusted, Branwen turned her gaze to the great stone cairn at Bryn Celli Ddu.

She stood only a few short steps away from the first protective circle surrounding the outer portion of the burial mound. Shards of slate and granite crowded a shallow trench, forming a moat of dark stones rather than water. Beyond the moat, a grassy hillock curved gently upward before leveling off to create a flat, circular expanse. Twelve standing stones, each half again as tall as Branwen, guarded the hill's peak. In the center, rose a massive cairn of rock and rubble with a single, narrow doorway leading down into darkness.

*I thought the tomb was supposed to be closed*, came the quiet mumble of Branwen's memory. The silver melody filled her mind, muddling her thoughts. The entire clearing rang with the sound, making it impossible to pinpoint as it danced between the standing stones and skipped along the rocky moat. Branwen had no choice but to go closer to the mound if she wanted to find the music's source. She could think of nothing else.

The stone moat was too wide to just step across, so she backed up a few paces and ran, hurling herself at the grass-carpeted embankment with a flying leap. She realized mid-air that she'd been overzealous on her take off, but no amount of flailing slowed her descent. Branwen slammed into the side of the small hill feet-first, then tumbled forward, catching her fall with her hands. The strain on her wrists popped a stitch, and she hissed in pain as she scrambled the rest of the way up the slope.

For a brief moment, the forest's ethereal song faded, and Branwen felt only the sharp, stabbing pain in her left wrist. Hot blood trickled from beneath her bandaging and down her hand. It dripped from her fingertips and onto the ground where the grassy mound drank it in like water. As she pressed the wound against her skirt to stem the flow, reality came rushing back and she realized exactly what was happening to her.

*The power at Bryn Celli Ddu is real!* she thought with burgeoning panic. *I've been lured here alone on the summer solstice with no one to know where I've gone!*

Granted, she had *intended* to do most of those things, but of her own volition and *not* at the will of the power at Bryn Celli Ddu. She'd only wanted to explore, to gain a taste of the forbidden before the duties of the village *iachäwr* smothered her adventurous spirit, but now....

*Is this how Eirlys felt right before she disappeared?* Branwen wondered frantically.

"Mother was right," she told herself as she rallied her nerves, ready to fight the pull of the music. "I shouldn't be here—this was a bad idea."

She spun on her heels quickly, ready to sprint down the hill and across the clearing, when the music came back full force—no longer fluting and melodic, but low and percussive like a battle march. Her feet became iron weights, refusing to move any closer to the edge of the embankment no matter how hard she tried. Drums pounded, matching and then beating over the rhythm of her own heart as they took control. She felt the bones in her ankles grind as the rest of her body slowly pivoted toward the sound coming from within the mound. Branwen wobbled, unable to keep her balance as her limbs and torso rebelled against her. With her concentration broken, her foot lifted, and the next thing she knew, she faced the mound and had taken one giant stride toward the cairn's dark entrance.

"Help!" Branwen shrieked. She tried to turn her head, throwing her voice over her shoulder and praying it carried down the path and into the woods where a Pathwalker might hear. "Dafydd! Thomas! Jacob! Someone, help!"

The drums thudded in her head, reverberating around in her skull, and she clamped her hands over her ears, physically screaming just to drown out the noise in her mind. The music seized control of her legs in the chaos and hurled her toward the sun-bathed mouth of the burial mound and its jet-black throat. She felt herself cross the boundary of light to dark with a stomach-lurching jerk. For a second the whole world spun, flipping inside and out, upside and down. Branwen's eyes slammed shut and she stumbled forward, reaching out with both hands to cling to the walls of the tiny cavern. For a brief moment, the drumbeats wavered, and she regained her footing long enough to stand straight.

Dry, warm air replaced the cool musk of the crypt in her nose, and Branwen opened her eyes. Gone was the reddish-gold glow from the morning sun that once funneled into the burial mound. Muted colors washed the narrow cavern walls, instead, painted pale by the light of a foreign sun trickling in from behind her. Branwen had no time to contemplate the sudden change as the music pulled her forward, marching her feet with each beat of the unseen drums.

Stone shelves and long, narrow benches lined the rough-hewn walls of the cairn. Branwen could see faint shadows of clay jars packed tightly on each shelf and a few urns tucked into every low, craggy corner. A massive urn jutted from a shallow nook in the wall to obstruct part of the passage, but the music forced Branwen onward, directly into the large jar's path. She braced herself as much as she could within the confines of the drums' spell in preparation for the collision, then ogled in disbelief as her body passed right through the urn as though it were only a ghost of the thing.

*Or maybe* I'm *the ghost*, her mind whispered. Cold danced up Branwen's spine, but her body remained too rigidly controlled to express her horror with a shudder.

The music marched her deeper and deeper into the cairn. As she went, the tunnel widened. Soon, the jars turned into cups and bowls, then bundles of cloth, and finally bare bones—some burnt, others untouched by flame. They littered the path before her, and unlike the urns earlier in the passage, these *crunched* under her heels, shattered by the pressure of her footfalls.

Some things were *real*, Branwen decided.

As long as she didn't try to stop her descent, the grip of the drums loosened enough for her to move her arms. Her fingers brushed over the rugged face of the walls, feeling which structures were truly solid and which only appeared that way. Within a few feet, she could start to tell them apart without having to touch them. The illusions, as Branwen chose to think of them, were almost see-through and had faint or absent shadows like the jars and urns at the entrance of the tunnel.

Ahead, the way flared and the walls curved, forming a circular chamber. In the center of the room, Branwen spied an oblong stone about four feet high with a jagged crack running from top to bottom. Serpentine patterns swirled across the stone's surface, forming concentric rings and waving, wriggling lines that stretched across the monolithic fissure.

At first, she thought the stone exuded its own radiance, but then she saw the narrow, angled slit in the far wall that allowed diluted light to filter though without exposing the chamber to direct sun. However, no light touched the split in the pattern-stone. Its serrated shape only grew darker—wider—as the drums pushed her forward: it had its own shadow.

Branwen realized, *This isn't a crack that exists in the rock. That crack exists in the* world, *and I'm heading right for it!*

She flailed, latching onto the archway created by the broadened tunnel. Her fingers dug into the crevasses of the rock, searching for purchase, but the drums of Bryn Celli Ddu overpowered her, ripping her free. The music flung her at the pattern-stone and she felt its yearning hands reaching for her through the fissure, trying to drag her in.

Her stomach lurched again as though pulled by a string though her navel, and Branwen yelped, craning her neck to get one last, fleeting glimpse of the world above. She caught only the weak, white light of a pale sun peering meekly through the crypt's oval entrance before utter darkness enveloped her.

# Chapter 4

Branwen stumbled through the blackness, her mind reeling with the sound of drums. Then, suddenly, the spinning stopped.

Breath whooshed out of Branwen's lungs in a startled shriek as she struggled to regain her balance within the disorienting dark. Beneath her boots, the crypt's jagged, bone-strewn floor gave way to a shifting, powder-fine softness. *Sand.* Branwen couldn't see it, but she recognized the texture just as her feet started to slide out from under her. She pitched forward, her arms flung out to break her fall. Her body tensed, preparing for the impact.

She never hit the ground.

Invisible hands snatched at her, grabbing her by the elbows. Another set of hands latched onto the back of her dress and wrapped around her waist, hauling her up. Branwen thrashed, trying to fight off her unseen captors, but their hold on her only tightened.

"Let me go!" she screamed, twisting and slamming her hands against the darkness. Her fingers collided with bare flesh and she dug her nails in. Branwen felt the bump-bump-bump of ribs jutting against too-taut skin as she raked her hands across her captor's chest.

A hot, metallic scent bloomed in the air and she knew she drew blood, but her captor didn't flinch.

"Play the drums, Sebastian!" a male voice rasped above her cries. His thin, almost-skeletal body braced against hers as she continued to struggle.

"Can't," retorted her second captor, his voice looming far above Branwen's head. He stood so close she could feel the reverberation of his words against her back. "Kinda need two hands for that, Bart," he said, his oil-slick tone oozing with contempt. "Besides, Celaeno said the music only helps pull those who are marked *through* the Veil. She didn't say anything about once they were on *this* side."

"Of course not." The first voice—Bart—sighed, exasperated, but Branwen's heart leapt in her chest.

No drums? No flute either? Her ears confirmed the truth of the statement, and hope soared, sending strength into her limbs. All she needed was for the taller of her kidnappers to relax for just a moment. Even now, she felt sure she could overpower the thinner one to break free.

*And then what?* she wondered desperately. She could think of only one option: run. Her spine trembled at the thought of darting through the inky terrain, and dryness pricked her eyes as she stared, trying to penetrate the black—looking for any sign of which way to go.

Nothing.

The cold, musky scent of the crypt faded, replaced by pungent, briny air. A faint breath of wind brushed across her back, cool against the heat of her skin. The feel of it made Branwen think of an open door.

*I can't have come far from the rift*, she reasoned. *That must be it behind me! It's still open—I can go home!* Branwen shifted her stance as best she could within her captors' grasp. Listening to them closely, she prepared to turn and bolt whenever an opportunity presented itself.

"How was I supposed to know who the Cù Sìth would send back?" the one called Sebastian rebutted. "Maybe something went wrong. He was supposed to find us a *little* girl—someone more malleable, someone less *feisty*—but he left his mark on this one instead."

A large, cool hand slid down Branwen's arm, then ripped the bandage from her injured wrist. Her stitches pulled at the contact, shooting needles of pain up her arm, and Branwen's body involuntarily froze. Her mind, however, did not. *The Cù Sìth? The shadow-wolf!* she realized, anger kindling within her. *They sent that beast after* Colwen*!*

In front of her, Branwen felt her smaller captor shrug. "Whatever. What's done is done. Let's tie her up and get this over with. *I* don't want to be the one to keep Celaeno waiting."

"Stars forbid *that* happen," Sebastian muttered.

Bart grunted. "Just help me with the rope."

His grip on her left elbow remained strong, but the pressure of his hand around her right disappeared briefly, and Branwen heard a faint rustle as her captor moved in the dark. Shrugging something—the rope—off his shoulder, she assumed. Sebastian's hold on her waist loosened, distracted, and she knew he must be reaching for the rope. Blood rushed in Branwen's ears, crashing like waves though her skull. This was her only chance; if they managed to tie her up, she'd never escape.

Branwen jabbed her right elbow up and across as hard as she could, crunching what felt like nasal cartilage and bone. Warm liquid gushed down her arm and she caught again the coppery scent of blood. The one called Bart shrieked and let go, allowing her to pivot and ram her knee into her second captor's side. A startled "oof" proved her aim was true, and Branwen reached out, clawing at where his face should be with her now-free hand, but Sebastian was even taller than she'd thought. Her nails skidded across the cool flesh of his throat before snagging on the thin chain of a necklace. She heard a faint *pop* as the metal links broke beneath her grip. She didn't think she'd done much damage, but her attack must have surprised Sebastian enough that he flinched, and she wrenched herself from his grasp.

Branwen spun on her heels and ran, diving into the pitch blackness. The air clung to her like tar, laying thick across her skin, but she pushed through it. Her arms waved madly in front of her, searching for the crack in the world that might lead her back home. It had to be close!

A light, cool wind brushed Branwen's face, urging her to go faster, faster. Was that a breeze from within the cairn leaking through? Would she know if she passed the rift by mistake? She couldn't see *anything*.

Behind her, Branwen heard cursing and the quick scramble of feet across sand. *They* could see. Her kidnappers' steady footfalls held no doubt, no hesitation, as they plunged after her. Yet, she couldn't help smiling: the texture of the sand under her feet had changed, growing compact and hard. She could sense the earthy dampness of the crypt. Any second now she knew she would feel the crunch of ancient bones. She squinted, preparing her eyes for the glorious onslaught of summer sun pouring through the cairn's passageway. Then—

SPLASH!

"No!" Branwen roared as warm, ocean surf swept her feet out from under her. She landed with an ignominious *ploosh* that fully soaked her hair and her woolen dress whose sodden skirts weighed down her legs like anchors. Her joy turned to sobs in an instant, but her broken voice was swallowed by the waves, their incessant lapping conveying the vastness of the body of water before her.

Her pursuers splashed lightly into the sea and hauled her out, supporting her weight unevenly between them. Branwen couldn't muster the will to stand, let alone struggle, and soon her two unseen captors lowered her tired, hope-crushed body to the sand.

"Well," said Sebastian, slightly out of breath, "that was fun."

"Thpeak for yourthelf," Bart retorted. "I hab thalt ub my nothe."

"Oh, I think it's a little worse than that," Sebastian quipped. "Looks broken."

A flutter of defiance awoke in Branwen, and she lifted her head. The small gesture of pleasure at her captor's injury was all she could manage against the wave of despair that shuddered through her heart and turned her bones to lead.

"I'll thay," grumbled Bart.

"I can fix that," Sebastian offered, his voice slick with charm. "For a price."

At his words, Branwen felt a sudden tension in the air like the moment before a lightning strike. The faint hairs on her arms and neck pricked to attention.

"No thankth," Bart said after a heavy pause. "I can fixth it mythelf." Branwen flinched as she heard the crack of cartilage realigning, followed by Bart's own hiss of pain. The normal rasp of his voice returned as he added, "I know better than to become indebted to a kelpie."

*A kelpie? Did I hear that right?* Branwen's thoughts whirred as the slight tingle in the air faded.

She tried to make sense of her captors' exchange—anything to keep her mind off the cool grit of sand between her fingers, the sop of her drowned dress, and burn of salt on her wounded wrist. Each sensation jabbed into her, a cruel reminder of her failure to escape. A drop of water trickled down the side of her face, curving with the weight of gravity to slip inside the corner of her mouth. She tasted salt, but not the overpowering tang of the sea. Instead, a unique brackishness assailed her tongue: tears.

She blinked. *Madden would make fun of me right now*, she thought. *He'd call me a weeping willow, then throw rocks at me. Little ones. Bigger ones if I didn't stop.*

Her tears flowed freely now; in the daylight, they would have blurred her vision, but they held no power in the dark.

Branwen stiffened. *No power in the dark.* Something about that phrase struck a chord. Her mind reached out, grasping at the half-formed notions floating inside her skull. Currently, her kidnappers held all the power. They outnumbered her. They could see.

She drooped in dismay, pressing her forehead into the invisible sand. She needed a way to shift the dynamic, something to give her an advantage or take away one of theirs. Numbers, darkness, power…

In her mind, a voice that sounded an awful lot like Madden suggested: *...rocks?*

*I don't have rocks,* Branwen thought, her fingers clawing at the damp sand in frustration. The tiny grains wedged underneath her fingernails, pressing into the tender quick like miniature boulders. *Wait...!*

Branwen's heart nearly galloped out of her chest. Sand. Sand could work, but not the wet, heavy stuff within her immediate reach. She needed dry sand. Light, fluffy, *inhalable* sand. Throat-shredding and eye-burning sand.

Slowly, she extended her arm, testing the moisture content with a brush of her fingers, and found herself in luck. Her captors had brought her a good ways away from the water. She could feel the line the tide made, where the sand shifted from its wave-compacted form to a slightly soggy mush.

*A few inches more and I'll have it,* she thought.

She lifted her body a little and used her other arm to push herself forward. Branwen sensed a slight movement to her right and heard the gritty *squish* of feet shifting on sea-soaked sand. The back of her neck burned and she knew one of her captors must be leaning over her, watching.

"What's she doing?" Sebastian asked, his voice suddenly close. Branwen tried to relax, keeping her limbs loose and flexible; she took comfort in the fact that her captor sounded more curious than alarmed.

Bart, on the other hand, answered dryly. "I think she's trying to crawl away."

Sebastian laughed. "Humans—do they never learn?"

A light, but firm weight settled onto Branwen's mid-back just above her kidneys, pinning her to the ground with the threat of organ-crushing pressure rather than actual heft. *Sebastian's foot*, she guessed by the angle and size. The weight seemed heavier toward the right, while she knew Bart stood on her left. Branwen eased back a little, heeding the unspoken command of *stay down*, but her fingers curled over a fist-sized dune of powder-dry sand, cupping as much as she could against her palm.

"Why don't you give her the Sight, Bart?" Sebastian continued cryptically. "One look at you and she'll think twice about her chances of running away."

*Sight!* Branwen clenched her jaw, forcing her face to remain neutral. In her excitement, she didn't hear the rest of Sebastian's statement. *If I can see, I can flee!*

"You're one to talk," Bart muttered, then he sighed, blowing out air in a single, long-suffering puff. "All right, all right," he said at last. "But *you* do it. I don't want to go near her. She might bite me or something next. Mangy human."

*Now, that's a thought*, Branwen considered as she heard Sebastian laugh again. She could sense the shift of his body in the dark. The weight on her back lifted and she felt the radiating warmth of his body hovering over her. One hand gripped her shoulder and the other her hip, pushing her onto her side and then her back. She didn't resist.

*Let them think I'm cowed,* she reasoned. *Broken. Abandoned. Weak. Then, strike.*

Sebastian knelt beside her; the rough fabric of his pants brushed against the bare skin of her arm. Branwen opened her eyes wide, innocent and straining in the dark. As close as she knew he was, she could still see nothing, but wanted to be prepared. Whatever this Sight revealed, she would take full advantage.

She heard a sudden inhale of his breath and then—*pppt!*

A brackish spray fanned across her cheeks and misted into her eyes.

"Ugh!" Branwen shouted in disgust as she flinched and jerked her head away, but a strong hand grabbed her chin and forced her to look straight. She slammed her eyelids shut in anticipation of another salivary assault. Then, she recognized Sebastian's laugh in the darkness; it matched his voice, low and slick. Bart's ear-grating rasp joined in, followed by a quick, sandy shuffle as though he'd stumbled away.

Branwen cracked open one eye to be safe.

The high afternoon sun glared off snow-bright sand, blinding her at first, so she turned to her other senses. In the darkness, everything had been muted, but now she could hear the soft caress of water against the shoreline. The taste of salt and fish rolled across her tongue and flooded her sinuses. She knew Sebastian still knelt beside her, so she turned back to him, squinting her eyes against the sun.

At first, his form remained shadowed, but as her eyes adjusted, she could pick out strange colors and textures. Sebastian's hair caught her attention first. Thick ropes of algae-green hung from his scalp and tangled around his shoulders like river weeds. The damp strands clung to the sides of his thin, coltish face, accentuating the razor-edge of his cheekbones and the narrow length of his jaw. His skin was a pale, swampy grayish-green, but his body was human-shaped and he wore human clothes: a loose, long-sleeved tunic under a black, eel-skin jerkin and matching breeches.

A long, silver chain hung from around his neck in a series of loops. The shortest loop was thicker than the rest and formed in the shape of a simple, jointed riding bit. The longest loop was broken; its loose ends dangled in front of Branwen's face, drawing her attention upward where she finally met Sebastian's gaze. Brilliant, golden eyes stared at her, their irises glowing like flames around eerie horizontal pupils.

*Goat's eyes*, Branwen thought, then, *The Devil's eyes.*

She suppressed a shudder.

Sebastian smiled down at her, his mouth curving into a wicked grin at her reaction. The expression exposed dark gray gums and unnaturally long, flat teeth that shone as iridescent as opals in the sun.

"Hello," the kelpie said.

Branwen screamed—then flung sand in his face.

Sebastian cursed loudly and twisted away, his hands clawing at the grit in his awful eyes. Branwen scurried backward to avoid his vicious flailing, then scrambled to her feet. To her left, she heard Bart's hoarse, rasping laugh and caught a glimpse of a pale, spindly creature with ink-black hands and the head of a surly black goat.

*Like a púka—from the faerie tales!* Branwen thought, but she didn't wait to see more. She bolted.

Her feet flew over the sand. She'd had no sense of direction in the dark, but now she could *see*. She raced along the line of her earlier footprints, plunging after the trail in the hope of reaching their origin—the point where she'd crossed into this strange and terrifying world. She felt encouraged by the firm wind that pushed at her back, urging her forward. The same wind carried her captors' voices, hurling them after her so they sounded only a few feet away.

"Stop her!" Sebastian shouted, but Bart just laughed again in defiance.

"Why?" he asked. "Just let her run. There's no way out. She won't get past the perimeter."

"I *know*," Sebastian shot back. "That's *why*. If she runs into Robin Redcap and the others—"

Branwen crested a dune at that exact moment and whatever else the kelpie said was lost as she tumbled down the other side of the sandy mound. For a moment, her world spun.

*This is it!* she thought, remembering the dizzying shift from before, but her heart sank as she quickly righted herself. The alien sun still shone bright overhead. Sand clogged her skin and her hair, a constant reminder that she was *not* in the grassy meadows of her home.

She'd followed her own footprints to the top of the dune, but on the other side—nothing. The only tracks she'd made were the log-shaped divots of her body rolling down the ridge. Branwen stared. If her footprints ended at the top of the dune, the rift between worlds should have been right behind them, but she saw no evidence of the fissure. She certainly hadn't passed through it.

*Should I try again?* she wondered, but concern for her hard-won freedom took precedence in her mind. *If I go back to look, they'll catch me again,* she knew. *If I keep running, maybe they'll give up and I can come back later to have another look.*

Branwen didn't see a better option. She put her back to the dune, gathered her sea-sopping skirts, and ran on, trying to put as much distance between herself and her captors as possible. Any moment, she expected to hear the shout of Sebastian and Bart's voices and the pounding of their feet against the sand. For every second she *didn't* register the sounds of their pursuit, her anxiety increased; it tightened like a serpent around her heart, constricting with every beat.

Why weren't they coming after her? Had Bart spoken the truth? Was there really no way out?

Unsure of how to proceed, Branwen slowed as she reached the beach's edge. The sand hardened under her feet as it mixed with dirt, and thick tufts of cordgrass sprouted at irregular intervals. Sprays of sea heather washed over the landscape, bathing the margin of the beach in shades of pink and bronze. In the distance, she could see a copse of trees—small, shrubby things, but even plants of that size indicated a good, clean source of water, which Branwen knew she would desperately need if she spent too much time in the midday sun.

She pointed herself toward the trees and started at an easy, ground-covering lope, hoping to save energy for a mad dash should she sense her captors' presence close behind her. Branwen had taken only a few strides when she spied a small, stoop-backed man wandering through the heather. He shuffled as he walked, each step slow and world-weary as he leaned on what looked like a short cane.

*A man like that can't have walked far,* she thought. *He must have a house somewhere nearby—someplace that I could stay or hide.* She made her decision.

"Help!" Branwen cried as she rushed toward him. "Please, help! I'm being chased!"

The small man stopped at the sound of her voice, but he didn't turn around. Instead, he made an odd sniffling sound and cocked his head to the side. Clumps of dingy white hair poked out from under the band of his vivid crimson skullcap and Branwen remembered the name Sebastian had used: Robin Redcap.

The wind shifted, taking away the salt of the ocean breeze, and Branwen's nose crinkled as she caught another scent—this one metallic and raw like freshly slaughtered meat from the butcher's shop. Warning bells sounded in her mind, and she skidded to a halt, her heels digging ruts in the sandy soil. She nearly tripped as her ankles got tangled in the cordgrass. Quickly, she stomped her feet to free herself, trampling the plants into a thin mat.

As she stood, the red-meat odor matured, gaining strength and substance. She could nearly feel it flow around her and cringed as it seeped into her pores. The sharpness of it stung the back of her throat.

*It's coming from him,* she realized as she watched the short, old man. The smell rolled off him in waves, mixing with the sweet scent of sea heather which added sickly floral notes to the sour tang of blood. *This cannot be good.*

Her eyes darted left, then right, looking for a swift exit—preferably one that did not take her any closer to the butcher stench—but found none. The man stood in the direct path between Branwen and the sparse gathering of beach shrubs that acted as the area's only cover. If she wanted to go around, she would have to backtrack and make a wide arc off to the right which would bring her far too close to her previous captors.

Branwen's adrenaline-tuned ears finally picked up the sound of sand-muffled steps behind her. She didn't have to turn back to know Sebastian and Bart approached. She caught snippets of banter growing louder and more distinct as they neared the top of the dune. They would be on her in moments.

*I don't have a choice,* she thought, gauging the distance between herself and the shrunken stand of trees. She moved forward, keeping an eye on Robin Redcap. He seemed preoccupied with…something. Branwen couldn't quite make it out; the hunch of the man's back and the protective curve of his shoulders obscured whatever he cradled from her view.

*He knows I'm here, but if I'm very quiet maybe he won't take interest. Surely, he wouldn't* chase *me,* she told herself. *He's got a cane—I could outrun him, anyway.*

Branwen picked up her pace, bounding through the dry beach grasses with feather-light strides. She gave the strange little man as wide a berth as she dared without sacrificing any of the distance she'd gained from Sebastian and Bart. She slowed as she circled around him, searching for any sign or reaction. Did the man see her? Hear her? From what she could tell, he was utterly absorbed in eating whatever he held in his hand.

She stared as Robin took voracious bites out of a stringy, green fruit. He made eager slurping noises, bright red juice flowing down the gray skin of his arms and staining his mouth.

As the angle of her path took her around, Branwen saw more. She felt her mind opening, much like her eyes had to the darkness when she gained the Sight. A veil she'd never known existed began pulling away, dismantling all her assumptions and exposing only truth. The longer she looked the more she understood—and feared.

What she had first mistaken for a cane became a sturdy poleaxe with an iron shaft loosely wrapped in crude leather strips. The axe's wicked head stabbed deep into the sandy ground. From a distance, plumes of sea heather had obscured the blade's sharp glint, but now she could see it clearly along with the dull sheen of iron shoes adorning the small man's feet. He leaned on the axe shaft for balance only because he'd planted one ironclad foot on the mutilated corpse of a small, emerald-skinned humanoid.

*Not a corpse,* Branwen realized as she saw the infant-sized thing flail under the weight of the man's metal boots.

Its limbs twitched and something else, too—wings as glassy and black-veined as a dragonfly's—struggled in vain for freedom. Large, multifaceted eyes looked up at her, their shimmery pink depths screaming with pain though the creature made no sound.

A loud *crunch* dragged Branwen's eyes higher, back to the man's mouth where sharp, yellow teeth sawed though the green flesh and near-translucent bone of his snack. Cartilage popped as Robin Redcap bit down, dislocating a miniature elbow joint.

*That man is eating an arm,* Branwen's brain calmly informed her, but the moral centers of her mind fought back, insisting, *That is* not *a man.*

Slowly, she eased back, not daring to let her eyes leave the evil creature and his morbid meal. She didn't know what Sebastian and Bart had planned for her, but she felt certain that if she hung around until the red-capped faerie had polished off his supper, he would come after her.

*Out of the pan and into the fire, as Great-Aunt Esther says.* The thought came unbidden to her mind and Branwen immediately regretted it. She knew she'd tempted fate too much because the capricious ocean wind shifted directions again, blowing from behind her. Just when Branwen thought the terrifying creature might have caught her scent, her two captors emerged over the top of the sand dune.

"There!" Sebastian yelled. His voice broke mid-syllable, cracking with alarm.

Hope sprang in Branwen's chest as she saw Sebastian leap down the side of the dune, his long legs eating up precious ground. Bart followed shortly behind him, his own spindly limbs sliding against the beige sand. Their noise and swift movements distracted the eerie red-capped fae, who turned his head so fast that Branwen heard the bones in his neck crackle.

She took advantage of the moment and ran, stretching her legs as far as they would go. Her calves burned as she struggled against the slight shift of sandy soil under her feet, and her heart thudded like Sebastian's drums, urging her onward.

From a distance, she heard the kelpie cry, "Feisty, watch out!"

*It's a trick,* Branwen thought, forcing her gaze to remain straight ahead as she ran, but doubt curdled in her stomach. Every time her foot left the ground, she heard a distinct *snap-snap* like the cracking of twigs, but she'd yet to see any wooden stems in her path. *If it's a trick, then* what *do I feel breathing down my back?*

She hazarded a glance behind her and nearly stumbled as she locked gazes with Robin Redcap. His obsidian-black eyes bored into Branwen, stealing the breath from her lungs, and he chomped his teeth in anticipation—*snap-snap!* Behind him, Branwen saw three more redcaps emerge from the edges of the field. Their thick, iron boots clomped through the stalks of cordgrass, moving slow at first, but they quickly gained speed, trying to pull even with Robin as they joined the chase.

Branwen ran faster. She reached the shrubby forest sooner than expected, but it didn't provide the safety she desired. Instead, her dress caught on a tangle of thorns nestled among the heather and salt-stunted trees, allowing small, nimble Robin to overtake her as she struggled to free herself. The others weren't far behind.

Robin Redcap swung his great axe wildly, slicing clean through the layers of her skirts. The blade nicked her heel, slicing through the leather of her boots and drawing blood, which threw Robin into a frenzy. He dropped his axe and lunged at her, teeth gnashing and foam dripping from the corners of his mouth as he committed to his course.

Branwen swerved, pivoting to dodge Robin then run toward the discarded weapon, but her movements were too fast, too desperate. As she spun, her boots slid over the sandy soil, twisting her weakened heel. The movement threw her off-balance, and she tumbled sideways, crashing into a nest of sea heather.

*NO!* Branwen's mind screamed at the same time the sound ripped from her throat. She'd lost all momentum and all hope of ever righting herself before Robin and his men would be upon her. Already, she could sense Robin scrambling to reverse his direction after he'd shot past her. She could feel the heavy thud of his iron boots through the sand. The fraction of a pause between each step felt like a millennium, the silent seconds dragging as she knew her doom approached.

Ahead, she could see Bart and Sebastian breaching the edge of the small, scrubby forest, their long strides overtaking the other redcaps.

As they ran, Bart raised his hand, his long ink-black fingers curling in the air. A spark of white-hot power shot down from the midday sky, forming a ball of sharp, pulsing light in his palm.

*Magic*, Branwen knew in an instant. *Danger.* She could feel the heady buzz of it against her skin—the same vibrant thrum of energy she'd sensed around Bryn Celli Ddu.

Beside him, Sebastian's form blurred, his limbs twisting and elongating as he surged forward. At this rate, her former captors were set to reach her in moments.

But Branwen didn't *have* moments; she was on her own.

Tears burned at the edge of her vision as she forced her body to move. *Too slow!* she knew but she couldn't give up. Flinging herself to her knees, she crossed one arm in front to shield her face, and the other she stretched out, her feeble human nails her only defense.

The traitorous ocean wind whipped around her, blowing her thick curls across her eyes and mouth, blinding her as she caught a glimpse of Robin's gaping, yellow-toothed maw and blood-red cap darting toward her. The putrid odor of his breath rolled over her and her own blood rushed in her ears—*whoosh, whoosh, whoosh!*

Bracing herself for flesh-rending, life-ending agony, Branwen heard Sebastian's oil-slick voice booming above the roar of her heart.

"Feisty!" he shouted. "DUCK!"

# Chapter 5

The hot, white light of Bart's magic exploded around Branwen as she immediately threw herself to the ground, thrusting her hands into a protective arch above her head. The hairs on her arms singed from the nearness of super-heated air. Beneath her, the earth shook as though struck by lightning, and the following crash of thunder deafened her.

She gasped in silence, her lungs seeking oxygen, but finding none. A jagged, black afterimage danced before her eyes, and she blinked rapidly, trying to sort out the electrified shapes as her body heaved for air.

A sudden gust cleared her thoughts and filled her lungs as strong hands encircled her waist, lifting her up. She smelled Sebastian's damp, brackish scent—for once, a relieving contrast to the dry scorch of lightning or the fetid reek of redcaps. He flinched as he touched her, residual magic crackling between her skin and his, but his grip didn't falter.

"Hold on," the kelpie commanded as he heaved her across his shoulder. "Robin and the others are just stunned, not dead. There's only one way to kill a redcap."

*Which is...?* Branwen wanted to know even as her body instinctively obeyed; the near-immediate threat of the redcaps overpowered any concerns of her recapture. *As long as I'm alive, I can fight back*, she reasoned as she grabbed onto the kelpie's eel-skin jerkin. *As long as I'm alive, there's a chance. Besides, I've escaped these two before—I can do it again.*

Doubt flooded her mind as she felt a swift surge of power beneath her. Sebastian's entire body hummed with magic, a raw, pulsing energy that bent and blurred the air. Branwen's eyes watered and her head throbbed when she tried to look at him. Her mind refused to focus on what she saw, warping her memory around it, but she could still *feel* the kelpie's form shifting and expanding.

Then, suddenly, the magic calmed, and Branwen found herself slung over the shoulders not of a lanky young man, but a massive, long-legged stallion whose slick, black coat glistened with a tinge of green under the afternoon sun. Faint rainbows of color rippled across his hide, swirling like oil over water as his muscles quivered with the final settling of his transformation. The kelpie shuddered and loosed a deep, whickering sigh.

Warily, Branwen slid her leg across his broad back. River weeds brushed against her palms as she twined her fingers through his damp, dark green mane to pull herself upright. As she adjusted her seat, Sebastian turned his head, the high crest of his neck arching proudly as he looked back at her. His golden eyes blazed with an unearthly light, sending shivers down Branwen's spine.

*This is his true form*, she realized, staring into the kelpie's eerie, horizontal pupils. The other was just a mask, a facade. *This* was where his true power lay; she could feel the ebb and flow of it beneath his skin, swift and deep as a river current. She realized something else, too—something dreaded: he'd been holding back.

*The both of them*, she thought as the memory of Bart's lightning bolt jolted across her mind. *From the very beginning. They* let *me go. I didn't just escape. They were toying with me. They still are.*

Branwen clenched her teeth in frustration, her hands digging deeper into Sebastian's mane as she considered her options. Even if she threw herself from the kelpie's back, there was nowhere to run. To her left, she could see Robin already stirring, his small body twitching among tufts of lightning-charred heather as he fought to stand. Tendrils of smoke rose from the soles of his iron-clad feet, but the redcap barely seemed to notice as he began to push himself upright, each movement more steady than the last. He would be fully mobile in moments, blocking her path to the east. And, then, of course, there was Bart....

Her eyes darted to the right, following the path of scorched earth to her other captor. She'd expected to find the goat-faced púka striding up to join Sebastian, his bestial mouth twisted into a wicked grin at the duo's apparent victory, but nothing could have been further from the truth. Unlike Sebastian whose strength had grown after releasing his sudden tide of magic, Bart had weakened, his thin body now nearly emaciated with the sudden expenditure of energy.

The púka swayed where he stood, his shoulders hunched and trembling against the gentle push of the sea breeze. His long, skeletal arms hung limply from his sides, and his bare chest heaved. Moisture beaded up on bone-white skin, his sweat too cold and clammy to evaporate even under the high-noon sun. Behind him, the three other redcaps lay sprawled out and groaning, their limbs spasming sporadically as they began to lurch to their feet. Bart saw them, too, and the gaze of his bulbous white eyes grew even more drained and weary.

"Damned iron fae," he rasped, his ragged voice shredding the air with scorn. "Damned spell."

He cursed again as he took a deep breath and staggered forward, weaving unsteadily across the sand. He paused by Robin's discarded axe, staring at it with open disgust before he flipped the leather-wrapped handle toward the kelpie with his toe.

"Keep an eye on that, why don't you?" Bart told him, then his gaze drifted past the kelpie to Robin. The goat-faced fae grinned, baring a pair of gleaming white fangs as he added, "I'm going have a little chat with our...*friend.*"

Sebastian snorted, his ears flicking to the side in annoyance, but he did as requested, prancing in a tight circle around the axe as Bart made his way toward Robin. The kelpie's partially webbed hooves left strange, three-toed prints in the sand.

Branwen leaned forward to keep her balance, her body pressing against Sebastian's strong, equine neck. Her legs clamped to his sides. The muscles in her thighs quivered, unused to the strain; she'd only gone riding a handful of times in her life and none of them bareback. The kelpie's damp and slippery skin didn't make matters any easier, but his gait was smooth. She adjusted to the rhythm of his movements quickly, her body's swift action freeing her mind to focus on other things—like the sudden shriek ripping from Robin's throat as Bart darted forward the last few feet and yanked the blood-dyed hat from the redcap's head.

The other redcaps exploded into a frenzy, clawing over each other as they staggered toward their leader with the buzz of Bart's lightning still lingering in their limbs. Robin himself froze, his beady black eyes never straying from the wadded-up cap in Bart's hands.

"Call off your men," Bart demanded, his gaze darting toward the approaching redcaps, but Robin only growled in response, his voice an obscene garble. Bart tightened his fists. Thick drops of red oozed from between his fingers as he began to squeeze the liquid from Robin's hat.

As the blood drained, the small man's already-gray face went ashen, leached of the vibrancy of life. Branwen stared as his skin shrank against his skull, growing paper-thin over the dark veins of his temples. His still-snarling lips split and cracked as though all the moisture had been drawn out of them and his hateful eyes grew dull and foggy, sinking into their sockets.

*Like a corpse*, Branwen thought, her heart racing with hope as she remembered Sebastian's earlier words: *There's only one way to kill a redcap.*

In moments, Robin dropped to his knees. His breath rattled in his throat as he tried to growl once more, but the sound weakened to a whimper.

Bart gave a single, short bark of a laugh, his bifurcated lips peeling back into a wicked grin. "Have you had enough?" he asked the floundering redcap. "Because I can do more. I swear by the Aegis Tree, I will wring out every last ounce of blood and leave you nothing more than a shriveled husk, if you don't *call—off—your—men!*"

Robin hissed at the threat, a spark of malice lighting in his eyes, but the vicious ember fizzled almost immediately as Bart gave the hat another squeeze. Robin grunted as he buckled, pitching forward onto his hands, then rolling to his side. All around him, the other redcaps stopped, their jet-black eyes wide and trembling—not in fear, Branwen thought, but in barely-contained rage.

Bart smiled. "That's better," he said, his body relaxing into a slouch.

Branwen couldn't do the same. Her back and shoulders were stiff with tension as she watched the scene unfold from her vantage point on Sebastian's back. She sensed that the slightest provocation would send the other three redcaps over the edge and they would launch themselves at the goat-like fae, but Bart clearly had a different opinion.

"Now, I'm certain this has all been just a misunderstanding," the púka insisted, holding Robin's cap aloft. It hung loosely from his hand, then he began to spin it slowly—*teasingly*—around his fingertips. Robin's gaze followed the hat, the sunlight glinting off the ink-black marbles of his eyes as they flicked in dizzying circles. Branwen followed the hat, too, her breath hitching in her lungs with every full rotation; each time she expected the cap's gathering momentum to fling itself from Bart's grip, but the púka remained in absolute, hypnotic control.

His low, rasping voice grated through the air as he told the shriveled and dying redcap, "I know Celaeno gave you permission to hunt down any humans that managed to escape, but I would hardly call *that*"—he made a vague, dismissive gesture toward Branwen and the boot-churned beach behind her—"a proper bid for freedom. Sebastian and I were just letting her stretch her legs. She would have never made it anywhere near the perimeter—which you were *supposed* to be guarding. You abandoned your post, dear Robin, forsook your duty, so you could take a bite out of that pixie...."

Branwen shuddered as Bart's words conjured the image of the small, winged creature Robin had been munching on when she'd first seen him. *Pixie*. The memory of its silent anguish still echoed in her mind, and she remembered the terror she'd seen in its multifaceted eyes as Robin's teeth gnashed through tender emerald skin, exposing the dripping red flesh beneath. *That could have been me,* she thought. *That could* still *be me if I don't find a way to get out of here—and soon!*

In front of her, two of the redcaps shifted, fanning out to either side of Bart. The third hung back, his head turned slightly to the side. His beetle-black eyes glanced down, lingering on the axe between the kelpie's feet. Sebastian caught the fiendish man's gaze, pinning him with his own golden stare, and snorted a warning as he continued to circle the axe. The kelpie picked up speed, the constant motion of his legs forming a near-impenetrable cage around the fallen weapon.

Bart caught the redcaps' movements, too—their blatant readiness to attack—but he didn't budge—not from his position or from his line of discussion.

"Oh, Robin," the púka tutted. "What would Celaeno do if she found out her favorite pet defied her orders all because he couldn't control a little bit of blood-lust?" He shook his shaggy black head, discretely eyeing the two redcaps within his periphery. The third stood directly behind him, out of sight, as Bart continued, "You'd be like a hunting dog who's developed a taste for his master's prey—*useless*—and I think we both know what our Lady does with useless things."

At Bart's words, Robin shuddered, his sunken black eyes suddenly losing focus as their malicious fires quelled in fear. His mouth spasmed, dry, cracked lips trying to clamp shut over yellow, half-rotted teeth. Still, a treacherous sound escaped—not a growl or hiss of defiance as Branwen might have expected, but something far more terrifying: a whimper.

*Uh-oh.* Branwen's heart lurched in her chest, its beat matching the rapid thudding of Sebastian's hooves on the sandy ground. *That's not good.* Out of all the other strange and horrible creatures she'd encountered—Cù Sìth, kelpie, púka, pixie—the redcaps were by far the worst, but to know that something—*someone*—in this nightmarish land was powerful enough, or evil enough, to frighten even them....

*Celaeno.* The name etched deeply into Branwen's mind, carving out the truth like granite. *She's the one behind all this. She sent the Cù Sìth to the human world. She gave Sebastian and Bart the flute and the drums to draw me over. She set the redcaps as guards, so I couldn't escape. But* why*? What* is *she? What does she* want*?* Branwen was certain of one thing: if she stayed with Bart and Sebastian, it wouldn't be long before she found out.

Bart's harsh laugh interrupted her thoughts as he stared down at the cowering redcap. "Don't worry. I won't tell Celaeno of your little lapse in judgment," the púka promised and the little man's eyes immediately brightened, his expression growing more eager with every word. "I'll even allow you to take back your axe and give you a chance to replenish your cap—"

"What?" Branwen blurted, the utter shock of Bart's statement loosening her tongue. Wasn't Sebastian guarding the axe to *prevent* that? Hadn't Bart drained the redcap's hat for a reason and not just to *give it back* to him? What in the world was the púka *doing*? Had he gone *mad*? If he returned the cap, they'd be right back where they started! Without that bit of leverage, there would be nothing to stop Robin and his men from carrying on with their merry murders! *He'll kill me!* Branwen knew.

"No!" she shouted in abject horror. Her stunned mind stumbled for words before settling on simply, "You can't!"

She looked to Sebastian. Surely, he understood, yet when the kelpie looked back at her, his eyes narrowed sharply and his nostrils flared. He bared his teeth at her, his meaning clear: *silence!*

"But—" Branwen began again, gesturing wildly at the ridiculousness of the scene.

Sebastian cut her off with a loud snort and sudden buck of his spine that forced her hands down, grasping his mane, and her attention on just trying to stay upright.

Bart didn't even spare her a glance. His bulbous, white eyes remained locked with Robin's beady black ones as he reiterated, "I *will*...under one condition." The skeletal-thin púka bent to Robin's level, leaning in close to whisper in the redcap's ear.

Branwen leaned, too, her newly-recovered balance tenuous as she strained to hear what Bart said without any luck. Sebastian's ears flicked forward, catching every word, but he kept his reaction guarded and unreadable.

Finally, Bart lifted his head, his voice steady as he asked, "Do we have a deal?"

Robin didn't hesitate. The little man grunted, his head bobbing frantically as he nodded and reached for his cap, his withered arms shaking with the effort.

Bart laughed again, taking obvious pleasure in the fiend's pathetic struggles. "All right," he said, holding the cap just above Robin's head. He peeled back his ink-black fingers from the blood-dyed fabric of the hat one-by-one until it dangled from the very tips of his curved nails.

Branwen's heart raced in her chest, thudding with the inevitable approach of their doom. "Don't!" she pleaded one last, desperate time. "You can't trust him! He's going to kill—"

Too late.

The hat fell, landing with a slightly-damp *splat* into Robin's grasping hands.

At its touch, a flush of life returned to the redcap's desiccated skin, flowing up from his arm and sweeping across his face. The pulsing, black veins at his temples receded beneath pale gray flesh, then were hidden completely as Robin settled the cap on his head, pressing it firmly over the lank, white strands of his hair.

The small man's back remained hunched as he staggered to his feet, still far from recovered, but no longer at death's door. As he raised his head, the sun cast shadows into the deep hollows of his cheeks and made caves of his eye sockets. His obsidian gaze gleamed from within, bright with malice and murder. He lunged straight for Bart.

"No!" Branwen shouted as the other three redcaps surged forward, taking the signal from their leader. Their guttural voices yipped with glee, shrieking in anticipation of bloodshed.

Branwen looked away, not wanting to witness the púka's fate as Robin and the middle redcap launched themselves at him from opposite sides. Still, she couldn't stop herself from hearing the loud thud of a collision, followed by a startled yelp that was cut off by the sickening crunch of bone and squelch of flesh.

"Sebastian, run!" Branwen screamed, suppressing a shudder. Instinctively, she kicked the kelpie's flanks with her heels, urging him to bolt while the others were distracted.

Instead, the kelpie slammed to an abrupt stop, his long legs still straddling the heavy, iron axe. Branwen slid forward at the sudden change in momentum, nearly smashing her face into the hard crest of his neck.

*"What are you doing?"* she hissed at the kelpie, holding tight to his mane. The river weeds squished under the pressure of her grip, dissolving into slime, so she grabbed another fistful, yanking it hard. "We need to go! Run! *I* don't want to be *next*!"

Sebastian snorted and shook his mane—whether protesting her grip or her words, Branwen didn't know—then he craned his equine head toward her and rolled his eyes. His golden gaze glinted with mischief as he reached down and nipped her knee, then he jerked his head forward again, motioning toward the slaughter.

*No, not just a slaughter—a massacre!* Branwen realized with horror as her eyes trailed across the sand. It had only been seconds since the fight had started, but already great spurts of blood drew dark, tangled lines across the dry, gritty soil. The body of the other redcap who had flung himself at Bart lay crumpled in a partially-ashen heap on the ground, his throat torn out and his cap ripped from his head. A short distance away, hunks of pale gray flesh littered the ground and strips of scarlet fabric hung from the feathery branches of surrounding sea heather, marking the site of another redcap's demise. And in the midst of all the gore, sat Bart resting comfortably atop a small boulder of sandstone—completely relaxed and unscathed.

*How?* Branwen's mind sputtered. *That's impossible! He could barely walk after using the lightning magic—there certainly wasn't time for him to dodge the first attack!*

As though sensing her gaze, the púka looked up, his pale eyes brimming with satisfaction. Beside him, stood Robin with fresh blood smeared across his mouth and drenching his clothes. *It was Robin!* Branwen realized. *He blocked the attack! He's killed his own men—well, not all of them.*

There was still one other redcap left. Robin had his iron-clad boot pressed into the back of the third and final redcap's neck, pinning the squalling creature to the ground. The captured redcap flailed, snarling with betrayal, but he had no strength as Robin held the blood-dyed hat aloft. He gave the cap a savage twist, wringing out the viscous fluid over his own head, but Robin's cap was nearly saturated from his previous two victims. Only a few drops of new blood soaked in before the excess dribbled off, forming thick, crimson rivulets that oozed down Robin's face and stained his collar.

The last redcap screamed as his hat drained. His skin shrank against his skull and his muscles wasted away as Robin's filled out, growing plump and strong with stolen blood. As the last drops squeezed out, the redcap's cry faded until it was nothing but a breath whispering through the wind. Robin stomped the creature's mummified form and it collapsed into a pile of dust.

Branwen stared in stunned silence. *So much for loyalty*, she thought, her eyes lingering on the sole-surviving redcap. A slight sea breeze stirred, slowly carrying the remains of his men away.

"Well done," Bart told Robin, still seated as he clapped his long, black-fingered hands in droll applause. "I believe that completes your end of the deal. Three for three—the lives of your men in exchange for your axe, your life, and my silence. That's quite a fair trade, don't you think?"

Robin merely grunted in response, his beady eyes now set on only one thing: the poleaxe lying at Sebastian's feet. Bart nodded toward the kelpie, and Sebastian took his cue, relinquishing his guard on the weapon. Branwen clung to his neck as he trotted toward Bart, his steps bouncing across the sand. She flinched as the redcap rushed past them and snatched up the iron-handled blade. He hefted it onto his shoulder and sighed, a guttural sound rumbling in his throat as he held the weapon covetously close.

"He never should have dropped it in the first place," Sebastian commented, and Branwen jumped, surprised by the sudden rumble of his voice.

"You can talk!" she blurted. "I mean, of course you can talk, but as a horse...." Her words staggered, then stumbled to a halt, embarrassed by her mundane assumption. *This is a realm of magic*, she chided herself, *where shadow-wolves and pixies and redcaps are real, where púkas can summon lightning from the air. Who knows what else is possible?*

Sebastian laughed, a throaty, whickering sound far more horse than human. "Kelpies can *always* talk," he said, "but in this form it requires a little bit of magic and a lot of concentration—not exactly something I had to spare a moment ago," he added, his voice waxing facetious. "I'm sure you can understand."

"Um, yes," Branwen mumbled, hazarding a glance back at the redcap. She regretted it immediately. With his axe restored, the small man had started to wander around, picking out gobs of gray redcap flesh from among the shrubs of sea heather and popping them into his mouth. He slurped at strings of sinews and chewed chunks of gristle with a loud smacking sound. Bile lurched at the back of Branwen's throat and she turned away.

Sebastian tossed his head, nickering at her discomfort, a playful light dancing in his golden eyes. He strutted over to Bart, his steps high and his neck arched in victory as he pranced around the púka's sandstone seat.

"Stop that!" Bart snapped irritably. The púka stood at last, his skeletal legs trembling as he climbed atop the chair-sized stone.

From there, he vaulted lightly onto Sebastian's back. Branwen suppressed a flinch as he settled behind her. Already, she could feel how much those small movements had cost him. The púka's breath rasped in her ears and his body slumped against hers, unable to hold himself fully upright. He wrapped one thin, quivering arm around her waist—less for her containment, she thought, and more for his support. Without her as an anchor, she was certain he would fall from the kelpie's back.

*And if I should give him a little push....* The idea was tempting, but short-lived as she considered the most probable outcome. It wasn't in her favor. *At best, Bart falls and distracts the redcap while I jump off and run a few feet before Sebastian catches up. More likely, Robin ignores the púka and comes straight after me.* She didn't think Bart's deal with the little man had said anything about not killing her if she escaped a second time, and she wasn't willing to take the chance. Branwen knew it didn't matter to the redcap whether his hat was saturated or not; he would bathe in her blood regardless.

*Wonderful,* she thought darkly. *Either way, I'm dead or re-captured—not exactly an improvement on my current situation.* Branwen clenched her teeth, biting back her frustration. She just wanted to be able to *do* something—*anything*—to fight back, but so far fighting had only made matters worse. *Just bide your time*, she told herself, rallying her thoughts. *Play along until Sebastian and Bart let their guard down, then maybe you'll have another chance.*

Behind her, the púka shifted, twisting in his seat as he turned his attention toward the redcap. "Enough snacking, Robin," he commanded as the little man scrounged through the sea heather for his men's remains. "It's time to go. I don't trust you behind us, so you lead the way."

Robin grunted, glaring at Bart as he plucked one final, gray morsel from the shrubs. He shoved the slick glob of flesh into his mouth, then swallowed it in one loathsome gulp before jogging over. His iron boots thudded in time with Branwen's heart as she cursed her luck.

She'd been hoping the redcap's job was done, that Sebastian and Bart would leave him behind to continue cleaning up the... debris. Then, she would only have two adversaries to contend with—one and a half if she took Bart's weakened state into account. Dealing with all three would make her next escape attempt almost impossible.

Suddenly, she didn't have any more time to think as Robin shot forward, his short legs churning through the sand. He veered to the east, barreling toward the shrubby copse of trees, and Sebastian bolted after him, following on his heels.

"Shouldn't we have waited for Kerebos?" the kelpie called back to Bart, his breath blowing hard between the words as he ran.

*Kerebos?* Branwen stiffened, her hands clenching in Sebastian's mane. *There's* another *one?* she thought in despair. How many fae did this Lady Celaeno task with capturing humans?

Behind her, the púka shrugged, unconcerned. "The Cù Sìth can find his own way," he said, pitching his voice above the rush of wind around them. "It's his business if he wants to stay in the Mundane. He's probably hunting up a present for Naunos. His mate is less than a week from whelping. A Cù Sìth would never miss that."

*Oh, he will this time*, Branwen thought, her spirits buoyed by a tiny spark of hope. The shadow-wolf—the Cù Sìth—had boiled to death when she'd pushed him into the crisp, clear water of her family's creek. She'd seen the way his flesh melted and his bones turned to vapor. He wasn't coming back. Not now. Not ever.

Branwen relaxed a little, her grip on the kelpie's mane slackening. She couldn't help it—a grim smile crept onto her lips. Sebastian glanced back at her, then, and Branwen startled, trying to mask her expression, but it was too late. The kelpie had seen it. His golden eyes narrowed at her for a split second before his gaze flicked forward once more.

*He knows! He knows the Cù Sìth is dead!* Branwen thought, her heart pounding in her chest again, then her rational mind took over. *So what if he knows? The shadow-wolf is still gone and Sebastian can't do anything about it.*

She stared at the kelpie, watching for any further reaction. Sebastian kept one ear pinned back, alert to her every movement even as the rest of his attention focused on keeping track of Robin as they crashed through the sparse undergrowth. Otherwise, he did nothing, and Branwen nearly sighed in relief.

It seemed the kelpie had come to the same conclusion as she had. Under their current circumstances, he was letting the matter pass, but Branwen had a feeling that strange mercy wouldn't last forever.

*Deal with that later*, she told herself as she pushed that looming fear out of her mind. A thousand more threatened to rush into its place, but she held them back with a single thought: *Alive!* As long as she was alive, she had hope—she had a chance.

Her newest conviction was put to the test as the sandy ground dipped abruptly, giving way to a steeply-sloped valley beneath Sebastian's feet. The kelpie leapt to keep his momentum, angling his long body as he flew through the air. For a moment, he soared over Robin's head, but the redcap caught up when he landed, his nimble limbs darting around Sebastian as the kelpie skidded sideways, half-sliding the rest of the way down the sand-strewn hill.

They barely stopped when they reached the bottom—only long enough for Branwen to adjust her grip on the kelpie's neck. Bart leaned heavily against her back, breathing curses down her neck as one arm coiled tight around her waist. His other hand had reached back during their flight and dug his long, midnight nails into the flesh of the kelpie's flank.

"Damn it, Sebastian!" he hissed, but the kelpie paid him no heed as he lurched forward again, hard, lean muscles bunching under his glistening black coat.

*He's enjoying this*, Branwen knew. A kelpie—just like a horse—was meant to *run*.

Sebastian plowed after Robin, the partially-webbed toes of his hooves gripping the hardening soil as sand gave way to loam and clay. Dark trees loomed before them, rising from the base of the valley. Robin disappeared beneath them, and the kelpie barely slowed as he, too, ducked between the shadowy branches.

# Chapter 6

"Nezzie, look out! Redcap!" cried a new, booming voice as soon as they breached the edge of the forest. Branwen glimpsed a tall, aquatic fae with pale blue skin and darker, half-shaved hair darting between the trees to her far left. His shirt of armored fish scales caught her eye, glinting in the speckled light of the woods as he angled toward the forest border. Ahead of him, Branwen saw what looked like a young girl with moss-green braids and broad, tawny wings launch herself upward just in time to evade Robin's grasping hands. The redcap swerved, chasing after the winged fae as she wove through the forest's low under-canopy.

Sebastian half-reared, throwing his weight on his heels as he pivoted to follow. His neck arched back and Branwen clung to it as tightly as Bart did to her own waist. As soon as the kelpie's hooves hit the ground again, an arrow sliced through the air just above his head. Sebastian flinched in surprise, prancing sideways to make himself a smaller target. His golden eyes rolled in their sockets, roving the forest for his attacker, but Branwen was the first to realize they weren't the target.

She heard a startled shriek of pain to her left and turned just in time to see the winged girl flounder, her small body careening through the forest as she fought to right herself mid-air. A short, black bolt protruded from the edge of her wing. Robin saw it and grinned, his legs pumping even faster.

"Don't let him catch her!" rasped another voice from Branwen's right—the source of the arrow.

*Another púka!* She knew even before she saw the bone-white body and black goat's head emerge from the underbrush. The creature was smaller than Bart with short, almost-delicate horns. Female. She had a distinct white star on her forehead and a miniature crossbow tucked against her shoulder. A second red-cap darted out from behind her, his black eyes focused only on Robin and the falling fae. He shot forward on a path to intercept the two.

Meanwhile, the new púka glared up at Bart and Sebastian. Her gaze skipped past Branwen entirely, disregarding her human presence.

*Which is fine by me*, Branwen thought. The last thing she wanted was another of the fae watching her every move. Her own attention was rapt with the plight of the winged girl. The two redcaps were almost upon her, so close Branwen knew the girl must smell their hot, fetid breath; her own memory of it almost made her retch. The second redcap veered, then, and he and Robin collided with a spine-shuddering snarl, tumbling to the side just as the girl finally landed. Sebastian and Bart's gazes flicked toward the sound—but only for a second—before returning to the simmering púka. Branwen kept watching just long enough to see the blue-skinned fae from earlier dash out and help the girl to her feet. The female púka never spared a glance.

"The bounty is *mine*," she hissed, ignoring the redcaps' tumult as she slung the crossbow into the holster on her back. Next, she drew out two silver daggers from the twin sheaths at her hips. The blades flashed in the dappled forest light, matching the sharp gleam in her eyes as she added, "For the strix and the merrow *both*."

Branwen blinked. *Merrow?* The word churned up memories of outlandish tales told to the village children by passing sailors: the merfolk—half-human, half-fish. *They're real, too,* she thought.

Behind her, she felt Bart bristle at the newcomer's defiance, but his voice was calm as he asked, "Is that so? Because it looks to me like they're *both* about to get away."

"What?" the smaller púka blurted. She spun toward her prey, her eyes wide with disbelief as she witnessed the truth.

The winged girl—*the strix*, Branwen thought, because the blue fae with the fish-scale shirt *had* to be the merrow—was already up and stumbling toward the edge of the forest. The bolt in her wing had dislodged and lay, splintered, on the ground. The merrow stayed close by the girl's side, glancing back at the redcaps ever few steps. The second redcap put up a good fight, but he was no match for the blood-glutted Robin and his long-reaching axe. Any moment now, she expected the second redcap's fiendish head to go flying.

The púka must have thought the same. "Call off your dog!" she demanded, rounding on Bart.

"Sure," Bart agreed amicably. "For half the bounty."

Branwen thought the other púka had nearly choked. The female's mouth opened and closed like a gaping fish. "Half?" she finally managed, then pushed a quick rebuttal. "A quarter."

Bart didn't budge. "Half," he said again. His gaze lingered on the scene beyond. Robin had forced the other redcap to the ground, leaning against the creature's throat with the iron handle of his axe. The strix and merrow were only a few yards from the border of the forest.

"Fine—half!" the female snapped. "I swear it on my name, Mina of Harth!"

Branwen felt the air crackle at her words as some kind of magic took hold. Bart smiled.

"Robin," he called. The redcap froze at the sound of his name, pinning the other redcap beneath him. His chest still heaved with excitement. "Leave him," Bart commanded, eyeing the fallen redcap, then he nodded toward the fleeing fae. "Catch the merrow."

Robin grunted, hefting his axe, then hurled himself after the blue-skinned fae. The thud of his boots echoed among the trees. The other redcap trembled, hacking up blood as he coughed, but otherwise unable to move.

Sebastian had craned his head to watch, but now looked down at the crossbow-bearing púka."I guess that means you're on your own for the strix," he commented dryly.

"*Mallacht an t-uisce*," the female—Mina—swore and spit at him before she turned and bolted after her bounty.

Bart laughed, his voice grating in Branwen's ears. "'Curse the water?'" he translated. "That's the best she could come up with?" His grip on Branwen relaxed, one hand dropping from her entirely to smack Sebastian's flank in jest.

The kelpie snorted, his weight shifting in a shrug as his attention focused on the chase ahead. Mina was fast—already she was halfway to the merrow and strix, her slender limbs carrying her like wind through the trees.

*This is it!* Branwen's mind screamed. The moment of distraction she'd been waiting for! *Now!* She slammed her elbow into Bart's side, knocking the precariously perched púka from Sebastian's back. She didn't wait to hear if he hit the ground, but leaned forward, her hands griping Sebastian's neck briefly as she started to roll off his other side. Her body shifted only an inch before suddenly it stopped. Her legs clung to Sebastian's sides. She couldn't pry them loose. The kelpie's once-slick flesh now stuck to her like glue, adhering her to his skin. She jerked her hands back, trying to peel them from his neck, then gasped in pain as her own flesh threatened to rip with the force.

Sebastian looked back at her, his golden eyes gleaming. "Nice try," the kelpie said, his oil-slick voice oozing with mockery.

Anger boiled inside Branwen, its blistering heat the only thing holding her despair at bay. She wanted to scream, to yell at the kelpie, to kick him and beat her fists against his neck, but she couldn't even do that. Her limbs were completely immobile. The only way to free herself was to physically tear the skin of her hands and thighs from the kelpie's hide. The pain would be excruciating—*debilitating*, Branwen thought. She couldn't bring herself to do it. Not yet. There *had* to be another way.

She stared at Sebastian, meeting his eerie gaze. "I will *never* give up," she told him. Magic crackled through the air, devouring the words of her oath.

Sebastian just laughed, a high, whinnying sound. Behind him, Bart had managed to pull himself to his feet. The púka glared at Branwen and started to say something when a rasping shriek cut him off, drawing everyone's attention to the edge of the forest.

Mina stumbled back from where she'd caught up with the strix, still clutching her silver daggers as she pressed the back of one hand against her cheek. Blood seeped out from behind her hand, dribbling down her bone-white neck and pooling at her collarbone. In front of her, the strix crouched low, poised to strike again. The winged girl's mouth bent into a small, grim smile as she flicked a tiny, hook-like blade out from between her nimble fingers. Branwen could tell from the look on her face that the strix knew the first hit had been a stroke of pure luck. With the element of surprise gone, her little knife would be no match for the púka's longer daggers.

And the púka knew it, too.

Mina grinned. A gush of blood flowed down her cheek as she peeled her hand away, but it soon slowed to a trickle as the liquid began to clot within the gash. She raised her silver daggers, positioning them for attack, their tips pointed at the strix, then she bolted forward.

The strix bolted, too—*into* the púka's whirling blades. She ducked at the last minute, narrowly missing a slash to the throat as she slid beneath Mina's reach, then kept running, not sparing a single glance back. She threw herself at the nearest tree, using her unbroken momentum to run halfway up the trunk. Her wings beat the air, giving her extra lift as she grasped onto the lower branches. By the time the púka had recovered from her lunge and spun around, the strix had pulled herself into the foliage of the upper canopy.

Below, Mina growled, sheathing her daggers. She unholstered her crossbow, aiming up at the tree, but couldn't get a clear shot as the strix shifted from branch to branch. The girl's green hair and brown skin blended in too well with her surroundings.

Only a few feet away, the merrow and Robin played cat and mouse, dodging through the trees. Unlike the strix, the merrow had no forged weapons to keep his adversary at bay. His only defenses were the shark-like rows of his needle-thin teeth and the barbed fins that ran along the outsides of his forearms—neither of which proved effective against a rampaging redcap. It didn't help that his attention was divided, too; he barely glanced at Robin, moving out of the redcap's reach half on instinct as his candle-yellow gaze kept flitting back to the strix.

*Nezzie*. Branwen remembered the fear in the merrow's voice when he'd first shouted the winged girl's name, warning her of Robin's approach. Something about the way he looked at the strix reminded Branwen of her brother Madden and his fiancée Ifanna, of the way their eyes always seemed to find each other even in a crowd. *He loves her*, she realized with a start. She hadn't even thought that was possible, given her experience with the fae so far. She'd assumed they were all pitiless monsters, but to witness something so *human*.... Branwen felt a sudden kinship with the strix and the merrow—both trying to escape whatever cruel plan the púkas and the others had in store for them. In that moment, it didn't matter whether the strix and merrow were innocent of their bounty or not, as long as they shared the same goal. *The enemy of my enemy*, Branwen thought.

A second later, she heard the taut *twang!* of the púka's crossbow as Mina finally took a shot at Nezzie. The bolt missed, embedding deep into the branch near the strix's left foot, but the sound was too much for the merrow. He turned away from Robin a moment too long and the redcap leapt at him, his axe raised high.

"Behind you!" Branwen shouted and the merrow jerked to attention.

He lunged to the side, but not fast enough. Robin's axe grazed his right arm, slicing a neat ribbon in his flesh. The merrow hissed, a breathy reptilian sound that made Branwen's skin crawl, and grasped his forearm. Smoke rose from between his fingers and the flesh beneath turned black and crisp where the blade had touched—had *burned.*

To Branwen's surprise, Robin didn't immediately attack again, giving the merrow time to reel back. He curled his injured arm to his chest, hunching protectively over the wound. Branwen glimpsed tendrils of black creeping up the veins of his forearm. *He's been poisoned!* the *iachäwr* in her realized, but Branwen knew she was in no position to help.

From the top of the tree, Nezzie saw it all, too.

"Destin!" she cried out. Her high, twittering voice sank into a moan as she spied the charred skin on the merrow's arm. "No, no, no...."

Robin grinned at the strix's response, exposing his rotted, yellow teeth. Then, the redcap lowered his axe, dragging it along the ground as he circled the merrow to block off any escape. The iron blade made an ominous scraping sound as it cut an arc into the roots of the forest floor. Robin's intent was clear: he didn't *need* to attack anymore. The poison would do his work for him. All he needed to do was wait.

"You bastard!" Destin growled, but not at the redcap as Branwen thought. The merrow's yellow eyes burned with hate as he looked past Robin to Bart. The púka smiled back at him.

"Oh, the beauty of iron-scorch!" Bart exclaimed, his own eyes lingering on the merrow's blackened arm as he approached. "You'll just *feel* like you're dying. It'll be *days* before you actually do, but in the meanwhile..." He approached the merrow in a few long, swift strides, moving faster than Branwen had seen since the lightning attack, though still not full speed. He wasn't recovered yet—far from it—but that didn't stop him from taking a swing at Destin.

Even injured, the merrow easily side-stepped Bart's attack, but he couldn't evade the magic that came after. A single spark crackled through the air, leaping from Bart to Destin. The merrow's muscles seized as the remnant of the púka's power coursed through him. Destin's eyes fluttered, half-rolling back in his head, and his body swayed as he tried and failed to regain control amid the shock.

In that moment of weakness, Bart struck again, grabbing Destin by the back of his neck. Branwen could see the merrow's half-shaved hair raise at the static of Bart's touch. The púka's grip tightened and he pressed down, forcing Destin to kneel under the weight of his electrifying threat. With the merrow seemingly cowed, Bart grinned and glanced at Mina who stood barely three feet away.

"Well, I've got my bounty," he gloated. "Now, what about yours?"

Mina sneered at him, then focused her attention on the strix. "Come down," she demanded, renewing her crossbow's aim at

Nezzie. The girl shook her head, her large, owlish eyes holding steady.

Mina looked at Nezzie for a full second, then swung her small crossbow toward Destin, pressing its tip just above the outer edge of his right collarbone—the same side as his iron-scorched arm.

Branwen gasped as the púka fired and a black bolt tore through the flesh of the merrow's shoulder. Destin screamed, his once-bleary gaze snapping into focus from the pain. Thick, blue blood oozed from the wound, its flow held in check by the still-embedded bolt.

"Hey!" Bart protested at his bounty's injury, but Mina utterly ignored him.

"How about now?" the female asked Nezzie, shifting the crossbow to the merrow's other shoulder. Her long, ink-black fingers wrapped around the trigger once more.

"No—stop!" the strix shouted, already halfway down the tree. She landed with a heavy thud, too rushed for her wings to break her fall. "Stop! I'll come with you—just don't hurt him!"

"Swear it," Mina rejoined, and Destin suddenly began to struggle against Bart's grip.

"Nezzie, don't," he pleaded, his once-booming voice now a broken whisper, but Branwen could tell from the strix's quivering, tear-filled eyes that she would give in.

"I swear!" Nezzie blurted, dropping her small, curved knife in surrender. As she spoke, the air buzzed with her oath.

*Magic,* Branwen knew. *It must make their promises binding somehow. Even Robin didn't dare go against his deal with Bart—*

Her thoughts were interrupted by a sudden rustle of bushes to her right. Sebastian pranced sideways, his body tense beneath her as he, too, braced for another intrusion.

A man-shaped fae stumbled out of the forest's undergrowth, his attention too focused on tidying his own appearance to be concerned about those around him. His handsome, sun-bronzed face grimaced as he looked down, plucking bits of twigs and leaf matter from his otherwise clean and well-tailored clothes. He turned slightly, then, his expression baleful as he glared at the offending bushes, and Branwen glimpsed the back of his shirt. Most of the fabric had been purposefully cut away to expose the gaping black hole that spread across the fae's shoulders and halfway down his spine.

*No, not a hole—a* hollow, Branwen thought, the word triggering a memory from her childhood, a tale of hollow-backed fae who came from forests beyond the North Sea. *He's one of the hulder. In the stories, the hulder are always women, but I guess not everything in the faeries tales has to be true.*

As Branwen watched, the hulder tilted his head back, ruffling a hand through his thick, chestnut hair to comb out any lingering debris.

At the gesture, Branwen felt Sebastian relax.

"Ronan!" the kelpie called out, clearly recognizing the intruder.

At his name, the fae glanced up, blood-red eyes burning in his otherwise human face. He smiled and raised a hand in greeting. "Sebastian! What are you doing here?" Ronan's gaze flicked to Branwen, sending a jolt of instinctual fear down her spine: yes, he was handsome, but everything about him also screamed *danger, danger, danger!* "Ah—same as me, I see," the hulder commented, reaching back into bushes from which he'd emerged. He yanked a gagged and cowering child out from the underbrush, his movements rough as he thrust the young girl forward.

*She's human, too!* Branwen realized with a start. She didn't know how she knew—she just *did*. When Branwen looked at the girl, something in her soul *twisted* and she couldn't stop staring. Her breath caught in her throat. *Colwen....*

The girl was only a few years older than Branwen's sister—eight or ten, at the most—but she had Colwen's same honey-blonde curls and peat-brown eyes. *Like Papa's eyes, too*, Branwen thought, her heart lurching in her chest. Those dark eyes widened when the girl finally saw Branwen, and she started to struggle within Ronan's hold. Her teeth gnawed at the gag in her mouth as she tried to speak.

The hulder slapped her across the face before she could get a single, muffled word out, his broad hand leaving a dark red mark on the child's pale skin. Blood oozed from the corner of her mouth where she had bitten herself, and tears sprung from her eyes, trickling down her cheeks. Her lips quivered against the gag.

"If you make one more sound...." Ronan threatened, drawing back his hand again.

The young girl flinched, cowering again in his grasp as she barely managed to hold back her sobs. Instinctively, Branwen lunged forward, trying to intervene, but pain shot through her limbs where her flesh met the kelpie's skin—a cruel reminder of her own captivity.

Sebastian rolled his eyes at her effort. Behind him, Mina stepped forward, glowering at Ronan.

"It's about time you got here," she snapped. "Thanks to you, we almost lost the bounty. As it is, I had to bargain off half—*your* half," she added pointedly.

"Of *course*, you did," Ronan muttered. His eyes narrowed, darting over to Bart and the spark-stunned merrow kneeling on the forest floor. Branwen could almost see the wheels churning in his mind, trying to concoct some plan to regain his stolen wealth. Then, the hulder saw Robin dragging his axe behind him as he paced beside Bart. The redcap still looked...hungry.

With some effort, Ronan sighed and shrugged—an unwilling capitulation. "Fine. Whatever. I've got the girl. You've got the bounty. We have what we need. Let's just go before *this* one"—he jerked his head toward the young girl—"starts wailing and attracts all the banshees in the forest—*again*."

*Banshees. Another faerie tale come to life,* Branwen thought, remembering the legends of the keening women, ghost-like apparitions that mourned for those about to die. In the stories, banshees were spooky, but mostly harmless. Judging by the sudden look of fear on the young girl's face, Branwen didn't think that was the case here. *Of course not*, she told herself. *Nearly everything in this place wants to* eat *people.*

To Ronan, Branwen said, "I bet if you stopped *hitting her*, that wouldn't be a problem."

"What did you say?" the handsome fae demanded as he whirled on her. His grip tightened on the girl as he spun. The child gasped in pain, her eyes pleading *stop!* as she looked up at Branwen, but Branwen knew she couldn't back down.

"You heard me," she said, pulling herself as upright as she could on Sebastian's back. The kelpie tossed his head, glancing at her out of the corners of his golden eyes, and she felt a slight rumble beneath her that she interpreted as a silent laugh.

"I told you we got us a feisty one, didn't I, Bart?" the kelpie said, breaking the tension. The púka gave a half-shrug, not committing one way or the other.

Ronan just stared at Sebastian. "You're lucky we're friends," he said, then he shoved the honey-haired girl toward the kelpie. "Since your human is so concerned about mine, why doesn't *she* keep her quiet? Every peep I hear out of the girl is an inch of flesh I get to flay from your *feisty one*'s hide once we reach the Red Keep—just so she'll have some incentive to do her job.

"And since you'd be bearing both our burdens, I'll even the scales by hauling the merrow to the Keep for Bart." Ronan nodded at the púka, eyeing his near-emaciated frame; the spark of magic Bart had used on Destin had already taken its toll, drawing the púka's black-furred flesh even tighter over the bones of his cheeks. "You know he's in no state to handle a merrow all on his own," the hulder commented to Sebastian, "so, how's that for a deal?"

"Seems fair," the kelpie agreed when Bart didn't immediately protest. In fact, Branwen thought the púka looked relieved.

"Excellent," Ronan said, his blood-red eyes gleaming brightly. In one quick motion, he boosted the young girl onto Sebastian's back. The child didn't settle, but half-climbed over Branwen until she'd nestled herself firmly between the cage of Branwen's kelpie-trapped arms.

"What's your name?" Branwen asked, and the girl twisted in her seat, her eyes wide as she tried to mouth the word. Branwen shook her head. "I want to hear your voice," she said, pinning Ronan with her gaze.

The hulder shrugged as if to say "your loss." Then, he grinned and silently began to trace a one-inch square on the delicate skin beside his right eye.

Sebastian grunted, displeased. He turned his head to Branwen, his golden eyes narrowing sharply. "Watch it," he warned. "Celaeno wants you *pretty*."

*Well, that's not good*, Branwen thought. There were only so many reasons why a *pretty girl* was more desirable, but as she looked at the young, frightened child in her lap—the one who reminded her so much of Colwen—she told him, "It's worth an inch of flesh." To the girl, she repeated, "Tell me your name."

"Ginny," the girl breathed. Her thick, Londoner's accent came through even at a whisper.

Branwen smiled at her. "Hello, Ginny," she said. "I'm Branwen and I'll keep you safe." She paused after saying the words, half-expecting a buzz of magic through the air, solidifying her promise, but none came. *What does that mean?* she wondered, but Mina didn't give her any more time to think.

"Glad that's settled," the púka said, her rasping voice sharp with sarcasm. "Now, grab the merrow and let's go," she commanded with only a perfunctory glace at Ronan.

The hulder followed her orders without protest, quickly pulling Destin to his feet. Nezzie rushed to the merrow's side, supporting him as he swayed slightly from the lingering effects of Bart's magic. Even when Destin regained his balance, the strix still clung to him, her expression wrought with concern as she refused to let go.

"The bolt," the merrow whispered.

Nezzie's owlish eyes widened as she realized what he was asking, but Ronan overheard and beat her to the merrow's request. Nezzie and Branwen both gasped as the hulder yanked the short, black shaft from Destin's shoulder.

The merrow hissed against the pain as the bolt ripped free. Dark blue blood spurted from the wound, then eased to a trickle as his swiftly-inflamed flesh closed over the puncture.

Ronan grinned, waving the indigo-stained bolt in front of Destin's face with sadistic pleasure. "Is that better?" he asked.

Destin merely cursed in response, his teeth clenched and the spiny fins along his jaw twitching with suppressed pain. Ronan laughed, tossing the crossbow bolt aside before he shoved the merrow—and Nezzie—forward, finally following after Mina.

Sebastian and Bart filed in behind them with Robin circling around to take the lead again. They passed by the second redcap, who still lay on the ground. His small body convulsed and he continued to wheeze and cough up blood.

*Punctured lung.* Branwen was certain. She'd seen it enough times when her mother treated villagers injured after boar hunting. The redcap was drowning as his lungs slowly filled with fluid. If he were human, he would be dead in a few more minutes. *But he's not human,* Branwen thought and she remembered Sebastian's earlier words. *Is there really only one way to kill a redcap?*

Mina tugged the little man's cap off his head as she walked by, giving it a sharp twist before flinging the wrung-out cap on the ground. "I hate redcaps," she muttered as her former companion shriveled and turned to dust.

"*Everyone* hates redcaps," Bart commented dryly. "That's why they're Celaeno's favorites—so she can torment the rest of us with their presence. Why else would she tell us to gather all the humans at the Red Keep, then hex the place so no one but her pets could find it?"

Mina snorted in agreement, her white eyes lingering on Robin as he led them deeper into the forest.

*That explains a few things*, Branwen thought, her gaze shifting to Robin, too. The redcap marched on, unfazed by his fellow fae's demise. Branwen couldn't say she was surprised by his reaction—or lack thereof. *After all*, she thought, *this is the same Robin Redcap who slaughtered and ate his own men less than an hour ago.*

The group walked on, their silence broken only by the snap of twigs beneath their feet and the steady stomping of Robin's iron boots. Sometimes, the dull thud echoed and Branwen would catch a glimpse of beetle-black eyes glinting in the shadows or blood-red caps shrouded in the bushes. At those moments, Robin would growl a warning, his guttural voice reverberating off the trees, and then the other redcaps would vanish back into the forest. Branwen tried to keep track of the twists and turns through the dark woods, but there was no use—all the trees looked the *same* and she suspected Robin had doubled back on his route more than once just out of spite. Then, suddenly they came upon a clearing.

Branwen blinked as the golden light of the late afternoon hit her eyes. When her vision adjusted, she found herself staring up at a vast, rotting structure that loomed in the midst of the clearing. Brown, slimy moss clung to the keep's crumbling black stones and streaks of rust oozed down the bricks like blood. *No, not* like *blood—some of it* is *blood!* she realized with horror as a sharp, metallic scent assailed her.

The ramparts and watchtowers, obviously once finely-crafted, were now nothing more than haphazard piles of wood and stone with bridges of bone and rope strung between them. Atop the half-collapsed bulwarks scampered scores of redcaps, their beady eyes gleaming with delight as they rushed to the front of the keep and looked down on their newest captives. In front of Branwen, Ginny whimpered. Quickly, the girl clamped her hands over her mouth to suppress the sound, but she couldn't stop her whole body from trembling. When Branwen looked down at her, she saw the girl's eyes had turned black with fear.

Ronan glanced at Ginny, too, then he looked at Branwen. The crimson-eyed fae grinned. He traced a second, one-inch square on his cheek as he said, "Welcome to the Red Keep."

Rusted chains screeched through stone eyelets as the redcaps lowered the Keep's half-rotted drawbridge over a moat of odd, iron-tipped pikes. The only treadable portions of the bridge were two, narrowly-spaced beams running its full length, their unstained wood marking the boards as a recent repair. Robin planted one foot on either beam, then marched straight across, his iron boots pinging against dozens of broken and protruding nail heads. At his approach, the other redcaps raised the first portcullis. Mina followed him first, reholstering her miniature crossbow before she set foot on the bridge. Ronan came after with Nezzie and Destin shuffling awkwardly behind as the boards forced them to walk in single-file. Sebastian went next with Branwen and Ginny on his back, while Bart brought up the rear, carefully picking his way along the planks.

*It's not just the nails giving them pause. It's the iron,* Branwen realized, staring at all of the fae's feet. Besides Robin, only Nezzie and Ronan wore any shoes—her, a pair of thin, strappy sandals that laced up her calves, and him a set of well-worn hunting boots. The rest walked barefooted—or bare-hoofed—and had to pay scrupulous attention in order to avoid scraping their heels on the bits of caustic metal. Even the shod fae weren't entirely safe: one firm misstep and even a blunted nail would puncture all but the sturdiest of soles.

*But what's the point? Why take such measures to guard against other fae when Celaeno clearly ordered them to come here?* Branwen wondered as they passed beneath the stone gatehouse. The guttural voices of the redcaps on the battlements echoed down into the partially-enclosed space, and Ginny shivered. The child twisted in her seat, wrapping her arms around Branwen and tucking her head against her shoulder.

Unable to hold her, Branwen comforted her as best she could. "Shh...shh...." she murmured into Ginny's hair, her soft, honey-blonde curls so achingly like Colwen's. She wanted to tell the girl that everything would be all right, that she would be safe, but the words just wouldn't come. She couldn't bear to offer such false hope, not when her own spirit was plagued with doubt. In the forest and on the beach, there had been a chance, however slim—a chance to run, to escape, to hide—but here, surrounded by iron and stone and fae upon *fae,* there was *nothing*.

*Or nothing I can* see, Branwen thought, desperate to fight off the despair. Her eyes darted around the gatehouse, looking for any openings or crevasses or even loose stone. For a structure that seemed near to ruins on the outside, the interior was remarkably well-fortified—far beyond anything she assumed the redcaps were capable of themselves. From what she'd seen, the wretched little men were just as likely to turn on each other as to cooperate. *This must be Celaeno's doing or something done on her orders,* Branwen thought, eyeing the second portcullis as it slowly cranked open. Its iron rivets gleamed dully in the slivers of light admitted through the murder holes in the gatehouse's roof. Beyond it, the redcaps lowered a second—also iron-studded—drawbridge over yet another pit of the same odd, iron-tipped pikes.

It wasn't until Sebastian and the others started crossing the second bridge that Branwen realized what had been bothering her about the pikes and the Keep's defenses as a whole. On both sides, the pikes faced inward—*toward* the Keep. *The double portcullis, the double drawbridge, the pikes, all the iron, iron,* iron...*it's not to stop other fae from* entering—*it's to stop them from* leaving. *This isn't just a keep,* she thought. *It's a faerie prison, and the redcaps are the jailers!*

# Chapter 7

Behind her, the second portcullis shut with a resounding *boom* that made Ginny startle and Branwen's heart skip a beat. With the exit sealed, Branwen felt Sebastian's adhesive hold on her loosen. Her legs still stuck firmly to his sides, but her hands slid free from his neck. She immediately wrapped her arms around Ginny, determined to protect the shivering girl from whatever might happen next. At the very end of the drawbridge, she could see a female Cù Sìth pacing incessantly, her shadow-black form huge and swollen in pregnancy.

*Naunos,* Branwen thought, remembering the name Sebastian had used. The beast's amber eyes glowed with a fierce light as she tracked the group's movement.

However, the shadow-wolf wasn't the only creature interested in their arrival, Branwen noticed. As she watched, three large, bird-like fae took flight from a half-toppled watchtower at the side of the Keep. At first, Branwen thought the new fae must be some kind of strix—they had wings and were a similar size to Nezzie—but as they drew nearer, she realized that was where the resemblance ended. Unlike the mostly humanoid strix, the three approaching fae were almost wholly avian with bodies like massive eagles and metallic wings that crashed with the sound of battle as they flew. The fae had human faces, however, with distinctly feminine features, and their long hair flowed behind them in the wind of their flight—one black, one flame-red, and the other a dark, earthy brown. Their knife-sharp feathers nearly matched their hair, glinting silver, brass, and a strange mahogany color in the sun.

The image of the bird-bodied women soaring above the waiting Cù Sìth burned in Branwen's mind, prompting a memory not of ancient stories told by firelight, but of a tavern in the neighboring town of Llanfairpwll. She remembered the pub sign clearly, its familiar iconography so eerily mirroring the scene before her—a female-faced eagle flying over a black dog. The name of the tavern had been painted above: The Hound and Harpy.

*That's it! These winged fae are harpies!* Branwen's certainty grew as the three birds began to circle overhead, their wild eyes watching the group cross the middle of the iron-studded bridge.

The brunette harpy dove first, swooping toward the drawbridge, but the others weren't far behind. While the mahogany-feathered harpy landed at the far edge of the bridge, perching on one of the wooden anchor post, the black harpy and the flame-haired harpy shot past her. Their silver and brass wings sliced through the air as they circled the drawbridge, the threat of them blocking Robin or Mina from moving forward and Bart, still at the rear of the group, from stepping back. Trapped between them, Ronan, Nezzie, Destin, and finally Sebastian—with Branwen and Ginny on his back—were all forced to stop, crowded together just past the center of the shoddily-repaired bridge.

The mahogany harpy smiled, her ruby lips curving in a droll expression. "Mina. Ronan. You're late," she chided, her honeyed voice at odds with the cruel light in her crimson-and-yellow eyes.

*Like marigolds*, Branwen thought inanely. In front of her, Ginny shivered and tried to bury herself further in Branwen's arms.

At the head of the group, Mina shrugged, adjusting the miniature crossbow on her back. "Something came up," the púka told the harpy. "Another opportunity presented itself, but we didn't think you'd mind, given the results." Branwen caught the flicker of a grin on Mina's goat-like face as the púka turned to gesture at Nezzie and Destin.

The harpy's eyes glittered with a malicious glee as she spied the strix and merrow. "Ah, Nezzie and Destin! How nice of you to join us again—and so soon!" she crooned. "My sister will be pleased. She missed you. We *all* missed you," the harpy added, tilting her chin to include the other two harpies who still circled the group in dizzying loops.

*What does she mean by* that*? And who is her sister?* Branwen wondered, alarmed by the harpy's familiarity with her co-captives. *They know each other? That can't be good. So much for allies,* she thought until she saw the way Destin bristled at the harpy's words. He took a step forward on the bridge, but Nezzie held him back with a glance, her owlish eyes pleading for him to stay still. The merrow obeyed, though his body still brimmed with a futile rage.

"Go to hell, Aello," the merrow growled instead. His hands clenched into fists at his side, but the fingers of his right hand only curled half-way, their strength sapped by the iron-scorch slowly spreading along his arm.

The dark harpy just laughed in response, dismissing the merrow's curse entirely as she looked past him and the strix to address Sebastian and Bart.

"The others found a bounty, but it seems you two have *lost* a few things...my *sister's* things," Aello said, her gaze suddenly sharp. "I thought Celaeno lent you her flute and her drums along with four of her redcaps, and yet I see no flute, no drums, and only one redcap."

*Wait*—Celaeno *is Aello's sister?* Branwen tried to keep her expression blank and her body still as she processed the unsettling revelation. *That means the "Lady" that Sebastian and the others have been talking about—the one that sent the shadow-wolf after Colwen but got me instead*—that *Lady Celaeno is a* harpy*!* Any of Branwen's further thoughts were cut short, however, as the dark harpy continued.

Aello's honeyed voice oozed with suspicion as she asked, "And where is Kerebos? His mate is waiting on him." The harpy flicked one mahogany wing toward the still-pacing she-wolf before adding, "Surely, capturing a human didn't give you *that* much trouble?"

Sebastian snorted, tossing his equine head, but otherwise said nothing. *All the stories claim the fae can't lie*, Branwen thought. *Is that why he's silent? Because he doesn't want to reveal how close Aello is to the truth?*

Bart seemed to have another tactic—distraction.

"I'll have you know *half* that bounty you mentioned is *mine*," he asserted, his mouth souring into a frown at the harpy's first assumption. "*I* captured the merrow. As for the rest..." The púka shrugged, mimicking Mina's earlier gesture and phrasing as he said, "Something came up. We saw Kerebos had marked this human, so we took her and left."

"Ah, yes. Celaeno's *humans,*" Aello commented, her full attention swiveling to Branwen and Ginny as they remained glued to Sebastian's back. The harpy had only glanced at them before, her wild eyes skimming past them as she'd addressed their captors first, but that didn't mean they hadn't been *seen.*

*She's been watching us this whole time*, Branwen knew. *Waiting. Measuring. Judging. And now it's time for the verdict.* Branwen braced herself, her arms wrapping even more protectively around Ginny. Then, she forced herself to sit up straight and meet the harpy's gaze.

Aello stared straight back. Her crimson-and-yellow eyes almost *burned* with their intensity, but Branwen refused to blink, refused to back down. *Ginny and I—we're here,* she wanted the harpy to know. *We're* alive. *And I will* fight *to keep us that way.*

That single moment stretched on into eternity until, at last, the dark harpy smiled. "Well, hello," Aello said, releasing Branwen from the beam of her gaze.

Out of shock and relief, Branwen found herself replying back automatically. "Hello."

Regret assailed her immediately. *Why did I do that?* She mentally kicked herself. *Of all the things to say when Ginny's life and mine are on the line—now is not the time for one of Great-Aunt Esther's lessons on etiquette and how to greet your host!* All around her, she felt the other fae stiffen as they, too, anticipated the harpy's reaction, but Aello merely laughed.

"How charming!" the dark harpy said, then looked to Bart. "My sister specifically asked for *young* girls, like the little blonde one there"—Aello nodded at Ginny, her red lips twisting into a smirk as the girl flinched—"but she might make an exception this time. What do you think, Sorcha?" she added as the flame-haired harpy circled by.

The brassy-winged harpy made a tight turn, her feathers scoring the air as she pivoted to make another pass over Branwen. Sorcha's black eyes narrowed in brief scrutiny before she concluded, "Better wait and see what a few days in the blockhouse does to her. Then, you'll know if she truly has any *grit*."

Aello nodded, obviously pleased with the red harpy's suggestion. "So be it," she said with a wicked gleam in her eyes. "Robin knows the way. Follow him," she told Mina. "Then, we'll just have to wait and see." The dark harpy caught Branwen's eye one last time and *winked* before launching herself skyward. The other two harpies stopped circling the bridge and followed, the sound of their wings crashing overhead as they flew back to the watchtower at the side of the Keep. The Cù Sìth remained, her dark presence looming ominously at the end of the bridge.

Robin strode past the shadow-wolf without any hesitation, but as the rest of the group neared, Naunos bared her fangs, issuing forth a long, low growl that made Branwen's skin crawl. The three lines of stitches across her left wrist twinged at the sound, and her hand spasmed—a not-so-subtle reminder of the last run-in she'd had with such a beast. *But I won,* Branwen told herself, clenching her fist until the twitching stopped. *I'm alive, Colwen is safe, and* that *Cù Sìth is definitely dead.*

The Cù Sìth in front of her was certainly *alive*, however, and Naunos' growl escalated as Sebastian and the others drew closer. When Mina tried to step around her, the shadow-wolf blocked their way, forcing the púka and everyone else back onto the iron-studded drawbridge, but it was obvious Naunos had no interest in Mina and her captives. Stopping the púka had just been the means to trap her real quarry on the narrow bridge: Bart and Sebastian. The Cù Sìth's burning, amber gaze bore into those two, ignoring all else. Magic rippled through the air around Naunos and suddenly words formed over the undercurrent of her snarling.

"You neverrr answerrred—wherrre is Kerrrebos?" the she-wolf demanded, her voice rumbling not through Branwen's ears, but through her mind. "Wherrre is my mate?"

Branwen froze, momentarily stunned by the unexpected invasion of her thoughts. Ginny yelped and clung to her, the girl's grip painfully tight on her ribs, but the surrounding fae seemed unalarmed.

*So, this is normal,* Branwen thought, then, *But Kerebos didn't speak—or did he, and I just couldn't hear it? Does this magic only work in the Sídhe? And if Naunos can speak into my mind, does that mean she can listen to me, too?* Dread filled her heart until she quickly followed the logic. *No, that's not possible*, she concluded. *Otherwise, Naunos would know about her mate and I would already be dead—though, it's not too late for that,* she reminded herself as she carefully gauged Sebastian's expression. He had at least an inkling of the other Cù Sìth's fate, but would he risk revealing it? To what end? Branwen could only guess, but she allowed herself to relax as the kelpie scrupulously avoided her gaze. His golden eyes focused entirely forward, settling on the seething Cù Sìth; only the slight backward twitch of his right ear belied the direction of his thoughts.

"How should I know?" Sebastian responded, his normally oil-slick voice now sharp with irritation. He tried to use the bulk of his body to push Nezzie, Destin, and Ronan all forward again, but the iron nails on the bridge made his footing too treacherous. One of his hooves brushed over a nail and Branwen felt the flinch travel through his whole body.

For a split second, he lost his hold on her entirely, but the bridge was too narrow for Branwen to take advantage of the opportunity. Even if she'd managed to hurl herself—and Ginny—from his back at that moment, they both would have simply plummeted to their deaths in the moat of iron pikes.

When Sebastian recovered, he continued.

"You heard what we told Aello. Kerebos was supposed to return after he sent the human through the Veil, but he didn't—at least, not before we left. You can ask *her* if you want," he offered unexpectedly. "She was the last one of us to see him."

Branwen nearly choked trying to stifle her surprise. *What are you* doing? she wanted to yell at him, but didn't dare as Naunos' gaze shifted to her for the first time.

However, before the Cù Sìth could respond, Sebastian spoke again, mentioning in an off-hand way, "Of course, she'll probably just lie to you. That's what humans do, you know. They aren't bound by the Rules of the Sídhe like we are. I wouldn't be surprised if she told some ridiculous story that Kerebos died just so she could provoke you."

Branwen tried to remain calm, but she couldn't keep her body from tensing at his words—at how close they hit to the actual truth. She knew the kelpie could sense her reaction, but he didn't let on. Instead, he grew more relaxed, more confident in the tale he wove for the Cù Sìth.

"She's feisty, this human," the kelpie said, nodding back at Branwen. "She's been trying to escape since the moment we caught her. She even tried to turn Robin and his redcaps against us." Sebastian snorted as though still in disbelief as he added, "It almost worked, too. I bet she thinks if she can get you to attack us out of revenge she'll finally have her chance. Isn't that right?" he addressed Branwen at last, tilting his head so that he stared back at her with one gleaming, golden eye. The other eye, she felt certain, kept Naunos in his peripheral vision.

*He* knows *Kerebos is dead, now*, Branwen thought. *But he also knows what would happen if Naunos finds out and it's not in either one of our best interests. Yet.* She was certain the kelpie would sacrifice her immediately if it meant saving his own hide or gaining some other advantage. She'd seen the same thing happen with the redcaps. *Just play along*, she told herself. *Play along and get through this.*

"Of course," she agreed, forcing the words through gritted teeth. She bared them in what she hoped was a devil-may-care smile while her heart beat frantically in her chest.

The Cù Sìth just stared at her, unrelenting and unimpressed.

From the back of the group, Bart spoke up, his rasping voice impatient. "What more do you want from us, Naunos? We're not Kerebos' keepers. As long as the human carries his mark, he can still cross over the Veil. It's not every day that one of us gets a chance to slip between worlds. He's probably just taking his time. You would, too, if you were in his place—"

"I had to wait for Ronan an extra *seven* days," Mina interjected, the bitterness fresh in her voice as she glared at the hulder.

Ronan half-turned and shrugged, pointedly showing the púka the dark hollow of his back. "I may have lingered a little longer than necessary," he admitted. "I wanted to have a good look around—see some sights, maybe cause some mischief, pass around a plague or two." The hulder glanced at Ginny and grinned, his red eyes flashing with some shared memory as he added, "I didn't even have to steal to get what I came for. This girl's family practically gave her away just as long as I promised to leave their little farm alone. It's a shame I had to go, really. I could have had so much more fun."

"Yes, yes, you're so clever," Bart said, rolling his white, bulbous eyes. To Naunos, he said, "See? It's easy to get carried away over there. The time passes more quickly than you'd think. When Kerebos comes back, you can ask *him* what took so long, but in the meanwhile—*let us off this damnable bridge.*"

"Hear, hear!" Ronan muttered, edging toward the end of the drawbridge along with Mina. Nezzie and Destin followed close behind. Naunos stared at them as they approached, indecision still burning fiercely in her amber eyes, but at the last moment she stepped aside. Branwen wasn't sure whether to be relieved or not as Sebastian continued to pick his way across the bridge.

*Every step he takes is one step closer to whatever plan he and Bart—and ultimately, Celaeno—have in store for us,* she thought, not daring to loosen her grip on Ginny.

Just as Sebastian passed from the iron-studded bridge onto the packed dirt of the Keep's bailey, Naunos darted in front of him once more. She allowed Mina and the others to slip by without comment, but her lips pulled back in a snarl as she eyed both the kelpie and Bart.

"Yourrr worrrds bought you passage—nothing morrre," she warned. "If Kerrrebos isn't back tomorrrow—"

"Then, we're going to have a much different conversation," Sebastian agreed.

The Cù Sìth nodded, staring at him one last time before slinking off into the shadows around the edge of the Keep. When the wolf disappeared, Branwen felt as though a weight had been lifted from her chest. She could finally breathe. Sebastian relaxed, too, his stride quick and easy as he caught up with Robin and the others crossing the dirt-paved bailey. All around them, more redcaps leered down from the Keep's battlements. As they drew deeper into the courtyard, Branwen noticed other fae milling about—most were púkas, but there was at least one other hulder and several squat, frog-mouthed fae with orange, warty skin.

*Kobolds*, Branwen thought as she dredged up fragments of folklore from her memory. *And where there are kobolds, there are...ah, dwarves!* She spied three short, swarthy men clothed in heavy leather aprons gathered around a fire, each taking turns as they roasted a skewer of pixies over the open flames. Bile lurched at the back of Branwen's throat, and she immediately looked away, focusing her attention ahead instead.

A towering, windowless blockhouse jutted from the back wall of the Keep, its dark structure streaked red with the heavy swirls of iron ore. *This is the place Sorcha mentioned—it's a prison!* Branwen knew as her eyes traced the extra scaffolding of iron bars that formed a network of narrow ramps and walkways around the outside of the building leading up to the roof. Three redcaps roamed the scaffolding, their iron boots clanging with every step as they each climbed to the prison roof and back down again. Two more redcaps stood guard at the very base of the blockhouse, one on each side of a single, low door made of pure iron. When they saw Robin, the pair immediately turned and began the process of prizing the door open; it took both of them to wrestle the heavy iron slab loose from its rust-fused hinges.

As the two worked, Sebastian eyed the entrance's stunted dimensions, then glanced back at Branwen. "You walk from here," he announced, and the slight buzz of magic across her skin was the only warning she got before the kelpie released his hold on her and started to transform.

Ginny yelped in surprise, flailing as she slid along Sebastian's spine, but Branwen was ready. Her arms wrapped around the girl's back, holding her tight as she half-leapt and half-fell from the kelpie's swiftly shrinking back. The two landed on their feet, but just barely. Branwen stumbled forward, trying to regain her balance and use her momentum to get as far away as possible, when Sebastian grabbed her arm, his long, newly-transformed fingers hooking into the bend of her elbow. His thumb dug into the joint—not enough to hurt, but just enough to remind her that he *could*.

"*Walk*," he repeated, clearly anticipating her desire. "Not *run*." The kelpie chuckled, his voice an incredulous rumble as he added, "Did you really think you could escape just now? The two of you? From a fortress full of redcaps and guarded by harpies?"

Branwen stared back at him, undaunted, as she promised, "I will *always* try."

Her words were punctuated by a spine-shuddering shriek as the rusted hinges of the blockhouse door finally gave way and the metal slab swung open, expelling a gust of cold, damp air thick with the scents of earth and iron and darkness.

As the breeze rippled past, it set off a cascade of reactions among her fae captors. As expected, Robin and the other iron-clad redcaps remained unfazed, but Mina and Ronan flinched, both shaking their heads and snorting as though they could clear the smell from their nostrils. Sweat broke out on Destin's forehead, and the merrow shivered, the spiny fins along his arms and the edge of his jaw spasming against the metallic chill. Beside him, Nezzie flapped her wings, trying to blow the air back, but she only managed to stir in dust.

"You can't take us in there!" the strix pleaded to Mina and Ronan. "Destin is already iron-scorched—that place will kill him!"

"I rather think that's the point," Sebastian muttered, struggling to suppress his own shudder. He stood close enough to Branwen that she could feel the way the kelpie twitched as the air slid across his skin. Behind him, Bart cringed, his jaws clenched as he tried not to breathe until the gust ebbed.

Near the head of the pack—and the first to recover from the iron-tainted air—Ronan scoffed. "Don't be ridiculous," the hulder said, then he grinned at Nezzie, flashing his gleaming white smile. "Celaeno will come to destroy you both long before the iron has a chance to do its work. Rumor has it she wants to deal with you personally—why else would the bounty be so high? Now, let's go."

Ronan proceeded to march toward the prison's dark entrance, pushing past Mina. He dragged Destin along with him, leaving Nezzie no choice but to follow them into the iron and stone blockhouse.

"You, too," Sebastian told Branwen, pushing her forward with his hand still on her elbow.

She nearly tripped as Ginny clung to her, the girl's weight like an anchor around her hip and leg. Branwen slid her free hand over Ginny's, twining their fingers together and giving them a comforting squeeze.

"It's going to be all right," she promised when the girl looked up at her with quivering eyes. Branwen hoped her own fear didn't show so brightly as she forced her lips into the semblance of smile. The small gesture was enough. Ginny loosened her vice grip on Branwen's skirts, and together—with Sebastian and Bart right behind them—they walked past the redcap guards, through the cold iron door, and into the gaping darkness. Robin trailed behind the group, pulling the door shut with an ominous boom.

For a moment, the blackness swallowed them. Branwen's heart sputtered and her stomach gave an unpleasant heave as the sudden void of light provoked another memory. In her mind, she careened through a vast nothingness—a place with no up or down, no left or right, no sense of sight or smell or touch—only sound—the pounding of drums that drew her through the pattern-stone at Bryn Celli Ddu and into the Sídhe.

*If only this were the same darkness, pulling me home instead,* Branwen thought, but she knew that wasn't the case. As the memory faded, she could feel the rough stone floor through the soles of her boots, grounding her in *this* reality. The scent of iron hung heavy in the air, but was soon overpowered by the acrid stench of sweat and fear billowing up from the depths of the blockhouse. It left a sour taste in Branwen's mouth, coating her tongue, so she clamped her mouth shut and tried to breathe as little as possible.

From just ahead, Branwen heard a dull thud followed by a sudden hiss as a few of the leading group seemed to bump into each other. One of them chuckled, while another—Mina—growled and cursed under her breath.

"Shut *up*, Ronan," the púka demanded, her rasping voice as sharp as knives. "Not all of us can see in the dark, you know. How about you give us some light?"

The hulder laughed again, his voice a throaty rumble in the dark, then with the strike of a match, a small, red flame appeared which he used to light a wall-mounted torch to his right. Mina shoved past Nezzie and Destin to pluck the torch from its sconce. The flickering light danced along the low entryway, making the thick veins of rust-red iron almost *pulse* across the tunnel's dark walls and floor. From beyond the halo of light, Branwen could hear the desperate, tortured moans of prisoners and the steady clomping of iron-clad shoes as nearly a dozen redcaps patrolled unseen corridors.

*Is this it? Is this the end*—my *end? To become another one of those moaning voices?* Branwen wondered with growing dread, but Sebastian didn't let her thoughts linger long.

"You're going first, Feisty," the kelpie told her. His fingers dug into Branwen's elbow, reminding her of his impossible strength as he maneuvered her in front of Mina and the others.

Branwen obeyed, keeping Ginny tight by her side. Whatever happened, they would not be separated. Nezzie and Destin followed close behind them, hemmed in by Ronan, Mina, and Bart with Robin still at the rear.

Within a few strides, the blockhouse's narrow, sloping entry ended, opening onto a platform in the midst of a vast, cylindrical vault made from the spiral of two helical staircases that spanned the walls of four stories—one above their current level and two below. Scores of iron-barred cells lined the outer walls of both sides of the vault, staggered with the downward curvature of the broad, shallow stairs so that each cell was slightly lower than the one before. The center of the prison was hollow—left open for ventilation. As Sebastian turned and marched her down the right-hand flight of stairs, Branwen could hear the faint whoosh of air rushing by their rail-less edge. A few hazy beams of sunlight trickled through the series of slits in the blockhouse ceiling, but they were too weak to truly penetrate the darkness.

Branwen caught the rhythm of the stairs quickly, allowing her attention to focus elsewhere. She tried to peer into each cell as she descended, taking note of their occupants—were they human or fae? Dead or alive? Were they fed? Were they starved? Were they tortured? She gleaned whatever she could from those brief moments, assessing her own likelihood of survival.

It didn't look good.

*But Ginny and I, we're different from all the other prisoners I've seen,* she told herself, drumming up her courage. *We're* human. *That has to mean something. Plus, Sebastian and Bart went through far too much effort to capture me alive if they knew I was just going to be brought here to die. Mina said she waited* seven days *for Ronan to bring Ginny back.*

Branwen knew they'd been captured for a specific purpose, and she didn't believe it was to rot away in the redcaps' jail cells. Nezzie and Destin, on the other hand.... She glanced back and caught the strix's wide, owlish eyes scanning the prison, just like hers. Destin followed right behind the winged girl, his towering form hovering protectively over her as he put himself between her and Ronan. The hulder merely grinned, his red eyes glowing in the light of Mina's torch. Branwen shuddered and looked ahead.

Beyond the ring of light, she could see dozens of *other* eyes gleaming from within the iron cells as many of the fae prisoners turned their attention toward the approaching group. The bravest ones shuffled close to their cell doors, leering out at Branwen and Ginny as they passed.

"Humans!" spat a looming, bark-skinned fae with thin, twiggy limbs and oak leaves for hair. *A dryad*, Branwen knew from her mother's stories. *A forest-guardian.* Tiny, butterfly-winged sylphs flitted about the dryad's branches, chittering in mirrored irritation. A patrolling redcap kicked the cell's iron bars, silencing the creatures with the threatening clang of his boot, but that didn't stop the other prisoners from talking. Branwen could hear their whispers echoing through the hollowed vault.

*"Two more of Celaeno's girls."*

*"What does she want with them?"*

*"Who cares? Tell Our Lady I'll bring her as many humans as she wants, just as long as she sets me* free!*"*

*Free!*

*Free!*

*Free!*

The word rang out, amplified by the curved, iron walls. The sound swelled as it traveled up the stairs. Branwen could feel the reverberations of it within her own heart—the final trumpet of hope for a hundred imprisoned fae—then, just as the cry was about to reach its crescendo, it crashed, plummeting to the bottom of the blockhouse's dark stairs. Silence reigned in the swift moment after, marking the death of that brief delusion, and Branwen heard the truth with deafeningly clarity: no one escapes from this place. No one ever goes free.

*But what would happen if they did?* she wondered, her mind suddenly churning. How many weakened, half-starved fae would it take to destroy the redcap guards? *Just about all of them*, she thought, remembering how easily Robin had dismembered his own men even in his partially-desiccated state. Besides him, there were at least ten other redcaps roaming near them on the blockhouse stairs; she could hear the steady clang of their boots against the stone. And would the other fae even turn on the redcaps or would they just single out the easiest prey—meaning Ginny and herself? The second scenario seemed more likely, judging by the hungry way some of them stared at her.

A coiling, snake-like fae hissed through the bars of his cell and his half-man, half-serpent body weaved back and forth as she and Sebastian neared. The creature's long, forked tongue slithered between the iron bars as he eagerly scented the prison air.

"Ssssso tassssty...." the creature breathed, his slitted, green eyes luminous in the dark. His gaze darted from Branwen to Sebastian. "Let me have a bite—jussst one...." the snake pleaded to Sebastian, but the kelpie just kept on walking, not even acknowledging his existence. The serpent glared at him, then quickly focused his attention on the next captive morsel. "How about the ssstrixxx, then?" he asked. His tongue flicked out in front of Nezzie's face.

Before the strix could even react, Destin flung out his arm and swatted the snake-like fae's tongue aside, but the action was weak and uncontrolled. It was obvious he'd lost even more strength to the iron-scorch whose black tendrils were slowly spreading up his arm. The muscles of Destin's shoulder tensed, and Branwen could see him trying to alter the momentum of his swing, but he failed. The back of his hand slammed against the iron of the cell, crushing the serpent's tongue between them.

The snake screamed, jerking back from the bars, but Destin barely flinched. *Can he even feel his arm anymore?* Branwen wondered as the merrow's hand dropped limply to his side. Wisps of smoke curled up from his skin where the iron had seared his flesh, but it was nothing compared to the char covering the serpent's mouth. The creature writhed in his cell, his own sickle-shaped teeth gnawing until they'd sheared off the scorched end of his tongue. In fury, the snake lunged at Destin, stopping just short of striking the iron bars. He hissed, spitting blood and foam at the merrow's face.

Behind Destin, Ronan laughed. "That's what you get, *naga*," he told the snake. "You should know how protective the merfolk are of their mates."

The naga glared at the hulder, unable to speak as iron-blackened blood continued to fill his mouth. The foul ichor gurgled from between his teeth, oozing down the creature's narrow chin and onto the pale green scales of his chest. His gnawed-off tongue still wriggled where it had fallen to the floor, squirming its way toward Nezzie. As it neared, the strix stomped on the flailing tongue, grinding it with the toe of her sandal before she kicked the crushed remains toward the edge of the stairs. Robin Redcap lunged forward from the back of the group, catching the chunk of flesh before it disappeared into the darkness below, then stuffed it into his own mouth, hardly chewing as he swallowed the organ whole.

Beside Branwen, Ginny retched at the sight. Her small body doubled over as her stomach convulsed in vain. Branwen struggled to hold back the bile rising in her own throat as she wrapped her one free arm around Ginny and physically lifted and turned the young girl away from the snacking redcap. For a brief moment, the hot, coppery scent overpowered the cold reek of iron and even more of the jailed fae roused. Their soft moans erupted into frenzied shouts and violent clanging as some of them even threw themselves against the walls and doors of their cells. Fae flesh sizzled against the iron, sending up spirals of acrid smoke followed by shrieks of fear.

From the next cell over, a fae with the giant ears and wings of a bat, rushed forward, his voice desperate as he shouted at them through the bars of his cell, "Get rid of the blood! You have to cover the scent of the blood before she wakes!"

"Before who wakes?" Sebastian bellowed over the rising din, but the bat-winged fae just shook his furry head. The great bells of his ears swiveled, pressing flat against his skull, and his small eyes widened as he glanced across to the other set of stairs.

"Too late!" he cried out, hurling himself away from the bars. His whole body trembled as he flew to the back upper corner of the cell. The bat fae cowered against the rough-hewn ceiling. His long, double-jointed toes and hooked wings twitched as they brushed against the veins of iron permeating the rock, but he refused to let go.

Sebastian's grip tightened on Branwen's arm as he traced the fae's quivering gaze to a cell across the prison and slightly below them on the second set of helix stairs. An impossible beast emerged from the dark, its alabaster hide gleaming like moonlight behind the prison's cold iron bars. As the soft glow spilled out into the stairwell, the fae in the surrounding cells screamed and shrank back. Like the bat, they huddled in the furthest corners, their bodies trembling as they clamped hands or paws or claws over their ears, but Branwen could only stare, transfixed by the creature's strange beauty.

The beast had the fine-boned body of a doe with the same long, dainty legs, wide eyes, and tapering jaw, but there the resemblance ended. Instead of a deer's short tuft, it had a tail like a lion's, twitching and flicking as the creature's nostrils scented the air. Cloven hooves as clear and sharp as diamonds cut tiny divots in the dark stone floor as it began to pace the front of its cell. The wind of its movement stirred the curls of its short, wispy mane, and the gossamer strands floated like spider's silk before settling once more against the serpentine curve of its long neck. A single, two-and-a-half-foot horn grew from the center of the beast's forehead, its tip sparking like flint as it scraped the ceiling of the cell.

Even without seeing the horn, Branwen would have known what the creature was. There could be no doubt.

# Chapter 8

"Unicorn...." She breathed the word like a dream, half-afraid the beast would vanish as she spoke, just as it did in all the village fables, but the creature remained as real as ever. Beside her, Ginny was equally enraptured.

"So pretty," the girl crooned, all fear of Ronan's promise apparently forgotten as she left Branwen's side. She took one step toward the edge of stairs and then another, reaching out to the beast. The girl's small hand stretched into the chasm between them, her pale skin bright against the darkness.

Branwen felt her own feet following, drawn toward the myth of her childhood. She just wanted to *touch* it—to feel its silky smooth fur beneath her fingertips. She wanted to look into its eyes—to see her mirrored reflection in its intense gaze. Somehow she knew—just *knew*—she would see her true self there, stripped of all the trappings and masks she wore for other people—where she wasn't Branwen the daughter or Branwen the sister, not even Branwen the shepherdess, Branwen the iachäwr, or Branwen the brave. To the unicorn, she would be simply...

*Branwen.*

To her right, Sebastian cursed, his grip on her arm like steel as he yanked her and Ginny back from where they teetered on the very edge of the stair. He nearly flung them against the prison wall with the excess of his force, and Branwen jolted to attention, suddenly realizing how close she'd come to walking out into the abyss.

After their commotion, the unicorn stopped, its whole body plunged into an abrupt and absolute stillness. Only its eyes flickered, glinting liquid silver as they honed in on the offending kelpie.

*No, not on Sebastian,* Branwen realized, watching closely but careful not to meet the unicorn's gaze. *She's looking past him—at the* naga. *At the* blood*!*

The unicorn's nostrils flared and its glistening white skin shivered as it inched toward the cell's iron bars, pressing as close as it could without touching. Then, slowly the creature lifted its head and started to keen. Its high, mournful cry echoed throughout the hollowed center of the blockhouse with an eerie, haunting beauty. Branwen felt the creature's longing. *Come to me—join me!* the unicorn seemed to plead, but Sebastian refused to let her go, his looming body blocking the way.

"Don't," the kelpie warned. "She'll kill you. Once a unicorn smells fresh blood, it will stop at nothing until it has prey of its very own."

As though hearing the kelpie's words, the unicorn's cry grew louder and more urgent. Branwen could sense the magic woven in its voice now—the hum of *want* that buzzed in her ears, trying to lull her into complacency. At the sound, the other fae went wild, banging against the walls and bars of their cells, oblivious to the sear of iron against their flesh as they all screamed, "Stop her! Someone stop her! Shut her up! Guards!"

For a moment, the tumult drowned out the unicorn's cry, and Branwen heard the thunder of the redcaps' iron boots on the stairs as half a dozen stormed toward the beast's cell, each carrying a long, iron-tipped spear. The unicorn saw them and immediately abandoned its luring tone, letting a desperate, furious shriek rip through the air. The sound pierced Branwen's heart and she felt it shudder to a stop for a single agonizing second. White-hot needles stabbed in her chest when her heart finally beat again and she gasped from the pain. Beside her, Ginny wept in fear, her own cries joining the frenzied calls of the fae.

Ronan, Mina, and Bart all staggered at the sound, stumbling and clutching their ears while Nezzie turned and pulled Destin down to her level. The strix clamped her hands over his ears as the merrow wrapped his un-scorched arm around her, burying Nezzie against his chest to block out the scream. Even Sebastian flinched, his grip on Branwen's arm faltering as his hands instinctively went to protect his ears, but before she could react, he caught himself, renewing his hold on her and Ginny. The unicorn's pitch continued to increase, soaring above the frequency meant for human ears, and Branwen and Ginny both sighed in relief at the sudden vacuum of noise while the fae around them continued to struggle. Sebastian growled, obviously trying to cancel out the sound with the low rumble of his voice; Branwen could feel the reverberation through his bones as he gripped her arm. When she glanced at him, she saw his eyes half roll back in his head and thick, swampy-green blood oozed from his ears.

Then, the redcaps arrived at the unicorn's cell, frantically thrusting their iron-tipped spears through the bars to distract the beast. The diversion worked and the unicorn stopped screaming just long enough to dodge their attacks within the narrow confines of its cell.

Out of the group, Sebastian recovered first in the brief soundless interval, and he pushed Branwen and Ginny forward, urging them down the stairs. The others rushed behind them, fleeing to the lower level, below the unicorn's piercing screams. Branwen glanced back every few steps, unable to truly look away. The beast fought back viciously, parrying the redcaps' spears with the tip of its horn. One of the wooden shafts splintered on impact, leaving an opening, and the beast lunged forward. Its horn impaled the closest redcap, lifting him up in the air as the unicorn raised its head. Only the width of the iron bars kept the beast from pulling the little man's flailing body into the cell as it quickly stepped back out of range of the remaining spears.

The skewered redcap slid off the unicorn's horn, falling into a crumpled heap on the ground outside its cell. The other redcaps stood back, eyeing their still-twitching comrade as blood drained from the hole in his chest. A few tried to dart forward long enough to retrieve the little man's cap and put him out of his misery, but each time the unicorn lunged at them, its deadly horn jutting through the bars.

In the end, they all just watched as the redcap's body desiccated, shriveling to a corpse-like state from loss of blood. The thick liquid seeped into the unicorn's cell and the beast arched its long, slender neck as it pranced in the growing pool. Crimson stained the unicorn's perfectly white fetlocks and coated its crystalline hooves like polish. Blood ran down the beast's horn, puddling at its base before dripping in a slow streak down the fae creature's face. When it reached the beast's nose, the unicorn snorted, blowing the blood into a fine mist, then at last, the unicorn calmed, standing in gratified silence.

The clamor of the imprisoned fae died down to a few quiet whimpers and shaky sighs as they realized their torment was over. The remaining redcaps turned away from the fallen guard, leaving him as they marched back up the stairs.

Behind her, Branwen could hear a steady stream of curses as Bart witnessed the final act.

"Who in all the seven Hells decided it was a good idea to bring a unicorn *here* in the middle of the *bloody Red Keep*?" he raged, still trying to shake the ringing from his ears.

"Oh, I think you know *exactly* who," Sebastian retorted, not missing a single beat as he moved briskly down the curve of the stairs.

The sudden knowing silence that followed proved him right, casting an ominous pall over the group that made Branwen take note.

"Damned harpy," Bart muttered, his rasping voice barely heard over the sound of their footsteps.

They followed the stairs for another half loop before the broad steps terminated at the final level of the blockhouse, dumping them into a wide, circular chamber lit by a ring of torches near the center of the room. In the middle of the torches gaped a perfectly round, black pit, plunging down into the earth like an oubliette.

The sickly-sweet smell of decay rose from the pit, drawn up by the breeze from the ventilation shaft, but Branwen couldn't see the actual source at the bottom. Only a soft sigh and a faint rustle within the dark told her that whatever—*who*ever—it was, wasn't quite dead yet. Beyond the pit, seven narrow, iron-barred jail cells lined the curved walls, but one was slightly larger than all the rest, and Branwen gasped in shock as she saw not one or two, but *thirteen* other human girls locked within the cell's cramped quarters.

*They've been stealing children from all over the world!* Branwen realized as she looked at the girls. They were all so different, representing every shade and shape and texture of humanity, and yet they stared at the incoming fae with identical expressions of terror. Most of the children were Ginny's age or younger—too small and weak to have defended themselves against the fae. Only two of the girls appeared to be older than ten; the younger girls huddled around them like lost chicks seeking anything that resembled the protection of their mothers. When the girls spied Branwen, their eyes sparked with tentative hope and some of them rose to their feet, taking a few brave steps toward the door of the cell.

"Save us!" begged a little tow-headed girl with dirt and flecks of dried blood smeared across her cheeks. Her clothes were ragged and stiff with sweat and mud.

Branwen's heart broke with the burden of the child's expectation. *How can I save you when I can't even save myself?* she thought. *They're looking to me because I'm the oldest. I'm the* adult *and they think I know what to do, but I don't! I'm trapped here, too, just not in a cage.* Branwen clenched her teeth, her grip on Ginny's hand tightening as she fought against the despair. *I'm still free*, she told herself. *Until those iron doors slam behind me, I'm free.* It wasn't over. Not yet.

Ginny's small fingers trembled against Branwen's palm, but still the girl squeezed back, her tiny gesture echoing the other child's hope—and her own belief—in Branwen.

Behind them, Ronan laughed, grinning wickedly. He pitched his voice higher to mimic the tow-headed girl's cry. "Save us! Save us!" he mocked as he sauntered around the edge of the group toward Branwen and the iron cell. His cruel tone resonated in the circular chamber. The younger girls shrieked as he neared, hiding their faces behind the older girls' skirts, which only made the hulder's smile broaden. Sebastian ignored his presence completely, pushing Branwen—and Ginny—forward.

"Door," the kelpie commanded, and suddenly another redcap appeared, stepping out of the shadows from beneath the spiraling stairs.

While all the other nearby redcaps had left their posts to attend the raging unicorn, this one had remained hidden below, guarding the girls even though he had been closest to the commotion. *Why?* Branwen wondered. *Are they—are* we—*that important? No, it's not us—it's* him, she realized as the little man approached. Like the other redcap guards, he carried a long, iron-tipped spear, but one thing set him apart from the rest: *keys*.

Two sets hung from around his neck, the dark iron clinking together as he moved. The first set had four nearly identical keys looped through a simple leather band. *One key for each level of the blockhouse*, Branwen guessed. Though how the redcap knew when one floor ended and another began, she could only speculate. The cells hadn't been numbered, at least not that she had seen. The second set had only two keys welded onto a long, thick, iron chain—only clearly brighter and newer than the other. Both keys were larger and more ornate than the other four with twisting iron leaves and sharp thorns that jutted along the shank. Even the key heads themselves were jagged with three bits instead of just one, each possessing backward-angled tines.

*Like snakes' teeth*, Branwen thought, easily imagining the fine points hooking and ripping into skin. *They're not just keys; they're weapons against the fae...well, any fae but the redcaps,* she amended, watching closely as the little man grasped the darker of the two vicious-looking keys. He didn't take the heavy chain off his neck, but simply leaned in as he unlocked the cell's iron-barred door. The hinges creaked as it swung inward and the imprisoned children flinched at the sound. Fear made them shy away from the door even as the redcap took a step back, leaving the way wide open. Not one of them tried to escape.

"You first," Sebastian said, thrusting Ginny toward the door.

Branwen clung to the girl with all her might, trying to draw her back, but Bart came along beside her and wrenched Ginny from her grasp, shoving the younger girl bodily through the door. Branwen balked as Sebastian pushed her forward next, throwing her weight back, but the kelpie out-muscled her and she staggered forward, nearly colliding with Bart until Ronan reached in and jerked her aside.

"Not so fast," the hulder said, still grinning as he spun Branwen toward him. His lithe body shifted, stepping in close, and his arms wrapped around her as she pivoted, crossing over her abdomen. The movement locked her in, forcing her to stop with her back pressed against his chest. His breath was hot in her ear as he whispered, "Did you think I'd forgotten about our little deal? You still owe me some flesh. It's *three* inches, now, by my count. One—" He lifted his hand, drawing a square by the corner of her eye. Next, he traced the line of her bottom lip.

"Two—" Then, his fingers drifted down, skimming beneath the collar of her blouse as he touched the edge of her collarbone. "Three—"

"That's enough," Sebastian said, smacking Ronan's hand away. "You're owed *one* inch, by *my* count. You should have watched your wording—our deal was only valid up until we reached the *Keep*, not the dungeon. Any noise your human made at the gates or after doesn't count."

At the kelpie's words, Branwen could feel Ronan's anger kindle, his body blazing hot against her back, but she knew Sebastian was right; the hulder had been caught in his own bargain.

"*Fine*," Ronan conceded, letting loose a sigh of frustration. "*One* inch."

A slim dagger flicked out from a sheath hidden beneath his wrist-sleeve. Its silvered edge glinted orange in the torchlight as he held it in front of Branwen. She could see her own gaze reflected in the narrow blade, her green eyes wide and terrified as the dagger drew near.

*You knew this was coming*, she reminded herself, calming the frantic beating of her heart. *You knew this was the price for learning Ginny's name and decided it was worth the pain.* She *is still worth the pain—every inch.*

Out of the corner of her eye, she could see Ginny try to move toward her, but Bart and the key-bearing redcap blocked her way out of the iron cell.

"No! Please, stop!" the little girl cried out now that she realized the ban on her voice had long since been lifted.

At the same time, Sebastian shouted, "Not the face!" His long stride carried him right up to the hulder, and he grabbed the other fae's bronze-skinned arm, halting the blade.

The kelpie's lanky form loomed over Ronan, but the hulder didn't back down; instead, he twirled the knife between his fingers, its tip slicing dangerously close to Branwen's cheek. She couldn't see Ronan's face from his position behind her, but she could hear the slick smile in his voice as he told Sebastian, "That wasn't part of the deal."

"Then, let's make a new one," the kelpie insisted, his golden eyes flashing as he realized Ronan had pulled his same trick of turning his words—or lack thereof—against him. "And this time, I'll make sure it's to your advantage."

*Wonderful*, Branwen thought with bitterness. *Once again, two fae are bickering over my fate as though I have no say in the matter.* Her jaw clenched, grinding her teeth. *Well, we'll see about that. The longer they talk, the longer I stay out of the cell. The longer I'm out of the cell, the more time I have to figure a way out of here!*

In front of her, the hulder's knife stilled, his interest obviously piqued as he said only, "I'm listening."

Sebastian's expression relaxed and he let go of Ronan's arm as he continued, "Celaeno sent out fifteen teams to capture fifteen human girls. Out of the fifteen, Celaeno will chose five and out of the five, only one. *She*"—the kelpie pointed firmly at Branwen—"is the *one*."

*The one for what?* Branwen wondered, only half-listening as she stared at the dark pit in the middle of the room. As she watched, the edge of the black rippled, sneaking a silent tendril toward Nezzie's foot. Destin spotted it and pulled the strix into the nearest circle of torchlight. When the shadow hit the light, it hissed and shriveled, retracting back into the pit with a familiar rustling sound. *There's no fae in that pit. It's the darkness that's alive!* Branwen realized, remembering one of the stories the old village women told—about a cave filled with unimaginable treasure guarded by a blackness so vast it ate heroes whole. *The Devouring Dark*, Branwen thought, recalling the name of the tale. Quickly, a plan formed in her mind, but first she knew she needed to be free of Ronan. She turned her attention back to the hulder and Sebastian, looking for the most opportune moment to act.

Ronan laughed. His blade drew a swift circle in air in front of Branwen's face as he asked, "Her? You really think Celaeno will chose *her*?"

From the side of the room, Mina butted in. "Our Lady wants young, beautiful, *biddable* girls. The younger the better, she said. At best, you've got one out of three, so what makes you think Celaeno will take her? What aren't you telling us? Do you know Celaeno's plan—why she wants these wretched humans in the first place?"

Sebastian shook his head. "I don't *know* anything," he said, "but I have my suspicions, and I think what Celaeno *wants* and what she *needs* are two different things."

"No surprise there," Bart muttered as he still stood guard in front of the open cell door. "Damned harpy *wanted* a unicorn."

"Exactly," the kelpie agreed, cringing at the memory. To Ronan, he said, "So you see why I can't just let you carve up her pretty face—not yet. All I'm asking is that you wait. As a hulder, you feed off pain. A mere inch won't be enough to satisfy you. It's just a taste. If I'm right, you won't miss much—just a bite—but if I'm wrong and Celaeno doesn't choose our Feisty here, then, you can have *every* inch of her. How does that sound?"

*Horrific*, Branwen thought, his skin creeping with dread. Her spine shuddered, unable to hold back her revulsion.

"Fantastic!" the hulder said, his voice rising with excitement. "But you'll forgive me if I don't entirely trust you. This isn't the first deal you've renegotiated with me, and I've learned since then. This time, I'm taking a down payment, just a reminder of what I'm owed—"

Before Sebastian could protest, the hulder's knife flicked down, toward Branwen's throat.

*NOW!* she thought and thrust her head forward as fast as she could, clamping her teeth on the side of the hulder's knife hand. She felt a crunch as the knuckle of his littlest finger popped out of joint. Ronan yelled in surprise, trying to jerk his hand away, but Branwen bit down harder. The hulder fed off others' pain, but it seemed he was vulnerable to his own. His grip on the knife weakened under the crushing pressure of Branwen's teeth, but he didn't quite let go. The blade stopped just shy of Branwen's collarbone, its tip pricking her chest as she inhaled.

Ronan recovered quickly, cursing in her ear as he shifted his grip. His took his left hand off her stomach, reaching up to take the dagger from his right, but in that moment, Branwen arched her neck, pulling his knife-hand up as she slammed the back of her head into his face. Next, she stomped her sturdy boot heel on his left instep, forcing him to widen his stance. She spun out of his grasp as quickly as she could, spitting his hand from her mouth in mid-rotation, then darted toward Ginny—and the red-cap with the keys.

Ronan lunged after her, but Sebastian caught Branwen first, yanking her away from the cell door with one hand and pivoting her behind his back. His other hand he thrust out at Ronan, shoving the hulder—*hard*. The shorter fae stumbled, dropping the knife in order to catch himself as he fell to the floor. He hissed as his hands brushed against a vein of iron embedded in the rock and immediately scrambled back to his feet. Angry red lines marked his palms where the iron had singed but not scorched his skin, and Branwen could see the crescent of her bite turning purple against his bronzed flesh. The hulder glared at her, his handsome face contorted with fury, but he didn't dare move against Sebastian so soon—not when Robin and Bart had both sauntered to his side. The second, key-bearing redcap remained at the girls' cell door, his face impassive but his black eyes glittering as he watched the proceedings.

Sebastian laughed, his low, smooth voice echoing in the chamber. Glancing at Mina, he asked, "What was that you said—she's only one out of three? That will be more than enough for Celaeno, don't you think? Our Lady loves pretty, spirited things."

From behind her, Branwen heard Nezzie mutter, "Yes, she loves to *break* them."

The other fae ignored the strix's comment—*because they all know it's true*, Branwen thought.

Ronan glowered at the kelpie, his red eyes bright in the torchlight. "If I didn't know better, I'd think you were a little *partial* to that human. Why else would you be so determined that she survive the culling?"

The word pricked Branwen's ears, setting a new urgency to her plan, and she heard several of the girls gasp from within their cell as they understood what the hulder was saying. *Culling? Well,* of course, *they're going to kill us,* Branwen scolded herself for ever thinking otherwise. *Then, they'll probably* eat *us. The fae certainly aren't going to just send everyone home, not after all the effort they went through to collect us.*

Bart scoffed at the hulder. "Don't be ridiculous," he said, giving Branwen a brief hope that he would deny Ronan's terrible implication, but the púka ruined it as he glanced at Sebastian and, with a sly grin, added, "She's not quite his type."

At Bart's words, Sebastian blanched, his expression suddenly and intensely blank. "Bart...." the kelpie warned, but the púka paid him no need.

"What? You know it's true," the goat-faced fae asserted in defiance, then turned to Ronan. "Our Sebastian likes them feisty like this one, sure," he continued, jerking his head toward Branwen. "But really he prefers his humans blonde and petite. That yellow-haired girl from last time was something else. She was small, but she fought like a devil." To Sebastian, he coyly admitted, "Even *I* could see why you liked her."

As Bart spoke, Branwen could feel Sebastian tense; his grip on her arm grew almost bone-crushingly tight and his whole body quivered with barely-contained rage.

"*What* did you say?" Sebastian growled, the words a grating rumble within his chest. Out of the corners of her eyes, Branwen could see Destin and Nezzie exchanging glances as the two backed away. Mina put her hands on her belt, her ink-black fingers hovering over the silver blades there. Even Ronan's own anger at the kelpie became tempered with caution, but Bart was too caught up in the apparent joy of provoking Sebastian to notice.

"I hadn't had that much fun in ages," the púka continued. "It was such a shame when she finally broke. Me and my men, we could have kept playing for *days,* using the power of her True Name to make her do whatever we wanted. It was a good Name, too—sweet, innocent, *pure*—just like her, but I can't seem to remember it exactly. What was it again? Some kind of flower. Oh, wait! I remember now! It was—"

Before he could finish, Sebastian snapped. He dropped Branwen's arm and threw himself at Bart, catching the púka off-guard, and the two tumbled to the side, shouting as they rolled across the iron-marbled floor. Branwen expected Ronan or Mina or even Robin and the other redcap to jump in and break them apart, but the other fae simply scooted out of the way, their message clear: this was between Bart and Sebastian alone. They wouldn't be dragged into anyone else's fight.

With the púka still weakened from the previous battle with Robin, Sebastian easily overpowered him, pinning him to the ground. The kelpie's long fingers wrapped almost completely around Bart's bony throat, choking the life out of him.

The púka's arms flailed, blindly grasping after Ronan's fallen knife to defend himself. His fingers bumped the blade and he grabbed it, swinging it toward Sebastian with all his might, but the kelpie caught the knife and wrenched it from the púka's grip. The kelpie leaned in close, almost eye-to-eye with Bart as he pressed the edge of the blade tight against the púka's throat.

"*You will* never *speak her name!*" Sebastian bellowed. The sound was almost deafening as the power and base of his voice reverberated off the blockhouse's curved walls.

"Okay! Okay! I swear! Now, let me up!" Bart said, choking out the words through his partially crushed throat. He lifted his head, trying to force his way up, but Sebastian didn't budge.

The kelpie's voice filled with an eerie calm as he next spoke, the words soft and low but undeniably clear.

"No. I don't think you understand," he told Bart as he slowly rotated the angle of the knife until only the tip rested just beneath the púka's chin. "That was *my* oath. *I* swear you will never speak her name again." At the last word, he thrust the blade upward, puncturing soft flesh.

# Chapter 9

Bart's mouth gaped as he tried to gasp in pain, but his throat had already filled with blood and he choked on it, unable to breathe. Then, Sebastian yanked the knife out. The crimson liquid drained, making a faint gurgling noise as it pulsed through the slit-shaped hole in Bart's neck and spilled across the floor. In seconds, the púka bled out, his body now truly nothing more than a skeleton.

Immediately, Robin lunged for Bart's corpse, whatever truce they'd struck clearly ending with the púka's life. Sebastian barely managed to fling himself out of the way before the fiendish little man leapt on top of the púka, ripping into pale flesh and smearing himself with glistening ruby gore. The key-bearing redcap was close behind him, the sudden flood of blood obviously too much for him to resist. His beetle-black eyes burned with hunger as he forsook his post by the girls' cell door and bolted toward Bart—but Robin wasn't in the mood to share. Already blood-glutted from earlier, he easily overpowered the second redcap, snarling as he lifted him bodily and hurled him through the air.

The girls screamed as the guard's body came flying toward their still-open cell, but at the last second Ginny darted forward, slamming the iron door shut and causing the redcap to rebound off the sturdy metal bars. Branwen's heart sank as she heard the secondary clang of the lock's pins dropping in place, trapping

Ginny and the other girls inside once more, but at least they'd kept the blood-hungry redcap out.

*For now,* Branwen thought ominously as she watched the guard scramble to his feet. *After all, he still has* the keys. Branwen widened her stance, preparing to launch herself at the guard should he turn to open the cell. *I'll do anything to protect these girls,* she told herself. *Anything! Otherwise, what has this all been* for*? Why did we fight so hard just for* this *to be the end?*

The redcap's dark gaze flitted toward the girls, drawn by the sound of fear as the younger children cried, but only for a second. The girls' continued whimpers weren't enough to hold his attention—not when there was another, living target right in front of him, covered in fresh blood.

*Sebastian.*

The kelpie stood off to the side, his head bowed and his tall, blood-splattered body slightly hunched. His chest heaved for air—far more than the effort of disposing of Bart required. He still held Ronan's knife, the short, blood-slickened hilt clenched in his fist. In the flickering light, Branwen thought she saw moisture glistening along the sharp planes of his cheeks, but when Sebastian looked up, his golden eyes were a blaze of hate. The kelpie was still spoiling for a fight, his rage barely diminished by Bart's death. The other fae, however, were not so eager.

To Sebastian's left, Ronan remained perfectly still as he watched both redcaps, clearly not wanting to attract their attention in his unarmed state. To the right and on the other side of the pit, Mina was just as wary. She had dropped her torch and pulled her crossbow from the holster on her back the moment Robin had lunged for Bart. In the commotion, she took the opportunity to jam her foot into the cocking stirrup, haul back on the string, and load a bolt before swinging the butt of the bow up against her shoulder, ready to fire. Weaponless, Nezzie and Destin had retreated behind her.

*No, not retreated*, Branwen realized as she saw the subtle way the strix and merrow had positioned themselves to either side of Mina, just beyond the púka's peripheral vision but still within range to attack. *They're regrouping. Strategizing. Waiting for a moment of distraction—and this is it!*

Sebastian and the key-bearing redcap locked eyes, each fuming with pent up rage and fury, and that was all it took.

The redcap moved first in an explosion of speed, but Sebastian was ready, slashing in low with Ronan's knife as he spun out of the way. The blade sliced through the edge of the guard's ear as he passed by. The redcap's feet scrambled to change directions but failed as he suddenly realized he was hurtling toward the pit just beyond where Sebastian had been. The redcap's iron boots screeched against the stone floor, sending up sparks as he flung his body to the ground and slid to a stop just inches away from the edge—and the Devouring Dark. The sudden reversal of his momentum caused the two sets of keys to swivel around his neck so they now dangled down his back, facing Branwen.

Just then, a familiar piercing shriek split the air, and humans and fae alike flinched, covering their ears.

*The unicorn—she's finally caught the scent of Bart's blood!* Branwen thought, dropping her hands as soon as the sound soared past her ability to hear it. All around her, Sebastian and the others shouted, trying to drown out the noise. Even Robin stopped his feasting on Bart to stuff his bloody hands against his ears.

While they were all distracted, Branwen bolted forward and grabbed both sets of keys from around the redcap guard's neck, yanking the leather cord and the iron chain over his head. The redcap growled, awkwardly trying to pivot and push to his feet to face her, but for once Branwen was quicker, her speed and strength born of desperation as she used all her might to shove the creature the last few inches into the pit. The Darkness hissed as the redcap's iron boots went over the side, but other than that, the guard disappeared without trace or sound, completely and utterly swallowed by the Dark.

Then, Branwen turned and ran as fast as she could, hoping the unicorn's bloodthirsty screams would keep the others occupied long enough for her to make it to the far set of spiral stairs. As she dashed past the girls' iron cell, she heard Ginny cry out in dismay, the girl obviously thinking Branwen was abandoning her to make her own bid for freedom, but nothing could have been further from the truth.

*I'm doing this for you—for us*, Branwen thought as she forced herself to turn her back on the girls and keep running. *There's no way me and fourteen little girls could defeat dozens of blood-raging redcaps. They would slaughter us! The fae would help if they were free, I think—I* hope*—but there's not enough time to release them all—not yet. I can only open one cell, so it has to be the one that* counts*!*

Branwen's heart raced as she neared the second twisting staircase, her muscles bunching as she prepared to leap, to take the steps two and three at time, hoping beyond hope that she could reach the unicorn before the redcaps—but she had forgotten about one thing.

Ronan.

As soon as Sebastian and the guard had attacked each other, the hulder had retreated to the side of the second stairs, half-hidden in the shadows of the spiral's curve. That same curve also shielded him from the worst of the unicorn's noise, leaving him only mildly incapacitated as Branwen approached. She saw him just a moment too late, unable to shift her stride to veer away from him. The hulder grabbed her, but with his focus split between her and the unicorn, his grip wasn't as strong as before. She easily twisted out of his grasp, but Ronan didn't give up. The hulder's red eyes flashed as he went for her again, so Branwen used the only weapon against the fae she had—the iron keys.

She swung the two tangled sets like she would a shepherd's sling, the heavy keys stretching the chain and leather cord taut, only she didn't let go and used the gathered momentum to bash the hulder across the face. The teeth of the two larger keys scraped his cheek, the marks turning instantly black as the iron scorched his flesh. Ronan shouted in pain, stumbling back, but Branwen knew that wasn't enough. It would only take him a minute to recover—not enough time for her to climb the stairs. She knew if she tried, he'd overtake her in moments and the next time her sling wouldn't catch him by surprise.

Branwen wrapped the iron chain around her right hand, gripping both sets of keys between her fingers, and swung her fist at the side of Ronan's head. The chain slammed into the hulder's temple and he staggered sideways, dazed and disoriented, so she hit him again, throwing her whole weight behind the blow and driving the hulder to the ground. His head smacked against the stone floor with a sharp thud, but Branwen could tell the force hadn't killed him, just knocked him unconscious.

*That will have to be enough,* she thought as she finally started her mad climb up the stairs. She didn't get very far before she heard the clamor of dozens of iron boots above her and knew it was too late. The redcaps were already at the unicorn's cell. Branwen couldn't see them from her position on the lower curve of the stairs, but judging by the unicorn's sudden silence she knew they must have come prepared with a sacrifice this time. She was proven right as she saw a gored pixie tumble off the side the stairs, its emerald green skin smeared with ruby blood. The dragonfly-like fae had served its purpose as an offering to calm the raging beast, and afterward the guards had thrown it away like so much garbage. The sight made Branwen sick.

*That's how much the fae value life*, she thought as she listened to the redcaps' steps recede as they quickly returned to their posts, their duty complete. *That's how much we're worth to them—a thing to be used and nothing more. Is it better to be dead than to be trapped here as their toy? Is that our final option? Death?*

*No!* She refused to believe it, taking firm strides up the stone stairs, her speed increasing with her resolve. *There's always another way. I will* make *another way. We are getting out of here and I* am *going to see my family again!*

As she darted up the stairs, the imprisoned fae took notice, their eyes drawn to the chain of keys still wrapped in her fist.

"Free us! Free us!" they hissed, reaching through the bars of their cells. "Give us the keys!"

Smoke wafted in the air as their skin burned against the iron, but Branwen continued to slip by them, dodging their grasping hands in silence. *Soon*, she wanted to promise them, but didn't dare speak her plan.

As she turned the first curve of the stairs, she heard half a dozen high-pitched shrieks from below.

*The girls! Ginny!* Branwen stopped in her tracks, her heart torn by their cries, but when she looked back, she saw it wasn't the humans who were in danger.

Destin and Nezzie had taken full advantage of the chaos and ambushed Mina, overpowering the skeletal-framed púka. Her miniature crossbow lay broken on the floor, but Nezzie had managed to steal the púka's twin daggers. The strix slammed both hilts against the back of Mina's horned head, knocking her unconscious. Then, Nezzie helped Destin lifted Mina up and unceremoniously dump her body into the pit in the center of the room.

Branwen didn't see her disappear into the Dark because in that short span of time Sebastian had recovered from the unicorn's screams.

The kelpie spotted Branwen on the stairs. "Oh, no you don't!" he called after her, then bolted up the stairs, his long legs eating up the distance between them.

Branwen ran faster, not daring to look back as she pushed herself to the limit. Her heart thundered in her chest, each beat slamming against her sternum. The rasping of her own ragged breath drowned out the sound of the kelpie's feet against the stone, so she couldn't even hear how close or how far he was behind her.

She was so focused on staying *ahead* that she almost flew past the unicorn's cell. At the last second, Branwen grabbed hold of one of the iron bars and flung herself back. She let go as soon as she could, twisting her body aside as she expected the beast's bloodstained horn to lunge through the bars of the cell toward her, but the unicorn merely tilted its head, looking at her calmly through the iron.

*It's still pacified from the pixie's death!* Branwen realized. *It won't attack! I need fresh blood—now!* From the corner of her eye, she could see Sebastian fast approaching. He'd be on her in seconds.

Branwen shifted her grip on the keys, holding the one that matched the lock to the unicorn's cell like a knife, then slashed its jagged teeth across her palm. The sharp, backward-facing tines ripped through her skin, and she blinked back tears as great ruby drops welled out of the cut and fell to the floor. With her other hand, she thrust the now-bloody key into the lock. Time seemed to slow as she turned the key. Below her, less than a dozen steps away, Sebastian cried out, his golden eyes going wide as he obviously realized what she was about to do. He skidded to a halt and immediately pivoted, cursing loudly as he raced back down the stairs. Above her, she knew the redcaps must have caught the scent of her blood; she could hear the harsh clanging of their boots as the group of them turned and stomped toward the unicorn's cell once more.

In front of her, the beast itself stood exceptionally still, and Branwen froze for half a second in shock, the key only a fraction of a turn away from unlocking the cell. She'd expected the unicorn to work itself into a frenzy as soon as it smelled her blood, the metallic tang in the air incensing the beast and provoking it to attack, but instead her blood seemed to have the opposite effect. The unicorn relaxed, the muscles of its moonlight body quivering as they released their tension. The creature's breath came out in soft puffs that tickled Branwen's face through the iron bars and she smelled the brisk scent of spring—of rain-soaked lavender and thyme. The unicorn stood so close Branwen could see herself reflected in the mirror-like surface of its eyes—her own expression so desperate and weak and afraid.

In that moment, Branwen remembered an old story told by the local hunters—a fable, really—that a unicorn once lived on the moors, slaughtering wolves and sheep alike. The beast was too wild and ferocious for the hunters to catch, but it became placid at the touch of a young maiden, obeying her every command, even remaining calm and quiet for its own death at the hands of the hunters.

Relying on nothing more than instinct and old stories, Branwen reached through the iron bars and touched her bloody hand to the unicorn's cheek, stroking it lightly. The creature was like a cloud beneath her fingertips, its substance so soft and ethereal she was afraid her hand might pass right through it and the beast would vanish as though it had been nothing more than a dream.

"*Help* me," she begged the unicorn. She didn't have to glance up the spiraling stairs to know the redcaps were coming down *fast*. She could hear Ginny shriek from below, crying out in warning. If she didn't act now, Branwen knew she would soon be dead, along with the girls' last chance at freedom. She gave the key one last twist and pulled open the door.

For a second, the unicorn did nothing—only stared at her—then it dipped its head, touching its bloodstained horn to Branwen's palm. She jolted as magic shot up her arm, burning through her veins. The hot spark of it reached her heart and she felt...*something* ignite within her like smoldering embers suddenly brought to life. A swift buzzing warmth bloomed in her chest, then spread through her body, revitalizing her and giving her a second wind. Her left hand tingled fiercely and when she looked down, she saw only a thin silver scar in the place of her jagged cut. The Cù Sìth's mark across her wrist had also nearly disappeared, its now-faint lines still dotted by her mother's neat stitches.

Branwen glanced back up at the unicorn, but before she could say anything else, the unicorn turned and bolted, its diamond hooves ringing against the stone as it charged up the stairs. The redcaps scattered before it, some even flinging themselves off the edge to avoid being impaled and instead fell into the oubliette below where they were consumed by the Devouring Dark. The beast's scarlet horn slashed through the remaining ranks, piercing the redcaps' leather armor and tough gray skin. With every kill, it cried out in victory and in vengeance, its silvery voice a clarion call through the entire blockhouse.

With the guards occupied, Branwen yanked the keys from the door and ran back down the stairs toward the girls. When she reached the bottom of the steps, she saw Ronan. The hulder groaned as he struggled to regain consciousness. Branwen gave him a swift kick to the head as she passed, knocking him back into oblivion. Sebastian was far ahead of her, sprinting across the circular chamber. He ignored Robin, Nezzie, and Destin completely as he headed for the first set of stairs—the ones that led *out*. His swift motion caught the redcap's attention and Robin lunged after him but Sebastian was too quick, leaping onto the stairs from the side in his desperation to flee. The redcap growled as he missed and hit the inner curved wall of the stairs instead.

Branwen skidded to a halt halfway to the girls' cell, backpedaling to keep out of Robin's peripheral vision as the little man rebounded off the stone. The last thing she needed was for the vicious fiend to catch a glimpse of her blood-smeared self and decide to change his target. However, before Robin regained his footing, Nezzie spread her wings and swooped in, snatching the cap from his head. The strix twisted the hat viciously between her fists, wringing out a waterfall of blood as she swerved and flew beyond his reach.

Robin collapsed as the liquid drained from his cap, his body becoming a half-desiccated husk. Branwen thought he had finally died until she saw the hateful gleam still burning in his pitch-black eyes. The redcap had been so blood-glutted from his meals of redcaps and of Bart that Nezzie couldn't come close to squeezing all the blood from his cap.

Still, she'd done enough. The strix haphazardly tossed the cap across the room, away from Robin. It landed in one of prison's empty cells, the still-damp fabric of the hat squelching as it hit the floor. With his limbs and joints shriveled, Robin could barely move. It would take him ages to crawl his way across the dungeon floor to the cell with his cap, and even if he made it, the door was closed and *locked*.

*Serves him right*, Branwen thought, a small, vindictive smile creeping onto her lips as she darted toward the girls' cell. Ginny saw her and rushed to the door, gripping the iron bars. As soon as Branwen unlocked the door, the younger girl flung it open and threw herself into Branwen's arms. The other girls stumbled out behind her, clinging to each other in a small, tight group.

"You came back!" Ginny cried, her voice choked with happy sobs. Tears streamed from her dark brown eyes. Branwen wiped them away even as she blinked back her own, her fingers brushing over the girl's honey-colored hair—so similar to her little sister Colwen's. She pulled her close.

"I will always come back," Branwen promised—to Ginny, to herself, to Colwen. "*Always*."

"That's nice," Destin commented dryly as he and Nezzie sidled up to the group.

Ginny and the other thirteen girls flinched at their approach, some of them cowering back into the cell, but Branwen stood her ground, her only movement the slight turn of her body as she put herself between the two fae and Ginny.

"What do you want?" she demanded, eyeing them warily. The strix and merrow had never offered to harm her, but that was *before,* when they'd had their own troubles. Now that they were free of Mina and Ronan, she didn't know what they would do. So far, every other fae had tried to kill or capture her.

Destin seemed to read the line of her thoughts. "We're not interested in whatever scheme Celaeno has going on. We just want what you want—to get *out* of here," the merrow stated. "Preferably alive. And you seem to have a plan, so do you want help with it or not?"

*Help?* The offer took Branwen aback, but not for long—not with the shouts and cries of redcaps echoing down from the upper floors. She looked toward the sound and saw the unicorn near the top of the stairs where the two spirals joined. The beast had killed or maimed many of the guards on the left side, but the other guards were still strong and had begun to rally their forces. As redcaps swarmed up the stairs toward the scent of blood and death, Branwen saw Sebastian. The kelpie's long, lean form was a shadow in the dark as he slipped into the now-unguarded corridor leading to the blockhouse entrance.

Branwen made her decision.

"We have to free the fae—as many as we can," she told Destin. "That's the only way we stand a chance against the redcaps, both here and in the Keep. With them and the harpies distracted, we might be able to escape."

"*Might*," Nezzie echoed, glancing up at Destin. The two shared an odd, knowing look as she said, "That sounds like a terrible idea."

"Absolutely," the merrow agreed, then his shark-like mouth curved into a wicked grin. "Let's do it. I'll start from the bottom. Nezzie, you work from the top. We'll meet at the door."

The strix nodded, her own mouth splitting into an eager, foolhardy smile, then she bent to the side, ripping two strips off the bottom edge of her blouse. Nezzie wrapped one around her right hand and the second around Destin's left, which the merrow then held out to Branwen.

"Give me the keys," he said.

Branwen obeyed, dropping the smaller set into his bandaged palm, all the while thinking, *Please, don't let this be a mistake!*

Together, Nezzie and Destin bent the key ring apart and split the keys between them—two for the top and two for the bottom floors. The strix leapt into the air immediately after, her tawny wings flapping furiously as she soared up through the air shaft.

"Wait to follow until the way is clear," the merrow told Branwen. "Not all the fae will be *rational*. They've been here too long. This place takes its toll and they may not recognize friend from foe from...food."

Branwen nodded, understanding the merrow's meaning all too well. She held the girls back and waited, watching for the right moment as Destin darted up the right-hand spiral of stairs, thrusting the keys into the nearest lock. The door sprang open and two half-starved hobgoblins stumbled out. The creatures didn't look back but rushed up the stairs as fast as they could, heading toward the only exit. At the sight of the newly-freed fae, those still imprisoned began to shout, bolting to the front of their cells and begging to be released. Destin obliged as fast as he could. Above him, Nezzie flitted from floor to floor, dodging redcaps as she freed fae from the upper levels.

The liberated prisoners stormed the stairs, trying to plow over each other and any redcap guards as they went. True to Destin's word, some of the fae were too far gone, their minds broken by the iron and the dark and the unicorn's piercing screams. Once freed, they attacked the nearest living being or even themselves—ripping, tearing, and biting—but still, few were a match for the redcaps. The little men were vicious fighters, throwing fae—and bits of fae—over the open side of the stairs where the prisoner's frail bodies made sickening splats as they hit the dungeon floor.

"Let's go!" Branwen commanded when she saw that the bulk of the fray had shifted far enough away. She wrapped the chain for the remaining two jagged iron keys around her right wrist, then took Ginny's hand. With her left, she grabbed the hand of the next nearest girl—a child of no more than seven with short, chestnut hair and pale green eyes. Together, they moved toward the first set of stairs, climbing the broad, shallow steps.

The rest of the girls followed behind them, some stumbling in their rush to leave. The second oldest girl—an olive-skinned beauty with wide, dark eyes and thick, black hair—bumped into one of the torches surrounding the pit, knocking it over. Branwen turned at the sound, looking back just in time to see the flame snuff out as the torch clattered to the ground, creating a gap in the circle of light.

"No!" she yelled, trying to force her way down the stairs again, but the crowd of girls behind her blocked her path. All she could do was cry out a warning. "Get back! Stay away from the pit!"

But it was too late. The Devouring Dark shot out from the edge of the oubliette, wrapping a shadowy tendril around the girl's ankle and dragging her toward its gaping blackness. The girl screamed, clawing and kicking against the Dark, but to no avail. As she struggled, she knocked over two more torches, widening the gap and allowing the Dark to grab one more child—the small, blonde girl who'd first cried out for Branwen to save them. This time, the girl didn't have a chance to make a sound before the Darkness swallowed her.

Pain stabbed through Branwen's chest, her heart breaking, but she knew she couldn't stop, couldn't turn back. "Run!" she shouted to the remaining girls, grabbing the nearest ones and pushing them in front of her in order to clear a path for the ones below. The girls obeyed, whether out of trust or panic, Branwen didn't care as long as they escaped the Dark. With a third of the torches gone, the blackness spread at an alarming pace, spilling out across the floor.

The shadowy pool stretched toward Ronan's unconscious form near the far side of the chamber, its dark tendrils reaching into the hole in his back. At their touch, the hulder woke, his whole body convulsing as the darkness invaded, pouring into him. His red eyes rolled back in his head at the pain and he wept and screamed—a sound of pure agony that sent chills down Branwen's spine as she and Ginny ran to catch up with the other girls. Then, after a few steps, there was only silence from below—a sudden echoing void of sound—and that, Branwen thought, was the worst of all.

She didn't look back, but kept pressing forward, guiding the girls from behind as they clamored up the spiral stairs, weaving past the fallen fae and ravaged redcaps that Destin and the other prisoners had left as they'd fought their way up. Several of the younger children lagged behind, having to wait for Branwen to lift them over some of the larger corpses that blocked the stairwell.

They made it to the entryway on the third floor without further incident. As Branwen ushered the girls into the sloped corridor leading to the blockhouse door, she glanced up, checking the level above. The last of the redcap guards were only a half-turn of the stairs away, but the unicorn kept them thoroughly occupied, leaping over them and charging from behind. Scarlet stained the beast's once-pure-white coat; now only small patches of moonlight remained, gleaming through the red. In a few more minutes, the unicorn would likely have the guards all gutted, their glistening entrails spilling down the stairs just like those of the fallen fiends behind them. Branwen looked away.

Ahead of her, the surviving prisoners crowded the dark tunnel, their bodies pressed against one another as they kept trying to move forward without success. Fae after fae threw themselves against the iron door—not caring how much it burned so long as they could get *out*—but each time, right before their flesh touched the metal, an invisible force exploded from the portal, propelling them backwards.

*Magic.* Branwen could feel the hum of it in the air. Her heart filled with dread as she thought, *There's a second safe-guard on the door! We're trapped!*

# Chapter 10

From the top of the corridor, the fae's panicked voices rebounded off the tunnel's iron-veined walls, channeling into Branwen's ears.

"The door is warded!"

"We can't get through!"

"There's no way out."

"We're all going to *die....*"

"*NO!*" Branwen hissed the word, the vehemence of her denial startling the girls around her; only Ginny remained calm, her grip on Branwen's hand unwavering.

The younger girl looked at her with absolute trust, and for a moment, Branwen could see Colwen gazing up at her with those same eyes.

*I'm coming, little one,* she promised, further steeling her will. *I did not fight* so hard *just for* this *to be the end!*

She spotted Nezzie and Destin standing only a few paces away, positioned in the back half of the group, and she pushed her way toward them with Ginny in tow. The other girls hesitated to follow, their fear of the fae holding them back. They huddled next to the wall, instead, their small bodies pressing against the stone.

As Branwen neared, she grabbed the strix's shoulder. The winged girl spun around at her touch, Mina's silver blades flashing in her hands, but Nezzie quickly lowered them as recognition set in.

"Feisty! You made it!" the strix exclaimed, her high voice gaining Destin's attention, too. The merrow looked back, his yellow gaze locking on Branwen. She caught a hint of surprise in his eyes, which soon turned to respect as he acknowledged her with a deep bow of his head.

Branwen wasn't sure how to interpret the gesture. *Are we friends, now?* she wondered, hazarding a nod back. *Is that even possible? No, maybe not friends, but* allies*, at least,* she decided. *In this place. At this time. As long as we're working toward a common goal.* Beyond that, she couldn't say. *First, we have to get out of here.*

She looked back at Nezzie. "Tell me what's going on," Branwen asked. "Why can't they open the door? Is it blocked? Do they already know we've escaped?"

"No." The strix shook her head hard, her moss-green braids whipping through the air. "If that were the case, the redcaps would be *swarming* in here," she said. "This is something else."

"Celaeno must have put some kind of enchantment on the iron," Destin added. "A ward against the prisoners, if I had to guess. None of them can even *touch* the door, let alone open it."

"Against the prisoners?" Branwen murmured, her thoughts churning until a sudden jolt of inspiration struck. "Then, what about *Sebastian*?" she asked. "He's not a prisoner. Have you seen him? Did he get through?"

"Not *yet*," came the kelpie's unexpected reply, his low voice rumbling just behind Branwen.

From the sides of the corridor, she heard the other girls' frightened gasps, and she whirled to face him, her only weapon—the two iron keys—thrust out before her just in case. However, Sebastian only glanced at her, his golden, goat-like eyes unreadable as he tried to shove his way past. Nezzie and Destin stepped forward to block him, their attention not on the kelpie, but the gray, shriveled *thing* draped across his arms.

*A desiccated redcap!* Branwen realized as the creature's iron boots dangled over the Sebastian's elbow. The metal shoes scraped against the nearest wall, sending up small sparks in the dark as the kelpie pulled up short.

"If you want to get out of here, *move*," Sebastian demanded. "That's not a ward against the prisoners," he added, jerking his head toward the door. "Damned harpy made a ward against everything but a living, breathing redcap. Thanks to *someone*"—he rolled his eyes at Branwen—"those are hard to come by, but I've managed it."

Destin snorted. "Just barely," he commented, eyeing the redcap's half-dried husk. The only sure sign of life was the hate still burning in the little man's gaze.

"Yes," Sebastian agreed. "*That* is why you need to move—before our only key *expires*. There's no time to get another one. The unicorn has seen to that, and when she's finished out there, she'll come here next."

The kelpie didn't have to say any more. Nezzie and Destin jumped out of his way, the strix flapping her wings briefly to rise above the crowd.

"Move!" she shouted, her high, clear voice cutting through the fae's frantic murmurs. "Make way!"

Below her, Destin started to clear a path, shoving the other prisoners aside as Sebastian pushed in after him. "He has the key!" the merrow bellowed. "Let him through!"

In seconds, their message spread through the crowd and all the fae suddenly parted before them, pressing their bodies flat against the iron-riddled walls despite the way it seared their flesh. With the path cleared, Sebastian shot out from behind Destin, gaining speed with every stride as he raced up the corridor. He shifted his grip on the redcap, holding the nearly-dried-out body before him like a shield. When he reached the top, he slammed the shriveled creature against the door, taking advantage of the redcap's iron-impervious skin as he pushed. All around him, the other fae joined in, placing their hands on the redcap's body and shoving with all their might until the heavy iron door behind it finally began to creak open.

At the sound, Branwen turned back, holding her left hand out to the girls still huddled against the wall. The scar from the unicorn gleamed faintly silver across her palm. *Like the mark from a blood oath*, Branwen thought, remembering the sign some of the village elders wore. *Well, this is my oath—what I swore to myself when I set the unicorn free—I will do everything in my power to protect these children and get us home!*

To the girls, she pleaded, "Come with me! We're safer together!"

Beside her, Ginny reached out, too, beckoning with her free hand; the other never let go of Branwen, not even once. "Come on!" the girl cried, spurring them to action.

One of the youngest took hold of Branwen, then turned and grabbed the girl next to her. The pattern continued, one girl taking hold of another until the last girl looped around and grabbed Ginny, forming a chain of interlocked hands with Branwen at the lead.

"Stay close and don't let go!" she warned, then began to pull them forward, moving up the corridor as fast as their shorter legs allowed while still remaining behind the crowd of fae. Nezzie and Destin hung back, too, letting the others push in front, and Branwen knew they shared the same strategy. *That's right*, she thought. *Stay inside the blockhouse just a little while longer. Let the other fae take the brunt of the first attack, then sneak out behind them in the chaos.*

Ahead of them, light spilled into the entryway as the door swung all the way open. While Branwen, Nezzie, Destin, and the girls still lingered in the shadows, the others rushed forward. In seconds, scores of hungry, vengeful prisoners poured out into the Keep's courtyard, their cries of freedom met with startled grunts from three new redcaps guarding the door. The escaping fae quickly overwhelmed them, ripping off their hats and wringing out the blood onto the dry ground of the Keep.

The commotion drew the attention of the nearest guards who turned toward the sounds, but they were no match for the sheer number of fae fleeing the blockhouse. Within moments, the area directly in front of the prison had been cleared, and the fae advanced into the center of the Keep, making their way steadily toward the front gate. Branwen squeezed Ginny's hand, preparing to dart out into the courtyard. She'd only gone half a stride when Destin thrust out his arm in front of her.

"Wait!" the merrow said, and Branwen skidded to a halt, the girls bumping into her from behind. Before she could even turned to ask him what was the matter, two dark shadows flew overhead, aiming for the gate.

*More harpies*, Branwen knew by the sound of their wings; their metallic feathers crashed together like swords, mimicking the din of battle. *They must have been above in the trees watching the back of the Keep.* She hoped there weren't any more—five was bad enough.

"Go!" Destin said, releasing her. At the same time, he and Nezzie bolted from the entryway. They immediately veered off to the side, keeping to the periphery as they ran along the far wall of the Keep.

Branwen followed them, the chain of girls trailing behind her. Without the heavy iron of the blockhouse around them, she could feel the buzz of magic in the air. It pulsed against her skin, stronger than ever, and a sudden heat flared in her chest as though the spark of the unicorn's magic within her burned anew.

*What exactly did that unicorn* do *to me?* she wondered, but her thoughts were interrupted by the *fwip* of an arrow shooting just above her head.

Immediately, she hurled herself and Ginny to the ground, pulling the other girls down, too, as she tried to make them all a smaller target. When she looked up, she saw an orange, warty-skinned kobold with a bow firing at a bulbous, spider-like fae off to her right. The eight-legged creature dodged easily and the second arrow flew past, clattering against the wall near the girls.

*An errant shot. They haven't seen us,* Branwen realized with relief. She scramble back to her feet, hauling Ginny up beside her.

"Go—and stay down!" she hissed, trying to keep her voice low, yet loud enough for the girls to hear over the shouts and cries of the fae battling toward the gate. She pushed forward, staying within the shadows of the Keep's walls. For now, the overhang of the Keep's crenellations would hide them from the view of any creature directly above, she knew, but soon they would have to cross the bailey to get to the first of the two gates.

Initially caught off-guard, the redcaps and other denizens of the Keep began forming the semblance of ranks with the aid of the harpies calling down orders from above. Still, the prisoners' sheer numbers and desperation continued to hold them off. The earth shook, knocking loose stones from the Keep's walls and towers as a newly-freed golem called forth more of its kind from the dirt. The creatures had only half-formed before the redcaps knocked them down, stomping them with their iron boots; however, the distraction was enough, allowing two fleet-footed fae to bolt for the bridge.

*The Cù Sìth is there!* Branwen remembered, but it was far too late.

Naunos darted in from the right, the shadow-wolf's mouth wide and gaping as she leapt for the first fae. She caught it by the throat, her powerful jaws crunching through flesh and bone. The creature went instantly limp and she tossed it aside, its body tumbling into the pit of iron spikes by the bridge as she lunged for the second fae.

Branwen couldn't watch the rest. Behind her, the younger girls were screaming and crying, terrified of the blood and chaos around them. Branwen tried to shush them, but their noise had already attracted the attention of another kobold, his toad-like eyes gleaming as he spotted them in the shadows. The creature grinned, his mouth opening far too wide for his face. He let out a loud croak, calling over three more warty fae.

"Run!" Branwen shouted at the girls, abandoning all efforts of stealth. *Run* where? her thoughts demanded, and she latched onto the last defensible place she'd seen. "Follow the wall and get into the moat!" she commanded, shoving as many girls as she could in that direction. She knew Naunos was by the moat on the right side of the iron-studded bridge, but if the girls were quick and stayed on the left—along the wall—the battling fae would be between them and the Cù Sìth, disrupting the wolf's line of sight.

They could make it.

*I just have to hold the kobolds off for a little while*, she thought, tightening her grip on the heavy iron keys. She tried to pry her other hand loose from Ginny, but the girl wouldn't budge. "Go!" Branwen pleaded. "The iron will help protect you! If you stay, I can't keep you safe!"

"No!" Ginny refused. The girl picked up a sharp, fist-sized stone from the ground—a piece of the Keep's crumbling walls veined with iron. "I can fight!" she insisted.

Branwen didn't have time to argue.

The kobolds leapt, their bowed legs launching them through the air.

Suddenly, a single, massive bolt of lightning exploded in the Keep, rocking the very foundations of the structure. The stone walls shook and some of the more shoddy scaffolding—already weakened from the golem's earlier attack—peeled away from the stone, tumbling into broken heaps on the ground. Brittle bone bridges snapped and collapsed as their meager supports gave way.

The force of the blast knocked almost everyone to their knees, including Branwen, and the violent gust of wind that followed blew the kobolds off-course, slamming them to the ground. One of the few creatures left standing was a púka near the center of the Keep. Haggard and beyond emaciated, he was clearly one of the prisoners. *And the source of the lightning*, Branwen knew, remembering how Bart had once summoned the same elemental force. Scorch marks blackened the ground around the goat-faced creature and beside him lay the burnt, still-smoking form of a harpy blasted from the sky.

The remaining four harpies circled overhead, shrieking in fury, then Aello tucked her wings and dove, slamming into the púka. He screamed as her talons pierced his skin, hooking through the bone and muscles of his shoulders as she lifted him into the air. Her sisters swooped down in rapid succession, slicing at him with the blades of their feathers until his pale flesh hung from him in ribbons. Then, Aello let him drop.

The púka screamed until his tattered body hit the ground. His cries stopped with a resounding *crunch.* By then, Branwen was already on her feet, running after the girls with Ginny in tow. The kobolds were slower to recover, their movements not fueled by the same utter desperation, but they weren't far behind.

"Go!" Branwen urged when some of the children looked back. Their terrified eyes told her the kobolds were almost upon her, and she spun around, lashing out with the jagged iron keys.

She caught one in the throat as it leapt at her, the sharp end of the keys ripping through the bloated membrane there. Air and blood sprayed out, misting Branwen's face as the punctured pouch deflated. She couldn't even wipe her eyes before the next creature attacked, hurling itself toward her. Ginny screamed and threw her rock at it, the iron scorching the kobold's warty skin as it made contact. The creature flinched, and in that moment before it could gather for a second attack, a crimson-stained horn burst through its chest, impaling the kobold from the other side.

*The unicorn! She made it out of the blockhouse!* Branwen nearly cried out in relief. The blood-splattered beast arched its slender neck, lifting the toad-like fae in triumph before slinging the creature aside and lunging for the next. The third kobold immediately fled, but its odd, hopping gait was no match for the unicorn's blood-frenzied swiftness.

Branwen didn't wait to see the end. She and Ginny turned and ran. The other girls were ahead of them, only a few yards from the moat of iron spikes and relative safety. Naunos was still on the other side preoccupied with the second, much larger group of fae making a run for the bridge—Destin and Nezzie were among them, keeping on the far edge of the mob, away from the Cù Sìth. When the wolf attacked, they dodged, scrambling onto the narrow bridge with twenty other prisoners. In the rush, some of the fae misstepped, jamming their unshod feet onto the sharp nails studding the bridge. Others fell off the side, landing gruesomely among the iron spikes, but the strix and merrow made it across.

*Please,* please, *let them get the gates open!* Branwen silently begged. With the twin portcullises in place, it didn't matter that they'd escaped the blockhouse—there was still nowhere to *go.*

When she and Ginny reached the iron-spiked moat, most of the girls had already climbed inside, the taller girls going first then lowering the smaller ones in after them. Branwen helped Ginny and the last two in before sliding down the steep bank herself, careful to avoid any of the inward-facing pikes. The iron-tipped shafts were closely spaced, giving Branwen, Ginny, and the other oldest girl some trouble, but the younger girls weaved right through them to huddle near the center of the moat. They were safe, shielded by the nest of iron, but Branwen knew they couldn't stay there forever.

Beyond the moat, she could see Nezzie, Destin, and three other fae fighting their way up a set of wooden stairs toward the top of the gatehouse where the mechanisms for raising the portcullises resided. The redcaps had already abandoned the area, drawn into battle by the sight and smell of blood. A few dwarves and kobolds remained, guarding the high walls, but they quickly fell under the prisoners' vicious onslaught, most literally tossed over the side of the Keep. Two of the weaker freed fae went with them, dragged over the edge by the guards' tenacious grip. Nezzie and Destin survived, reaching the winches at top of the gatehouse. They and the other surviving fae—another merrow—began raising the portcullises. Hope surged in Branwen's chest as she saw the double iron gates slowly lift.

"We have to keep going!" she told the girls around her, pointing to the gates—and freedom—beyond. They couldn't wait for the portcullises to be fully raised. They need to move *now*—to get out before the harpies noticed. The wretched birds were currently their biggest threat, able to swoop down on them from above; all the other fae would have to cross the moat or the bridge first.

The girls moved, squeezing between the iron spikes with Branwen right behind them. Her skirts ripped as she yanked her way through, but she didn't slow. When they reached the steep, far edge of the moat, Branwen boosted the girls up, one by one, the smallest ones standing on her shoulders.

"Don't wait for me—run!" she commanded as she thrust the girls out of the pit.

The children obeyed, scrambling to their feet and bolting out of her limited range of sight. She hoped they made it through at least the first portcullis, but she couldn't even see that from her position at the bottom of the moat. Instead, Branwen kept her eyes on the sky, watching the harpies.

The foul creatures were otherwise engaged, busy following Aello's example of plucking up the fleeing prisoners and dropping them from a bone-shattering height. Sorcha even scooped up a guard by mistake, but she didn't seem to care. The flame-haired harpy sent him plummeting to his death like all the rest, laughing as he fell. The low, throaty sound sent shivers down Branwen's spine.

She worked faster.

Ginny was the last girl Branwen pushed out of the moat before beginning to claw her own way up. She slid almost immediately, the dry dirt crumbling beneath her fingers and the toes of her boots, but then Ginny's pale hands reached over the edge of the moat, grabbing her wrists. The younger girl helped haul Branwen up, and together they ran toward the portcullis.

The other children were just ahead, ducking under the first, half-raised gate.

Then, Branwen heard a scream of pain from above the gatehouse. Before she could react, a body fell from the sky, its scaled skin rupturing as it hit the ground in front of her. She could hear Sorcha's laughter as the murdered fae's blue blood gushed out, soaking into the thirsty earth.

*Destin!* Branwen thought as she pressed herself and Ginny against the nearest wall to avoid any further carnage from above, then she noticed the dead merrow's skin was shimmery green, not pale blue. She glanced up, looking for Destin and Nezzie at the top of the gatehouse, but the strix and merrow were nowhere to be seen. *They've either escaped over the wall or they're dead*, Branwen knew; there weren't any other options, not with the red harpy circling so close. Sorcha swooped low, eyeing the partially open portcullis.

"Oh, Aello!" the flame-haired harpy called, her voice pitched in an eerie, sing-song tone. "The humans are escaping!"

"Then, kill them!" came Aello's swift reply as she dove after a hobgoblin near the center of the Keep. She swerved at the last second, abandoning her prey to veer toward the gates.

"But Celaeno will *see*—" the red harpy protested.

"No, she won't," Aello snapped, exposing dagger-like teeth behind the curl of her blood-red lips. "Forget her. We'll get more humans later, but we can't let *these* loose in the Sídhe. They'll destroy everything we've worked for—*kill them all!*"

The harpy's last words sliced through the air, electrified with magic. Sorcha shouted, too, adding her power, and in an instant, they conjured a hurricane of wind that exploded against the gatehouse, ripping the stones apart.

"NO!" Branwen screamed as the whole structure began to collapse, the mass of it crushing the girls beneath. She could hear their brief, terrified shrieks, carried to her on the wind, then suddenly the edge of the storm caught her and Ginny. They tried to hold onto each other, but the wind was too strong, prying their hands apart as it flung them across the moat and back into the bailey. Branwen landed first, slamming down inches away from the iron spikes. Ginny went further, beyond Branwen's line of sight, her smaller body easily tossed by the fierce gale.

Chunks of rock and iron rained down, pelting human and fae alike, followed by thick clouds of gray and red dust that swirled in the air as the winds finally died. The dark clouds blocked the sun, plunging the Keep into an eerie twilight. The metallic crashing of harpy wings rang out from above as the birds flew beyond the reach of the choking dust. All around her, Branwen could hear the hacking, retching coughs of the surviving fae as they breathed in pulverized iron and stone. Her own lungs wheezed as she stood, so she yanked the collar of her linen blouse over her mouth and nose to filter the worst of it. Still, the fine particles stung her eyes as she peered through the dust.

"Ginny!" She shouted the girl's name, not caring what other attention she might attract. *I* have *to find her!* Branwen knew, tears streaming down her cheeks. *I can't leave without her—I* won't. *We're the only ones left, and if something has happened to her....* Her heart seized in her chest at the thought of losing Ginny—of losing *Colwen.* In her mind, the two girls' fates tangled together, compounding her desperation.

"GINNY!" Branwen screamed again, her voice going hoarse with the effort. "*GINNY!*"

A dark shape hurtled toward her out of the dust, too squat and broad to be the young girl, and Branwen braced herself for the impact, unable to move out of the way in time. She lifted her right hand, clutching at the iron keys that still dangled from the chain wrapped around her wrist.

An orange-skinned kobold crashed into her, knocking her off her feet. Branwen panicked, flailing violently against the creature as she fought to stand, trying to regain her only advantage—height. From her kneeling position, she slashed out with a key, scoring a line across the fae's warty arm.

After the strike, she flinched back, expecting the creature to lunge at her, but instead the kobold shoved her even further away, bolting as soon as Branwen twisted out of its path. The fae ignored her prone form and fled, disappearing into the gray shroud of dust.

Branwen stared after it, confused. As she struggled to her feet, she saw more shapes darting through the clouds of iron and stone—dwarves, redcaps, kobolds, hobgoblins, pixies, merrows, and dozens of other fae she didn't have names for—all fleeing to the front of the Keep.

*Like they're being chased*, Branwen thought. *Like there's something* behind *them. The unicorn? No.* She would have seen the beast's white coat gleaming even through the dust. *This is something else.*

Whatever it was didn't matter. She wasn't leaving until she found Ginny. She called the girl's name again, half-choking on the dust before she remembered to re-cover her mouth. To her left, she heard a faint, all-too-human cry in response. Branwen ran toward the sound.

She found Ginny sitting amid the rubble, her right arm curled to her chest—clearly broken—but the girl hardly seemed to notice as she flung herself at Branwen. Tears stained Ginny's face, leaving dark trails through the dirt and dust there which smudged on Branwen's clothes as she held the girl close. Branwen let out a sob of relief, her own cry matching Ginny's as she helped her to her feet.

"We have to go," Branwen whispered, "before the dust clears." Already, she could see the shadows of the harpies circling above. *Waiting to see the extent of their wreckage*, Branwen thought.

Ginny nodded, sniffling back her tears. She grabbed Branwen's right hand with her uninjured left and the two started toward the fallen gatehouse, picking their way across the rock-strewn ground. Branwen would have given nearly anything not to go back there—not to face the deaths of the girls she'd tried to lead to freedom—but the gatehouse, collapsed into rubble as it was, still remained the only way out of the Keep. The rest of the fortress' had withstood the brunt of the harpies' storm; some of the weaker sections had tilted or crumbled, but none had shattered so fully as the gates.

The dust began to settle and Branwen could see more clearly around her. Things she had assumed were broken stones and debris were actually bodies—fae slaughtered in the first assault. Their blood and gore had soaked into the ground turning it to a soft mud that made faint sucking noises beneath Branwen's boots. After that, she didn't look down.

Branwen kept her eyes ahead, focusing on the bridge. Naunos was nowhere to be seen. The she-wolf had presumably fled from the wind or succumbed to the fae trying to fight past her to the portcullises. Most of the remaining fae had vanished, too, clamoring over the pile of stone and iron that had once been the gatehouse. Even the guards had pulled out of the Keep.

*Why?* Branwen thought as she and Ginny crossed the narrow, nail-studded drawbridge and began climbing over the ruins of the gatehouse unobstructed. *Why would even the redcaps leave? And why is it so...*quiet*?*

Ahead, she could hear the clash of harpy wings followed by their raucous cries as they flew through the thin, upper layer of the dust, undoubtedly searching for what remained of the prisoners—yet behind her, Branwen heard nothing. An eerie silence had settled over the Red Keep. The vacancy of sound pressed against Branwen's back like an unseen force, but still she refused to turn around. She hastened her movements, half-lifting and half-dragging Ginny over the mound of the gatehouse. They'd breached the crest and had started scrambling down the other side, when Branwen heard a high-pitched scream and felt a sudden jerk on her right arm, pulling her to a stop.

*Ginny!*

Branwen spun around, teetering precariously on the rocky debris to look at the girl. The cloud of dust hovered just above their heads and at any moment Branwen knew Aello or the flame-haired harpy would see them, but when her gaze locked on Ginny all thoughts of the harpies left her.

The girl's dark brown eyes, so like Colwen's, filled with tears as she stood just below the crest of the ruins, barely two feet away from Branwen—the distance spanned by their joined hands. Behind her, impossibly—*illogically*—stood Ronan, his bronze-colored arms wrapped around the young girl's waist and injured limb, holding her back.

Branwen hissed at the sight of him, something primal—something *feral*—waking within her.

"You're dead," she growled at the hulder, sure of what she'd seen in the blockhouse. "You were swallowed by the Dark!"

From behind Ginny, Ronan smirked, tilting his head to rest his cheek against the top of the child's head. "And?" he said, his breath stirring through her honey-blonde curls.

Branwen flinched at the sound; the hulder's lips had moved, but it wasn't Ronan's voice that had answered. His eyes, when he stared at her, were no longer a bright, bloody red, but deepest black—twin voids in his sickeningly handsome face.

"Who are you?" Branwen demanded, her grip on Ginny not slackening in the least.

She refused to let go even though her only weapons, the iron keys, were wrapped around that wrist. With the chain twisted, it wasn't long enough for her to use with her left hand. Instead, Branwen tried to tug Ginny forward, testing the hulder's strength, but his arms were cinched tight.

"Let her go!" she yelled, but the Ronan-not-Ronan only laughed, his mouth opening wide and dark. When he spoke, his voice echoed through his chest as though it were a vast, empty cavern.

"I'm afraid I can't do that," the thing within Ronan said, "though I suppose I owe you for leaving me this vessel"—he gestured briefly to the hulder's body, his hand leaving Ginny for a mere fraction of second—"and for that tasty redcap, too," he added with a slick, knowing smile.

Branwen stared at him, finally understanding the truth. "You're the Dark," she whispered, horror filling her soul. No wonder the fae had ignored her and run. Now, with the dust settling, she and Ginny were clearly visible atop the gatehouse ruins, yet still none dared come near—not even the harpies who shrieked with frustration as they soared in the sky.

The hulder glanced at them, then winked at Branwen, his jet black eyes flashing briefly scarlet.

"I'm *mostly* the Dark," he corrected, pulling on Ginny's injured arm when she started to squirm. The girl cried out in pain, and Branwen lurched forward, wanting to protect her, but froze as the Dark shot her a warning look. "That's it—not so *feisty*," he commented as she settled down. The hulder grinned at the play on her fae-given name, then continued. "You see, Ronan and I have made an *arrangement.* We both wanted out of that hellhole, but I can't survive the light, so Ronan kindly loaned me the hollow in his back, and I promised not to devour him, body and soul. It seemed like a fair trade to me, but Ronan had two more provisions. Can you guess the first one?"

Branwen didn't have to guess; she *knew*. For a moment, she thought about playing dumb—anything to prolong the conversation, to give her more time to think, more time to set Ginny free—but she knew, too, that Ronan, if not the Dark, would immediately see through her charade. She told the truth instead, lifting her head to meet the hulder's gaze.

"To kill me," she said. It was a statement of fact, not a question. As she spoke, she could see Ronan's hatred for her burning through, another flicker of red in the black of his eyes, but this time it didn't fade away.

The Dark laughed, the cold echo of his voice making Branwen's skin crawl. Ginny whimpered, shuddering in his grasp. Branwen squeezed her hand, trying to comfort the girl as much as she could, and the hulder's grin widened.

"Oh, you were so *close*," he told Branwen. "That was Ronan's *second* request. His first request was this—"

For a split second, the Dark released Ginny from the cage of his arms. In that brief moment, Branwen saw hope flare to life in the little girl's eyes—*she was free, she could go!* Then, the hulder placed his long, strong hands on either side of Ginny's head and, with a quick *twist*, he snapped her neck.

# Chapter 11

"GINNY!" Branwen shrieked as she lunged for the girl, but it was too late. The light in Ginny's eyes suddenly and irrevocably extinguished. Her small hand went limp in Branwen's grasp, and the girl's whole body sagged, held upright only by the Dark's vice-like grip on her skull.

At the sight, a sharp arrow of grief pierced Branwen's heart, ripping through to her core. She abandoned all caution, all reason, to rush at the hulder, screaming with rage and sorrow as she tried to pull Ginny away. Hot, stinging tears flooded her eyes as she clawed at his hands. She could barely see as she attempted to pry his fingers loose, but the Dark was far too strong.

The hulder laughed at her efforts, easily slinging Branwen aside as he yanked Ginny's body from her grip. His movements made the child's lifeless limbs jostle back and forth as though she were one of Colwen's rag dolls and not a once-living girl.

Branwen lost her balance on the rocky ruins of the gatehouse and tumbled to the ground. Her back slammed against the compact earth, knocking the breath from her lungs for three agonizing seconds—just enough time for the Dark to clamber down after her.

As he skidded across the rubble, he shifted his grip on Ginny to free one hand; with the other, he grabbed the dead child by the hair, dragging her body along beside him.

Before Branwen could roll to her feet, the Dark was upon her. He stepped on her shoulder, pinning her to the ground with his weight. As he leaned in, the heel of his boot dug into the joint sending stabs of pain up and down her arm, but Branwen hardly felt them compared to the agony of seeing Ginny's vacant, death-drawn face so close to her own. The hulder held the child's head just above Branwen's, his tight grip on Ginny's scalp pulling her brow into a permanently surprised expression. The girl's mouth gaped open and her tongue lolled slightly forward as though issuing one final, silent scream.

*I'm sorry! I am* so *sorry! Ginny, forgive me!* Branwen wanted to cry out—to *beg*—but she knew the words wouldn't bring Ginny back—wouldn't bring any of the girls back. *They're all* dead *because of me, because I thought I could* save *them when I can't even save myself! Now, they're all gone and I don't even know their* names. Somehow, on top of everything else, that sin seemed the worst of all. Branwen shuddered, tears blurring her vision as she struggled to hold back the torrent of gut-wrenching sobs that threatened to overwhelm her. Only her guilt kept her silent, its voice blaring within her, *No! You don't deserve to cry!*

Above her, the hulder grinned. Branwen caught the bright red glare of his eyes even through the mist of unshed tears. When he spoke, Ronan's low, throaty voice rose above the cold echo of the Dark.

"The look on your face right now is worth a thousand deals with the Dark," the hulder whispered, leaning in so close that his lips brushed the edge of her cheek. She could hear the click of his teeth when he talked. "I can't *wait* to see what happens when you figure out what I—what *we*—are going to do *next*."

With that, the hulder stood, lifting Ginny away from Branwen's face and removing his boot from her shoulder. Numb from pain, that arm flopped uselessly at Branwen's side as she quickly righted herself. Only as she lurched to her feet did the feeling begin to return.

In front of her, Ronan took a step back, and then another, placing himself within the faint shadow of the Red Keep cast by the late afternoon sun. As soon as the shade of the penumbra touched his skin, the Dark resurfaced, swirling the hulder's crimson eyes with inky black.

The eerie echo resonated in his voice once more as he told Branwen, "I was in that pit for *such* a long time, and I'm still... so...*hungry*...."

At the last word, night-dark tendrils shot out from the hollow of his back and wrapped around Ginny's body. The little girl's joints popped and her bones broke as the hulder twisted and bent her small form, compressing it into an even smaller shape which he began to draw into the gaping hole at his back.

"No! Leave her alone!" Branwen screamed, throwing herself at the Dark. She didn't care that everyone feared him. She didn't care that his touch could mean her death. She didn't care about anything except Ginny. She hadn't been able to save the girl's life, but she'd be damned if she let that precious child suffer this one final indignity.

Branwen grabbed at the thick ropes of darkness, but her fingers immediately slid off, unable to grasp the shadows.

The hulder laughed again, his cold, cave-like breath blowing in her face. "Just give up," he told her. "You'll be joining her soon enough."

"Never!" Branwen growled, but her words sounded hollow as the Dark continued to pull Ginny away. He shifted the girl behind his back, and, in moments, Ginny's left side disappeared into the hole there, swallowed by the Dark.

Clearly confident in his success, the hulder didn't even try to block Branwen as she sidestepped him and reached for Ginny. She took hold of the girl's wrist just before it vanished into the black abyss, her own hand plunging after it. When the raw, elemental darkness touched her skin, Branwen felt something within her break—not *apart*, but *open*, exposing a place of blazing light and heat and *power* that she'd never known existed.

*Is this...mine?* she wondered as the magic burned through her veins like fire. In her heart, the spark of the unicorn's magic flared to life, too, its white-hot light different from the first raging, red heat. Both spread from the center of her being, coursing through all her limbs, but the bulk of the power flowed to her hands, burning where the Dark touched her.

The hulder flinched, trying to squirm away from her, but Branwen refused to let go. She could see a faint, fist-sized glow in the hollow of his back where she still clung to Ginny. With every passing second, the glow grew brighter and brighter.

"What are you doing?" the Dark hissed, twisting to look at her. His jet-and-scarlet eyes widened when he saw her free hand, now radiating light, and Branwen allowed herself a small, grim smile.

"*This*," she said, then thrust her sun-bright hand into the hulder's back.

She felt the magic within her surge. The white spark of the unicorn's power seemed magnified by the darkness around it, and light exploded in the black hollow. Flames followed as the heat sizzling in Branwen's own veins became a wildfire, roaring out of her control; the blaze burst through the hulder's skin, searing flesh from bone. Beams of light shot through the cracks, shining out like the sun as they invaded every part of him.

The Dark screamed, his and Ronan's voices peeling apart into two separate, agonized cries as they succumbed to the immolation—one burned from within, the other from without. The sound tore into Branwen's heart, but she didn't stop—couldn't stop—*wouldn't* stop.

*Not even if I knew how*, she thought, shoving her hands in further. *This is for Ginny. This is for the thirteen girls whose names I'll never know. This is for every girl, every human, every innocent stolen from their homes and forced into the Sídhe.* Though her conscious mind would deny it, her heart whispered the final truth: *This is for* me.

The last shadowy tendrils of the Dark vanished like smoke on the wind, shredded by the force of light. Soon, Ronan's husk of a body followed, crumbling into a pile of embers. Amid the smoldering ash of his corpse, lay Ginny, her body broken but undevoured by the Dark. Branwen cried out in relief, then collapsed beside the child, still holding her cool, limp hand. Above her, she heard the harpies shriek and squawk, but she couldn't bring herself to look, or even *care*. At any moment, they could swoop down on her, and there was nothing she could do to stop them.

Destroying the Dark had completely and utterly drained her, consuming the unicorn's magic within. She could feel the lack of it—the empty space where the bright spark once burned. She ached for its loss, but knew the power was never really hers to begin with. *It was only ever borrowed,* Branwen thought, remembering the way the unicorn had looked at her—looked *into* her. *I asked her for help and she* knew. *She knew what it would take.*

Branwen's own magic was gone, too. Or near enough. The faint warmth of it kindled near her heart; its tiny flame was only a breath away from extinction, yet it refused to go out.

*Just like me*, Branwen thought, struggling against the fatigue that threatened to overwhelm her. She wanted nothing more than to give in—to give *up*—to remain curled next to Ginny until the harpies finally took her, but something within her just wouldn't allow it. *This is not over*. You *are not over,* it whispered, stoking the embers of determination. They caught fire, slowly burning through her exhaustion. Branwen sucked in a deep, ragged breath and pushed herself up, rising to her knees.

The world spun for a dizzying second as she lifted her head, then her vision snapped into focus as a shadow fell over her. *Harpies!* she thought, flinging herself protectively over Ginny's body. She tensed, expecting to hear the crash of their wings—to feel the agony of their razor claws hooking into her back—but neither happened. Instead, a soft *whuff* of air brushed the back of her neck, cool and gentle and...familiar. Branwen looked up.

*The unicorn!* The beast's finely sculpted head hovered just above hers, its nose almost touching her cheek. Its silver eyes stared into her.

"You came back," Branwen whispered in disbelief. She'd thought the unicorn had left, chasing after the other fae as they'd fled the crumbling Keep—the fresh blood on the creature's horn told her that was at least partially true. The rest of its coat gleamed in the late afternoon sun, shining white even through layers of blood and dust.

*She's the only reason the harpies aren't attacking yet*, Branwen realized, glancing toward the sky. The beast's position blocked Aello and the others' view of her from above, but as soon as she moved out of the unicorn's shadow, the harpies would know she was still alive. *And how long after that will their fear of the unicorn keep them at bay?* Branwen wondered. *A minute? A few seconds?*

Not long enough, she knew, still holding tight to Ginny's hand. She sat up and pulled the child's small body into her lap, unable to let go. When she looked back at the unicorn, she saw not one, but two poor, broken girls reflected in its mirror-like eyes.

"I can't leave her," she told the beast. "I just—*can't*."

For a moment, the unicorn remained motionless, continuing to stare into Branwen's eyes, and she found she couldn't look away—didn't *want* to look away. In the unicorn's eyes, there was just her and Ginny in the forest clearing. There were no harpies, no redcaps, no Keep—nothing to indicate they were even still in the Sídhe at all. *We could be anywhere*, Branwen thought. *We could be* home *in the lower pastures at a spot where the sheep have overgrazed.*

Tears stung Branwen's eyes at the notion, blurring the scene, which only made her imagination more vivid, replacing what she saw with what she wanted. It wasn't Ginny who lay in her lap so still and so perfect, but Colwen, fast asleep after a long morning chasing the lambs. Any moment now, the six-year-old would wake up and start jabbering away, insisting that they visit their brother Madden on the other side of the hill—

But Colwen didn't wake. *Because this is not Colwen*, Branwen remembered, feeling the young girl's body grow cold and heavy in her lap. *This is Ginny. And she's not asleep, she's—*

*Dead.*

The word blasted through Branwen's mind like lightning, jolting her out of her trance-like state. She blinked and the rest of the vision shattered, thrusting her back into the cruel reality. She gasped at the shock, her heart lurching within her chest. But there was something else there, too—a new and painful understanding. As much as Branwen had cared for Ginny, had fought for her, had fought *with* her, she wasn't Colwen. She wasn't her sister. Thinking of Ginny in that way had given Branwen the strength—the courage—to do otherwise impossible things, but now that same bond was holding her back. If she wanted to have even a fraction of chance of getting home—of getting back to her family, to Mother, Papa, Madden, Colwen, and little Magrid—she had to let Ginny go.

She *had* to, but she didn't know *how*.

"Help me," Branwen pleaded again, echoing her cry in the prison as she looked to the unicorn once more.

The beast blinked back at her slowly, its long, nearly-translucent eyelashes flickering in the sun. Branwen couldn't begin to imagine what was going through its mind. Did it even understand what she was asking? How could it when she barely understood herself?

Branwen suppressed a flinch as the unicorn lowered its head, its blood-stained horn passing perilously close to her face. The beast had never threatened to harm her, but it was still one of the fae and therefore unpredictable. She wouldn't forget that the same unicorn who had saved her could just as easily impale her in a blood-crazed fit of rage like it had done to so many others, redcaps and prisoners alike. This time though, the unicorn was utterly calm as it touched the tip of its dripping, scarlet horn to the center of Ginny's forehead. A brilliant white light flashed at the contact, filling the air with the buzz of magic. It hummed along Branwen's skin, and she shivered as it sent crackles of energy though her nerves. In her lap, Ginny's whole body glowed as though the light of the sun burned within her, searing away any taint of the Dark. As the light warmed her flesh, the child's death-startled expression relaxed into one of peace. Branwen held Ginny close, gently brushing the honey-colored curls from the younger girl's face and kissing her brow.

"I'm so sorry," Branwen told her one last time, then, as she held her, the girl's body dissolved into thousands of tiny, white sparks that glittered like diamonds as they soared up into the sky. One spark trailed behind the rest, drifting quietly by Branwen's head. It touched her brow, its warmth mirroring the kiss she'd given Ginny, before it rose toward the sun and disappeared.

Above them, the four harpies had veered away from the column of light, loath to touch any part of the unicorn's magic, but now that it had vanished, they closed ranks. The unicorn snorted, arching its neck to look at the birds, then it reared back, its horn stabbing the air in challenge. Branwen took the signal and staggered to her feet, ducking to stay clear of the beast's diamond-sharp hooves. The harpies spotted her immediately, crying out to one another, "The other human! She's alive!"

"Not for long!" a black-haired harpy shrieked, her matching ebony feathers crashing together as she snapped her wings into a dive.

Branwen ran, bolting toward the forest at the edge of the clearing, but she wasn't fast enough. The black harpy hurtled toward her, her jet wings barely unfurled to break her descent. Her talons remained tucked against her body for speed, and instead she stretched her head and neck forward, her razor-toothed maw wide open for the attack. Branwen didn't stop, didn't slow, didn't dodge. There was no time.

She fought the urge to squeeze her eyes shut as the black shape of death barreled toward her, the sound of the harpy's victory scream deafeningly close. Then, suddenly—WHAM! The scream stopped with a gut-wrenching crack and a splatter as the unicorn leapt in front of the harpy at the last moment, thrusting its horn toward the bird's gaping mouth.

Too late to turn, the harpy impaled herself on the scarlet horn, the impact crunching every bone in her neck and bending her head back at a terrible angle. Fresh, hot blood spurted from the hole in the harpy's mouth and skull, dripping down the unicorn's horn and onto its face, framing its silver eyes with red. The color reflected off the mirrored pupils making them seem to glow with a lurid light. Then, the unicorn screamed, the full breadth of its blood-lust awakened and shrieking through the air.

Aello answered with her own cry of fury. Her marigold eyes blazed with vengeance as she led the other two harpies in a wild charge against the unicorn, their pursuit of Branwen momentarily forgotten. The unicorn slung the black harpy's corpse free of its horn with a toss of its head, then lunged forward, ready for the attack. As she watched, hope surged in Branwen's veins, filling her limbs with renewed vigor. Branwen turned and ran. Her legs pumped, her heart raced, and her lungs blew like bellows as she made the last sprint toward the edge of the clearing. The forest was her only chance at cover with its jagged branches far too close together for the broad-winged harpies to fly between.

Branwen hurled herself through the spindly outer trees, fighting past the scraggly bits of undergrowth that grabbed at her, trying to pull her back. She broke free, stomping through the reaching brambles and into the depths of the woods. Beneath the forest's dense canopy, the world plunged into a false twilight, blinding Branwen's sun-adjusted eyes for a fraction of second. In that moment, she heard the sharp snap of twigs in the treetops as something small, but *fast* dove toward her. Branwen threw herself to the side while swinging out with her right arm, hoping to use the iron chain and keys still wrapped around her wrist as a flail. The attack missed, but just barely, as the fae pulled up short with a frantic flap of her tawny wings.

"Whoa, Feisty—it's me!" a familiar twittering voice proclaimed, and Branwen finally *looked* at her assailant, her brain catching up to her eyes.

"Nezzie! You're alive!" Branwen exclaimed, straightening from her defensive crouch. The last she'd seen, the strix had been atop the gatehouse with Destin. The two had disappeared only moments before the harpies struck. In all the chaos after the windstorm, she hadn't seen whether they'd managed to escape the Red Keep or had fallen during the collapse of the gatehouse. The smudges of sap and iron-tainted dust that inflamed the strix's skin told a likely story, however.

*She must have flown or jumped after all*, Branwen reasoned. The strix could have easily glided from the Keep to the first thin line of trees in the forest. The merrow, on the other hand....

Her eyes scanned the woods, looking for a glimpse of pale blue among the rich greens and browns. "Where's Destin?" she asked, trying to ignore the sinking feeling in the pit of her stomach. "Is he—?"

"Right here," the merrow interrupted from above.

Branwen startled at the sound, her gaze drawn upward. She relaxed as she saw Destin clambering down from the same tree the strix had occupied. *Of course,* she thought, breathing in relief. *I should have known Nezzie would never leave him behind.*

Destin landed with a heavy thud, staggering slightly as he stood. Like Nezzie, sap and dust clung to him, raising ugly red weals where the fine particles of iron slowly burned his flesh—only his wounds were far more aggravated, seeping blue-tinged lymph onto his skin.

*Is it because he's already iron-scorched?* Branwen wondered. *Does one exposure to iron make the fae more sensitive to another?* She gripped the iron keys in her hand, certain it wouldn't be long before she found out. All around her, she could hear the rustling of other creatures in the woods—of other fae fleeing the Keep and the redcaps and kobolds who pursued them.

"Let's go," Destin said, his own expression wary as he, too, listened to the forest. The merrow moved protectively toward Nezzie, but before he reached her, a furious, ear-piercing scream split the air, freezing them all in place.

*The unicorn!* Branwen knew the sound at once—that eerie, visceral shriek that demanded blood and vengeance. Her eyes darted back to the clearing, peering at it through the forest's dark trees.

She could see a second harpy had fallen to the beast, her bronze-feathered body trampled beneath the unicorn's diamond hooves. Only Aello and Sorcha remained, their rage doubled at the loss of their comrades. The two ducked and dove around the beast, their wings lashing out like swords and slicing into the unicorn's flanks and neck. Thick, silver blood pulsed from the gashes, painting over the stains of red on the unicorn's once-white coat.

Branwen's heart wrenched at the sight and a wail of despair rose up within her. She had to clamp a hand over her mouth to suppress the mortified sound, lest she draw the harpies' attention. Beside her, Destin grabbed her shoulders, his iron-scorched hand hot against her skin as he jerked her around to face him. His candle-yellow eyes burned with urgency as he spoke.

"You can't help her," he told Branwen. "She's doing this for you—the unicorn will take care of herself. We need to leave. *Now.*"

Branwen could only nod. The merrow was right. She couldn't go up against the harpies—not with only two iron keys and a flicker of magic she didn't know how to use. There was nothing she could do but try to save her own self and hope the unicorn could do the same. She peered through the trees one last time, engraving the image of the beast in her mind—of its power and majesty, of its blood-lust and beauty, of its ferocity...and its kindness.

"I will *never* forget," she whispered, knowing the magic of the Sídhe would make it so, turning her words into an oath. She could feel it even now—the strange power crackling through the air, binding the memory and the debt to her soul.

"Come on!" Nezzie said, urging Branwen forward as the magic settled. The strix half-ran and half-flew as she weaved between the trees with Branwen following close behind her. Destin brought up the rear, using his tall form to shield their backs.

Together, they plunged deeper into the woods, fleeing the sharp, shearing sound of harpy wings and the unicorn's subsequent bellows of rage. Their path zigzagged wildly as they tried to avoid the dozens of other fae still roaming near the Keep. The escaping prisoners mostly ignored them, too focused on their own safety and survival to be concerned, but some of the guards had other ideas.

"Nezzie—to the right!" Destin shouted a warning as a kobold leapt at the strix. The creature's wide, warty lips peeled back in a hungry grin.

With a quick snap of her wings, Nezzie pivoted mid-stride and drew Mina's daggers from her belt. Silver flashed as the twin blades lashed forward, slicing into rubbery orange flesh. The kobold gave a surprised grunt, then immediately crashed to the ground as his throat and belly split open.

Branwen and Destin jumped over the fae creature's corpse as it tumbled into their path spilling brown blood across the forest floor. They kept running, knowing that in seconds the closest redcaps would catch the scent and converge upon the freshly slaughtered kobold.

Already, Branwen could hear the crash of iron-shod boots behind them as the redcaps were drawn to the smell of blood.

She just hoped the kobold would occupy them long enough for her, Nezzie, and Destin to escape.

Ahead of them, the trees grew larger, leaving wider gaps between the trunks, and Destin surged forward, finally able to stretch his long legs. As he drew even with Nezzie, the strix automatically fell back, giving him the lead as she took up the rearguard.

"This way," the merrow indicated, veering slightly left. His stride was steady and sure as he angled through the trees.

*He knows where he's going*, Branwen thought as she turned with him. *Does that mean he has a plan?* She hoped so, but couldn't waste the breath to ask. She needed every huff of air to fuel her mad sprint.

Her lungs burned, her sides ached, and the muscles of her legs screamed in pain, yet she kept pushing forward, knowing only death lay behind her. To either side, she could still hear the frantic cries of other fae trying to fight their way through the woods and failing.

The prisoners' spirits were willing and ready for escape, but their bodies were still weak, their energy and flesh depleted from days and days spent in the dark, iron-riddled cells of the blockhouse. Those that made it past the lingering guards climbed the trees for shelter like Nezzie and Destin had done at first.

As Branwen ran, she saw a beetle-like fae burrow into the ground beneath a briar thicket for protection. Up ahead, a gray and brown scaled naga had coiled himself within the hollow of a fallen log. When a kobold rushed by unaware, the serpent struck, sinking long fangs into the toady fae's throat. The kobold made only a faint croak of sound before the naga unhinged his jaw and began shoving the creature into his mouth even as he slithered back into the log.

Branwen startled at the suddenness of the attack, tripping over one of the many tree roots that tangled the forest floor. Nezzie grabbed her from behind, righting her before she could fall.

Branwen nodded her thanks to the strix as she staggered forward, regaining her stride, but her earlier momentum was lost. Her limbs felt as though they weighed a thousand pounds as she tried to pull them forward, each step born in labored agony. Her heart hammered against her sternum and her lungs heaved, growing tighter in her chest with every breath. Still, she fought on, struggling to keep pace with Destin.

*I'm doing this for Mother, for Papa, for Madden*, she reminded herself with every stride. *For Colwen, for Magrid, for Ginny, for all the lost girls, for the unicorn, for* me. She chanted the names over and over in her mind until they drowned out her pain.

Everything else around her faded away except for three things: the sight of Destin running before of her, his pale blue skin streaked with sweat and iron, the pressure of Nezzie's hand at the small of her back urging her forward, and the pounding of her boots against the forest's rocky, root-strewn soil.

She didn't know how long the words carried her, only that they *did*, and when she finally came to the end of herself—just when she thought she could go no further—the merrow stopped. Branwen and Nezzie both nearly ran into him, suppressing their startled *oof*s and gasping breaths as he held up his hand for silence.

“Listen,” he said amid his own shallow panting as he, too, struggled to catch his breath. He cocked his head to the side and slowly turned it back and forth, searching. “Do you hear that?”

“Hear what?” Nezzie asked, her voice high and gasping with fatigue. Branwen could barely hear either of them speak over the sound of her own blood pulsing in her ears.

“Bells,” the merrow said. “We must be close.”

He tilted his head in the other direction, slowly turning his body as he tried to pinpoint a sound only he could hear. Nezzie mirrored his example, stepping out from behind Branwen to listen. After a moment, the strix just shook her head, rubbing both her ears, and began pacing the forest. Her owlish eyes squinted in concentration as she examined every rock and tree trunk.

“What exactly are you looking for?” Branwen asked, following the strix.

“Destin has tracked down a naiad grove,” Nezzie explained as she peered into the black center of a half-rotten stump. “It’s a place of healing and rest, which we’re going to need if we want to make it much further. Only the water fae can sense them from a distance. The rest of us just have to look for the signs. The groves are usually hidden, marked only by a cracked stone or tree with a split in its trunk. Sometimes, when you’re very close, you can hear the sound of bells.”

“Well, I don’t hear any bells,” Branwen admitted, “but what about a ring of clover? Could that be one of the signs?”

“Clover? Where?” Nezzie suddenly lifted her head from the stump, her huge eyes scanning the ground.

Branwen pointed to a patch just ahead and to their left. The circle was so wide it hadn’t been obvious at first, but little by little she had connected the path, tracing the thin trail of the plants' bright green leaves against a carpet of yellow moss. *A faerie ring*, she thought, remembering the stories from the old women of Llanddaniel Bryn: *Beware a circle of mushrooms or overgrown grass*, they'd warned. *Those who enter a faerie's ring rarely make it back.*

*It's a bit too late for that, now isn't it?* Branwen thought, narrowing her eyes at the line of clover. Beside her, Nezzie grinned excitedly.

"Destin, come look at this!" the strix crowed, waving the merrow over.

At her summons, Destin immediately abandoned his search and headed in Nezzie's direction. As he neared, his expression piqued. "The bells *are* getting louder," he confirmed.

"So, I was right?" Branwen asked. "This is the place—the naiad grove?"

The merrow shrugged. "It could be a troll hole instead," he said. "Sometimes they nest in abandoned groves, but there's only one way to find out—"

He took a deep breath and stepped into the ring of clover. Destin vanished as soon as both feet touched the other side.

# Chapter 12

Branwen blinked at the sudden void of the merrow's presence, her mind still churning over the notion of a "troll hole." Then, Nezzie darted forward, grabbing her by the arm and tugging her into the circle, too. Branwen didn't resist; a part of her realized she was probably safer with Nezzie and Destin, even in a troll hole, than she would be roaming the woods alone.

As she crossed into the ring of clover, a mist rose up from the ground and swirled around her, obscuring the forest. For a brief moment, all she could see was Nezzie's wings in front of her, their tawny feathers bright against the pale vapor, then the mist cleared, revealing a sparkling grove and Destin only a few feet away. A circle of vibrant, white-barked birch trees surrounded a moderate clearing, their strong, straight limbs so unlike the dark, twisted specimens in the rest of the forest.

A small stream burbled up from beneath a large stone near the middle of the grove. A massive oak grew atop the stone, its roots twisting over and around the stony mass. The tree's wide-reaching branches shaded the vast majority of the clearing, blocking most of the evening sun—*and the view from above*, Branwen noted with relief, her thoughts never far from the harpies. In front of her, the grove's diamond-clear waters pooled along a wide, shallow bank, rippling against a bed of jewel-toned pebbles as she and the others approached.

Destin sighed, the tension easing from the harsh features of his face as he stepped into the stream. Ribbons of black trailed through the water as the gentle current washed the dust from his feet. Slowly, the merrow lowered himself into the stream, submerging every inch he could. Beneath the water's surface, the merrow's pale skin flushed a healthier blue as the iron rinsed from his scales.

Nezzie simply jumped into the water, rolling her small body through the knee-deep pools. She laughed as she sat up, fluttering her wings like a bird in a puddle. Gray droplets sprayed in every direction, showering Branwen who couldn't help but laugh. The strix's high, rolling giggles were infectious, revealing a jubilant, carefree side as she continued to splash in the stream.

Branwen joined them at the water's edge, positioning herself upstream from the frolicking fae. She washed her face and hands before cupping them to her mouth to drink. The cool liquid slid down her throat, its crystal crispness reviving something inside her. She could feel the fire in her heart begin to stir, its flicker of power not doused, but *inflamed,* strengthened by the tingle of magic Branwen could sense permeating the water. She took another sip and another, quenching her thirst.

*A naiad grove*, she thought, glancing around as she let the last half-finished scoop of water dribble through her fingers. *That must mean there is a water nymph nearby, but where?* She saw nothing but soft moss and fine, feathery grasses surrounding the stream, their emerald greens still brilliant in the evening sun.

Then, she looked at the oak tree, perched atop the stone like a king on his throne. As she watched, the pattern in the oak's bark shifted, carving out the shape of a soft, lovely face with blue river stones for eyes. The naiad smiled at Branwen, her wood-colored lips forming a gentle curve, but the expression didn't last long. The water nymph's eyes widened suddenly and she disappeared back into the tree just before Branwen caught the sound of something heavy crashing through the birch trees on the other side of the stream.

"Nezzie, Destin—watch out!" she called as she sprang to her feet, raising her right wrist in defense. She griped the two keys like knives, their jagged edges jutting between her fingers.

At her warning, the merrow and strix surged from the water, weapons braced and ready to fight. Destin grimaced, his needle-like teeth bared to the air. Purple poison dripped from the spiny fins on his forearms. Nezzie drew both of Mina's daggers, their silver blades flashing in the light of the setting sun.

A dwarf staggered out from the trees directly across from them, his short, stocky body broadened by layer upon layer of leather armor. He skidded to a halt when he saw Nezzie and Destin, his earth-brown eyes narrowing suspiciously. Iron dust coated his already swarthy skin, marking him as one of the dwarves from the Red Keep. He carried a gleaming, tungsten-headed war hammer at his side, twirling the slim, wooden handle between his thick, nimble fingers as he sized up the two fae. Branwen edged closer to Nezzie and Destin, trying to position herself well within the range of their protection, but as she moved, she drew the dwarf's attention.

The dwarf's eyes widened when he saw her, filling with rage and recognition. His lips peeled back in a sneer and his grip on his hammer tightened.

"*N'zadak-tem!*" the armored fae spat, slinging his words at Branwen.

*A curse*, she realized as she felt the air around her ripple with heat. She thought it would burn, but instead it sank into her skin, warming her. The flame in her heart crackled in delight, its fire growing. Across from her, the dwarf stared, his small, brown eyes nearly bulging from his skull in surprise, then he abruptly turned and ran, his feet thudding heavily on the mossy ground.

Branwen blinked, stunned by what had transpired. When she recovered, she turned to Nezzie and Destin who simply watched as the intruder fled.

"Shouldn't we stop him?" Branwen sputtered, surprised at their inaction. "He could give away our position!"

Destin shrugged away her concern. "I doubt it," the merrow said, bending down again to the creek. He cupped water in his hands and began to splash it on his upper arms and face, washing away the last remnants of dust as he continued. "Dwarves aren't as malicious as redcaps and kobolds. At least, not *usually*. He and the others were probably only in the Keep to do repairs. With the harpies gone, it wouldn't benefit him to expose us."

"Plus," Nezzie added, looking at Branwen with a mischievous twinkle in her lichen-green eyes, "I think he was afraid of you."

"Of *me*?" Branwen blurted, taken aback.

The strix laughed, the twittering sound ringing through the air. "Of course!" she said. "Every fae near the Keep saw you take a stand against the Devouring Dark. Most fled before the end, but they still would have felt the explosion and known something had happened—something *big*. I don't think any of them would have ever assumed you'd survived, though." Nezzie shook her head, her voice incredulous as she admitted, "I can hardly believe it myself and I *saw* it."

Destin nodded as he straightened, his own expression more reserved. To Branwen, he said, "No doubt the dwarf thought the Dark had won and was inhabiting you like it had Ronan. That's probably why he tried to curse you. *N'zadak-tem* is a dwarvish oath to invoke the flames of the mother forge. Fire and light are the only elements that can harm the Dark, yet they did nothing."

"Because I'm not the Dark," Branwen asserted, but the merrow shook his head.

"No," he said slowly. "The curse would have burnt you regardless. The only reason you're not a pile of ashes right now is because you have a strong affinity for fire magic, and fire mages can't be burned."

"But I'm not a—" Branwen began to protest, then stopped as Destin and Nezzie both stared at her. Instinctively, she cupped a hand over her heart as though she could hide the tiny flame that kindled there, but the strix and merrow's knowing gazes pierced through her denial. "I mean, I wasn't," she amended. "Not until today."

At her admission, Destin rocked back on his heels slightly, his lips pursed as he glanced at Nezzie, engaged in a silent consultation. After a moment, the strix just shrugged, and Destin sighed, looking back at Branwen.

"We thought that might be the case," he said at last. "No one with the slightest *hint* of magical knowledge would have tried what you did. Shoving your hands into the Dark like that...it should have killed you. It *would* have if not for that extra burst of power. The unicorn—she gave you some of her magic, didn't she? At the Keep. Right before all hell broke loose."

Branwen nodded, taken aback by the accuracy of his assumptions. "How did you know?"

"Water fae are good at sensing the ebb and flow of things, particularly magic," the merrow told her. "When you came down those stairs after freeing the unicorn, you were nearly glowing with power. You still have a trace of it right...*here.*" Destin reached for Branwen's hand, flipping it over to expose the long scar across her palm where the unicorn had healed her. "A tiny fraction of her power is embedded in you now," the merrow said. "Not enough to use, but enough to leave its mark. As long as you have that scar, you two will always be connected."

"Oh," Branwen breathed, staring down at her palm as Destin released her hand. The scar shimmered faintly silver in the grove's slowly dimming light. She'd thought all the unicorn's magic was lost—burned up in the same explosion of power that had destroyed the Dark. Any other remnant should have vanished with the unicorn after the harpies' brutal attack unless.... "She's alive," Branwen whispered, clenching her hand into a fist. Her fingers curled protectively over the shimmering scar. "The unicorn is still alive!"

Beside her, Nezzie laughed, her high, twittering voice ringing like jubilant bells. "Of course!" the strix said. "It would take far more than a few harpies to bring down a unicorn, especially once she's worked herself into a rage."

Destin nodded. "I think that's why Sebastian helped us escape from the blockhouse in the end," he added. "That kelpie would do anything to save his own skin. He weighed his options and decided he'd rather risk Aello's wrath after freeing the prisoners than be trapped in a dungeon with a rampaging unicorn. Frankly, I would have chosen the same."

"Didn't you? I mean, isn't that why you helped me, too?" Branwen asked, her questions pointed as she sought to clarify the merrow's motives.

Until now, she had trusted Nezzie and Destin out of necessity, but without any imminent peril currently binding the three of them together, she couldn't help but wonder how much further that trust could go. In her limited experience, the fae helped others only as long as it also benefited themselves, so why should she expect Nezzie and Destin to be any different?

The merrow gave her a slow, appraising look. "Yes," he admitted, his angular features devoid of any guilt or shame. "At first. You offered our best chance to get out of the Red Keep alive—our only chance, really—so we took it."

"And now?" Branwen prodded, knowing she couldn't stop until she reached the truth—not when her very life could depend upon the strix and merrow's answer. "You both could have left after Aello destroyed the gatehouse—hidden in the dust while the harpies and everyone else were distracted. You could have fled when the Dark came, but you stayed. Why? Why do you keep risking your lives to help me?"

Nezzie snapped her wings for attention. "We're risking our lives if we *don't* help you," the strix asserted, her lighthearted tone suddenly serious. "If we don't help *each other*. Our best chance is to stay together. There's something you don't understand—this isn't over, Feisty. Far from it. You think we're free, but we're not. Destin and I still have a bounty on our heads and that price will only go higher when Celaeno learns we had a part in the fall of her precious Red Keep. And then there's you...."

"Me?" Branwen's heart seized in her chest, the flame of magic there sputtering with a dark premonition as she watched the strix and merrow exchange another weighted glance.

When Nezzie looked back at Branwen, her owlish eyes were soft, their corners crinkled with concern. "By now, I think you know there's something bigger going on here," the strix said. "This was more than just a few simple kidnappings gone awry. Celaeno has a grander scheme at play and somehow you've ended up right in the middle of it."

"Well, I don't *want* to be in the middle of it," Branwen said, her words emboldened by her frustration. "I want to go *home.* How can I make *that* happen?"

For once, Nezzie hesitated to answer, her silence speaking volumes in itself. Destin, on the other hand, held no such compunction.

"That's not an option right now—for any of us," he told Branwen with hope-crushing honesty. "Once Celaeno sets her mind on something, she doesn't give up. She went through a great deal of trouble to have not *one* but *fifteen* humans girls brought across the Veil. Now, you're the only one left, and Celaeno is going to want to know *why.*"

Nezzie confirmed the truth of the merrow's words with a solemn nod. "There are few things our Lady hates more than wasted effort," the strix told Branwen, her voice embittered. "Celaeno would come after you for no other reason than that, but once she hears Aello's report of what happened at the Keep, how you single-handedly defeated the Dark, she's going to have a whole new motivation to find you."

"But all of that was just a fluke!" Branwen protested. "It's not something I can just *do*. I'm nowhere near strong enough. Destin said it himself—without the unicorn's power, I would have died when I faced the Dark."

The strix shook her head, her mossy braids swinging over her shoulders. "None of that matters to Celaeno. She won't be interested in your magic, but in what your magic represents."

Destin concurred. "I said you would have died—I didn't say you would have *failed*," the merrow clarified, stunning Branwen into silence. She stared at him and he stared right back, his yellow eyes like twin beacons peering into her soul. "There is an immense power in the ability to sacrifice yourself for someone else," the merrow told her. "That's something Celaeno has never been able to understand."

Beside him, Nezzie nodded, turning her attention back to Branwen. "As much as I hate to admit it, Sebastian was right," the strix confessed, her cupid's bow lips curling with distaste as she spoke the kelpie's name. "You're different from the others, Feisty," she continued. "There's more than just fire magic burning inside of you. Your will to survive is indomitable, and Celaeno is going to *want* that. She's going to want *you*. She won't be able to help herself. It's a compulsion she has—the need to bend every free-spirited thing until it comes under her control."

"And what Celaeno can't bend, she *breaks*," Destin added. Anger seethed beneath the knife's edge of his voice, slicing straight to the bone of irrefutable *fact*. "She'll want to crush you like she has done to so many others—to shatter everything in your being until there's nothing left, and she can mold you into whatever image she likes. Only, she's never satisfied. Oh, no, not *our* queen." The merrow shook his head, his mouth twisting into a grimace of both loathing and despair.

"Celaeno *can't* be satisfied," he iterated, the words rising like a growl in his throat. "She just keeps molding and breaking until there's nothing left, not even a whimpering blob of your former self. Only then does she allow you peace. Only then does she allow you to *die*—" Destin stopped, the veins in his neck throbbing as a surge of raw emotion suddenly constricted his voice. The merrow looked away quickly, but not before Branwen caught a glimpse of the truth in his eyes.

*He's afraid*, she realized with a gut-wrenching jolt of certainty. *More than afraid. He's terrified. This isn't just some imagined scenario to him.* "You've seen it," Branwen stated. "Both of you. You've witnessed Celaeno break someone."

Destin's only response was an ugly, strangled laugh, so Branwen turned to Nezzie for elaboration, but she found the strix wouldn't quite meet her gaze. The winged girl ducked her head, her eyes lowered in...*shame?* Branwen wondered. *Guilt?* Both were such human emotions that she hadn't expected to see them among the fae and least of all from the two that had risked so much to save her.

"You deserve to know the truth about us," Nezzie said, finally looking up at Branwen. "About who—no, *what*—we are and where we came from."

*No, stop! Don't tell me!* Branwen wanted to plead, but it was far too late. A part of her already knew at least some of what the strix was going to say. She'd been picking up subtle hints of it for a long time, but now the evidence was overwhelming—from Nezzie's intimate knowledge of the workings of harpy court to Destin's visceral reaction when he spoke of Celaeno. *How deeply is the fear of her power and authority ingrained in him that even in his hatred he calls her "our queen?"* she thought, remembering the merrow's words with terrifying awe.

Nezzie confirmed her suspicions, filling in the last wretched details. "We didn't just *see* the atrocities Celaeno committed," the strix confessed. "We were a *part* of them—because up until two days ago we were soldiers in her elite guard."

Branwen's heart sank at the news, filling with a slow, choking dread. It was worse than she'd thought. She'd expected Nezzie and Destin to have belonged to Celaeno's court, but to have been a part of the harpy queen's guard on par with Aello and her fiendish allies.... Doubt crept into Branwen's mind. Had Nezzie and Destin's humaneness been an act all along? Was it part of some elaborate scheme to win their way back into Celaeno's graces?

*No!* she thought, her spirit surging in denial. They had been through too much together for it all to have been a ruse. There had been too many times Nezzie or Destin could have simply *let* the harpies have her, but instead they protected her. *I have to believe in them*, she told herself. *Otherwise, there is nothing left for me. No life, no hope, no future.*

Still, she couldn't shake her sense of unease. If Nezzie and Destin had hidden such an important fact from her until now, what else could they be hiding? She had to dig deeper. She had to ask the hard questions even though she knew the answers might hurt.

She looked to Nezzie, her voice pleading for truth as she asked, "Why? If you know what Celaeno is like, then why would you join her guard? What did she promise you? And how can I trust that you won't use me to go back to her?"

"It wasn't a choice," the strix responded, the pain of that statement evident in her wide, green eyes. "Celaeno forced it on us with nothing in return. Every seven years, she demands a Tithe from each of the thirteen houses presiding in her court. They draw lots and the chosen ones must serve the queen loyally for the rest of their days. That's how Destin and I became part of the harpy guard. If we had refused, Celaeno would have slaughtered every member of our families until someone willing stepped forward. That is her idea of mercy."

Branwen shuddered, her own thoughts turning dark as she wondered, *Is that the choice I face, too? Even if I escape the Sídhe, will Celaeno still pursue me out of spite? Will she go after my family thinking she could force me back into her clutches? Because it would work,* she knew without hesitation. Like Nezzie and Destin, she would have no choice other than to concede to whatever the harpy queen desired, and yet.... Her spirit balked at the notion of surrender, kindling a flame of defiance in her heart. Her magic responded, its faint flicker sizzling back to life as she thought, *Celaeno might win in the end, but first we would fight. Mama, Papa, Madden...they would all fight for me, just as I would fight for them. That's what families do. We don't give up on each other. I can't give up!*

To Nezzie and Destin, she asked, "How were you able to leave the Guard with Celaeno still threatening your families? Did you free them, too? Did any of them come with you?"

Already, Nezzie was shaking her head. "No one came with us," the strix said, her tone and expression perplexed. "Why would they?

"Because you're family!" Branwen exclaimed in astonishment. "How could you leave them behind?"

"Because they left us first," Destin said, his sharp words cutting into the conversation. "Once we were selected to join the Guard, our families severed all ties to us. Our names were blotted out of every registry—struck from every record of lineage. We became dead to them—no, worse than dead. It was as if we had never existed at all. If I passed my sister on the street, she would not even be allowed to look at me, let alone call my name. It's the same for all the guards. That's part of the sacrifice of the Tithe as well."

Nezzie nodded. "It's another one of Celaeno's tactics to ensure the Guard's loyalty and bind them only to her. She creates a scenario where you give up everything to save the ones you love, only to have them turn on you in the end. Even when you know better, you begin to doubt, but by then it's too late. Celaeno already has her hooks in you, sinking into your mind, and you find yourself thinking you were *right* to join the Guard, that you *belong* there, that you're *grateful*. As cruel as Celaeno's Guard is, you know they'll never leave you because they *can't* leave you. Your old identity is stripped away and the Guard becomes your new identity, your new family. You'll do anything for them—for *her*—as along as it means you're not alone."

A cold chill ran up Branwen's spine as the strix spoke, every word cementing the harpy queen's vileness in her heart. The sheer magnitude of mental sabotage and manipulation nearly took her breath away.

"That's terrible," she whispered in response.

Nezzie shrugged, her tawny wings fluttering behind her nonchalantly. "That was our life. We didn't know of any different. By the end of our first year of training, we no longer had any concept of freedom."

"Even if we had, we wouldn't have wanted it," Destin admitted, his voice tight as he continued to struggle reining in his emotions. "That's how much control Celaeno had over us—how much control she has over the Guard still."

"Then, what changed?" Branwen asked, carefully gauging the merrow's response. "What happened two days ago that you were finally able to break free?"

Destin gritted his teeth, anger and fear rising up within him again as he spat out two words: "The Cull."

"It's how Celaeno gets rid of the weaklings and the troublemakers within the Guard," Nezzie explained, sparing the merrow from answering further. "The summer after every seventh Tithe, Celaeno holds a tournament where she chooses fourteen guards—two from each of the previous Tithe years—and pits them against their Tithe-mate in a fight to the death. Whoever wins their match is no longer bound to her service." The strix took a deep, bracing breath before she added, "Destin and I are from the same Tithe, and this year Celaeno chose *us*."

"Oh...." Branwen murmured as the implications of what Nezzie said sank in. She realized the impossible decision they would have faced. Nezzie and Destin were more than just friends, she knew. Their every action toward each other screamed of a deeper bond—of a connection forged through war and trauma of their shared time in the Guard, but also something more.

*They love each other*, she thought without any doubt. The strix and merrow's feelings were written on every fleeting look, exposing their hearts at every glance. In that moment, Branwen realized something else: *Celaeno knew. That's why she chose them for the Cull—because what could be more devastating than forcing someone to destroy the person they care about the most?*

"Celaeno meant for Nezzie and me to turn against one another on the battlefield," Destin stated. "When we refused, she tried to force us, using the power of the oath we swore as guards to bend our will to hers." The merrow shuddered, his eyes losing focus as the memory threatened to overtake him. "All I could hear was Celaeno screaming, *Kill! Kill! Kill!"* he said, his voice torn by guilt and shame. "She flooded my mind with visions of death, of my hands around Nezzie's neck, crushing. I almost gave in. I almost—"

Nezzie refused to let him finish, stepping between Destin and Branwen as if to block the merrow's words. She grabbed his hands, her small fingers barely wrapping around his palms, but with that single gesture she had his complete attention. Nezzie locked eyes with Destin, then, her lichen-green orbs burning with determination as she told him, "But you didn't give in. You *didn't* and that's what matters. We both fought back and we *won,*" she insisted. "Our bond proved stronger than Celaeno's magic. We escaped!"

As Nezzie spoke, Destin was already shaking his head. "Celaeno *let* us go and you know it," he countered. "Our lives were just another game to her. She was growing bored of the

Cull after all these years and wanted something new to entertain her, something *exciting* for her harpies to chase."

"So what if she did?" the strix argued. "The end result is the same whether she let us go or we escaped by our own efforts. We're still free of her for however long this lasts. From the beginning, we both knew it was a long shot. We were just trying to buy some time—just one more day together, even if it was spent running for our lives. We never thought we'd actually succeed, but here we are. We've had three more days than we were due, Destin." Nezzie reached up and touched the merrow's face. Her nut-brown fingers brushed along the spiked fins at the edge of his jaw, smoothing them down against his skin. "Whatever lies ahead, wasn't that worth it? Isn't every second we're still alive a victory?"

Destin stared at the little strix, the fear and pain in his luminous eyes shifting to something else as he wordlessly succumbed to her reasoning. The merrow laid his hand over Nezzie's, twining their fingers together tightly as he leaned into her caress.

Behind them, Branwen stood momentarily forgotten in the surge of her companions' emotions. She didn't mind the lack of scrutiny; it gave her a chance to observe and to *think*. Any doubts she'd had about trusting Nezzie and Destin had nearly vanished. *They have just as much to lose as I do if Celaeno and her harpies find us. Maybe even more,* Branwen considered as she looked at the desperate way Destin and Nezzie clung to each other.

*They are the only thing each of them has left,* she realized. *They've been abandoned by their family, their friends, the Guard. Because of the bounty Celaeno placed on their heads, even the whole harpy court is against them, while I still have my family. Mama, Papa, Madden, Colwen, Magrid. They are all* alive *and* safe *outside of the Sídhe,* she told herself, using that fact as an anchor for her hope, her reason to keep fighting.

Branwen opened her mouth, resolving to ask about the next step in Nezzie and Destin's plan—if they even *had* one—when she noticed something far more concerning. One of the scabs along the merrow's iron-scorched arm had just burst, releasing a gush of dark liquid, but Destin didn't even seem to notice. *He can't feel it!* Branwen thought in alarm.

"Destin, you're bleeding!" she blurted, staring in horror as the droplets steamed when they hit the ground.

The two fae startled at her comment, breaking slightly apart as they finally remembered they weren't alone. Destin shifted away from Nezzie first, reflexively trying to hide his wounded arm from her sight, but the strix was too quick and pivoted with him.

"Destin," she began. Her brows furrowed with concern as she reached for his arm.

"I'm fi—" Destin choked, trying to force out the lie, but it lodged in his throat.

At the sound, Nezzie's gaze narrowed in a glare. "You are *not* 'fine,'" the strix insisted. "Far from it!" She darted to the side, grabbing his arm before he could dodge again, and turned the limb scorch-side up.

Finally, the merrow winced as the sudden movement caused the rest of the thick, black scabs along his forearm to crack open, draining a gray-streaked discharge along with iron-blackened blood across his pale blue skin.

Nezzie gasped, her light green eyes growing vivid with fear. "Why didn't you tell me it was this bad? You could lose your arm if we don't do something soon!"

Branwen stepped forward, then, her years of *iachäwr* training compelling her to *do* something, even if she wasn't sure *what*. "Is there any way I can help?" she asked, but Destin just shook his head.

"Fire magic isn't exactly the most conducive for healing," he told her. "A skilled mage might be able to burn the poison out, but I'd say that's beyond your level of control, wouldn't you?"

Branwen nodded meekly. She couldn't argue with that. The last thing she wanted was for the fiery flicker of her magic to suddenly explode into a blazing inferno and roar through Destin as it had done to the Dark. And that was if it did anything at all. Most likely, the tiny flame would simply sputter out at the effort, leaving nothing but dying embers in her heart. Still, she couldn't give up.

To Destin, she said, "There must be *something*. Some other way."

The merrow sighed, weariness and dejection heavy in his voice. "The only other treatment for iron-scorch is salt," he continued. "A lot of it. So, unless you just happen to be carrying around about two pounds of salt...?"

Branwen shook her head, patting the apron of her skirt out of reflex. "No, I—wait." Her fingers drifted over a soggy lump in her left pocket. Hastily, she dug out the contents, revealing the wad of long-forgotten willow bark, a gift from her mother only that morning. It felt like a lifetime ago. *Several lifetimes*, Branwen corrected, holding the damp bark out to Destin. It still smelled of salt and sea water from when she had plunged into the ocean trying to get away from Bart and Sebastian that first time on the beach. "It's not much, but will this help? It's willow bark," she added. "If nothing else, you could chew it to ease the pain."

Destin stared at her, the thin, nictitating membranes of his second eyelids blinking across his candle-yellow eyes in mild shock. "I didn't expect you to actually *have* something," he blurted in surprise. Beside him, Nezzie nudged the merrow into silence.

"We'll take it," she said, accepting the briny bark on Destin's behalf. "Whatever it is, it can't hurt to try."

"A poultice might work best," Branwen suggested. "Something that can be spread over the entire wound. I have plenty of material for bandages." She pulled up the edge of her woolen dress, gesturing to the lighter, linen skirt beneath—slightly water-stained and rumpled from her tumble at the beach, but otherwise preserved from dirt and grime. Nezzie handed her one of Mina's silver daggers without question, and the two set to work with Destin hovering between them.

Using two palm-sized rocks from the creek bed, Nezzie quickly ground the bark, along with a few other herbs from the grove, into a fibrous mash while Branwen sliced strips from her underskirt. When they finished, Nezzie motioned for Destin to sit and he obeyed, slowly lowering himself onto the upper slope of the bank.

His long legs stretched out in front of him, dipping his bare feet into the water. For the first time, Branwen noticed a slight webbing between his toes.

Nezzie waved Branwen over next, holding out the stone containing the paste of willow bark in her other hand. "I can't touch the iron-scorch without getting burned myself," Nezzie told her, "so you'll need to apply the poultice. Can you do that?"

Branwen nodded. "Of course," she said. Before accepting the strix's make-shift bowl, Branwen unlooped the iron keys from her wrist, conscious of how the dangling metal could accidentally burn the merrow further as she worked. With the keys stowed safely in the right-hand pocket of her skirt, she was nearly ready. Branwen placed the bowl down beside her, along with her stack of bandages and Mina's knife, as she knelt by Destin's side.

The merrow looked at her dubiously, but said nothing as she re-positioned his injured arm, holding it gingerly with her left hand. Her right hand dipped into the salve, ready to apply it, when suddenly she stopped, her attention drawn back to her hand on Destin's arm. The merrow's skin blazed beneath her fingertips, hot and raging with infection. Black lymph seeped from his pores, leaking from the inflamed vessels beneath his skin even under the light pressure of her touch, and she knew the poultice was not going to be enough. She pulled her right hand back from the salve and took up Mina's dagger instead, bringing it to Destin's wound.

The merrow's eyes flashed wide. "*What* are you *doing*?" he protested, suddenly trying to wrench his arm away. Branwen tightened her grip, the threat of pain holding him in place, but Nezzie was another story.

"I'm not going to hurt him!" Branwen shouted before the strix could lunge at her in Destin's defense. "I need to debride the wound first," she quickly explained. "There's no point in applying a poultice if it can't reach the infection. Trust me," she insisted. "I was an *iachäwr* in my village—a healer." They didn't need to know about the "in-training" part of her title. Besides, she told herself, she had helped her mother debride dozens of wound before, some even worse than Destin's.

The merrow frowned at her, the corners of his dark blue lips turning down in skepticism. "I know what an *iachäwr* is," he muttered, making Branwen wonder if he could sense the slight untruth to her words.

"Then, you know I know what's best," she said, pushing against his reluctance with a confidence she didn't quite feel. She steeled her gaze before looking up at Destin and pressed her lips into a thin, stubborn line. "You need to let me try to clear some of the infection now. Otherwise, at the rate this is spreading, it'll be more than your arm that needs saving. Come morning, you could be *dead*."

Nezzie gasped at Branwen's ominous proclamation, the strix's sharp intake of breath drawing Destin's eyes. The barely audible sound sparked something within the merrow and his face grew resolute.

"That won't happen," Destin declared. "I won't *let* that happen—no matter what it takes."

"This is going to hurt," Branwen warned him.

"Just do it," the merrow commanded, his muscles already clenched beneath Branwen's grip.

Nezzie knelt by his other side, resting her small hand atop his for comfort. At her touch, Destin's tension eased, but only slightly.

Branwen twisted her head from side to side, stretching her own neck and shoulders and forcing them to relax. Her hold on the dagger steadied, then she took a deep breath and deftly flicked the blade forward, slicing just beneath the edge of the necrotic tissue.

Destin grunted at the pain of the first cut, but otherwise remained remarkably stoic as she pried away the iron-blackened flesh. The only tell for the agony she knew he must be enduring was the instant sheen of sweat on his brow and the intermittent tremor in his cheek.

Branwen moved quickly, peeling off the thick scabs and using some of the strips cut from her skirt to wipe away the infection that drained from beneath. With the merrow's raw and festering flesh exposed, she could finally apply the poultice.

"This is going to hurt *worse*," she told Destin, then before he could protest, she pressed the willow bark into the fissure of his skin.

A stream of curses hissed from Destin's lips as the salt stung his already-tender wound. The spiny fins on his arms and the sides of his face flared in agony, but Branwen kept her grip steady, not allowing him to flinch away. After the initial shock, the merrow collected himself, shoving all his pain behind a mask of calm where Nezzie couldn't see.

Branwen could feel the effort it took as the muscles in his forearm quivered beneath her hand. Destin's eyes flicked to the worried strix and he smiled, the corners of his lips pulling tight with pain.

"It's not so bad," he said, forcing his words through gritted teeth. "I've had worse."

"Oh, yeah? When?" Nezzie asked, sniffling back her own tears of sympathy to scoff at his bravado.

Destin hesitated a moment before answering. Branwen could sense the debate within him. As a fae, he couldn't lie, so whatever he said next would be a true indicator of the level of pain he was so vainly trying to hide. "Remember that time I was nearly gored by a leviathan?" he said at last. "Or when we were new guards and Celaeno sent all the water fae to clear out a nest of spriggans, only it turned out to be a nest of fire salamanders? Those were definitely worse."

Nezzie's eyes widened. "Both times you nearly died!"

"Yes, well...." Destin gave a sheepish, half-shrug, not daring to move his injured arm as Branwen began gingerly wrapping it with the cloth bandages. When she finished, the merrow rose to his feet, refusing any offer of assistance as Branwen and Nezzie scrambled to stand beside him.

Above them, the sun dipped just below the treeline, its fading glow partially hidden by the vast canopy of the single oak in the center of the naiad's grove. Before long, it would vanish entirely.

"What do we do now?" Branwen asked, looking to her companions.

Destin shrugged again, fiddling absently with his bandage. "Sleep," he said. "If you can. Since I'm not likely to doze off anytime soon, I'll take first watch. Nezzie, you're on second."

The strix accepted the order with a nod, the perfunctory gesture another tell of her life in the Guard. *A soldier's life*, Branwen thought as she watched Nezzie begin to make a nest in the grass, methodically flattening a wide swath just beyond the stream-dampened soil. The strix picked out stones and other sleep-hampering debris as she went, her owlish eyes perfect for seeing in the growing dark.

"I can take third watch," Branwen offered, eager to keep herself preoccupied. Her body was exhausted but her mind still whirled, trying to focus on anything but what she felt and all the horrors she'd seen. The idea of the dark and the quiet terrified her. Without something to distract her, she knew all the memories of the day would come rushing back, forcing her to live them all over again. "I doubt I'll be able to sleep," she added honestly, but Destin just shook his head.

"Nezzie and I are trained for this," he told her. "We know the dangers of this world—and how to fight them should it come to that. You don't. It's safer for all of us if you just rest. Tomorrow will be a long day."

Branwen couldn't let go that easily. She opened her mouth to protest, but Nezzie cut her off before she could say a word.

"You've done your part," the strix insisted, pausing briefly in her work. "Rescuing us from the Dark and from the Red Keep... we owe you our lives. That's not an easy debt in the Sídhe. Let us do what we can to repay it. Plus, Destin and I are both better at seeing in the dark," she added, tossing Branwen a teasing wink as she settled into one side of her grass bed.

"Exactly," the merrow agreed, overlooking Nezzie's humor to validate his point. "Leave the guarding to the guards. We'll figure out the rest in the morning. For now, *sleep*."

Nezzie nodded, smiling up at Branwen from within the nest of grass. She patted the empty space to her right, and reluctantly, Branwen gave in, knowing there was no use arguing with the two fae. She lay down next to Nezzie, but with her back to the strix so she could keep a clear view of the far side of the grove—where the dwarf had stumbled in. *If it happened once, it could happen again*, she reasoned, her body curling tightly within the circle of the nest. *Destin and Nezzie don't want me to keep watch, but it doesn't hurt to have an extra set of eyes on things.*

Behind her, she could hear the light sound of Destin's footsteps through the grass and the faint scrape of bark as he positioned himself in a tree near the edge of the grove.

*That would be the best place to keep watch*, she thought, trying to distract herself with the minutia. *Somewhere he can see, but not be seen. I wonder...if he stands on the border of the fairy ring, can he see past the grove and into the forest? Or is the forest not visible beyond the ring just like the grove wasn't visible from the other side?*

As she pondered, the evening turned to night. Her spine tensed as moon-cooled air caressed her skin. Behind her, she felt Nezzie shudder, too, and the strix scooted closer until her wings pressed against Branwen's back.

The nearness of the soft down feathers warmed Branwen instantly, and she could feel her own heat shared with Nezzie. She heard the strix sigh and in seconds the winged girl relaxed, her breath deep and even in sleep.

Branwen wished she were so lucky.

As the night and quiet grew, she could feel her thoughts drifting toward the past, replaying the day's terrors across her mind's eye. The Cù Sìth. Robin. The redcaps. Bart and Sebastian. Ronan and Mina. The harpies, the kobolds, the dwarves, the naga. The unicorn. The Devouring Dark.

Wherever Branwen went, death and destruction followed her, carving new wounds in her flesh and in her heart. Every time she closed her eyes, she could see Ginny's face—her dread as the Dark first took hold of her, the way her head lolled after he snapped her neck, her lifeless stare as Dark-Ronan dangled the child's body over Branwen in taunting victory—

*Think about something else! Anything else!* Branwen commanded herself, trying to retreat to the haven of family and friends in her mind. *Mama. Papa. Madden. Colwen. Magrid. Ifanna....* But this time, the litany of names was not enough. Ginny's face kept pushing through followed by images of the thirteen nameless girls who had died under Branwen's watch—some of whom she'd never seen under the light of day. Each face burned in her mind, so young and so frightened, yet willing to put all of their trust in *her* to set them free.

Branwen gasped as she opened her eyes, her heart racing as the night deepened around her. The dark of the grove did nothing to banish her ghosts. She could still see the girls standing against the deep shadows of the woods, looking to her, pleading for help she couldn't give. Tears filled her vision, blurring the trees, but not the girls' faces—those existed only in her mind.

"I'm sorry!" she breathed, her voice strained with regret and remorse; she could feel the weight of it crushing her, pressing the remaining air from her lungs.

Out of the crowd of girls, one of them stepped closer. *Ginny*, Branwen thought, but as the specter drew nearer she realized it wasn't the dead, honey-haired girl, but the living naiad emerging from the massive oak by the stream and coming to stand by her side. For a long moment, the naiad simply watched Branwen, gazing at her with those gentle, blue river-stone eyes. Somehow, they seemed to see *through* her, piercing the tangle of hurt and fear in her heart and absorbing some of her pain. Thick sap began to ooze from the corners of the naiad's eyes, dripping down the crevasses of the fae's face like tears to mirror Branwen's own. Then, slowly, the bark-skinned fae leaned over her, touching a long, twig-like finger to her forehead.

"Sleep, child," the naiad whispered. The creature's kind, quiet voice swept through Branwen's mind, blowing away the tumult of her thoughts like leaves on the wind. With her visions dissipated and the desperate cries of her memories silenced, exhaustion swiftly enveloped her, dragging her consciousness into its void.

She slept and did not dream.

# Chapter 13

The next morning, Branwen woke with a start, her eyes wide as they took in the pale light trickling through the grove's canopy. Immediately, she knew it wasn't the dawn that had stirred her, but the cool breeze running across her back where Nezzie's warm form had once been.

Branwen jolted upright, frantically looking around the clearing for any sign of the strix or the merrow. Her mind raced, conjuring her deepest fear. *They've left me!* she panicked. *This is why they didn't want to me take a watch. They were planning to leave me! Now, I'm all alone!*

A strangled sob rose in her throat, but before she could give it utterance, she caught the familiar twitter of Nezzie's laughter, the strix's high tone chiming above the quiet burble of the nearby creek. In the next instant, the winged girl fluttered down from the top branches of the naiad's oak tree, landing lightly in front of Branwen.

"Breakfast," the strix announced, holding out a handful of small, date-like fruits with reddish wrinkled skin.

Branwen blinked, swallowing her earlier panic with an audible gulp as she reflexively reached out to accept the proffered fruit. Her stomach already gurgled with anticipation. The sound drowned out the anxious beating of her heart as it ardently reminded her that she had eaten nothing but willow bark since her porridge breakfast at home the previous dawn. She could smell the sweet and tangy scent wafting off the wizened berries. Her mouthed watered, yet she hesitated to bring the fruit to her lips as the warning of an ancient folk tale sang in her mind: *When in the land of Faerie, eat no food and drink no wine if you ever wish to see your home again.*

"They're not poisoned if that's what you're thinking," came Destin's wry comment as the merrow peeled away from the faint morning shadows beneath the trees at the edge of the naiad's grove.

Branwen winced at how easily he had been able to read her expression and glean the wary gist of her thoughts even from a distance. *I want to trust Nezzie and Destin, I* need *to trust them,* she told herself. *They have done nothing but help me, so why do I keep having these doubts?*

*Maybe it's not because* you *don't trust* them, whispered the dark voice of her fear. *Maybe it's because you know* they *shouldn't trust* you. *After all,* who *has shown the most disregard for others' lives?* Who *intentionally provoked the unicorn's blood-lust to drive it into a killing frenzy?* Who *released the fae from the blockhouse with the sole purpose of using them as fodder for an escape?* Whose *rash actions ultimately freed the Dark?* Who *promised life and hope, then led fourteen innocent young girls to their deaths?* Who?

Branwen shook her head violently as though that simple action could deny the truth...and her guilt. "That's not it!" she insisted with far too much vehemence, earning a sideways glance from Destin and a worried look from Nezzie who still stood in front of her. Branwen struggled to regain her composure, pushing back the black thoughts that threatened to devour her more completely than the Dark ever could. She'd hoped the light of day would vanquish some of the horrors that had lurked in her mind during the night, but instead she found them even more vivid as everything around her reminded her that this world was *real*.

Cool, hard ground pressed against her as she sat, its unyielding foundation softened by flattened blades of dew-strewn grass. The constant trickling of the creek chimed in Branwen's ears, carried to her by the faint breeze that flowed from its crystalline waters. Her nose caught the pungent scent of earth and stone and wood and water and.... *Magic*, Branwen thought, recognizing the almost indiscernible fragrance—not a smell, exactly, but the *sensation* of a smell—drifting through the crisp air of the grove. Its power hummed gently against her skin, stoking the tiny flame within her heart.

*That, too, is real*, she thought, focusing on the flicker of warmth within her to steady her emotions. The small flame roared to life, the magnitude of its power so vastly different from the fragile embers she'd expected. The magic blazed with the fuel of her attention, and the heat of it spread like a wildfire through her veins and in her mind. There, the flames seared each dark thought and memory from the day before, not destroying them—nothing could destroy them for those memories were a part of her now—but cauterizing them like edges of a wound so they wouldn't bleed into her every waking moment. The image of fire grew so strong in her mind's eye that she could feel the scorching heat of it against her palms as she clenched her hands into fists and her nose stung with the acrid scent of smoke, then—

*SPLASH!*

Branwen gasped as cold water hit her face, extinguishing the mesmerizing flames in her mind and hurling her back into the brisk reality of the naiad's grove. She looked around with a start, her gaze clouded by the fog of steam that rose from her skin. When it cleared, she could see Destin and Nezzie standing in the creek with the merrow's outer armored shirt stretched between them like a tarp pooling water in its tightly-woven scales as they readied to douse her a second time. They paused when they saw Branwen looking at them, their eyes still wary until she had collected her senses enough to ask, "What happened?"

At her words, the two relaxed.

"I don't know. You tell me," Nezzie said, gesturing vaguely toward Branwen as she released her grip on Destin's shirt and let the gathered water flow back into the creek. The merrow drew the garment to himself, shaking out the excess liquid as he and Nezzie waded the last few steps to the shallow embankment.

Branwen stared at them both, confused, until she looked down at her hands which still tingled with the remnants of magic. Slowly, she uncurled her fingers, revealing a pile of now-slightly-soggy ash in her right hand.

*The fruit*, Branwen realized as Nezzie and Destin came to stand beside her. *I burnt the fruit and I didn't even know it.* From her still-seated position, she looked up at her companions, dumbfounded. When they had told her she was a fire mage now, she hadn't envisioned *this.*

A long moment of silence lingered between them until finally Destin shrugged and said, "You could have just told us you weren't hungry."

His words brought Branwen back out of her thoughts and she groaned, mortified. "That's not what I—I didn't intend to—I mean—I-I'm sorry," she sputtered lamely, looking to Nezzie for forgiveness.

The strix merely sighed and nodded, her owlish eyes gentle as she reached down and patted Branwen on the shoulder. "I'm sure the naiad will give me some more," Nezzie assured her. "She seems very keen on you, though maybe not as much now," she added as she peered again at the immolated fruit. Only the pits remained, charred into a cluster of ebony shards. Nezzie just shook her head, then moseyed back to the naiad's oak, her tawny wings fluttering almost playfully behind her.

Branwen caught Destin's gaze following the strix, too, his tense, angular features softening briefly as his eyes lingered on her carefree movements. When he noticed Branwen watching him, he didn't flinch under her scrutiny like her brother Madden had done so many times when his love for Ifanna was still shy and new. Instead, Destin stared back at her boldly, his confidence forbidding any doubts as to how he felt about Nezzie.

"We'll leave within the half-hour," the merrow announced. "Wash. Eat. Prepare as much as you can. It could be a long time before it's safe for us to stop like this again."

"Leave?" Branwen surged to her feet, half-expecting her legs to be wobbly from sleep, but glad to find they were not. In fact, her whole body felt oddly refreshed and energized. *The naiad's doing?* Branwen wondered as the image of blue river-stone eyes flickered through her mind and she heard again the half-dreamed memory of the woodland fae's hushed and gentle voice: *Sleep, child.* Then, her own healing instincts kicked in—

once an *iachäwr*, always an *iachäwr*, she thought. To Destin, she pointed at his linen-wrapped arm and said, "You're not going anywhere until I've had a look at those bandages."

The merrow frowned as though he were going to protest. Branwen could almost hear the words "I'm fine" on the tip of his tongue, but his fae nature choked them back, not allowing him to tell an outright lie. He made an odd, strangled noise, then gave in, holding out his injured arm to Branwen. He barely managed to raise the limb above a forty-five degree angle from his side.

Branwen worked within his range, stooping to carefully peel back the layers of cloth. The outer most bandages had remained clean and dry through the night, which made Branwen cautiously hopeful until she reached the inner layers. Thick, gray pus saturated the last two strips of cloth and continued to ooze out from around the edges of the poultice. The wound itself looked better than Branwen had expected, especially given the amount and color of its drainage. The salt and willow bark poultice had done its job drawing out some of the infection and reducing the inflammation, but the results could hardly be called *good.* Disheartened, Branwen cleaned what she could and slowly began to redress Destin's wound with the remaining unsoiled cloths.

"I had wondered if we would stay here a few days," she admitted quietly. "To give us all a chance to recover in safety before moving on, but..."

"But I don't have a few days," the merrow stated, shifting his iron-scorched arm ever so slightly in her grasp. With his outer shirt off, Branwen could clearly see the black trail of iron-infected veins crawling up his forearm. The furthest tendrils reached nearly to Destin's shoulder and showed no sign of slowing. Unless something drastic happened, Branwen knew it could be only a matter of *hours*, rather than *days*, before the poison reached the merrow's heart.

"That's why we can't afford any delays," Destin continued. "It's going to be a close call as it is, but we don't have any choice. There's only one place in all the Sídhe where we can be *free* of the harpies."

Branwen's heart rose in her throat at the merrow's words, buoyed by hope. *Freedom! That's one step closer to home!* The thought sang in her very bones, stirring up a nervous energy that made the flame within her flicker in wild anticipation. She tamped it down as best she could, conscious of her hands on Destin's iron-scorched forearm. The last thing she needed was to burn him further as she tied off the last of his bandages.

She finished quickly, letting his arm drop before she asked, "Where is that? Where are we going?"

For the first time, Destin looked at her and smiled. The gesture was genuine, but far from comforting as the corners of his lips curved not upward but downward in a distinctive shark-like grin. The needles of his teeth scissored together as he spoke, lending an air of finality to his words as he told Branwen, "We're going across the Shimmer Sea and down the Bone Road to a place where Lady Celaeno can never touch us. We're going to the Black Throne at *Gcroílár an Sídhe*—the Heart of the Sídhe. We're going to see the *King*."

*The King?* Branwen's mind raced, instinctively recalling the brief history lessons of her childhood. There had been no king over Wales for forty years—not since the death of young

Edward VI. Queen Elizabeth reigned now and had for as long as Branwen could remember, but the merrow certainly wasn't talking about *her*.

*He means whatever fae...creature...rules over the Sídhe,* she realized and had to suppress a shudder. With the likes of kobolds, púkas, and redcaps as his subjects, the King couldn't be anything close to human. *And how fierce and powerful must he be if even Celaeno, the queen of the harpies, doesn't dare cross him?*

Her heart thudded in her chest as her brain conjured images of the ancient forest-god whose myth still haunted village firesides on cold, moonless nights. Cernunnos, the horned one—a tall, dark being with a crown of antlers on his head and cloven hooves for feet. In Branwen's mind, the vision mutated and the false god-King grew vast black wings, veined and fleshy like a bat's. His teeth became fangs and their sharp tips pierced his lower lip, coating his mouth with blood—

*No!* Branwen banished the manifestation of fear from her thoughts. *I've made it this far—I can't give in now. I* won't. *Mother, Papa, Madden, Colwen, Magrid...I'm coming! Whatever it takes, I will find a way!*

To Destin, Branwen asked, "Will the King really help us?" She could barely breathe as she voiced her next—and most important—question. "Can he...can he send me *home*?"

Her hopes plummeted when the merrow didn't answer right away. His brief smile faded, and when next he spoke, Branwen could tell he chose his words carefully. *A sign of fae deception?* she wondered, yet sensed no guile from her companion. *What would be the point?* she reasoned. *We're in this together.*

"As one of the Firstborn, the King *can* return you to the Mundane, but *will* he?" Destin shook his head, the spiny fins at the edges of his jaw twitching restlessly as he admitted, "I don't know. I don't even know if the King will accept Nezzie and me into his Court when and *if* we get there, but still we have to try.

"Because I *do* know this," the merrow continued, his tallow-yellow eyes now burning with certainty. "Without the King's help, we are all *dead*. Few other fae, even among the Firstborn, are strong enough or bold enough to defy Celaeno and her harpy court, yet the King can act with impunity because he knows she doesn't dare strike him back. He and our Lady have a long-standing feud, so he won't easily turn down an opportunity to expose Celaeno's schemes and put her in her place."

Branwen thought she understood Destin's reasoning. "So, the enemy of our enemy is our...?"

"Friend," the merrow confirmed, hesitating just a fraction too long before adding, "We hope."

"That's a terrible plan," she told him, mirroring Nezzie's earlier sentiments about Branwen's own vaguely formed idea on how to escape the Keep. *It worked*, she knew, *but at what cost?* Whether she made it out of the Sídhe or died trying, would she ever look back and think *this was worth it*?

*It* has *to be*, Branwen told herself, otherwise she didn't think she could bear it.

Beside her, Destin laughed—a short, sharp, humorless sound—as he recognized Branwen's reference. "Do you have a better idea, then?" he asked.

"No," Branwen asserted. Then, plucking up her courage, she adjusted her skirts, nominally brushing away the dirt and grime before she settled the rumpled, ragged layers around her. She straightened her shoulders and lifted her head, looking Destin directly in the eyes as she said, "Let's go see the King."

The merrow grinned at her response, the rows of his needle-like teeth glinting in the morning's dawning light, but when she tried to move past him toward the edge of the naiad's grove, he grabbed her arm with his non-scorched hand and pulled her back.

"Not so fast, Feisty," he said, then nodded to Nezzie, calling the strix over for support. "We have to set a few ground rules before we leave—for our safety and yours. There are things you still don't know that could mean the difference between life and death for all of us. And, besides," the merrow continued, "it wouldn't surprise me if Celaeno ordered her minions to keep scouring the woods, seeking to eliminate all of the Red Keep survivors on sight. Three separate hunting parties passed us during the night. If it weren't for Nezzie's quick wits and the naiad's illusions we would have been found already."

"O-oh?" Branwen sucked in a shuddering breath, her body tensing at the revelation. *I could have gone my whole life without knowing that*, she thought as she tried to calm the sudden, frantic beating of her heart.

Nezzie nodded to confirm, her mossy braids bobbing against her small shoulders. "We *have* to stay together," she said. "Otherwise, Celaeno will *see.*"

"See?" Branwen stared at the strix, confused. "See what?"

"She'll *see* us," Nezzie said. "Destin mentioned the Firstborn, right?"

"Yes..." Branwen answered hesitantly, unsure of where the strix was leading. "He said the King was one of them."

Nezzie nodded again, her tone matter-of-fact as she stated, "Yes, the King is the first of the Firstborn, but there are four others with powers that rival his."

"Celaeno is one of them," Branwen said with certainty. "But her sister Aello is not."

"That's right," Nezzie said, a look of surprise flashing across her face. Her owlish eyes darted over to Destin for an explanation, but the merrow only gave a one-sided shrug.

Branwen didn't know how to explain it, either. She just *knew*. She had witnessed the might of Aello and Sorcha's magic as the two harpies had conjured a hurricane of wind strong enough to obliterate the gates of the Red Keep. While they were both undeniably powerful, neither was a match for the Devouring Dark who had been bound within the blockhouse's oubliette by Celaeno herself. *The unicorn, too,* Branwen realized. Once freed from the iron of the Red Keep, the beautiful, savage beast had held her ground against not one, but *three* harpies including Aello, yet despite the unicorn's obvious power, Celaeno had managed to capture and imprison her as well.

*Looking back, I can reason it out—that Aello isn't a Firstborn,* Branwen thought, *but how did I know in the first place? I can't sense levels of magic in the fae like Destin...or can I?*

Unconsciously, her hand rose to her heart, feeling the flicker of magic there brighten at her touch. For just a second, she let her eyes slide out of focus, and when she looked at Nezzie and Destin again, she could see a faint ripple in the air around them. *Like the shimmer of heat over a vat of oil just before it starts to boil*, she thought. The ripple around Destin spread further than Nezzie's except for along his entire right arm and shoulder where the strange aura collapsed into almost nothing.

Branwen blinked and the ripples vanished like a dream—not just from her sight, but from her mind. She found she couldn't even recall the exact shape of them anymore, as though she were trying to remember something that just didn't exist.

*But the ripples* did *exist—they* do *exist*, Branwen knew as her thoughts snapped back into focus along with her vision. *It's just that my ability to see them, or to even comprehend them, comes and goes. This...sixth sense...is magical, not physical, but somehow it manifests in a physical way? Where I* hear, *but not with my ears,* feel, *but not with my skin,* see, *but not with my—*

"When you said Celaeno would *see* us, you didn't mean with her *eyes*, did you?" Branwen blurted as the realization struck. She saw another *look* pass between Nezzie and Destin and knew she'd guessed right.

"How?" she asked, not waiting for their response. "What can she *see*? Does she know where we are? Is she coming for us?" Panic rose in her throat, choking out her words so she couldn't even voice her true fears: *How long has Celaeno been watching? Can she* see *across the Veil? Did she* see *what happened to the Cù Sìth? Has she* seen *my family? Has she* seen *Colwen?*

"Whoa, Feisty, relax," Nezzie said, grabbing Branwen's hand in a comforting gesture. The strix's small fingers barely reached across her palm, yet even her slight grip exuded a confidence and warmth that slowly began to calm Branwen's frazzled nerves.

Destin was less compassionate.

"Yes, don't be ridiculous," he chided. "If Celaeno could *see* us right now, we'd already be dead."

Rather than frightening her more, the merrow's blunt statement quelled the storm of Branwen's emotions far more effectively than Nezzie's kind actions ever could. His cold logic forced her to look past her fears and acknowledge the truth. Rational once more, Branwen's mind began churning, trying to digest everything Destin and Nezzie had told her so far.

"Three of the Firstborn possess what's called the Second Sight, meaning they can *see* beyond the here and now," the merrow said, adding fodder to the mill of her thoughts. "Celaeno has the ability to see into the future—and not just the current future, but the *changing* future and every *possible* future in-between. She constantly uses that knowledge to manipulate other fae and events in the Sídhe until she can guarantee the outcome of the future she wants. Our Lady is so adept at reading the web of fate and predicting the actions of those around her that it's almost as if she can hear their very thoughts. However, there are limits even to her great power."

*Oh, good,* Branwen thought, but didn't get her hopes up. She'd known escaping Celaeno would be difficult, but the merrow's description of the harpy queen's Sight made it seem nigh impossible. *How can we hide from or out-maneuver someone who can* see *our every possible move? If that's the case, how have we even managed to make it this far? How could she have not* seen *our escape of the Red Keep? Did she* see *it and let it happen? For what purpose?*

Nezzie seemed to follow her line of thought, giving Branwen's hand a final, comforting squeeze before letting go.

"There are things Celaeno can't *see*, no matter how hard she tries," the strix chimed in. "She can't *see* other Firstborn, for example. Most of the Firstborn can't use their powers against one another. To do so would violate the Rules of the Sídhe and their own life would be forfeit. No Firstborn is willing to risk that. As the oldest and most powerful of all the fae, the Firstborn value their own lives above anything else. Even Celaeno, who has lusted after the power of the King's Throne for eons, would never risk sacrificing herself to take it."

"And that's why she never will," Destin added. "The Sídhe operates on the Law of Equal Exchange. Celaeno will never be able to take what rightfully belongs to the King without offering something of equal or greater value in return. Yet, she never stops trying. I don't know what she was planning when she had you and those other young humans brought into the Sídhe, but it is undoubtedly connected to another scheme to overthrow the King. This time, though, I think our Lady has gone too far. She's pushed past the limits of her Sight and, hopefully, that limit will allow us to move un*seen*."

"What is it, then?" Branwen asked. "What is her limit?"

Destin looked at her, his yellow eyes almost glowing as he smiled and said, "It's *you*."

Branwen blinked, stunned for half a second before blurting out, "Me?"

"Well, not you specifically," the merrow amended. "Any human from the Mundane would do. Celaeno can't *see* the fate of anything or anyone that is not of the Sídhe. Your presence is her blind spot and as long as Nezzie's fate and mine are entwined with yours, we're in her blind spot, too."

Nezzie nodded. "That's why I said we need to stay together," the strix explained. "With your magic so new and uncontrolled, you don't stand a chance of making it to the King's Court on your own—not with Celaeno's redcaps looking for you, nevermind any other less-than-friendly fae you might run across along the way. Plus, if we separate, Celaeno will *see* me and Destin immediately. Her court in the Shard Forest is not far from here as the harpy flies. She and her harpy guard would be on us in a matter of minutes, and while our Lady may not be able to *see* you with her Second Sight, she can still see you with her *eyes*. You wouldn't be safe."

Branwen couldn't deny the strix's reasoning. Every word she spoke rang with truth, adding to the foreboding reality of Celaeno's power and emphasizing the inherent dangers of the Sídhe.

*I should be terrified*, Branwen thought, *but I'm not.* Something about Nezzie's stark honesty calmed her instead, assuaging her lingering doubts about her companions' sincerity. At least for now.

*Nezzie and Destin* need *me,* Branwen told herself. *We* need *each other—and as long as that holds true, they will never abandon me.*

*But would* you *abandon* them*?* came with whisper of the darkness within. *Would you sacrifice Nezzie and Destin to the harpies as long as* you *could escape? If circumstances were different, would you leave them behind like you did those nameless, innocent girls at the Red Keep? Like you left Ronan to be devoured by the Dark? If it had been Ginny instead of Ronan lying there, would you have still turned your back?*

*But it wasn't Ginny!* Branwen mentally countered. Her jaw clenched as she fought back, letting rage kindle in her heart. The searing heat scorched through the black thoughts that threatened to overtake her. *It wasn't Ginny,* she affirmed again, *and I'll be* damned *before I let anything make me feel guilty about Ronan! As for Nezzie and Destin—*

Branwen took a determined step forward, positioning herself firmly between her two companions as she vowed, "I'll do whatever it takes. Just tell me how."

Destin snorted, his expression bemused as he stated, "To start, you don't have to be so close. Distance is less important than association," the merrow explained. "Our fates will be intertwined as long as we must depend on one another to evade Celaeno and survive the journey to the King's Court."

"Oh," Branwen said, but she didn't back away, didn't retreat. If she did, she was afraid her resolve might weaken and she couldn't risk that—not even a fraction of a percent. Beside her, Nezzie smiled, patting her on the shoulder.

"Here." The strix offered another handful of the naiad's reddish, date-like fruit to Branwen. "You really should eat before we go. It's a long way to the King's Court and it may not be safe enough to stop once we've started."

Again, Branwen hesitated. "There are tales in my village warning people not to eat or drink anything in the Sídhe," she told Nezzie even as her stomach gurgled at the sight of the ripe, wrinkle-skinned berries. The strix only laughed in response, her high voice twittering through the clearing.

"Let me guess," Nezzie said. "It must be something like—eat no food and drink no wine, lest you never go home again?"

"That's right," Branwen said, startled by the strix's accuracy.

A smile danced on the winged girl's lips. "Of course," she said. "But it's just a trick—a prank," she clarified. "One of the oldest the fae ever pulled. It started ages ago, back when the gates between worlds were kept open and humans could simply stumble across the Veil. Those first fae to encounter humans found them amusing, but were wary of any iron-wielders overstaying their welcome. As a precaution, the fae agreed to spread a rumor to discourage humans from lingering in the Sídhe for more than a day."

"Well, it worked," Branwen told the strix. "Though I don't understand how, if the fae can't lie."

Beside her, Destin shook his head. "No fae can tell an *outright* lie," he corrected, "but that doesn't mean we can't encourage a...misunderstanding. I'm sure the original rumor only left the consequences *implied*. The humans would have filled in the rest as they spread the story among themselves. Therein, lay the real deception.

"But now you know the truth, so eat," the merrow insisted, taking the fruit from Nezzie and pressing them into Branwen's palm. "I can't guarantee there will be another grove for us to take refuge in if you suddenly faint from hunger in the middle of our journey."

Feeling both reprimanded and reassured, Branwen obeyed. The red, shriveled fruit practically dissolved on her tongue, its slightly grainy texture and sweet flavor reminiscent of dried dates. The handful of berries was nowhere near enough to fill her, but even that small amount was able to lift her spirits and renew her energy. As she ate, Nezzie and Destin tidied the clearing, disguising any evidence of their stay. When they finished, they motioned Branwen to join them by the oak tree near the center of the clearing.

As she approached, the naiad emerged, and Nezzie and Destin bowed to the bark-skinned fae. Branwen quickly followed suit, wanting to show respect to their gracious host. When she glanced up, she found the naiad staring at her. The water nymph blinked, her blue, river-stone eyes closing in a brief and subtle greeting.

"Rise," the naiad told her. The fae's soft voice rustled like the sigh of wind through trees. "You and your companions owe me no gratitude. I am aware of your deeds—how you destroyed the Dark and freed some of my kinsmen from Celaeno's Red Keep." The naiad extended her branch-like hand, gesturing beyond Branwen to the entirety of the grove as she added, "As long as these waters flow and my tree still stands, your kindness will not be forgotten. Go in peace, my child." Then, the naiad turned and faded back into the oak tree.

With the water nymph's blessing and dismissal complete, Branwen, Nezzie, and Destin left the grove. They passed through the brief shroud of mist beyond the naiad's white birch trees and emerged into the dark forest on the other side. The woods were quiet—*worryingly so*, Branwen thought as she and Nezzie oriented themselves with Destin. They set off in silence, trusting the merrow's infallible sense of the sea to lead them out of the forest.

With every step, Branwen could feel her tension growing as she expected one of Celaeno's redcaps or kobolds or even a púka to ambush them at any moment, but none did. Other than spying the heavy tracks of redcaps who'd passed by the grove in the night, their journey through the forest remained eerily uneventful.

Hours passed and the gloom of the forest lightened as the trees thinned, telling Branwen they neared the edge of the woods. She could sense the subtle shift in the air as it grew heavy with moisture from the ocean. A faint sea breeze wafted through the trees carrying the tang of salt to her nose. In minutes, they reached the boundary of the forest, pausing only briefly to listen for the telltale thud of iron boots or the distinctive scraping sound of harpy wings. Hearing none, they plunged ahead, bursting into the glare of the noon-day sun as it reflected off a pale, sandy shore in the near distance. Branwen expected Nezzie and Destin to turn and follow the line of the forest, staying near the cover of the trees, but the two made directly for the water and Branwen rushed to follow. They stopped at the shoreline, toeing the line where the sparkling water met the sand.

Standing beside Branwen, Nezzie raised a hand to her owlish eyes, shading them as she stared across the vast body of water. Branwen followed the strix's gaze. On the horizon, she saw the shadow of land.

Nezzie turned and looked at her, squinting against the sun. "Do you swim?"

Branwen nearly gaped at her. She had to be joking, right? But Nezzie didn't laugh or smile, and Branwen quickly re-evaluated. As a child, she'd spent plenty of summer days swimming laps around the village pond, but this.... "Not *that* well," she replied.

The strix shrugged. "Just thought I'd ask. Guess you're coming with me, then. Hold still," Nezzie commanded. "This might hurt a little."

Branwen froze as the strix reached up and yanked four strands of hair from her dark braid. She winced and tears pricked behind her eyes, but she blinked them away. "What's that for?" she asked as Nezzie plucked four strands from her own moss-colored hair.

"You're too heavy for me to carry by myself," the strix said, "but I know something that will help."

With a few deft movements, Nezzie twisted two strands together—one each of black and green—then looped the thin braid around Branwen's right wrist. She did the same for Branwen's other wrist and both ankles, chanting, "Light as dust, swift as rain," every time she tied the ends of the braids together.

The fine hairs on Branwen's arms and the back of her neck raised, responding to the gathering sizzle in the air that she recognized as magic. When Nezzie tied the last loop, a sharp *zap* ran through each of Branwen's limbs, and she suddenly felt lighter. Floating, almost.

"There," Nezzie chirped, looking all-too-pleased with herself. "Much better. Now, you're portable." She shrugged again. "At least, until the braids break, anyway."

"Then what happens?" Branwen couldn't stop herself from asking.

Nezzie just looked at her, her lichen-green eyes blinking exactly once as she mimed a violent crash-and-splash into the ocean.

*Oh.* Branwen couldn't argue with that. She glanced at Destin who had wandered further into the sea, but she could still see the yellow gleam of his eyes flashing back toward the shore. He seemed to be watching the whole affair with a perverse sense of glee.

"What about him?" she asked, jerking her head in his direction. The rest of her body remained paralyzed, too afraid to move lest she float away. She could feel the wind off the ocean tugging at her.

The merrow grinned at her response; now she knew for certain he'd been watching.

"Don't worry about me," Destin said, then he dove into the oncoming surf.

The waves didn't break around him, but instead rose up, wrapping him in a translucent, turquoise cocoon. The faint buzz of magic raced along Branwen's skin as she watched the merrow's clothes ripple and meld into his already-shark-like skin, adding an extra layer of protective scales. The next instant, his legs fused and his feet splayed, stretching out until they morphed into two stiff, angular fins. Webs grew between his fingers, joining them together. A single triangular fin and smaller spiked fins—like the ones on his arms and face—jutted from his spine, and slits opened along his rib cage, exposing feathery red membranes.

*Gills*, Branwen thought as the water-cocoon burst and Destin quickly ducked under the sea. *Well, of course.*

"Show off!" Nezzie called after him. Her lip curled and her small nose scrunched with disdain, but Branwen saw the sparkle of excitement in her owlish eyes.

In response, Destin surfaced, careful to keep his chest just below the waterline.

"Race you to the other side!" he shouted above the lapping sound of the waves. Then, the merrow spun and dove into the sea. A quick flick of his tail splashed brine in Nezzie's direction.

The droplets didn't come anywhere near the shore, and the strix laughed, taking hold of Branwen's wrist.

"Come on," Nezzie said, tugging her along. "We can't let him win. He'll gloat for*ever*."

Before she could react, the strix thrust her arms under Branwen's, wrapping them around her chest and pulling her tight. She could feel Nezzie's pointed chin resting between her shoulder blades.

"Hold on," Nezzie said.

"To what?" Branwen blurted, then scrambled to obey as she saw the arching forms of the strix's wings stretching to either side of her. She crossed her arms over Nezzie's, and then, with one, two, three massive beats, they were airborne.

Branwen sucked in a shuddering breath as she watched her feet leave the damp sand of the shore. Her legs grew lighter and lighter, drifting up until they were parallel with Nezzie's so her body was positioned in an odd, dead man's float. Their grip on each other was awkward and would have never worked without Nezzie's magic, but as it was, Branwen felt comfort at the light pressure of the strix against her back. Without it, she was certain she would be tossed to and fro in the ocean breeze.

With a few more flaps of Nezzie's tawny wings, they soared into the sky. A world of blue engulfed Branwen, swirling with shades of cerulean and azure as she cruised between water and air. Wind bit at her cheeks and salt spray burned her eyes. Her heart trembled in her chest, threatening utter capitulation out of sheer terror. *Humans were never meant to fly!* her mind screamed, yet she found she couldn't stop smiling.

The distance had seemed so vast from the other side, but now that she was above it all, Branwen realized the body of water wasn't a true ocean at all, but a large bay partially surrounded by land. A dense, emerald wood sprouted not far from the eastern shoreline, fed freshwater by one of the bay's inlet streams, she assumed. Beyond that, she thought she saw a strange glimmer of white snaking across the terrain, but couldn't make it out clearly.

"Celaeno lives in that forest," Nezzie said, her high, chirping voice flying against the wind. "On the other side is part of the river court, and then...the King."

*It sounds so close when she says it like that,* Branwen thought, wishing it could all be that simple. Her short time in the Sídhe had taught her that would not likely be the case, but for now she clung to that faint hope—her *only* hope—of returning home.

As they approached the midpoint of the bay, Nezzie swooped low, hugging so close to the water that Branwen could have skimmed her fingers across the surface if she had been so brave—or so foolish—to let go. She had no doubt why they called it the Shimmer Sea. The water was such a clear, reflective blue that she imagined even a single beam of moonlight would turn every ripple into a galaxy of stars. Under the noon sun, the spray of Destin's wake glinted with the light of ten thousand diamonds.

"Haha!" Nezzie crowed, arching her back and soaring upward as they rocketed past the wave-leaping merrow.

They flew by so fast and so high, Branwen almost didn't catch Destin's desperate shouts of, "Nezzie, behind you!"

A mass of dark shapes eclipsed the sun, sending a flock of shadows to dance over the sparkling sea.

"*Harpies*." Nezzie spat the word like a curse. "They didn't leave. They were just *waiting* on us," she muttered, her normally cheerful voice deepening into a growl of frustration.

Her wings furled and she dove again, twisting sideways to come out from beneath the flutter of shadows, but the three dark shapes followed her, growing larger as they drew near. A powerful wind rushed around Branwen, stirred by the beats of a half dozen new wings. Their feathers made the sound of hundreds of knives sharpening as they rent the air.

# Chapter 14

The strix darted forward, her tawny wings flapping furiously as she tried to pull ahead, but the harpies matched Nezzie's pace, beat for beat, obviously taunting. Then, the nearest one dipped lower, her deep mahogany feathers slicing through the air by Branwen's cheek as she slowly came into view.

*Aello!*

The dark harpy stared at Branwen, her wild crimson and yellow eyes burning into her soul.

"Hello...*again*," the harpy whispered, her velvet-soft voice somehow drowning out all the noise around them. A gentle smile caressed her mouth, gradually widening until the perfect mask of her face cracked. Branwen couldn't take her eyes away as the blood-red curtain of Aello's lips parted, displaying two rows of gleaming white daggers.

*Why must everything in the Sídhe always have* teeth*?* Branwen lamented, but she had no time for other thoughts as the harpy lunged, chomping down on Nezzie's shoulder.

Nezzie screamed. The strength in her arm failed, and Branwen could feel herself slipping from one side of the strix's grasp. She scrambled to hold on. The tendons in her wrists strained, pressing their bulging cords against her bruised skin as she clung to Nezzie's wounded arm with the strength of sheer desperation.

Branwen looked down, searching frantically for Destin, hoping he might be swimming close enough to help—to provide a distraction at least—but she saw no trace of him in the sparkling sea. *We've outdistanced him*, she realized. *It's just me and Nezzie now. And the harpies.*

Branwen felt the scrape of talons against her ankles and knew Aello sought to rip the hair-loops of Nezzie's spell. After one more try, she succeeded and Branwen's right leg dropped, suddenly in possession of its natural weight. Nezzie swerved as she tried to re-balance the load, but careened into one of the other harpies instead. In that instant, Branwen felt the thin braid on her left ankle snap.

Nezzie fell twenty feet before she could recover. They were balanced now, but Branwen could feel the strain in the strix's body and hear her cursing between each ragged breath. Blood ran down from Nezzie's shoulder and onto Branwen's arm. Mist-fine droplets sprayed into the air with every beat of her wings.

They had almost reached the other side of the bay. A copse of trees loomed ahead of them, dipping in and out of their line of flight as Nezzie struggled to stay aloft. Silver and gold branches jutted toward the sky like giant grasping hands, each covered with jagged emerald leaves glinting sharply in the midday sun. Branwen couldn't help imagining what would happen to her body if she rammed into those spiny limbs.

Her best chance was to drop before she hit the trees, but Nezzie was still too high up. From the current distance, Branwen knew she was sure to break a foot or an ankle upon landing—*No good for running from harpies,* chimed her thoughts unhelpfully—but if she could just get a dozen feet lower, she might survive with only a few more bruises and scrapes.

On the beach beneath her, Branwen saw two more shadows circling their own, each growing bigger by the second. *Bigger means closer,* she thought frantically and watched in horror as one harpy-shaped shadow dived into the Nezzie-and-Branwen-shaped one. She felt Nezzie lurch with the added weight, and the strix could no longer stay airborne. She plummeted toward the ground...and the trees.

"Nezzie!" Branwen shrieked, twisting her body against the strix's grasp. Fear clogged her throat as the trees rushed toward them, their sharp points gleaming. She couldn't even get the words out: *Let me go!*

Branwen slammed her eyes shut and forced her fingers to go limp, releasing their hold on Nezzie's wrists, but the strix still stubbornly clung on. All Branwen could do was count the seconds until impact.

*One, two, thr—!*

Nezzie let go.

Branwen didn't drop. She drifted—down, down, down—approaching the forest at an angle. Her shoulders ached as the power of the woven-hair bracelets jerked her arms directly upward, pulling them straight over her head.

Her descent slowed just enough for her to get a good, long look at the spiny branches waiting to impale her. She twisted her dangling body, desperately trying to maneuver away from the trees' gleaming limbs, but to no avail. Her course was set straight for a tall, poplar-shaped tree with wild, cork-screwing branches.

*If only Nezzie had let go sooner*, she thought. With speed born of mortal regret, her brain calculated that, had the strix released her two seconds earlier, she would have sailed right under the lower boughs of the forest. However, her current rate of travel meant a short, skin-shredding journey through the razor-leafed woods right before her soft, organ-filled belly collided with the sharp end of a silver branch. Skewered like so much meat.

Branwen knew she didn't stand a chance. She'd seen the way Aello had looked at her. The blood-lipped bird and her flock would pick her bones clean. She would never reach the King. She would never find a way home. She'd never see her family again. They'd never even know what had happened to her. She'd be gone forever—just like Eirlys.

*No.* The word reverberated through Branwen's skull. Something inside her snapped—not into pieces, but into *place.* Her will steeled. *I killed the Cù Sìth. I've survived red caps and kobolds and púkas and dwarves. Since coming here, I've turned potential enemies into allies and together we escaped the Red Keep and defeated the Devouring Dark. I will not be done in by harpies. I will* not *disappear.*

She looked up, staring at the thin strands of hair around her wrists. She could feel the power in them struggling to keep her afloat. The faint *zing* against her skin had turned into a constant prickling current that encircled her wrists and radiated down her arms. If only she had something to cut the loops—then, she'd drop like a stone! It would be a bumpy way down, but she'd miss the spear-like branch entirely. She remembered the jagged iron keys still stowed in her right pocket, but she couldn't reach them as long as her arms were held above her head. Branwen looked around for another option. The forest's emerald leaves were probably sharp enough to do the job, but, again, the positioning of her hands made grabbing them impossible, and the likelihood of any stray leaves cutting through both braids by accident was slim.

*There* has *to be a way!* Branwen thought. *I just need to free* one *hand! Could I burn the braids?* she wondered in desperation, but she knew she didn't have that kind of control over her magic. Not yet. Right now, she struggled just to focus beyond the panic and chaos of her surroundings.

Above her, she could hear Nezzie's shouts of pain and defiance as the strix fought with the harpy Aello. The other two circled nearby, watching events unfold with vicious glee in their eyes. Branwen recognized one of them from the Keep—the flame-haired harpy who'd helped Aello destroy the gate, crushing eleven helpless girls beneath its debris. *Sorcha*. The harpy's name burned in her mind.

The strix was doomed. Aello was only playing with her, taking her time until the final blow. *And I'm doomed, too*, Branwen thought, her mind whirring. If she could distract some of the harpies, Nezzie might have a chance to escape—a slim chance, but still a chance, which was better than what she had now. *And* w*hat difference does it make if a harpy kills me or I get impaled by a branch?* Branwen told herself. *I'll still be dead, either way.*

She needed to act fast. Any second now, she would duck under the cover of emerald-leafed trees—out of sight and out of easy reach of the harpies. Branwen only had a moment to provoke the woman-faced birds into action, so how...? Inspiration struck in the form of her little sister, Magrid, sticking out her tongue, putting her thumbs in her ears, and waggling her small fingers. Taunting. *Of course!*

"Hey!" Branwen shouted, trusting in her years as an older sister to provide the rest. "Leave her alone, you—you fat, ugly chickens!"

*That* got their attention. The unfamiliar harpy shrieked her indignation, but it was Sorcha whose wings snapped shut with a clap of thunder as she dove after Branwen. The harpy plummeted, zooming past her fellow fiends with murder carved into her porcelain features.

Branwen sucked in a terrified breath. *Too close!* Sorcha flew much faster than she'd anticipated—faster even than Aello. She thought the flame-haired bird would simply barrel into her with talons extended and ready to disembowel, but at the last instant, the harpy spread her wings, slowing so she didn't shoot past Branwen and smash through the glinting, green overgrowth. The harpy came in at an angle, catching hold of Branwen's right arm in mid-flight.

The creature's claws punctured the sides of her wrist, and Branwen flailed from the pain. Her movements jerked her left arm forward just as the harpy sought to grab it, too, and the bird missed by a mere fraction of an inch. The tip of creature's longest outstretched claw hooked the thin braid of hair around Branwen's wrist.

*Please, break-break-break-break-*break! Branwen's mind screamed as she watched the loop pull taut—then snap! *Yes!* She yanked her newly-liberated arm down and tried to stretch it across her body, reaching for the iron keys in her pocket on the opposite side. The tips of her fingers brushed tantalizingly close to the iron chain, but she couldn't quite grasp it. Then, it was too late.

Branwen curled her freed, left arm over her face, trying to protect herself from knife-sharp leaves as she and the flame-haired harpy plunged beneath the edge of the forest canopy. Silver branches reached out and their emerald leaves smacked against Branwen's shoulder, slicing the sleeve of her dress to ribbons. Beneath the fabric, blood bloomed. Tendrils of scarlet trickled down her arm and pooled in the cradle of her elbow.

Sorcha laughed at the sight, her black eyes glittering. She swerved, slinging Branwen like a pendulum toward the nearest razor-leafed tree, but this time, Branwen was ready. She thrust out her free arm, and her hand closed around a cluster of leaves, ripping them loose as she flew by. Their glass-like edges cut deep into her palm, just above the unicorn's silver scar, but she didn't let go.

Branwen swung her bloody fistful of leaves upward, slashing with the pieces that protruded from between her fingers. At first, they clattered across the harpy's metallic feathers, but then Branwen felt something give beneath the leaves' sharp edges. The harpy screamed, thrashing wildly, and Branwen felt the bird's grip on her other wrist weaken. She looked up.

The harpy's foot dangled—half-severed—from the rest of her feathered leg. Branwen had cut most of the creature's tendons in that first swipe and the harpy now held onto her by the strength of only two claws. Branwen wasted no time—she swung again, slicing through the thin, hollow bones above Sorcha's ankle.

The harpy's foot fell and so did Branwen, plunging down through the forest's canopy with one arm still held straight in the air as the failing magic of Nezzie's braid tried to keep her aloft. Above her, she heard Sorcha's terrible shrieking and the crash of metallic wings against the glass treetops as the sudden release of her weight must have rocketed the red-haired harpy upward.

*Yes!* Branwen thought, rejoicing in the reprieve, but she knew everything was far from over. Emerald leaves cut her skin, leaving trails of blood behind as she half-glided, half-fell between the forest's grasping silver limbs. Ahead of her and fast approaching, she could see another dreaded tree. Thanks to the harpy's unintentional intervention, she had missed the first gut-skewering branch, but now the jagged limbs of this new tree aligned with her throat. *Great.*

*Only one option*, she thought in desperation. She reached up and cut the loop of hair from her other wrist. The effect was immediate.

The full force of gravity took over and she fell straight down. Wind whooshed around her, roaring in her ears, as she zipped by the deadly silver branch. Impalement averted, Branwen's thoughts jumped to the next crisis: landing. Instinctively, she flung aside the leaf shards she held and tucked her head into the curl of her arms. She bent her knees mid-air, bracing for impact. Just before she slammed her eyes shut, she caught a glimpse of something strange and wonderful.

She'd been so focused on Nezzie's and her own peril that she hadn't given any thought to Destin. Now, a single image burned hopeful behind her eyelids: the merrow darting through the woods, leaping over fallen logs and rocky outcroppings. His long legs devoured the distance between them, rushing to her aid.

*Not fast enough*, Branwen thought, then hit the ground with a joint-jarring crunch.

Her knees buckled with an explosion of pain, pitching her forward. Branwen managed to twist her torso at the last second and narrowly avoided a collision with the trunk of the silver tree. Bronze roots scraped her forearms as she landed, but her head remained protected from the brunt of the fall.

"Up, up up!" she heard Destin yell, his voice growing louder as he drew near. "Get up!"

Branwen struggled to obey. Every bone in her body ached and her muscles screamed as she tried to push herself off the ground, but she did it anyway. With a vengeful, one-footed harpy still loose in the woods, she knew her very life was at stake if she didn't *move.*

The forest spun as Branwen pulled herself upright, leaning against the tree trunk for support. She'd nearly recovered her balance, when something strong clamped around her arm. Branwen shrieked, desperately flailing and clawing for the terrifying second it took her to realize it was a *hand* and not a taloned foot gripping her.

"Go!" Destin commanded, pushing her deeper into the woods. He stayed close behind her, blocking the way back.

His momentum carried Branwen forward a few steps, but her conscience wouldn't let her go any further.

"But—Nezzie!" she protested, digging her heels into the forest's loamy soil. "We can't just leave her!"

"Don't worry about Nezzie right now," Destin said, his voice sharp as he forced her onward, yet Branwen caught a glimpse of pain burning in his yellow eyes. "Worry about *us.* Any second now, that harpy you wounded is going to come back—with *friends*."

*I guess my plan worked a little too well,* Branwen thought, holding her wrist where Sorcha's claw had dug into her flesh. Her eyes darted up to the forest canopy. The leaves rustled with the sound of broken glass and, above it, she could hear the slice of harpy feathers cutting through the wind.

"If they're coming after us, then maybe Nezzie can escape... right?" She wanted to hope for the best, but her experiences in the Sídhe gave her plenty of doubt, which Destin did nothing to dispel.

"Even with the others gone," he said, "Aello is more than a match for Nezzie." Destin's jaw clenched and his eyes fluttered closed, damming back tears before they snapped open again, now lit with a new fire. "But she won't kill her," he declared. "Not yet. Celaeno will want to torture her first."

*What a comfort,* thought Branwen.

The merrow's gait hitched for half a second as he fished something out of his back pocket. "Here, I picked this up after you fell. If you want a chance at surviving, take it. By all rights, it's yours, anyway." Destin thrust the severed harpy foot in her direction. "Harpy claws can slice through nearly anything. They won't burn like your iron, but they're longer, sharper—they'll cut deeper."

*And do more immediate damage*, Branwen thought, following the merrow's logic. Still, she cringed as she grabbed the back of Sorcha's severed foot with her right, uninjured hand, locking her fingers between the long, eagle-like talons. The scaly flesh still felt warm and pliable against her skin, but the claws were one of her more reliable means of defense against the viscous birds and she wasn't about to go against them unarmed. The iron keys she let remain in her pocket, afraid she might drop them if she tried to wield them with her leaf-sliced left hand.

Then, Branwen and Destin ran on, darting between the silvery trees. The branches thickened and the under-canopy rose as they dove deeper into the forest. Minutes passed. Branwen kept her eyes downward, concentrating on her footing in the unfamiliar woods, but her ears were tuned to the slightest sound. Above them, she could hear the faint *sschick, sschick* of sharpening knives; however, the noise grew no louder as she and the merrow raced through the forest.

Soon, Destin slowed. His eyes flicked upward and Branwen followed his gaze, watching the gentle swaying of the forest's upper boughs.

"Where are they?" the merrow muttered. The short fins on his jaw flashed, their webbing stretched taut in agitation. "The harpies should have attacked by now."

Branwen tilted her head from side to side, listening for a pattern in the harpies' wing beats. *Louder means closer and softer means further away,* she thought, but the noise she heard was cyclical. First, loud for two beats, silence for two beats, then soft for two beats. Repeat. *Silence is soaring,* Branwen realized and the pattern suddenly made terrible sense.

"The harpies are circling," she said. "Waiting on us. Why?"

Her eyes grew wide as she turned to look at the merrow for answers—this wasn't her world; she couldn't comprehend the motives behind such foreign creatures—but Destin only shuddered under the weight of her gaze.

"It's because of Celaeno," he said at last. "She *knows* we're here. She knows we're close and she's *waiting*."

"What?" Branwen sputtered. "How? I thought you said she wouldn't be able to *see* us."

"She can't," the merrow insisted. "It's not possible unless..." Destin put a hand over his eyes, then slowly dragged it down his face in a gesture of realization and despair. "She's looking for the blind spots," he said. "Celaeno can't *see* us, but she can *see* around us. Your human presence creates a void that she must be able to track. I should have thought—damn it!"

The merrow lashed out, swinging his fist at the nearest tree. Branwen heard his knuckles crack on impact, but they weren't the only thing broken. Tiny fissures radiated through the silver bark beneath his hand. Flecks of metal chipped off, hitting the ground in a series of quiet *plink*s.

"Destin...." Branwen reached out a tentative hand, then stopped, not sure of what she meant to do. Comfort him? On what authority? How could she ease his pain in any way—she whose very presence was the reason they were in this situation in the first place? The moment passed and Branwen let her arm drop just as Destin turned around.

He stared at the forest floor for a long moment. When he spoke, his voice was incredibly calm and even. "This is all my fault. I wanted to be free. I wanted Nezzie to be free. I should have never...." The merrow closed his eyes and his mouth pinched tight as he shook his head.

*Never what?* Branwen wondered. *Never left the court? Never helped me? Never agreed to flee?* Now was not the time she wanted him to have regrets, not when she was otherwise lost and alone in a strange forest with death-dealing harpies circling above her. Yet, when he looked up, Branwen didn't feel the sting of accusation in his eyes, but the low smolder of determination.

"Aello will take Nezzie to the Aegis Tree for judgment," the merrow told her. "She knows I'll try to save her."

Branwen nodded. She thought she understood. "It's a trap."

"Yes."

"And you're going anyway."

Destin didn't answer, but Branwen supposed it hadn't really been a question. Of course, he was going. His continued silence told her she, too, had a decision to make.

*This is it,* her dark thoughts whispered. *This is what you feared, what you've been dreading, all along.* Branwen knew that until now she had mostly let her circumstances dictate her actions, always choosing the path that she thought had the highest outcome of her own personal survival. Even her reckless plan to escape from the Red Keep, even her defeat of the Dark, had been born in the face of a greater threat—death. Until now she had been willing to risk everything just to live. To live was *hope*. To live was the possibility of returning *home*, no matter how slim. To live was to see her *family* again, no matter what it took. To live...

*What are you willing to become?* the darkness within her questioned. *This is when you must decide: who* are *you? Are you willing to go with Destin to rescue Nezzie knowing you will likely die a horrible death? Or will you abandon them and attempt to find the King's Court on your own before Celaeno sends her harpies back to kill you? Will you continue to throw away the lives of those around you just so long as* you *have a chance to survive? Or will you sacrifice everything you've worked for so far to appease the guilt within your soul? Was Ginny's life lost in vain?*

*NO!* The fire in Branwen's heart roared, rejecting her own dark voice and searing it from her mind. *I will* not *die—and* no one else *will die for me! I will find a way. I have* always *found a way.* That *is my choice.*

Branwen straightened her shoulders, pulling herself up tall, then thrust her arm out before her, gesturing toward the depths of the forest. She still held the severed harpy foot clenched between her fingers as she told Destin, "Lead on."

# Chapter 15

Destin plunged ahead, and Branwen followed close behind him. Growing dizzy with the twists and turns as they navigated the forest, she put a hand on the merrow's shoulder to steady herself. When she regained her balance, she didn't let go, but kept her arm outstretched like a tether between them. Destin didn't stop or slow for her; instead, he started calling out directions—left, right, straight—warning her before he made any sudden changes in their path. With his help, Branwen no longer struggled to maintain their swift pace, and the two made bounding strides into the woods.

Above them, she could still hear the steady shearing sound of harpy wings, muffled only by the soft clink of emerald leaves swaying in the breeze. Then—*boom, crash*—the forest's under-canopy shattered as a dark shape burst through. Neither she nor Destin had time to duck before the vibrant green shards rained down, their jagged edges catching on the creases of skin and clothing. A sharp shower pelted Branwen's scalp and she felt the warm itch of blood trickle through her hair.

When she looked up, she saw Aello weaving between the forest boughs with short, powerful flaps of her wings. The strix dangled from her talons, as limp as Colwen's rag doll.

"Nezzie!" Destin lunged after the flighted figures, but his long legs were no match for the airborne harpy.

Aello laughed, her voice oozing with devious satisfaction. "Too slow," she taunted. "Your lover's fate belongs to Celaeno now, but my sister might—*might*—be merciful...for the right price." The harpy's wild eyes flicked pointedly toward Branwen. Aello grinned, satisfied that her meaning had been made perfectly clear, then she shot upward, dragging Nezzie through the razored under-canopy again. The strix cried out as the foliage cut her flesh.

Destin hissed a curse between his teeth and ran. He tore through the underbrush without regard to stabbing branches and slicing leaves, but the harpy was gone—disappeared through the dense cover of the forest. Branwen caught a glimpse of red flashing over the hole punched into the canopy, and knew Sorcha followed directly behind Aello. However, the continuing clatter of wings told her the third harpy had stayed behind, keeping watch over her and the merrow's pursuit.

"Wait!" she called out. Branwen bolted after Destin, but the merrow had already come to a panting halt. She caught up quickly.

"Which way? Which way?" Destin muttered, his eyes frantically scanning the air and the ground. His movements grew more desperate with each passing second, putting Branwen's nerves on edge.

"What do you mean, *which* way?" she asked with a terrible feeling settling in her stomach. "They're still going to the Aegis Tree, aren't they? I thought you knew where that was."

Destin laughed, the sound sharp and desolate as it escaped his lips. "The Aegis Tree doesn't have a set location," he said. "Only the avian fae can find it easily. As queen of the Shard

Forest, Celaeno can move the Tree at will, so long as it remains within the bounds of her land. I was following Nezzie," he continued. "I could sense her familiar magic, but she's so far away now. Aello saw to that. Nothing flies faster than a harpy."

"But Aello and Sorcha still want us to follow them," Branwen observed, gesturing upward to the faint clashing of harpy wings. "They left the other one here like"—she blurted the first thing that came to mind—"like a sheepdog to herd us, right? So there has to be a way."

Destin shook his head. "Aello left that harpy here to toy with us—toy with *me*. The harpies are all sisters, in name and in power, and this one's presence is muddying Aello's tracks. On a good day, I might be able to distinguish one harpy's magic from another, but with the iron-scorch dulling my senses, it's impossible. I can't even track them like I can track Nezzie. There's no link for me to—"

His words cut off so abruptly that Branwen thought he'd choked on his own despair, but when she looked she saw the merrow staring at her right hand—the one that still clung to the severed harpy foot. With all her attention focused on following Destin through the glass-sharp forest, she'd forgotten about Sorcha's claws.

"Take it," she insisted, thrusting the foot out to him. She barely had time to loosen her grasp before the merrow snatched it from her.

"What Nezzie and I have, we forged over years," he said as he cracked the harpy's knuckle-bones and twisted. "Trading debt for debt and magic for magic until it wasn't always just mine or hers. Sometimes, it became *ours*." He broke off each vicious talon and tossed the claws back to Branwen who caught them with fumbling fingers, then stuffed them into her pockets. "But there's more than one way to create a bond like that," the merrow added, brandishing the bare-knuckled foot. "Even if it's only for a little while."

Destin smiled, his eyes burning with an eerie yellow fire. Then, he tilted his head back, stretched open his shark-toothed maw, and dropped the foot in.

Branwen's stomach lurched, throwing bile at the back of her mouth. She nearly vomited at the splintery, bone-crunching sounds Destin made as he chewed. Fatty marrow dripped from the corner of his mouth and he licked it up. His head bobbed as he swallowed, forcing large chunks down his throat.

"What kind of *bond* is *that*?" She spat out the words, then covered her mouth, afraid she might spit out something else.

Destin grimaced, too, rubbing his neck to move things along. "The most basic," he answered when his throat cleared. "The bond between consumer and consumed, where one literally becomes a part of the other. It's very strong, but short-lived, so we have to act fast."

The merrow closed his eyes and pressed a hand to his stomach. He turned slowly on his heels, first left, then right, until finally he stopped. "That way." His eyes snapped open and he pointed north.

They didn't run at first, but gathered speed as Destin became more and more sure of the pull of magic in his gut. After a few minutes, Branwen noticed he no longer hesitated at every crook in the forest. They kept a steady pace north by northeast. The constant *shriing* of harpy feathers and intermittent shrieks and squawks following them from above the forest confirmed the truth of their path.

"Nezzie...." She heard Destin whisper suddenly, his voice hissing in her ear as he loped beside her. The merrow veered sharply west, exploding into a full sprint.

*Wait!* Branwen thought, but didn't waste her breath on futile words. Instead, she ducked her head and bolted after him. Spiny underbrush tore at her skirts and nipped at her bare arms and ankles, but she didn't dare stop for fear of losing sight of Destin in the maze of the forest.

Then, just as suddenly, Destin stopped, grabbing onto the nearest tree trunk and swinging around to slow his momentum. Branwen zoomed on, her feet frantically skipping over the bronze roots that jutted in her path. She saw the candle-yellow of Destin's eyes flare as she stumbled past and the merrow's pale blue arm shot out. His fingers wrapped around her wrist. Branwen's feet flew out from under her as Destin yanked her back. The two skidded a dozen feet before landing in a jumbled pile near a line of slim, brassy trees, so different from the jagged silver and emerald ones that made up the rest of the forest.

*Almost like they mark some sort of boundary,* Branwen thought absently as she and Destin untangled themselves. The merrow collapsed against one of the trees to catch his breath. Branwen grabbed a low branch in an attempt to pull herself up, but only managed halfway before she gave up and plunked down next to Destin.

"What...was that?" she asked him between hiccuping breaths. The collision had sent her diaphragm into spasms.

Destin lifted a hand and waved, gesturing behind them to the stand of densely-packed saplings, but words still escaped him. Branwen saw that blue blood decorated the merrow's knuckles—the result of when he'd punched one of the silver trees earlier. His movements flicked droplets onto their current tree, coloring the brass bark an eerie shade of green. His other arm lay across his lap, its sea-drenched bandage sliding down to expose the top half of his wound. The saltwater from Destin's swim across the bay should have slowed the spread of his infection, but their wild run through the forest seemed to have reversed any good effects. The once-gray wound had blackened and festered, oozing murky green pus around the edges. Dark tendrils continued to snake further up his arm and shoulder, mapping the course of his poisoned veins.

*Is it too late already?* Branwen wondered. *Was he doomed from the start?*

Destin caught Branwen's line of sight and hastily readjusted the bandage, unable to contain a wince as the damp cloth dragged over his inflamed skin.

"It's Nezzie," he said at last, ignoring her worried glance. "She's here. Just beyond these trees. And so are a hundred harpies."

Branwen sat straight up, her concern for Destin temporarily overridden by their greater plight. "A hundred! How are we supposed to—" She shook her head, unable to finish the thought. Supposed to what? Rescue Nezzie? Get out of the forest alive? Return home? Each outcome seemed increasingly remote. *You already knew your chance of success was slim at best, but you agreed to help Destin anyway*, Branwen reminded herself. *Nothing about* that *has changed.*

She looked at Destin again—at the grim, yet determined set of his mouth, at the spiny fins jutting along his clenched jaw. She could see the ragged pulse in his neck, the artery there thrumming beneath his pale blue skin as his body still fought to recover from their mad dash through the woods. Every beat brought the taint of iron closer and closer to the merrow's heart, yet the flame of his candle-yellow gaze never wavered—never gave up. *And neither can I*, she thought.

"Tell me you have a plan," she said, her voice nearly begging.

"I do," Destin confirmed—too quickly, Branwen thought, noting the way the merrow's gaze slid away from hers briefly.

A sudden seed of dread sprouted in her stomach, watered by her intuition, and she asked, "I'm not going to like this plan, am I?"

Destin glanced back at her, then, heavy lids hooding his eyes. "No," he said, "Probably not."

Branwen took a deep breath. She wanted to close her own eyes, to pretend she wasn't in this strange, wretched world if only for an instant, but she knew denial would do her no good. She let out her breath in a gusty sigh, then straightened her shoulders, bracing herself for whatever the merrow might say. After all, any plan had to be better than nothing, right? To Destin, she said, "Tell me, anyway."

The merrow obliged. "Once in a lifetime, any fae of the Sídhe may petition the King for a favor," he began. "It doesn't matter what it is or where they are—the King's magic ensures he'll hear them. Once his Favor is called, the King's Treaty is invoked, and the petitioner and any parties directly involved are under the King's protection and must then be allowed a fair chance to proceed to his Court for judgment."

Whatever Branwen had expected Destin to say, that wasn't it. She stared at the merrow, stunned, as the implications of his words slowly sank in.

"Do you mean to tell me that you or Nezzie could have called on the King's Favor *this whole time*?" she asked, her voice rising, but Destin cut her off, dousing the outrage kindling within her with cold, harsh truth.

"It's not that simple," the merrow stated. "If it were, don't you think every prisoner at the Red Keep would have called on the King to rescue them from that place? But they didn't, did they? Even when they were being slaughtered by redcaps or sacrificed to the unicorn or thrown into the Devouring Dark. Not a single prisoner, guilty or innocent, called on the King—*why?*

"Because the King hasn't granted his Favor in over a hundred years," Destin continued, his pale yellow eyes boring into her. "Like everything else in the Sídhe, the King's Favor must have a price. He cannot grant it without receiving something of equal value in return. The greater the Favor, the higher the cost—those are the Rules of the Sídhe, and even the King can't defy them. That's why Nezzie and I didn't invoke the King's Favor when we fled Celaeno the *first* time. We already knew we had nothing to offer that would satisfy the Law of Equal Exchange and guarantee our acceptance into his Court. As fae, we would only get *one shot* at earning the King's Favor. When we failed to obtain it, he would have no choice but to send us back to the harpy court where we would receive whatever punishment Celaeno deemed fit for our desertion."

*Punishment? He means torture and then death—if they're lucky,* Branwen translated even as her mind soaked up the rest of the merrow's words, trying to make sense of the deluge of information.

"If calling the King's Favor wouldn't work then, what makes you think it would work now?" she questioned. "Nothing has changed. You're still in the same—oh." Suddenly, she understood why the merrow had said she wouldn't like his new plan. "It's me." *Again*, Branwen thought. "You want *me* to be the price for the King's Favor."

"Yes, that was the idea," Destin readily admitted. "If we had reached the King's Court on our own merit like Nezzie and I initially planned, the three of us could have claimed asylum without invoking the King's Favor, but"—he gestured to the line of thin, bronze trees in front of them, their only shield against the eyes of a hundred harpies—"that option is clearly beyond us. Right now, calling on the King's Favor is the only move we have left that is not outright suicide."

"But will it be enough?" Branwen interjected. "Will *I* be enough? You said it had to be an equal exchange."

The merrow shrugged, wincing at the movement of his iron-scorched shoulder. "We'll have to hope so. Humans are rare in the Sídhe," he explained, "and the King has always been oddly fascinated by them. Also, never underestimate a faerie grudge. When the King learns of Celaeno's interest in you, he'll want you to join his Court even more, simply out of spite. That's why offering you gives the best chance of survival, of freedom...for *all* of us."

Branwen nodded in grim agreement. There didn't seem to be any other option—not one where she came out alive, anyway. *I cut off Sorcha's foot*, she reminded herself, patting the hard, curved shapes of the harpy's claws in her pockets. *I saw the look in her eyes. She'll kill me unless I find a way to escape, and this is* it. *Instead of being Celaeno's prisoner, I will be captive to the King.* She had to hope that was the better choice. She just *had* to.

"What will happen to me?" she asked. "The King, if he accepts...will he ever let me go home?"

Destin was quiet for a moment before he spoke, and in the silence, Branwen's heart plummeted.

"I don't know," the merrow admitted at last. "The King is a Firstborn—the *first* of the Firstborn. He has lived since the dawning of the Sídhe. I can't begin to fathom why he does what he does, but I know this: whatever he chooses for you will be far better than what the harpies have in store. If all goes well, he'll accept the three of us into his Court and we'll be under his protection, even from Celaeno. And if not...."

Destin didn't need to finish; Branwen knew. She could still hear the steady, grating wing beats of the harpy circling overhead. Waiting on them. Waiting *for* them.

"How do we do this, then?" she asked, sitting up in attention. Beside her, she felt Destin's body relax for the briefest instant before he leaned forward eagerly.

"We need to get close to Nezzie," he said. "Since she is the one Celaeno captured, she must be the one to call for the King's Favor. As the price for the Favor, you just need to be in her line of sight, but I need to be *touching* her for the magic to include me in the contract. Nezzie knows that—she won't call the King's Favor without me. Your proximity should prevent Celaeno from *seeing* any of our intentions until too late. She'll think I've come to try to trade you for Nezzie like Aello implied, but by the time she realizes the truth, we'll all be protected under the King's Treaty until his Favor is decided."

"What if Celaeno does *see*?" Branwen had to ask. The queen of the harpy court had managed it before by looking for blank spots, Destin had said. What if she could do something like that again? Another dreadful thought entered Branwen's mind and she spoke it without thinking, "What if Nezzie's already...?" She saw the look on Destin's face and couldn't bring herself to finish.

The spiny fins along the merrow's jaw flashed and his tallow-colored eyes hardened to topaz. "She won't," he said. "And she's not—I would *feel* it. Nezzie's alive and she's going to stay that way. I'll make sure of it."

The merrow's tone brokered no arguments. Branwen nodded, taking a deep breath. She didn't know if Destin had an actual plan for that eventuality, but it didn't really matter. Whatever the case, their only way *out* was *forward.*

The sharp flutter of feathers told her their harpy guard had finally abandoned her post to join the others at the Aegis Tree. Beyond the thin curtain of forest that hid them from view, she could hear the clatter of knives and a dozen raucous calls of greeting. She recognized the smooth purr of Aello's voice sliding through the clamor. Branwen couldn't make out the words, but under the dark harpy's influence, the others quieted, and the woods grew somber with silence.

Then, a new voice came, vaulting through the trees and breaking the soundless void with a timbre as rich and dark as ebony.

"I know you're there, my...*lovelies*." The words oozed into Branwen's ears and seeped into her pores. "You might as well join us."

Destin's jaw clenched. "Celaeno." He muttered the name like a curse. The merrow glared through the veil of trees with such intensity that Branwen thought his candle-light gaze would catch the whole forest on fire. "Let's go," he said, offering her his unscorched hand.

Branwen grabbed it without hesitation, and the merrow surged to his feet, using his momentum to pull her up behind him. His grip loosened as they stood, releasing her, but Branwen clung on, squeezing his hand tight. A look of understanding passed between them, and together, they strode through the thin line of brassy trees that separated them from the harpy court.

She blinked as they emerged on the other side, startled by the sudden light after what felt like ages in the emerald-tinted forest. A vast clearing opened before them and in the center stood a massive white tree. Sunlight bounced off the ivory bark and burned through diamond leaves veined with gold. Branwen put a hand to her eyes, shading them from the brilliance. That's when she saw the dark blot crowning the otherwise radiant tree.

At the top of the tree on one of the tallest branches, loomed the harpy queen. The sun painted her black as it shone behind her, casting her into silhouette. Scores of other harpies nested beneath her, decorating the Aegis Tree like nightmarish ornaments. Branwen didn't see Nezzie or Aello anywhere.

"Greetings," called the harpy queen as she spread her wings. The swords of her feathers clashed together and she took flight with the sound of battle.

Now that Celaeno was no longer back-lit by the sun, Branwen could see the harpy queen clearly as she descended. Where Aello was dark, Celaeno was pure light. Her porcelain skin glowed. Wreathes of gold and diamonds wove through her white-blonde hair which billowed like a cloak behind her. Lips as bright and soft as peonies smiled down on them as her corn-flower-blue eyes glittered with excitement. Her golden feathers marveled in the sun. She circled the Aegis Tree, once, twice, then landed on a branch just high enough to force Branwen and Destin to crane their necks to look at her.

"The second prodigal has returned," the queen declared, her lips still pressed into a gentle smile as she looked down at the merrow. "And you've brought the human, too. How delightful!" As she spoke, her intense gaze swiveled over to Branwen, and the harpy's petal-soft mouth split into a razor-sharp grin, exposing the same vicious teeth as her sister.

Branwen's spine cringed and her skin crawled as though preparing to flee her body under Celaeno's dark scrutiny, but she held her ground, gripping Destin's hand with fierce determination. He returned the gesture with equal strength, never once taking his eyes from the Aegis Tree; they darted from branch to gleaming branch as he searched for Nezzie and the dark harpy Aello. By his taut expression, Branwen knew he must not have seen them yet, either.

"Where's Nezzie?" the merrow demanded. A muscle under his eye twitched as he stared back at Celaeno, but that was the only outward sign of the gut-wrenching revulsion Branwen knew he must feel toward the harpy queen.

"So impatient," Celaeno chided, shaking her glorious head. Her hair fell like moonbeams across the golden feathers of her shoulders. "You'll see your dear Nestyria soon enough," came her ominous promise, "but first I want to have a look at *her.*"

The queen tilted her head, pinning Branwen with her bright stare. As she watched, the harpy's eyes faded, first the left, then the right, until they both shone milky white. Only Celaeno's pupils stayed black, sucking Branwen into their twin abysses. Magic buzzed in the air, tickling the hairs on the back of her neck. She could almost see it—not with her eyes, but with some other sense. Curling tendrils of power radiated out from the harpy, casting impossible shadows in Branwen's mind's eye, yet none of them actually touched her. They parted before her, flowing around her, instead. She looked up and saw the harpy's magic did the same for Destin, hovering just beyond his pale blue skin. When she caught his eye, the merrow flashed her a grim smile.

*She really can't* see *us,* Branwen thought, but the feeling of astonished relief faded quickly. *Celaeno knows that, but she's looking anyway—why? What* else *can she* see*?*

Suddenly, the coils of magic retracted, converging on the harpy queen in a moment of frenzy. The magic glowed with an intense, near-visible light. *She's turned her power onto herself—she's looking at her own future!* Branwen realized, then Celaeno blinked. The harpy's eyes returned to their vibrant blue and the tendrils vanished.

"Interesting," the harpy queen said, clicking her tongue against her teeth. She looked at Branwen with an eerie, simpering smile. "I like you," Celaeno told her, but the words sent a chill through Branwen's bones. "I heard what you did at my Keep," the harpy continued in the same deadly sweet tone. "By all accounts, you are resourceful, and I can see there's a fire in your eyes. You've shown a lot of pluck—all traits admired in my court..."

*Where is this going?* Branwen wondered, taken aback. She could feel Destin tense beside her. The slight flick of the fins along his face belied his carefully crafted stoicism. Apparently, he didn't think getting complements from the harpy queen was a good sign, either.

Celaeno continued without a single change in her cloying expression, "...which is why it's such a shame that I've *seen* enough to know your presence here is against my best interest."

A faint, treacherous hope bloomed in Branwen's chest. "Does that mean you'll let me go?" she dared to ask the harpy queen. Half of her truly wanted to know the answer, while the other half knew she was only buying time for Destin to continue searching for Nezzie.

Celaeno laughed, a high, fluting sound that filled Branwen's heart with dread. "Of course not!" she said. "I can't have you running loose in the Sídhe, blocking my Sight with your humanity. Besides"—Celaeno gestured to Branwen and Destin's clasped hands with the tip of her wing—"it's clear you have colluded with traitors to my court. Together, you led an insurrection at the Red Keep, freeing my prisoners, my *enemies*, so you shall share in their punishment. But, I am not without mercy," the harpy continued, her eyes gleaming with a vicious light. "Your bravery has earned you this much—I will allow my sister Aello to decide your fate and the fates of your companions, not I. Her methods will be far more *humane*. That is my final judgment."

The harpy queen shuffled her feathers dismissively, then launched from her branch. With a few beats of her wings, she returned to the top of the Aegis Tree, but Branwen thought she could still see the blue glow of Celaeno's eyes, watching. She and Destin followed the harpy's gaze to the far branches of the Tree.

On the lowest bough perched Aello, her dark shape shrouded within the Aegis Tree's radiant light. On the ground beneath her, Branwen spied Nezzie's prone form. The strix's green and tawny coloring had blended in with the grass and dirt of the clearing, making her nearly impossible to detect.

Destin spied Nezzie at the same time and made to go to her, but Aello had other ideas. The dark harpy swooped down and grabbed the strix by the ropes of her braids. Nezzie cried out as the harpy's claws scraped the back of her neck, drawing fresh blood from the strix's already sliced and battered body.

Aello returned to her perch, dragging Nezzie with her. When she landed, the strix dangled beneath her, pinned to the same branch by the harpy's talons twining through her hair. The strix's toes barely touched the ground and her wings fluttered, trying to maintain her balance. One flap too many sent her into a spin. Branwen could see pain in Nezzie's owlish eyes as her braids twisted and the hairs pulled tight against her scalp.

"Let's play a game, shall we?" the honey-voiced harpy purred. Around her, the other harpies chattered with excitement.

Branwen could feel their fiery eyes weighing her, measuring out cuts of meat like a butcher. "How about Bloodybones? Or maybe Slitherskin?"

The nearby harpies cast their votes.

"Bones! Bones!" cried some. "We want to hear them crunch!"

"Tear them to ribbons in Slitherskin!" shouted others.

A shock of red caught Branwen's attention as Sorcha hobbled into view. "The human is *mine*," she growled, lifting her bloody stump of a leg. "I'm owed a flesh-debt!"

"Wait!" Destin stepped in front of Branwen. His hand still remained wrapped around hers. "I have a debt to collect first," he demanded, glaring at the gathering crowd of hungry harpies. "A life-debt owed to me—no claim can trump mine!"

"What is it, then?" snapped the red harpy. "Get on with it!"

Destin said nothing. Branwen watched in fascination as he turned to stare at Aello. For a moment, the harpy stared back. The longer she looked, the more agitated she became.

*Almost...nervous*, Branwen thought.

The bird flexed her grip on her perch and ruffled her wings, then Destin began to speak.

"By the Rules of the Sídhe, I, Destin, merrow of the Gaadin clan, claim life-debt on Aello, daughter of the North Wind—"

Aello shrieked, trying to drown out the merrow's voice. Her claws dug into the ivory tree bark, and ruby sap leaked out as thick and dark as blood. The harpy's wings crashed in protest, stirring up strong winds that ripped leaves from the Aegis Tree. Diamonds scattered on the ground, set ablaze by the light of the sun. Rainbows flashed into Branwen's eyes, nearly blinding her, but Destin led her forward through the wind and pelting leaves until they stood right under the furious harpy as he shouted.

"—in repayment for the murder of my father, Keiphas, son of the sea. Your life be spared for Nestyria's. Let her go!"

Branwen went momentarily deaf from Aello's scream, but the harpy had no choice except to comply. She released her hold on the strix's braids. Destin bolted, dropping Branwen's hand as he reached for Nezzie.

Aello might have been momentarily cowed, but Sorcha was under no such compunction, Branwen realized as she heard the vengeful bird's sudden cry of triumph. With Destin distracted and no longer at her side, Branwen was vulnerable and the harpy took full advantage, diving straight toward her with her unmaimed foot grasping and extended.

Branwen didn't have time to think; she reacted on pure instinct, spinning to the left to avoid the collision. Her hands plunged into her pockets, grasping the first things they touched—the harpy's own dismembered claws. She clasped them between her fingers, then lashed out.

She wasn't quick enough.

The flame-haired harpy swerved and smashed into her, the force of the impact flinging both of them to the ground. Branwen rolled away as fast as she could, trying to avoid the harpy's piercing talons, but she didn't get far. Powerful wings buffeted her from either side and sharp feathers scraped across her skin. She threw one arm over her head to protect her face and slashed out blindly with the other, knowing that in such close quarters the severed harpy claws would surely connect with avian flesh.

The first blow caught the harpy's outstretched foot, severing another toe, but it didn't matter; Sorcha was so full of fury Branwen doubted she felt any pain. With one hand, Branwen grabbed the toe from the grass, adding it to her arsenal as she continued to slash with her other hand. Despite her new injury, the frenzy of the harpy's attack only increased, forcing Branwen into a defensive position. She crouched with her hands over her head and her knees curled against her chest, making herself as small as possible, but it was no use. The harpy landed on her exposed back, pinning Branwen to the ground with her surprising bulk. Branwen screamed as Sorcha's talons ripped through the thick wool of her dress and gouged her flesh. Searing pain shot all the way along her spine as her skin split open, and she felt a hot gush of blood.

"Destin! Nezzie!" she shrieked in desperation. Every muscles strained as she looked toward the Aegis Tree, searching for the fae who were supposed to be her saviors. What was taking so long? Why hadn't the strix called King's Favor yet? Any second now, she expected Sorcha to lunge for the back of her neck, ready to bite through the bones and nerves at the base of her skull. She was running out of time!

She spotted Destin standing only yards away with his arms wrapped around the strix, supporting Nezzie with his whole frame. The strix clutched at his shoulder, sucking in horrible, ragged breaths. Her owlish eyes were black with pain and her right wing hung broken at her side. She looked barely conscious—let alone able to cry King's Favor. Despite that, Branwen could sense a faint *zing* of magic surrounding Nezzie.

*Destin is doing everything in his iron-weakened power to* heal *her*, she realized. *And it's working!* Hope flickered in her chest until Sorcha's malevolent laugh snuffed it out. *Too late!* she thought as fresh pain stabbed into her back. The flame-haired harpy had adjusted her now-three-toed grip on Branwen's skin, carving fresh lines into her flesh. She felt the harpy's rancid breath warming the back of her neck. In one last act of defiance, Branwen punched upward with her harpy-taloned fist, aiming to puncture one of Sorcha's eyes.

She missed and the harpy laughed again, pinning Branwen's arm down with edge of her bladed wings.

"You are *mine*," Sorcha whispered in her ear. "Time to pay your debts."

Branwen sobbed, slamming her eyes shut and burying her face into the grass of the clearing. *Mother, Papa—I'm so sorry!* She prayed, *Please, make it quick.* Her fingers grasped at the ground as though she could throw it over herself like a blanket, her childhood protection against monsters. Only these monsters were *real*, and she could do nothing but brace herself for the death blow.

# Chapter 16

"Favor! We call King's Favor!"

The impossible gasp of Nezzie's voice punctuated the air followed by the flame-haired harpy's shriek of wordless fury. Branwen's eyes snapped open just as she felt the whoosh of blade-like wings scissoring over her head. The tips of Sorcha's wicked talons pierced her skin as the harpy tightened her grip. Branwen could barely breathe from the pain. The stump of Sorcha's severed leg pressed into her other shoulder, hard and blunt and bony, but the final attack never came.

"The human is our oath-price. Release her or you will be in violation of the King's Treaty," Destin snapped. Branwen could see his bare feet out of the corner of her eye. "Death awaits those who break the King's laws."

"Rot and ruin on the King and his laws!" Sorcha spat back. Her voice dripped with vengeance and burned in Branwen's ears.

Around her, she could hear the other harpies gasp and murmur among themselves:

"She's cursed the King!"

"Fool!"

"If he finds out, he could have her head!"

Then, from high above, Celaeno's voice blotted out all others.

"Sorcha!"

The clamor of harpies stilled instantly. Branwen carefully craned her neck, risking a look upward as the queen took to the air once more. Her great golden wings folded and she plummeted, breaking her momentum at the last minute by a few strong flaps of her wings. The wind of her descent flattened the grass and made dervishes of the light, loamy dirt of the clearing. Celaeno settled on the ground. She looked smaller now that she wasn't amid the grandeur of the Aegis Tree—barely hip-height on Destin, Branwen guessed—however, the harpy queen was no less terrifying.

"It is treason to speak against the King," Celaeno told the flame-haired harpy. Her voice pounded like a judge's gavel and her eyes flashed tombstone-white for a second as she warned, "Never do it again."

Branwen couldn't see Sorcha on her back, but she felt the uneasy shift in the red harpy's weight and heard the slight ruffle of her feathers.

"Yes, my Lady," Sorcha said, her tone no longer harsh, but cowed. "Forgive me. I spoke only in anger."

"Anger can be a valuable asset," the harpy queen said, "but it's one you have always wielded poorly. Release the human as he said. By the Rules of the Sídhe, we must allow them to attempt an audience with the King."

Branwen could hardly believe what she'd heard. The harpies were letting them go! Destin's plan had worked. Euphoria flooded her veins as she felt the weight of the flesh-debted harpy lift from her back. The bird shuffled off, slicing further ribbons in Branwen's skin with her remaining three talons. Branwen bit her lip to keep in an agonized scream, then as soon as she could, she scrambled away.

Every movement ignited her back with pain. The skin felt hot and damp, so she knew she must be covered in blood, but she stood anyway, stuffing the harpy's severed claws back in her pockets to free her hands. Behind her, she heard the scuff of feet across dirt and knew Destin and Nezzie edged closer. Soon, a cool, shark-skinned hand touched her shoulder, leeching away the heat and pain.

Magic *zing*ed across her skin. She felt her flesh crawl as it tried to knit itself together, but the wounds refused to heal completely. She could hear Destin's labored breathing, though Nezzie's harsh wheezing had eased.

One glance at the merrow's pale skin and hollowed-out eyes told Branwen everything. She didn't fully understand the ways of magic, but she could clearly see Destin had drained much of his vital force to heal Nezzie in the last moment before Sorcha's attack. The strix's eyes were bright and her wings straight and unbroken.

With Nezzie no longer critical, he had turned his attention on Branwen, but she could see what it had cost him. Iron-scorch blackened the web of veins along the side of his neck.

"That's enough," she said, taking hold of Destin's hand. She pried it from her shoulder. The merrow made a small moue of protest, but he didn't fight her any further.

"That's right—don't bother wasting your energy," the harpy queen said, eyeing their brief exchange. "The King will not accept your gift."

"You don't know that," came Nezzie's swift and sharp reply. Defiance glared in her voice as she held Destin up, instead of the other way around. "You can't *see* that."

Celaeno shrugged, the slight shift of her feathers chiming in the air. "I don't need to *see* it. You aren't bringing anything the King doesn't already have. What need has he for another human?"

*Another?* Panic flooded Branwen's mind. Was the harpy right? The rarity of humans in the Sídhe added to her value, but if the King already had one, would she still be enough to buy their freedom?

Nezzie interrupted before her thoughts could go much further. "Need has nothing to do with it," the strix snipped. "Besides, that's *our* business, not yours."

The harpy queen stared at her for a long moment, tilting her head from side to side, but her eyes remained cornflower blue.

"So be it," Celaeno said at last. She turned her gaze to the Tree where her sister still perched. "Aello—you owe no more debts to this merrow?"

The dark harpy cringed at the thought. "He has no more hold over me," she confirmed. "I am free."

Celaeno nodded. "Good. Then, we can begin the *negotiations*." Branwen suppressed a shudder as the harpy queen looked back at them, her peony lips peeling back in a far-too-knowing smile. "In accordance with the King's Treaty, I am obligated to allow the three of you nothing more and nothing less than a fair chance to reach the King's Court, but what is 'fair,' I wonder?

"It is at least a day's journey to the Heart of the Sídhe," Celaeno continued. "I could let you try to make it there yourselves, but sadly I don't think our darling Destin would last that long." The harpy tutted softly, her features arranging themselves in a facade of concern as she watched the merrow. Her eyes belied the expression, however, gleaming with perverse glee as she told Destin, "Iron-scorch is *such* a nasty way to die."

Beside her, Branwen could sense the merrow tense—could feel the heat of his indignation rising from his skin. *But is it* anger *or* fever*?* the *iachäwr* in her wondered. She didn't dare take her eyes off Celaeno long enough to check. The return of the harpy's simpering smile told her enough.

Nezzie protested immediately. "That's hardly a fair offer when one of us is guaranteed death," the strix said, unable to keep her voice from quivering at the mention of the merrow's fate. She took a deep breath before she continued. "Destin is included in the King's Favor, too, and is subject to the same terms of the Treaty. The only 'fair' option is the one in which all three of us can survive."

"Yes, it does seem time is of the essence," Celaeno agreed—*too easily*, Branwen thought. *She is planning something.* The harpy didn't disappoint. "That is why I will offer you the Mirror Way," Celaeno continued. "It can take you to the very edge of the Shard Forest. From there, the King's Court is only one mile away, which I think is far more than a *fair* offer. I'm practically gifting you to the King, but in return, I have one condition."

"Name it," Nezzie demanded. Her patience for the harpy's theatrics had clearly worn thin, and Branwen understood why. With every moment they delayed, Destin weakened. The use of his magic had sped up the effects of the iron-scorch. Branwen could feel the merrow's muscles quiver as he stood beside her, fighting to suppress the agony of poison burning through his veins.

Celaeno smiled, her blue eyes glinting with devious delight. "Once you exit the Mirror Way, I will allow three minutes for you to cross the boundary of the King's Court unhindered by any fae of my court. During that time, Sorcha and Aello will remain with me at the Aegis Tree, forbidden from any interference. But after three minutes, if you haven't reached his Court, I will release my two sisters and they may do with you whatever they wish.

"I'm being generous, really," the harpy queen asserted. "A few minutes won't matter to me, but to you they are precious. They are your *last*. Remember—if you arrive at the King's Court, you must also face his judgment. Then, I will still *win* and you will still *die*."

Branwen swallowed. The harpy sounded so sure, but Nezzie appeared unfazed by the queen's proclamation. Her pale green eyes narrowed and her cherubic mouth pinched with resolution.

"We'll see," the strix said.

Celaeno paid no heed to her bravado. "This way, then," she commanded and started walking.

The harpy, fierce and free when flying, hobbled on the ground, her body bobbing from side to side with each flat-footed step. Her claws pierced the dirt as she trod, leaving two-inch divots in her wake, and Branwen tried not to think about the aching wounds in her back. Destin's efforts had taken away much of the pain, but she didn't know how long the magic's analgesic effect would last. She could still feel the stickiness of blood on her dress and the pull of skin beneath the damp fabric, reminding her that the wounds had not fully healed. Without proper attention, she knew they could fester, but that was the least of her worries. Branwen set her attention on surviving the next few moments.

She, Nezzie, and Destin followed the harpy queen around the edge of the Aegis Tree, circling its massive ivory trunk. When they passed under Aello's branch, the dark harpy hopped down, her wings cutting the air as she flapped them to control her descent. She landed so close behind Branwen that the harpy's talons caught the hem of her dress, shredding it.

Branwen flinched at the harpy's proximity, imagining her claws lashing out in revenge for Sorcha. The redheaded harpy remained at a distance, nursing her injured leg. However, Aello only smiled when she caught Branwen glancing back at her. The harpy gnashed her teeth suggestively, but otherwise did nothing.

*She'd kill me, too, if it weren't for the King's Favor,* Branwen thought, quickening her pace so that she nearly stepped on Nezzie and Destin's heels as the group curved around the base of the Aegis Tree.

A great crack split the back side of the Tree, marring the pristine bark. The fissure formed a small alcove, which the afternoon sun flooded, burning away the shadows from its hollow corners. Something else gleamed, nestled inside the once-hidden flaw of the Aegis Tree. Branwen nearly yelped as she saw the light flicker and caught movement from within the crevice.

*Another harpy!* Her heart slammed in her chest. Her fingers clenched around Sorcha's severed talons within her pockets. She would have backpedaled, but she knew the action would have forced her to collide directly into Aello. She had no choice but to keep walking.

As they drew nearer, realization dawned and Branwen felt her heartbeat slow from a raging gallop to a brisk trot. There was a harpy within the Tree all right—one with white-blonde hair and golden wings. Behind the harpy stood a green-eyed, tawny strix and a lanky merrow with skin the gray-blue color of a shallow sea. Branwen saw her own pale face and wide, green gaze staring back at her—a reflection off an eight-foot oval mirror mounted within the crack in the Tree.

Branwen sucked in a deep, shuddering breath.

*Mirror Way. Of course.*

She would have felt silly if she hadn't still been so terrified.

Celaeno approached the mirror first. She lifted one taloned foot and scratched strange symbols on the broad, glassy surface, then blew on them with a soft, gentle breath. The mirror fogged and then rippled, coming to life. Their reflections faded and a new scene replaced them: a wide, open road edged by ruby-studded trees and topaz undergrowth.

Branwen fought the urge to look behind her—she knew she would find none of the gemstone trees nor the dazzling white road that she saw in the mirror, but the rational part of her mind insisted that the image *must* be true—that was how real mirrors worked, after all. *But this is far from a real mirror,* she reminded herself and kept her gaze facing forward. She didn't want Nezzie or Destin to leave her sight for one second—not with Aello so eager at her heels.

"Go on," the harpy queen said, stepping aside, and Nezzie obeyed.

The strix shuffled forward, still supporting part of Destin's weight. A little bit of color had returned to the merrow's cheeks, but he looked far from recovered. Branwen huddled close on Nezzie's other side. Together, they stepped into the mirror.

A shiver of cold ran down Branwen's spine and she heard the sound of breaking glass as she passed through the barrier. She saw Destin flinch, and Nezzie's feathers ruffled. The strix stretched out her wings to insulate them both from the chill and sudden soft rain of silver shards. The glass fell to the ground, clinking against the small pile that lay at their feet. The shattered remains of emerald leaves were scattered among the debris. Beyond them, the silver trees of the Shard Forest glinted in the mid-afternoon sun.

*We burst out of the trees,* Branwen realized as she looked down at a small, jagged stump just behind her. The cracked silver bark reflected a dozen images of her face, and she thought again of what Celaeno had said. *The Mirror Way...does it work for* all *mirrors?* she wondered, dread filling her heart as she looked around the edge of the forest. Hundreds of silver and emerald trees shone back at her, each a potential passageway for the harpy queen and her army.

Then, Branwen could think no further as Nezzie grabbed her hand, pulling her forward.

"Run!"

Branwen stumbled after the strix, regaining her stride just as they emerged from the Shard Forest. Together, they plunged ahead, feet pounding along the wide, chalk-white road that cut through the glimmering landscape of the Sídhe. Amber foliage and stained-glass wildflowers flashed by, their ethereal beauty lost on Branwen as she focused only on the path before her. Every step she took sent a jolt of pain across her spine as the half-healed wounds there stretched with her movements. She could feel them slowly ripping open again, trickling blood and lymph down her back, but she didn't dare slow down. Instead, she used the pain like the lash of a whip to spur her onward because she knew that what she felt now would be nothing compared to the agony Sorcha or Aello would inflict if they caught her.

Beside her, Nezzie kept up, her shorter legs pumping furiously with her tawny wings tucked tight against her back to reduce drag. The strix could easily outstrip them all, Branwen knew. If she flew, she could reach the King's Court long before the harpy-imposed time limit, but Branwen also knew Nezzie would never abandon Destin like that. Even now, Branwen could feel the buzz of power around the strix, flowing through her and the merrow's joined hands as Nezzie tried to lend him her strength.

It wasn't working.

Destin struggled to match their blistering pace, his long-legged gait slowing a fraction of a second with every stride. In moments, he would start to lag behind.

*What difference does it make?* Branwen wondered, darkness rising in her thoughts. *This was an impossible task to begin with—a three-minute mile? I couldn't run that even on a good day, and this is* not *a good day.* Despair began to fill her, threatening to weigh down her own limbs, but she fought against it. Branwen conjured images of her family and friends in her mind's eye, envisioning everyone she ever held dear. *Mama, Papa, Madden, Colwen, Magrid. Ifanna. Ginny.* The litany of names burned in her soul with a brightness that pushed back the dark. *You owe them*, she told herself. *You owe it to them to* try. *Get as close to the King's Court as you can, then, when the harpies come, stand and* fight.

The fire within her kindled at the thought, its flames coursing through her veins and searing away the weariness in her bones. The heat of it spread like a wildfire, pushing at the very boundaries of her self. Branwen tried to rein it in, but she was already too late.

Her palm sizzled where she touched Nezzie, her magic spilling over into the strix. Afraid her power would physically manifest as it had in the naiad's grove, Branwen frantically tried to release her grip; however, Nezzie held on tight, purposefully twining her fingers through Branwen's instead.

"Let it go," the strix commanded, clearly not meaning her hand, but Branwen shook her head. She couldn't. She just *couldn't*. She didn't trust herself enough—didn't trust her magic enough—to let it run free.

"I'll lose control!" she protested, her voice cracking with fear. "I'll burn you like I burned the Dark!" Tears blurred the edges of Branwen's vision at even the possibility of harming Nezzie. *I can't lose anyone else,* she thought. *I can't have another innocent's death be—all—my—fault!*

Nezzie didn't accept her answer.

"No, you won't," the strix asserted between ragged breaths as she ran. "Trust me. Trust yourself. You said you were an *iachäwr*—a healer. Destin was wrong before. I don't think your magic wants to *burn,* I think it wants to *heal*—so, let it heal *us*."

As Nezzie spoke, Branwen could sense the truth of her words. She knew the fae couldn't lie—at least not outright—but it was more than that. What the strix said resonated within her, plucking some unknown chord within her soul. *Yes*, the flames in her heart whispered in response. *Yes!*

Branwen took as deep a breath as she could and, in the next stride, released it along with her tenuous hold over her magic. The flames within her surged, leaping across her connection to Nezzie. The strix flinched, but didn't falter as Branwen's magic flowed through her. In seconds, she even relaxed, her own short stride lengthening as Branwen sensed her fire consuming the strix's fatigue and burning away any lingering aches and pains. Next, the flames spread to Destin through his and Nezzie's joined hands with the strix acting as a conduit between him and Branwen.

The merrow screamed, collapsing to the ground when Branwen's magic reached his iron-scorch. His movement jerked Nezzie and Branwen back, pulling them all to a sudden and jarring stop.

"Destin!" Nezzie shouted as she crashed to her knees beside him. The merrow writhed in agony, steam rising from his pale blue skin. Branwen panicked, trying to yank herself free of Nezzie's grip—trying to break her connection to Destin, trying to stop his pain—but Nezzie held on tighter, her small fingers clenching desperately over Branwen's knuckles. The strix's grip on Destin was just as strong, turning his fingertips nearly white with the pressure.

"Don't stop!" Nezzie ordered only half-turning back to Branwen. Her green eyes remained fixed on Destin as his body convulsed in the middle of the wide, white road.

"I have to!" Branwen cried out, terrified that her worst fears were coming to life before her very eyes. She tried to focus on her magic, to calm the flames and call them back to herself, but the fire had grown too strong, taking on a will of its own and ignoring her frantic plea. "It's killing him! *I'm* killing him!"

"No," Nezzie interrupted. "Look! Your magic—it's starting to heal his iron-scorch!"

The strix nodded toward Destin's injured arm. The merrow held the limb close to his chest, but Branwen's eyes could still trace the iron-tainted lines across his skin—only now the very edges glowed with a fierce white light. The light burned along the path of his veins, leaving a trail of ash in its wake.

Beneath the ash, gleamed a map of silvery scars, their flesh still raw but free of the corrupting iron. Then, the light reached the boundaries of the merrow's original wound where the scorch ran deepest.

Branwen felt the fire of her magic surge forward, exploding where it touched iron-putrid flesh. The bandage on Destin's arm turned to smoke with the heat, and the merrow screamed again, the sound ripping all the way up from his gut.

"Enough!" he roared, violently twisting away. Destin tried to wrench himself free from Nezzie's grip, desperate to stop the pain, but the strix refused to let go. She dropped Branwen's hand, instead, severing the connection at its source.

Branwen flinched, her vision flashing white as her own power rebounded, the furnace-bright flames doubling back on themselves since they no longer had anywhere else to go. The heat of them ignited her bones and turned her blood to lava. The power overflowed and burst from her hands, its fiery tongues reaching toward Nezzie and Destin with a ravenous desire even as Branwen could feel her magic begin to burn itself out. *Feed us!* hissed the withering fire within her. *We hunger! We must consume!*

"No!" Branwen yelled as she crouched and slammed her hands to the ground. Her fingers dug into the chalky dirt of the road, pressing the fine, white powder against her palms in an attempt to squelch the flames. The dirt turned to soot at her touch, coating her hands with a slick, black film, but at last the fire of her magic fizzled out, reaching the end of its power. Only a spark remained, that tiny light glowing merrily among the ashes within her—ready to reignite at a moment's notice.

When she looked up, she met Destin's gaze. Sweat dripped from the merrow's brow and his breath came in labored gasps from the shock of what he'd experienced, but for the first time in a long while, his eyes burned bright not with fever, but with *hope*. Her magic hadn't healed him completely—Branwen could still see the ugly black slash across his forearm, but it no longer oozed foul gray pus. Silvery scars gleamed at the edges of the wound, forming a border that seemed to keep the iron-scorch from spreading further, at least for now.

"I keep underestimating you," the merrow told Branwen, his expression wry as he staggered back to his feet. Nezzie leapt up beside him, offering her help, but Destin didn't need it. His movements steadied as he stood, growing tall and strong once more.

"Let's hope Celaeno does the same," Branwen added as she, too, rose. Her hands remained clenched into fists even after she pushed herself up. She didn't dare risk loosening her grip—not with Nezzie and Destin so near and her magic still so unstable. She could feel the heat of it slowly building within her, fueled by her attention. *Think of something else—anything else!* Branwen told herself.

Destin's keen eyes didn't miss her struggle. He glanced at Nezzie and nodded. At his signal, the three of them took off running with equal parts desperation and hope propelling them forward. Branwen focused on the sound of her own footsteps, drowning out the soft crackle of her fire with the harsh pounding of her boots against the bone-white road. Healing Destin had cost them precious time. Branwen prayed their renewed vigor would help make up the difference, but even if it didn't, she couldn't regret her actions. It was a necessary sacrifice—and one that Branwen had been more than willing to make. With the iron-scorch still ravaging his body, she knew the merrow would have fallen further and further behind. Even if he had managed to survive the impossible race to the King's Court, he would have been too weak to aid her and Nezzie in their inevitable last stand against Aello and Sorcha.

*At least now we have a chance*, she thought. *A small one—a* very *small one—but it's still a chance.* Branwen tried to stay strong, but as she stared down the long, straight road with no end in sight, dismay crept in, polluting her thoughts. *How?* she wondered. *How are we going to fight them? And for how long?* Visions of the harpies' attack on the Red Keep flashed though her mind, reminding her of the cruel reality. *We'll be lucky if we survive the first strike.*

*Don't think about that yet!* Branwen scolded herself as she sensed her will begin to falter. *Just— keep—running!*

Determined, Branwen redoubled her efforts, pouring everything she had into conquering Celaeno's time limit. She emptied her thoughts, focusing on nothing but quickening the drum of her feet against the gleaming white path in front of her. The spark within her flared, eager to be set free, and Branwen finally relaxed her hold, allowing the hungry flames just enough room to burn away her fatigue. She concentrated so deeply on keeping the destructive aspect of her magic in check that she didn't notice that she had pulled away from Nezzie and Destin, leaving the strix and merrow several paces behind.

She also didn't notice the sudden bend in the road until it was almost too late.

"Watch out!" Nezzie shouted, her high voice piercing the air.

Branwen snapped to attention, but couldn't slow in time to take the curve. Instead, she careened off to the side of the road, wasting valuable seconds before she could correct her course. Nezzie and Destin almost caught up with her, both their faces breaking into wide smiles as they pointed ahead.

"There!" Destin cried out to Branwen. "That's the King's Court! That's the Heart of the Sídhe! Can you see it?"

Branwen looked straight ahead, her eyes following the line of his hand as they ran. At first, she only saw more ruby and topaz-leafed trees casting their long shadows along the far end of the road, but there was something strange about the dark shapes. The lines didn't correspond to the angle and intensity of the late afternoon sun at all—they were all too straight and too black. Then, she realized, *Those aren't shadows! Those are standing stones! Like the ones near my village—like the ones at Bryn Celli Ddu!*

Now that she knew what they were, she could estimate the scale and distance. *A quarter of a mile!* she thought, spurring herself onward. Already, she could hear music drifting through the air followed by the muffled sounds of dancing and laughter, their joyous noise so different from the bloodthirsty shrieks of Celaeno's court. *We're so close! Can we make it?*

The crash of harpy wings answered for her, shattering her hope. Above and behind her, she could hear Aello's honeyed laugh, so confident and sure of victory. The sound dripped into Branwen's ears blocking out all other noise, but she knew Sorcha, too, must be close behind her. She could sense the flame-haired harpy's gathering magic. It buzzed against Branwen's skin, bringing back memories of the Red Keep—of the tornado Sorcha had conjured to destroy the gates. Already, Branwen could feel a breeze rising as the harpy drew the air in toward herself. The gusts of it tugged at the fabric of Branwen's dress, slowing her down. Out of the corner of her eye, she saw Nezzie flap her wings, her small body fighting against the growing gale. Destin ran beside the strix, his hand on the small of her back, pushing her forward, but their efforts were in vain.

For the span of a breath, the wind stopped, but Branwen knew that wasn't the end. The pressure of the air around them soared, popping her ears, and in the next second, Sorcha's magic exploded in a pointed blast of wind.

Then, impossibly, the wind *missed.* Branwen' spirits soared as she only caught the edge of the blast and used the force of the gale to fling herself forward. She tucked and rolled as she went, landing in a sprinter's crouch that allowed her to bolt ahead. *Yes! Finally!* Branwen thought, overjoyed at her stroke of fortune, but the feeling didn't last long.

She'd barely made it three paces before she realized Nezzie and Destin were no longer close behind her. Immediately, she skidded to a halt, her heels kicking up fine, white dust from the road as she instinctively turned back and saw Sorcha's wind had hurled the strix and merrow to the ground. Overhead, she heard Sorcha and Aello's malicious cackles and realized the truth. *Sorcha didn't miss!* Branwen thought, watching the two harpies circle lazily above the treetops. *She aimed for Nezzie and Destin on purpose! She and Aello are toying with us!*

She didn't have time to contemplate further as Nezzie's voice broke into her thoughts.

"Keep going, Feisty!" the strix yelled, pushing herself up from the dusty road. She tried to stand, but failed, her ankle twisting at an odd angle beneath her. Destin caught her just before she fell.

*I can't leave them!* Branwen thought, panic rising in her chest.

"You're the Favor-price!" the merrow shouted at Branwen when she hesitated. "If you don't make it to the King's Court, we don't stand a chance!"

*He's right*, Branwen knew with the dreaded sound of harpy wings ringing in her ears. *If I die, Nezzie and Destin's fate is sealed! I have to survive! I have to* try*!*

She turned and ran.

# Chapter 17

The standing stones at the boundary of the King's Court loomed large in front of her, so close and yet so impossibly far away. Vibrant green peeked from between the stone frames, promising a wide, open field beyond. Branwen even caught a glimpse of fae figures dancing, their twirling, fluid movements matching the melody of harps and flutes, oblivious to her plight just outside their border.

"Help!" Branwen yelled in a desperate effort to attract any of the fae's attention. She didn't expect a response—why would the fae of the King's Court risk their lives for hers with nothing promised in return? They wouldn't, she knew, but she had hoped at least one of them would stop and *look* at her. *If this is how I die, then at least let me be* seen, she thought. *Let someone witness our end—how hard we fought and how close we came!*

Above her, Aello laughed, drowning out her plea. "Useless!" the dark harpy crowed as she and Sorcha swooped low, turning tight, taunting circles over Branwen's head. The wind from their wings stirred up a dervish of dust from the road. Branwen nearly choked as the white power entered her lungs, clogging her airways with every wheezing breath, but she couldn't stop—*didn't* stop. *You can stop when you're dead*, she thought with grim determination. *Until then, you and Nezzie and Destin are all still alive, alive,* alive!

She ran faster.

In response, Aello dipped even lower, the tips of her mahogany wings scraping the ground as she flew across the road directly in front of Branwen. The dark harpy's sudden nearness forced Branwen to backpedal or be sliced by the blades of her feathers.

"You *are* a feisty thing, but enough is enough," Aello commented as she circled again, her swift flight cutting off Branwen's path once more.

She was trapped, caged by the harpies' dizzying revolutions.

Aello grinned, her blood-red lips and marigold eyes streaking Branwen's vision as the harpy flashed by. "No one can save you now, puny human," the dark harpy purred. "Why don't you just give up? Say the word and I could give you an easy death."

The very thought made Branwen's stomach churn, revolted by the idea of throwing away all the sacrifices she and so many others had made to get even this far. Nezzie. Destin. Ginny. The thirteen nameless girls. The unicorn. Their pain and suffering would not—*could* not—be in vain! Anger burned within Branwen and she felt her own lips curl in a snarl.

"Never!" she spat back at the harpy in defiance. Branwen thrust her hand into the pocket of her dress, her fingers ignoring the curve of Sorcha's severed claws as she pulled out something far more effective: the iron keys she'd stolen from the Red Keep. She looped the keys' long metal chain around her wrist, letting the keys themselves drop to form a make-shift flail, which she swung with all her might as Aello circled past. She nearly missed the timing, but at the last second the keys' jagged teeth made contact, catching the dark harpy in the face and slicing the skin just above her left eye.

Iron-darkened blood gushed from the shallow wound, splattering across the bone-white road as Aello shrieked, spinning up and away in a feat of frantic aerial acrobatics. However, Branwen barely had time to move before Aello recovered from the initial shock of her attack, the harpy's pain numbed by raw fury.

Aello's earlier facade of mercy shattered. Now, her gaze blazed with hatred as she righted herself mid-air, her unbloodied eye never losing sight of Branwen. "You'll pay for this!" the harpy screamed, then tucked her wings and dove once more, her mahogany form barreling toward Branwen who could do nothing but brace herself for the impact.

"NO! The human is MINE!" Sorcha roared, plunging after Aello. The redheaded harpy summoned a storm of wind, the force of it slowing Aello down, and the two harpies collided with the crashing sound of war.

The swords of their feathers scraped together, sheering the air as they battled for supremacy. Aello was faster and stronger with the full use of her claws, but Sorcha's ambush had caught her off-guard, giving the flame-haired harpy a moment's upper-hand—which was all she needed.

Sorcha used her own body weight to slam Aello into the ground, temporarily stunning the dark harpy. The impact made the earth beneath Branwen rumble, spurring her tensed limbs into action. She bolted. The fire in her heart raged, fueled by even the smallest glimmer of hope. Power flowed through her every vein and sinew, pushing her body to its limit. She felt as if she were burning from the inside out, but she didn't care. She had only seconds before Sorcha left Aello and turned on her—she wouldn't waste them.

The standing stones of the King's Court drew near with an aching slowness, and Branwen realized they were bigger than she'd thought—*farther away* than she'd thought. Despair began to creep into her heart, threatening to sap her strength, but she ran on, focusing only on the goal ahead. She could make out more details of the clearing beyond the standing stones now. A cluster of butterfly-winged fae stood near the entrance, their backs to Branwen as they talked among themselves and sipped from gem-studded goblets. A ruddy-cheeked faun skipped by, summoning them to dance with a set of silver pipes, and the butterfly fae obliged. Their brilliant wings and jeweled clothing glinted in the afternoon sun as they fluttered across the open field.

*Come back!* Branwen wanted to call after them. She opened her mouth to do so, then—*WHAM!*

"NO!" Branwen screamed as she felt Sorcha's few remaining claws pierce her left shoulder from behind, anchoring deep into her flesh. The harpy hooked the joint of her footless leg under Branwen's other arm and yanked her into the air. Sorcha staggered under the added weight but remained aloft, her powerful wings gaining lift with every beat.

Branwen flailed in the harpy's grasp, screaming in agony as Sorcha's claws gouged deeper into the muscle and bone of her shoulder. The half-healed skin of her back began to tear open as she twisted and swung her body, trying to use her own weight to throw the harpy off course or, better yet, bring them both crashing down—anything to stop Sorcha from turning around and taking her away from the King's Court. Branwen tried to grab the iron keys that still swung from her wrist, hoping to used them like she had against Aello, but she fumbled. The chain loosened, nearly slipping off her hand. She caught it just before it fell, pinching the links of the chain tight between two fingers.

Below her, Branwen heard Nezzie and Destin cry out. When she glanced down, she saw the strix and merrow had recovered and were running toward her. As Nezzie passed Aello's downed form, the dark harpy stirred, lashing out at the strix with the blades of her wings, but Nezzie dodged the attack. Destin followed, rushing Aello from behind. His long legs swung out, kicking Aello in the back of the head. The harpy's marigold eyes rolled in their sockets and she crumpled to the ground, unconscious. With the threat of Aello out of the way, Nezzie launched herself into the air, her tawny wings flapping wildly as she sought to catch up with Sorcha.

The redheaded harpy laughed, her voice brazen with victory as she flew higher, rising above the ruby and topaz trees. The wind from her wings pushed Nezzie back and it was everything the winged girl could do just to stay airborne.

"You're too late, little strix," Sorcha taunted. "Did you really think any of you stood a chance? Did you really think you could win? Against me? Against Celaeno?"

Nezzie glared at the harpy, but didn't answer. *Couldn't answer? Couldn't lie?* Branwen wondered. Instead, the strix focused her energy solely on her flight. "Feisty, hold on!" Nezzie shouted, straining to gain ground.

*I'm trying!* Branwen wanted to shout, but couldn't. Pain had stolen her voice, stabbing into her back with every breath.

Beyond the agony, the fire of her magic blazed, its flames fanned by her life-or-death struggle. The heat of it coursed through her body, testing the limits of her control. She could hear the roaring crackle of it in her ears, demanding, *Feed us!* Before, she'd held off the fire's hunger by sheer force of will, but now even that wouldn't be enough. If she didn't do something, her own magic would devour her. *Whenever we* heal, *we must also* burn, the flames hissed. *You cannot escape the Law of Equal Exchange.*

*Then, I won't,* Branwen thought, strengthening her grip on the chain to the iron keys that still dangled from her pinched fingers. With a few quick flicks of her wrist, she twisted the chain tighter, shortening its length and drawing the iron keys to her palm. The fire within her lunged at the touch of the hated metal, screaming *Burn, burn, burn!* And Branwen let it, loosening her tenuous hold over the flames. Her magic engulfed the iron, turning it molten-red in an instant, and Branwen struck, punching up with the keys clenched between her fingers.

Her fist smashed into Sorcha's jaw, the keys' forge-hot iron puncturing through skin and bone.

Branwen had been aiming for a deathblow to the harpy's temple, but her reach had fallen short. *Missed!* she cursed inwardly as Sorcha's scream nearly deafened her. Still, Branwen clung to the iron keys, pressing them upward with all her might. She felt their jagged teeth hook into the flesh at the back of Sorcha's throat, and the harpy's shriek became garbled as the heat charred her airways.

Despite her pain, Sorcha didn't let Branwen go. Instead, her grip tightened, sending a clear message: *If I'm going down, I'm taking you with me!*

*That's the plan!* Branwen thought, her teeth gritted against the stab of Sorcha's claws in her shoulder. Her whole left arm went limp, but that didn't matter. The keys were in her right hand and she gave them another twist.

Sorcha spasmed at the renewed pain, her wings shuddering still. Without the upward thrust, she dropped below the treeline and within Nezzie's range. Freed from Sorcha's wind, the strix shot forward, ramming into the harpy's chest. The blades of Sorcha's feathers shredded Nezzie's arms and hands, but the strix kept going, her momentum pushing Sorcha—and Branwen—closer and closer to the boundary of the King's Court. Destin ran below them, his long strides devouring the distance as he, too, surged toward the border of stones.

*He's going to make it! We're all going to make it!* Branwen thought, watching as her, Nezzie's, and Sorcha's conjoined shadow touched the top of the first standing stone. *Just a little further!*

Branwen kicked out her legs, straining to reach across whatever invisible line marked the end of Celaeno's domain and the beginning of the King's, but just then Sorcha recovered from the jolt of Nezzie's assault.

With her failure so near, the harpy fought back with a vengeance. Nezzie ducked just as Sorcha lashed out, narrowly missing a blow from the harpy's wings as they sliced through the air with decapitating force.

*Next time, Nezzie won't stand a chance!* Branwen thought with horror. *The keys are killing Sorcha, but they're not fast enough! I need to do more! I need more power!* Her thoughts turned inward, begging the fire within her for every ounce of its strength. *Whenever you heal, you must also burn, so heal* me—*and BURN!*

The flames roared at the chance, devouring her pain as she relinquished her control. Their heat blazed in her back and her shoulder, knitting her flesh together even as the tension from Sorcha's talons continued to tear it apart. Branwen could feel the pressure—the *debt*—of her magic building, building, building—demanding a release. She tried to channel her power into the keys to sear Sorcha's skull from the inside out, but the metal wouldn't go any hotter. Had she reached her limit?

*No!* Branwen refused to give up, pouring all of her will into stoking the inferno in her heart. *The iron—it's acting like a stopper*, she realized. *My magic can burn through iron-scorch but it can't destroy pure iron. It will never be enough unless....*

"Nezzie, Destin—get down!" Branwen shouted, but she couldn't wait to see if they obeyed.

She yanked the keys out of Sorcha's jaw, throwing them to the ground, then shoved her hand directly against the harpy's face.

Without the iron to contain it, her magic erupted, spewing white-hot flames into Sorcha's body.

The harpy exploded.

The force sent Branwen flying, her body sailing over the standing stones and into the King's Court before gravity took hold and she began to fall. Flaming shards of bone and flesh and feathers followed her, pelting her back and shoulders with their gruesome rain, but Branwen had no time to think of victory. The ground rushed up to meet her, its soft, grassy appearance belying the truth—which was the promise of a sudden and excruciating end to her hard-won battle. Whether she died on impact or not, Branwen was certain she wouldn't be walking away from such a collision.

*Will the King still accept me if I am broken?* she wondered, a detached part of herself still clinging to hope. *And if so, into how many pieces?* she thought, her body too exhausted to even brace for the impending crash.

Then, just before she hit, she caught a familiar streak of blue out of the corner of her eye—Destin!

The merrow lunged after her, leaping to catch her mid-air. His arms wrapped around her tightly, ignoring the scalding hiss of his flesh where it touched her still-searing-hot skin. Destin twisted his body in an attempt to redirect her momentum, and, together, they rolled as they hit the ground.

The merrow's scaled shirt bruised Branwen's skin, but he succeeded in absorbing most of the impact from her fall before they broke apart, coming to a stop in the middle of the grassy clearing of the King's Court.

Still, pain ripped through Branwen as she landed on her back, her half-healed wounds screaming at the sudden pressure of the ground against her spine. She found she couldn't move, couldn't even speak. Her cries strangled in her throat as her lungs heaved for air and failed. She couldn't *breathe.*

"Feisty!" she heard Nezzie call as the strix rushed to her side. Destin was close behind her, barely recovered from his own fall.

"Don't touch her!" the merrow warned just as Nezzie reached for Branwen's hand. The strix flinched back just in time, seeing the angry red weals on Destin's neck and arms where he had touched her. Destin grabbed Branwen's hand, instead, trying to used his water magic to help her, but it turned to steam against her skin, forcing him to let go.

Desperately, Branwen reached for her own magic, begging once again for it to heal her, to take away her pain, but the fire within her was gone—burned beyond ashes. There was nothing left in her heart but a wisp of smoke which vanished when she tried to touch it.

Tears stung in Branwen's eyes as she stared past Nezzie and Destin and up at the blue, blue sky above her. Its vastness mirrored the emptiness inside her now, but she couldn't regret the loss—not really. She knew she would do the same thing—make all the same sacrifices—as long as it meant getting herself and her companions safely into the King's Court.

*But this is not over, yet*, she thought as her diaphragm continued to spasm, cutting off her air. The edges of her vision began to blur and the sound of her own heartbeat pounded in her ears, but she fought back, forcing herself to focus not on her pain but on all the sights and noises around her. Beyond Nezzie and Destin, she caught glimpses of dozens of fae creatures crowding around her. The laughter and music of the King's Court had stopped, replaced by gasps and whispers as the other fae drew near.

*A human! In the King's Court!*

*She can't be! Did you see what she* did*?*

*Is that even possible? To attack a harpy and live....*

Then, one voice boomed above the rest, quelling them all into silence. The very air rippled with its power, leaving no doubt as to whom it belonged.

"Nestyria. Destin. I've been expecting you," the King said. "As former guards of Celaeno's court, you've made quite the entrance. I see you brought a human as the price for my Favor. I have one of the Mundane in my Court already. This one seems a bit...*different,* but I have to ask, is she even still alive?"

*This is it,* Branwen thought. She knew an ultimatum when she heard one.

"Yes!" she gasped, answering for herself as air finally rushed back into her lungs. Gathering every last ounce of her energy, she rolled over and pushed herself up. Her worn and torn body screamed in pain, but Branwen knew that agony was nothing compared to what Celaeno had in store for her if she failed to gain the King's Favor.

Her joints popped and her bones ached as she turned toward the King. She kept her gaze on the ground as long as she could in an attempt to hide her pain. She had to be *strong*. The skin of her back felt as if it were on fire, but she fought through it all, biting back every whimper and groan until she stood completely upright. Her movements drew excited and disbelieving murmurs from the fae within the King's Court. Nezzie and Destin rose beside her. A daring hope gleamed in their eyes, giving Branwen courage. She took another fortifying breath.

"I live, Your Majesty," she announced in a clear and steady voice.

Then, she raised her own eyes.

A great black throne loomed before her, its high back gleaming obsidian-dark in the midday sun.

And there sat the King.

Branwen's heart thundered in her chest, its beat intense and erratic as her eyes drank him in. The King was nothing like she'd imagined. He was no dark forest god, no ancient horned beast or winged fiend. *He's* human*!* came Branwen's first shocked thought, but she knew that couldn't be true—no mortal man could be so achingly beautiful.

His skin glowed alabaster-pure against the black of his throne, limning his chiseled features with traces of moonlight even under the afternoon-bright sky. Faint shadows hid beneath the cliffs of his cheeks and accentuated the perfect bow of his lips. Waves of thick, red hair tumbled down to his broad shoulders. *No, not merely red*, Branwen's mind asserted, mentally shuddering as she thought of Sorcha's flaming tresses. The King's hair was nothing like that. His was the color of fox fur—not just red, but orange and gold and black and brown. Thin braids twisted from his temples, weaving like beaten brass into the crown of holly adorning his head. Spring's white flowers and winter's crimson berries sprouted from the circlet, existing impossibly together on a single intertwining branch that perched just above his coppery brows.

The King did not sit straight and stately upon his throne, but slouched comfortably into the deep seat, cutting sharp creases in his black-and-gold tunic. He leaned on one elbow, allowing the sculpture of his body to sprawl possessively across the rest of the throne—so much so, that his left leg draped over the seat's carved obsidian arm, dangling above the dais. The black fabric of his breeches pulled tight over the muscles of his thigh and calf as he absently tapped that same heel against the side of the throne. His casual bearing screamed of authority and pride.

Branwen had never seen anything so majestic, so *regal*. Her heart stuttered and her chest grew tight. For a moment, the world spun. *What's happening?* She panicked as everything around her began to blur and fade—everything but the King—then she realized: *You've forgotten to breathe!* She clenched her jaw to keep from gasping as she filled her lungs anew.

Slowly, the King rose to his feet, and the quiet murmur of the crowd behind Branwen stopped immediately. She could almost feel their collective intake of breath; it mirrored her own.

*What have I done?* she thought, but didn't dare take her eyes off the King in order to glance at Destin or Nezzie. The King's deerskin boots didn't make a whisper of sound against the velvet-black stone as he walked down the shallow steps of the dais. Where his feet finally touched the grass of the clearing, wildflowers sprang up, blooming bright and full.

As he drew nearer, Branwen could feel the magic radiating from him. She gathered all her courage and looked directly into his eyes. *I will be seen,* she thought, *and I will see you.* She would not let the man who determined her fate count her as nothing. *I fought so hard and gave up so much, so I could be* alive, she silently pleaded. *Don't take that from me.*

The King stared back at her, meeting her gaze with eyes that held the colors of the woods on a summer evening—all deep greens and shadowy purples. Gold flecked his irises like the light of the setting sun scattering though leaf-laden branches. His dark eyes bore into Branwen and she felt herself becoming lost in the forest of his gaze.

*No human could ever have eyes like that*, Branwen thought. Reality sank in, drawing her back to herself. For all the King's human form and features, he was no "man," but another creature of the Sídhe. How could she comprehend his needs and desires? How could she make him want to keep her and her companions alive? Despair began to set in, but Branwen fought against it. She threw back her shoulders, biting back the pain, and stood straight and tall.

Amazingly, the King smiled at her actions, displaying his dazzling white teeth.

*Look, no fangs!* Branwen noted in relief. Still, she sensed something feral about his face—maybe it was the sly, fox-like curl of his lips as he grinned at her. His eyes sparkled.

The King laughed, his voice ringing through the air like a gong. Branwen could smell the cinnamon of his breath caressing her cheeks as he spoke.

"You *are* feisty," he said, addressing her directly. The light in eyes danced as he looked at her and his voice was teasing. Or mocking. Branwen couldn't quite tell. Either way, she felt he had made his decision and there was nothing more she could do. Now, she only had to hear the verdict.

"Tell me you name," he asked.

She told him.

"Branwen," the King repeated. Her heart skipped a beat as he rolled the syllables across his tongue. "You have earned my Favor—you and your companions. Welcome to *Gcroílár an Sídhe.* Welcome to the Heart of the Sídhe."

# About the Author

Miranda Gaines lives in Greenville, SC. She has a BS in Biology from North Greenville University. When she is not haunting the aisles of her local library, Miranda enjoys binge-watching Korean dramas and being a pet-butler for her six cats, two goldfish, and the family's immortal fire-bellied newt, David. *Fearless* is her debut novel.

*www.mirandagaines.com*

# Dauntless

*Book 2, Heart of the Sidhe*

*Coming in 2024*

"Branwen, you have earned my Favor," said the King with a smile dancing at his lips. "You and your companions. Welcome to *Gcroílár an Sídhe.* Welcome to the Heart of the Sídhe."

Relief washed over Branwen. Her knees threatened to buckle as the long-carried burden of fear and dread began to lift. Tears burned at the backs of her eyes as she thought of her family, of the hope that she might actually see them again. *Mother, Papa, Madden, Colwen, Magrid, my dear friend Ifanna...I'm one step closer to home!*

Branwen turned toward Nezzie and Destin as soon as she could, forcing her tired, wobbly legs into motion, and watched as grins of pure joy spread over their faces. The corner of her own mouth twitched in response, wanting to rejoice, but not quite believing.

*Are we safe? Are we really safe?* It didn't seem possible after everything they'd been through. Since their capture by the servants of the harpy-queen Celaeno, they had managed to survive multiple attacks—from iron-wielding redcaps and a crossbow-bearing púka to razor-winged harpies and the Devouring Dark. Together, they had escaped the Red Keep and taken refuge in the naiad's grove, only for the harpy Aello to kidnap Nezzie the next day, luring Destin and Branwen to the Aegis Tree where Celaeno plotted their execution. Only the harpy queen's arrogance, along with the King's miraculous Favor, had saved them from certain death.

While Branwen's doubts lingered, one look at Destin and Nezzie told her they had put all such concerns behind them. The merrow grabbed the little strix in a fierce embrace, crumpling some of her feathers in his excitement. But Nezzie didn't seem to care—she laughed and cried, burying her head into the merrow's chest. The two spun in a dizzy, happy circle, then Destin hoisted Nezzie up, his un-scorched arm crossing under the backs of her legs to lift her to eye level. The strix leaned into him, straddling his waist for balance. She grinned and pulled Destin's face to hers in a passionate kiss.

Branwen grinned, too, then blushed as her companions' kiss grew more intense. When she looked away, she caught the King's eye. He'd been watching Nezzie and Destin as well. Their gazes met and Branwen saw that the colors in his magnificent eyes had shifted, growing darker as shades of purple flooded over the green. His expression hadn't changed—he still wore the same inscrutable smile as when he'd proclaimed his Favor—yet Branwen felt her breath quicken and her heart flutter. Her blush burned deeper into her skin.

A sudden raucous sound caught Branwen off-guard and she ducked, thinking the sharp clatter was the sound of Aello, or even Celaeno herself, coming for revenge. Her eyes darted to the crystalline skies, but found them as clear and bright as sapphires with not a harpy in sight. Then, the realization hit: the sound came from *around* her, not above. As she lowered her gaze, she caught sight of the crowd of fae before the throne. Hundreds of hands, claws, and paws crashed together in a roar of applause. Dozens of voices cried out.

"A Favor from the King!"

"Blessed be!"

"A Feast! Let there be a Feast!"

"Feast! Feast! Feast!"

The entire gathering took up the chant. The words smashed into Branwen in waves. She could feel the heat of their voices and the breath of a hundred lungs shouting their will at the King. Beside her, the King raised one hand, his wrist and fingers curving as though he caressed the very air his people breathed. Their sound rose to a fevered pitch as the King lifted his arm, conducting their voices like a frenzied orchestra. Then, his hand slowly closed, his fingers curling into a fist, and the fae's shouts faded into silence.

"There *will* be a Feast," the King announced, his jovial voice booming over the crowd. "A Feast of Celebration for our fine members of the Court. But first I must have my obeisance—a vow of loyalty from my bold, new subjects."

He turned to Nezzie and Destin first, who broke apart under his gaze, each trying to adopt a reverential pose and expression. Branwen witnessed the strix's struggle to master her emotions. Nezzie set her mouth into a thin, firm line, but her bow-shaped lips kept bending into a smile.

"Your word is Law," the strix said, curtsying so deeply her grass-green braids brushed the ground. "My life is yours to command."

Destin knelt beside her, his tall frame folded in humility. "As is mine," the merrow said fervently. "May you reign eternal, my King."

Branwen could barely breathe as the King turned his attention to her and only her. His dark forest gaze focused intently, crushing her heart with the weight of his beauty and majesty. Her already-flushed skin burned anew where his eyes touched—her wrist, her shoulder, her throat, her lips....

"My King," she gasped, unable to formulate any more coherent thoughts. She dipped as low as her battered muscles would allow, then pushed a little further. Her back screamed with pain and tears flooded her eyes, but she knew her agony was nothing compared to what the King had saved her from. "My life," she murmured to the grass by the King's boots. Tiny white flowers bloomed at the binding magic of her words, but Branwen didn't dare lift her head. Each second seemed like an hour, and fear bubbled in her chest again. *Did I get the words wrong? Was that not enough? What else can I say? I owe him my life, but I still need to find a way home!*

She nearly toppled when a light, firm hand touched her shoulder. She could feel a strong, steady pulse through the pressure of each fingertip, and the pain in her back eased.

"Rise," the King said, a smile gracing his voice. "Rise and greet your Court."

Branwen obeyed. She straightened slowly, testing every muscle and joint on the way up. Everything still *hurt*, but the most piercing pains had subsided to dull throbs, though she was by no means healed. While the place where fire magic once burned within her heart now felt void and barren, she could sense the remnants of those flames still coursing through her veins. *Just like when the unicorn first woke my power at the Red Keep*, Branwen thought. The stubborn sparks of magic refused to die, glowing like tiny embers under her skin. Suddenly, she was glad the King had healed her as little as he did. Any more and he might have reignited her power, stoking an inferno that would have consumed her from the inside out.

Branwen took a deep, shuddering breath, pushing the morbid thoughts away as she turned to face the gathering crowd. She could hear the excited shuffle of their feet through the grass of the clearing, and their expectant whispers washed over her in waves. Then, she lifted her eyes once more. The words perched on her lips, only she had no chance to utter them as the King's Court erupted into another cheer.

"Welcome and well met, Nestyria, Destin, and Lady Branwen!" shouted a lion-faced fae with a ruff of ruby-red roses instead of a mane. His proclamation was followed by a volley of "Hear, hear!"

Beside him, a golden-haired nymph giggled, her eyes bright as she twirled a charred and bloodied harpy feather between her hands. Sorcha's remains littered the clearing, having rained down from above after her immolation. Smoke still rose from the scattered chunks of her flesh, creating an eerie haze, and the pungent scent of burned hair and feathers lingered in the air.

Some of the fae in the King's Court had been injured in the blast as well. Branwen could see a few with nicks and scrapes, mostly on their arms and backs where flying bone shards and razor-sharp feathers must have sliced as they fell. A group of fauns pushed their way through the rousing crowd, stubbornly butting aside larger fae with their nubby horns until they stood directly in front of Branwen. At their arrival, Nezzie and Destin broke apart, warily positioning themselves to protect her flanks. The King remained behind her, but she could feel him silently watching.

The small herd of fauns bowed to the King, then the first two stepped aside, revealing an injured member in the center of their group. This faun was shorter and younger than the others with speckled fur on his goat-like legs. A mop of curly brown hair fell across his freckled face, but it could do nothing to hide the vicious red blisters splashed across his ruddy-colored cheeks. They trailed down his neck and across his chest and left shoulder. Several of his companions had smaller blisters on their arms and torsos, but nothing as severe as his. Looking at them, Branwen recognized the pattern in their marks; she had a few such scars herself—battle wounds from the kitchen where as a young girl she had sloshed scalding-hot oil while trying to help her mother cook. All of the fauns' blisters were the same, although the youngest had clearly taken the brunt of the mishap.

*He was closest to the source,* Branwen thought. *But what could have caused—oh!* She closed her eyes as the realization struck. *The burns aren't from hot oil. They're from blood. Harpy blood.* Sorcha's *blood.* She had thought everything liquid had vaporized in the blast, but she was wrong. *How many others?* she wondered, opening her eyes to look once more among the crowd. *How many others were hurt because of me?*

The *iachäwr*—the healer—within her ached with sympathy, and tears began to mar her vision, blurring all the fae together. She reached out to the young faun, her fingers hovering by his swollen cheek, but she didn't dare touch him, not with the flicker of fire still in her veins.

"I am sorry," she began, but the faun shook his head, wincing at the small movement.

When he looked up at her, his large, hazel eyes shone with awe and wonder. "It is an honor," he told her. Gingerly, he placed his hand on his chest, avoiding the worst of the burns over his heart, and bobbed in a small bow. "To have witnessed the defeat of one of Celaeno's cursed harpies...." His voice trailed in disbelief before rallying. "In time, these scars will fade," the faun said, gesturing to the vivid marks. "But my memory of this day will not. Hail, harpy-slayer!"

His fellow fauns echoed his cry, which was soon taken up by the rest of the fae. Branwen flinched as Nezzie and Destin grabbed her hands, one on each side. She expected the sizzle of heat, but none came as they hoisted her arms high in victory.

"Hail, harpy-slayer!" Nezzie repeated, her high voice fluting above the crowd. Destin joined her, his lower register adding power to the declaration. "Hail, harpy-slayer! Hail, Branwen!"

From behind Branwen, the King stepped closer. She could feel the warmth of his nearness, of his magic. His powerful solidity comforted her, like a shield at her back. For the first time in a long while, she felt absolutely safe.

"Hail, harpy-slayer," the King whispered. His soft, rich voice penetrated the roar of the crowd for her and her alone. "Hail, Branwen, my fearless one."

Branwen glanced back at him just as his lips slipped into their signature fox-like grin. Whatever expression he'd worn before was lost, though hints of it lingered in the depths of his half-hooded eyes, in the hitch of his breath, and in the faint flush of color across his alabaster skin.

She felt her own face flush in response, and her heartbeat quickened in her chest, matching the rise of the cries from the King's Court.

As the fae's jubilant shouts reached a fever pitch, another sound rose above them—a shriek of devastating pain and fury. Branwen recognized the voice at once with Destin and Nezzie only a fraction of a second behind her.

"Aello," the merrow growled. "I'd hoped she was dead."

Nezzie and Branwen both shook their heads, dismayed, but not surprised. They all knew it would have taken a lot more than a kick to the back of the head to kill one of Celaeno's guards.

"What have you *done?*" the mahogany-plumed harpy screamed. Branwen could see her dark form circling just beyond the border of the King's Court, soaring high above the first standing stone.

*She won't dare cross...will she?* Branwen wondered. Fear pounded in her chest, but also defiance. *In the Sídhe, an oath is an oath. Celaeno promised us freedom if we reached the King's Court and obtained his Favor. Nezzie, Destin, and I have fulfilled our end of the bargain, now Aello has no choice but to keep hers.* Branwen took a step forward, her shoulders squared and ready, but the King held her back, placing himself between Branwen and the raging harpy.

"You're too late, Aello!" he called out, smiling at the dark harpy's frustration. "Sorcha is dead, and these three"—he gestured to include Nezzie and Destin—"are pledged to my Court now!"

Aello snapped her wings sharply as she flew, making the blades of her feathers crash together in a cacophony of contempt. "Damn the strix and the merrow!" she shrieked, abandoning her usual honeyed tone for one of sheer fury. "I want the girl! She is *mine*! I am owed a life-debt for my sister! You cannot deny me!"

For a moment, Branwen panicked. *Is that true?* she wondered, remembering the life-debt Destin had so recently claimed on Aello for the death of his father. *No, not death, but murder*, she reminded herself. *It makes sense that an unjust killing could invoke a life-debt, but not a justified one, surely?* she thought. *Because Sorcha's death was certainly justifiable!*

The King's response, though, refuted both Aello's and Branwen's assumptions. "Sister?" he scoffed. "Come now, Aello, you know better than that. You and Sorcha were no more sisters than you and Celaeno, for all you harpies call yourselves that. Celaeno is a Firstborn. She *created* you and all her other harpy ilk. Only *she* can claim a life-debt over her creations."

Aello snarled, her ruby lips curling back from razor teeth. "Then, I claim the life-debt on Celaeno's behalf!" she demanded, her crimson and yellow eyes seething with malice. "Even the King's Favor cannot void such a claim!"

*No!* Branwen thought. *That can't be!* With the King's back to her, Branwen's eyes darted to Nezzie and Destin, desperately looking for answers, but the two avoided her gaze.

The King sighed, harsh and exasperated. "Of course," he conceded. "The debt remains."

Branwen's spirit plummeted. So, she wasn't safe after all. Then, *why*, she wondered, had they tried so hard to make it to the King's Court, to earn his Favor, if with a few words, Aello could take everything away? What had it all been *for*? *I have not bled and cried for this to be the end!* she thought with growing fury. *Ginny and thirteen other girls did not* die *at the Red Keep just for me to become harpy fodder!*

Enraged at his hypocrisy, she grabbed the King's arm, ignoring the shocked looks from everyone around her. She could hardly believe the audacity of her own actions, but if the King was really willing to give her up to the harpies so easily, then these were the last moments of her life. *King or not, Firstborn or not, I won't leave without a fight!* she thought with desperate determination.

Though the strength of Branwen's grip dug divots in his flesh, the King appeared unfazed. Instead of prying her fingers loose, he calmly laid his hand on top of hers and gave it a gentle squeeze. His eyes flicked back to meet hers. *Trust me*, they said.

To Aello, the King repeated, "The debt remains, but this one is under my protection now. Any attempt to claim her life-debt while she remains within the bounds of my Court will count as an attack on *me*. Only death awaits traitors to the throne," he added with solemn assurance.

Aello beat her wings, shrieking and squawking in protest, but the King's words rang true, even to Branwen's unpracticed ears. Aello would have no choice but to obey his constraints.

*Those were the Rules*, Branwen was beginning to learn. Her grip on the King relaxed. Ashamed now at her lack of trust, she started to let her hand fall away, but the King caught it, resting her fingers on the crook of his arm. *He does me a great honor*, Branwen thought at the gesture. *Treating me like an actual court lady and not the daughter of a shepherd, but why? What am I to him?* Her musings were cut short as Aello made her opinion of the King's ruling known.

"Fie!" the harpy spat, then glared at Branwen. "Enjoy his Favor while it lasts," she said, venom dripping from every word. "The moment you step out of this Court, you are *mine*. Celaeno and I will suck the marrow from your bones, and that, *my dear*, is a promise!"

# To be continued...

Made in the USA
Columbia, SC
20 September 2023

6d5ad7e6-b988-409d-a94c-ce2f49237871R02